Peter Townsend is Professor of Social Policy at Bristol University. From 1963 until 1982 he was Professor of Sociology at the University of Essex, where he was also Pro-Vice Chancellor between 1975 and 1978. He has been Chairman of the Child Poverty Action Group since 1969 and of the Disability Alliance since 1974, and he was a member of the Government Working Group on Inequalities and Health from 1977 until 1980. His books include *The Family Life of Old People* (1957), *The Last Refuge* (1962), *The Social Minority* (1973), *Sociology and Social Policy* (1975), *Poverty in the United Kingdom* (1979) and, as co-author, *Disability in Britain* (1981), *Responses to Poverty: Lessons from Europe* (1984), *Poverty and Labour in London* (1987) and *Health and Deprivation: Inequality and the North* (1988).

Nick Davidson is a journalist, writer and documentary film maker who has written widely about the national health service and social policy. He is co-author of *Out of Our Hands* (1982) and author of *A Question of Care* (1987).

The Health Divide:

Margaret Whitehead is a biologist with a background in medical and health education research, having worked for the Medical Research Council in London and Edinburgh and the Scottish Health Education Group before becoming a freelance researcher and writer. She has been involved in a wide range of projects concerned with health and preventive medicine, and is the author of numerous articles, pamphlets and research reviews including *Book of the Child* (1980), *The Best of Health?* (1982) and *A Change for the Better* (1986).

Inequalities in Health

The Black Report

Sir Douglas Black, Professor J. N. Morris,
Dr Cyril Smith, Professor Peter Townsend
Edited by Peter Townsend and Nick Davidson

The Health Divide

Margaret Whitehead

Penguin Books

PENGUIN BOOKS

Published by the Penguin Group
27 Wrights Lane, London W8 5TZ, England
Viking Penguin Inc., 40 West 23rd Street, New York, New York 10010, USA
Penguin Books Australia Ltd, Ringwood, Victoria, Australia
Penguin Books Canada Ltd, 2801 John Street, Markham, Ontario, Canada L3R 1B4
Penguin Books (NZ) Ltd, 182–190 Wairau Road, Auckland 10, New Zealand

Penguin Books Ltd, Registered Offices: Harmondsworth, Middlesex, England

First published, containing *The Black Report* only, 1982
Reprinted 1982, 1983, 1985, 1986
This edition, comprising *The Black Report* and *The Health Divide*,
first published 1988
10 9 8 7 6 5 4 3 2

Made and printed in Great Britain by
Richard Clay Ltd, Bungay, Suffolk
Typeset in 9 on 11pt Times

Contents

List of Figures   vii
List of Tables   viii
Preface   xi
Acknowledgements   xiii
Introduction to *Inequalities in Health* by Peter Townsend, Nick Davidson
and Margaret Whitehead   1
List of Abbreviations and Definitions   28

The Black Report

Foreword by Patrick Jenkin   31
1. Concepts of Health and Inequality   33
2. The Pattern of Present Health Inequalities   43
3. Trends in Inequality of Health   57
4. Inequality in the Availability and Use of the Health Service   68
5. International Comparisons   82
6. Towards an Explanation of Health Inequalities   104
7. The Need for More Information and Research   127
8. Planning the Health and Personal Social Services   133
9. The Wider Strategy   165
Summary and Recommendations   198
Appendix of Tables   209

The Health Divide

Preface by Dr David Player   217
Foreword by Sir Douglas Black, Professor J. N. Morris,
Dr Cyril Smith and Professor Peter Townsend   219
1. Setting the Scene   221
2. Health Inequalities Today   227
3. Recent Trends   256
4. Health Services: Equal Access for Equal Need?   267
5. International Comparisons   274
6. Explaining Health Inequalities   286
7. The Research Response   306
8. What Are the Health and Social Services Doing?   316
9. The Wider Strategy and Beyond   332
Summary   351
References   357
Index   383

List of Figures

The Black Report

1. Mortality by occupational class and age   44
2. Infant mortality by sex, occupational class and cause of death   45
3. Class and mortality in childhood   46
4. Occupational class and mortality in adult life   47
5. Death rates, standardized to 1901 population   57
6. Percentage excess of male over female death rates by age, 1841–1970   58
7. Infant mortality in five Swedish counties, 1916–60   96
8. Mortality ratios by occupational class, age and cause of death   123

The Health Divide

1. Occupational class and mortality in babies and adults, early 1980s   229
2. Mortality of men by social class and broad age groups, 1976–81   230
3. Percentage of population reporting limiting long-standing illness by age and socio-economic group, 1984   233
4. Percentage of males and females reporting (a) long-standing illness; (b) limiting long-standing illness; (c) restricted activity, 1972–84   244
5. Outcome of pregnancy by mother's country of birth, 1984   253
6. Post-neonatal mortality by father's social class, 1970–84   260
7. Standardized mortality ratios for select causes of death, manual and non-manual groups, 1970–72 and 1979–83   261
8. Percentage of males and females reporting long-standing illness and limiting long-standing illness by whether non-manual or manual socio-economic group, 1974, 1979, 1984
Percentage of persons reporting restricted activity in the 14 days before the interview by sex and whether non-manual or manual socio-economic group, 1974, 1979, 1984   263
9. Percentage of males and females consulting a NHS GP by whether non-manual or manual socio-economic group, 1974, 1979, 1984   270
10. Some examples of social trends in chronic illness, in five countries   277

List of Tables

The Black Report

A. Resources available for services (1980/81 to 1985/6)   20
1. Death rates by sex and social class   49
2. Regional variations in mortality   50
3. Mortality by country of birth and occupational class   51
4. Mortality by tenure and class   52
5. Comparison of distribution of standardized patient consultation ratios and standardized mortality ratios   54
6. Sickness and medical consultation in early adulthood   55
7. Mortality of men by occupational class   59
8. Mortality rates per 100,000 and as percentage of rates for occupational classes I and II   60
9. Mortality of women by occupational class   62
10. Trends in infant mortality by occupational class   63
11. Working males absent from work owing to illness or injury   64
12. Rates of long-standing and acute illness and consultations of occupational classes IV and V, as a percentage of class I   65
13. 'Use/need ratios' by social group   69
14. Morbidity and GP attendance indicators for socio-economic groups   70
15. Hospital standardized discharge ratios and standardized bed-day ratios by occupational class   73
16. Late ante-natal booking   74
17. Use of health services by children under 7 by occupational class of father   75
18. Percentage of old persons of different occupational class who receive or feel the need for chiropody treatment   75
19. Percentage of old persons of different occupational class who were receiving public or private domestic help, or who said help was needed   76
20. Perinatal and infant mortality in Europe   83
21. Adult mortality in Europe   84
22. Mortality rates under 1 year per 1,000 live births, for selected causes (Sweden, and England and Wales)   86
23. Physicians, nurses and hospital beds in Europe   87
24. Regional variations in number of physicians   88
25. Denmark: neonatal mortality rate by occupation   89
26. Finland: age-adjusted mortality indices by social group   90

27. France: rates of infant, neonatal and post-neonatal death by socio-professional group of father   90
28. France 1968: mortality rates among economically active men   91
29. West Germany 1974: infant mortality and early neonatal mortality rates, by *Land*   93
30. Netherlands 1971: age-standardized adult mortality   94
31. Norway 1975: morbidity by age and income   95
32. Numbers of persons in poverty and on the margins of poverty   108
33. Household food consumption by income group   111
34. Cigarette-smoking by socio-economic group   111
35. Active leisure pursuits by males   112
36. Causes of death from accidents of children   117
37. Planned and recommended revenue expenditure on selected services   137
38. Highest-ranking local authority areas on each of eight 1971 census and mortality indicators   141
39. Evidence of capacity of elderly residents in homes for self-care   150
40. Desire for day provisions for under-5s by occupational class   173
41. Numbers and percentage of total and disabled population living in poverty or on the margins of poverty   184
42. Mortality by occupation unit   186

The Health Divide

A. Resources available for services   20
1. SMRs for select causes of death, 1979–83   231
2. Mortality of men and women by housing tenure, education and access to cars   237
3. Mortality of males in selected clusters by housing tenure   238
4. Mortality of men and women in different regions of Britain, 1979–83   246
5. SMRs for all causes by region and occupational class, 1979–83   247
6. Deprivation and ill-health. Small area analyses   249
7. Summary of main findings of Immigrant Mortality Study   251
8. Infant mortality by occupational class, 1975–84   259
9. Mortality from all causes in selected countries, 1983   275
10. Denmark: neonatal mortality, 1974 and 1977   278
11. Prevalence of cigarette-smoking by sex and socio-economic group, 1972–84   290
12. Prevalence of cigarette-smoking by region, 1984   291
13. Food consumption by income group, 1976 and 1984   293
14. Exercise in leisure-time by socio-economic group, 1977 and 1984   294
15. Relative risk of CHD death, controlled for risk factors   295
16. A comparison of the social indicators used in five area-based studies   310
17. Children in or on the margin of poverty, 1979 and 1983   334
18. Changes in the extent of poverty in Great Britain, 1979, 1981, 1983   334

Preface

This publication brings together two major reports on inequalities in health, with an introduction which sets them both in context and spells out what needs to be done in the future.

The first is the 1980 Report of the Working Group on Inequalities in Health (known as the Black Report after its Chairman, Sir Douglas Black). A slightly slimmed-down version is presented here which has been read and approved in general terms by the original Working Group of four members: Sir Douglas Black (Chairman), Chief Scientist at the DHSS (to April 1978) and later President of the Royal College of Physicians; Professor J. N. Morris, Professor of Community Health in the University of London at the London School of Hygiene and Tropical Medicine; Dr Cyril Smith, Secretary of the Social Science Research Council; and Professor Peter Townsend, Professor of Sociology at the University of Essex, now Professor of Social Policy, University of Bristol. Dr Stuart Blume was Scientific Secretary to the Group, and the Administrative Secretary was Mr A. J. Forsdick. Dr Nicky Hart was seconded by the University of Essex to act as Research Fellow to the Group. Some statistical and technical details and elaborations of the text have been cut, but a large body of information remains in this version, which is nearly two-thirds of the length of the original report.

The terms of reference of the Working Group, which had been appointed in April 1977, were: (i) To assemble available information about the differences in health status among the social classes and about factors which might contribute to these, including relevant data from other industrial countries; (ii) To analyse this material in order to identify possible causal relationships, to examine the hypotheses that have been formulated and the testing of them, and to assess the implications for policy; and (iii) to suggest what further research should be initiated.

The second is a review of the studies on the same subject which have appeared since the Black Report was published in 1980. This review was originally published in 1987 by the Health Education Council under the title *The Health Divide: Inequalities in Health in the 1980s*. In this book the review has been substantially extended to expand the treatment of topics which attracted particular public interest in 1987 and also to add new evidence appearing during 1987–8.

Between them the two reports provide much of the evidence from the last twenty or thirty years required to allow informed discussion of this national issue.

Acknowledgements

Peter Townsend and Nick Davidson would like to thank the Controller of Her Majesty's Stationery Office for permission to reproduce sections of the original Black Report. The Department of Health and Social Security wish to make it clear that this permission in no way implies their authorization or approval of this book.

Margaret Whitehead expresses her thanks to the many people who helped bring *The Health Divide* into the light of day, not least to David Player for identifying the need for a review and guiding its progress, and the Health Education Council for funding the initial research. It should be stressed that the views expressed and the conclusions drawn are those of the author and not necessarily those of the Council. Special thanks are due to the informal group who gave invaluable support and critical comment throughout, including Alex Scott-Samuel, Bobbie Jacobson, Professor Peter Townsend, Professor J. N. Morris, Madeleine Gantley, Pattie White and Richard Wilkinson. Professor John Fox, Professor Michael Marmot and Dr Mildred Blaxter have also been of great help. Fast and efficient back-up services were provided by Christina Coltart, Fiona Martin, Jeannie Sloman, Edna Patterson, Margaret Hatton, Rachel Austin and the staff of the Shropshire Information Service. The author is grateful to the following, who kindly gave permission to reproduce their illustrations in *The Health Divide*: Mildred Blaxter and Gower Press; M. G. Marmot and colleagues, and the *Lancet*; John Fox and colleagues, and the Office of Population Censuses and Surveys; Peter Townsend and colleagues, and Bristol University/Northern Regional Health Authority; Alison Macfarlane; Peter Goldblatt; Otto Andersen; the World Health Organization, and Her Majesty's Stationery Office.

Introduction to *Inequalities* in Health

Peter Townsend, Nick Davidson and Margaret Whitehead

The Black Report: why was it necessary?

Inequalities in health are of concern to the whole nation and represent one of the biggest possible challenges to the conduct of government policy. The Black Report provides an example, which is rare anywhere in the world, of an attempt authorized by a government to explain trends in inequalities in health and to relate these to the policies intended to promote health. Because it concentrates on Britain, the report also provides a commentary on the achievements of forty years of a National Health Service in reducing these inequalities, and, by the same token, a standard by which to judge the current attempts of the government to develop a new mixture of private and public services.

We begin with some necessary background to the preparation of the report. In its publications the Department of Health and Social Security has frequently expressed concern with Britain's failure to match the improvement in health observed in some other countries and has acknowledged the relationship of this to persistent internal inequalities of health (for example, *Prevention and Health: Everybody's Business*, 1976, especially Chapters 1 and 4). In a speech on 27 March 1977, David Ennals, the Secretary of State for Social Services, stated:

... the crude differences in mortality rates between the various social classes are worrying. To take the extreme example, in 1971 the death rate for adult men in social class V (unskilled workers) was nearly twice that of adult men in social class I (professional workers) ... when you look at death rates for specific diseases the gap is even wider ... the first step towards remedial action is to put together what is already known about the problem ... it is a major challenge for the next ten or more years to try to narrow the gap in health standards between different social classes.

There were those like Sir John Brotherston, the Chief Medical Officer of Scotland, who in 1976 voiced the concern of many working in the health services and who had called the nation's attention to the social gulf in health which still existed and were calling for action. Many of those inside as well as outside the National Health Service were also aware that such inequalities might account for the failure of mortality rates in Britain to improve as far or as fast as in some other rich societies. Thus among the countries of the world having the lowest infant mortality Britain ranked eighth in 1960 but had slipped to fifteenth by 1978. In the latter year, the infant mortality rates for Hong Kong and Singapore were slightly lower than the rate for Britain (World Bank, 1981).

Accordingly, in 1977 the Secretary of State for Social Services of the Labour government appointed a Research Working Group to assess the national and international evidence and draw some of the implications for policy from the evidence on inequalities in health. The group consisted of Sir Douglas Black, formerly Chief Scientist at the Department of Health and at that time President of the Royal College of Physicians; Professor J. N. Morris of the Department of Community Health, London University; Dr Cyril Smith, Secretary of the Social Science Research Council; and Professor Peter Townsend, at that time Professor of Sociology at the University of Essex.

The Working Group completed its review in 1980. In essence it concluded that the poorer health experience of the lower occupational groups applied at all stages of life. If the mortality rates of occupational class I (professional workers and members of their families) had applied to classes IV and V (partly skilled and unskilled manual workers and members of their families) during 1970–72, 74,000 lives of people aged under seventy-five would not have been lost. This estimate included nearly 10,000 children and 32,000 men aged 15 to 64. The class gradient seemed to be greater than in some comparable countries (though it must be said that the data for the United Kingdom almost invariably are fuller) and was becoming more marked. During the twenty years up to the early 1970s covered by the Black Report the mortality rates for both men and women aged 35 and over in occupational classes I and II had steadily diminished while those in IV and V changed very little or had even deteriorated.

What had gone wrong? The Working Group argued that much of the problem lay outside the scope of the NHS. Social and economic factors like income, work (or lack of it), environment, education, housing, transport and what are today called 'life-styles' all affect health and all favour the better-off. Yet they have largely remained outside the ambit of national health policy. The Group also found that those belonging to the manual classes made smaller use of the health care system in a number of different respects, yet needed it more. Its thirty-seven recommendations included giving effect to improvements in information, research and organization so that better plans might be drawn up, redressing the balance of the health care system so that more emphasis was given to prevention, primary care and community health, and, most important of all, radically improving the material conditions of life of poorer groups, especially children and people with disabilities, by increasing or introducing certain cash benefits, like child benefit, maternity grant and infant care allowance, and a comprehensive disablement allowance, and developing new schemes for day nurseries, ante-natal clinics, sheltered housing, home improvements, improved conditions at work and community services. So there were two policy thrusts:

(i) calling for a total and not merely a service-oriented approach to the problems of health;

(ii) calling for a radical overhaul of the balance of activity and proportionate distribution of resources within the health and associated services.

A frosty reception

In April 1980 the report was submitted to the Secretary of State of the new Conservative administration. But how were the findings received by the new government? Instead of being properly printed and published by the DHSS or HMSO, only 260 duplicated copies of the typescript were made available. No press release or press conference was arranged but a few copies were sent to selected journalists on the Friday before the August Bank Holiday – a date which virtually guaranteed the lowest possible level of publicity. However, this led to an unforeseen reaction when one of the journalists realized the significance of the report and persuaded the Working Group to call an alternative press conference which, because it was not allowed at the DHSS, was duly held at the Royal College of Physicians. Both the specialist and general press began to display a keen interest in the manner of the appearance of the report and its substance. The *Lancet* referred to the Secretary of State's reception as 'frosty', and pointed out that publicity for the report was 'in the lowest possible key' and that Ministers and officials gave the impression of being 'keen to reduce the report's impact to a minimum' (6 September 1980, pp. 513 and 545). The *British Medical Journal* wrote angrily of the failure to take measured account of the work of experts and urged that the report 'should be examined more closely than Patrick Jenkin's foreword suggests that it has been' (6 September 1980, p. 690, and 20 September 1980, p. 763). It said that, like the Short Report of 1980, it had been discarded with 'shallow indifference' (20 December, p. 1663).

The Secretary of State's dismissal was brief. After stating in two short paragraphs the scope of the Working Group's task he went on:

I must make it clear that additional expenditure on the scale which could result from the report's recommendations – the amount involved could be upwards of £2 billion a year – is quite unrealistic in present or any foreseeable economic circumstances, quite apart from any judgement that may be formed of the effectiveness of such expenditure in dealing with the problems identified. I cannot, therefore, endorse the Group's recommendations.

There followed vigorous correspondence within the pages of the medical journals. Interested trade unions, and the TUC itself, published summaries for their members (COHSE, 1980; TUC, 1981), and quite exceptional efforts were made by bodies connected with the health and welfare services to bring the evidence and arguments in the report to a wide audience (for example, Gray, 1981; Black, 1981a; Deitch, 1981; Watkins and Elton, 1981; Townsend, 1981; and Radical Community Medicine, 1980). In July 1981, following a special conference devoted to the report, the Association of Community Health Councils for England and Wales adopted a resolution which deplored 'the negative response of Her Majesty's Government ... We call upon the Secretary of State for Health and Social Services to present a report to Parliament and to allow a debate on the important issues raised. We call upon the Minister to press for the necessary resources to provide the services and to analyse and give guidance to health authorities on the many recommendations which have little or no revenue consequences.' Partly at the prompting of bodies like the Socialist Health Association, the Labour Party took an active interest in the report and a resolution passed in October at the annual conference called on the next Labour government to give priority to the implementation of its recommendations and, since many measures in the report could be introduced by local authorities, Labour representatives on councils and health authorities should 'do all in their power to ensure the implementation of these recommendations'. The General Secretary wrote to all Labour Groups accordingly (*Labour Weekly*, 4 December 1981).

By the spring of 1981 the Secretary of State found it necessary to elaborate on his first reaction and in a speech in Cardiff he drew attention to what he considered to be the report's three principal shortcomings. First, he claimed it did not adequately explain the causes of inequalities in health, and 'its enormously expensive' programme of recommendations could not therefore be accepted.

Secondly, Mr Jenkin argued that new evidence disproved the thesis that the working class suffered poorer access to the health services.

My department has looked at a whole lot more evidence. We have compared the total use of the health services and we have found that people with lower incomes, more of whom are likely to be elderly, tend to receive proportionately more services than the average for the population as a whole. Moreover, there is support for this finding from an independent source – a recent analysis by two researchers at Bath University who have used quite different data based on the General Household Survey. The widely held view, therefore, that the poor do not have a proper crack of the whip when it comes to using the National Health Service is simply not supported by the facts. This is a very encouraging finding. (Cardiff, 13 March 1981)

Thirdly, Mr Jenkin argued in his Cardiff speech, and elsewhere (Deitch, 1981, p. 159), that there was no evidence that more money would make any difference (so missing the main point of the report).

We have been spending money in ever-increasing amounts on the NHS for thirty years and it has not actually had much effect on increasing people's health. (Deitch, 1981, p. 159)

The first and third of these objections were reiterated by Sir George Young, the Under-Secretary of State for Health and Social Security, on 31 July, in a short adjournment debate in the House of Commons, when replying to Mr William Hamilton, M P for Fife Central, who had drawn attention to the report. He repeated the costs given in the report (for November 1979), but suggested that by November 1980 the costs would be up to £4.8 billion. He did, however, go on to say that the government agreed with some of the recommendations, particularly those on prevention. But, disappointingly, he did not seem to have recognized the gulf between the Working Group's concept of prevention and that of the government.

I see the progress being made by encouraging health education, personal responsibility for health, and encouraging voluntary organizations to help in the personal social services and helping to complement the NHS. That is the right way forward, given the difficult economic circumstances in which we find ourselves, rather than committing ourselves to the rather expensive solutions outlined by the Black Report, which we are not absolutely convinced would deliver the goods. (*British Medical Journal*, 22 August 1981)

All three objections raised by government Ministers – explanation, access and money – have been strongly contested by the members of the Working Group, who have not only reaffirmed the original findings, but called attention to new evidence that has become available since the publication of the report (Black, 1981a and 1981b; Morris, 1980a, 1980b and 1980c; Townsend, 1981).

Members of the Working Group were wary of claiming too much for their analysis of the *causes* of inequalities in health. Too little work of a wide-ranging kind on different age groups, and on the interrelationships between mortality or, even more, morbidity, and social and economic as well as biological and clinical factors has been carried out. But the Working Group were convinced that it was difficult to begin to explain the pattern of inequalities except by invoking material deprivation as a key concept. In looking at the causes of death for different age-groups where differences between the classes are at their greatest, it is particularly difficult to deny the relevance of socio-economic variables. While it is as yet often impossible to pinpoint exactly how poverty and the class structure *cause* ill-health and death, there is little doubt about the kind of strategy which deserves to be pursued – a theme we shall return to later when policies for the future are discussed.

The review of evidence on causes of inequalities and on access to the NHS has been brought up to date in *The Health Divide* in this volume, and such evidence clearly confirms the main conclusions drawn in the Black Report. The one study quoted by the Secretary of State to cast doubt on the health service findings has itself been severely criticized (see p. 270). *The Health Divide* also charts the progress of the Black Report's recommendations up to the present day, so let us now turn to the treatment that that report received at the hands of the media, the politicians and the professionals.

The Health Divide surfaces

To understand some of the responses to the publication of *The Health Divide* it is necessary to know something of the events leading up to it.

In January 1986 the Health Education Council's Director General, David Player, commissioned Margaret Whitehead to update the evidence on inequalities in health which had accumulated since 1980 and to assess the progress made on the thirty-seven recommendations of the Black Report. This update was prepared during 1986 and finally published in March 1987 as an HEC occasional report. But in the intervening months between commission and publication there were two unforeseen developments: plans were announced to disband the HEC from 31 March 1987, and many political commentators were convinced that an early General Election would be called.

The plans to disband the Health Education Council (which was theoretically an independent body funded by the DHSS) came as a complete surprise to almost everybody – staff, Council members and fellow professionals in the health services alike. The Secretary of State for Social Services, Norman Fowler, announced in November 1986 the plan to dissolve the HEC, which had been responsible for a wide range of health education programmes at a national level, and to reconstitute a special

Health Education Authority within the NHS. Some members of staff would be transferred automatically to the new Authority, but senior members would be asked to re-apply for the top posts. The Authority was to carry on the responsibilities of the old HEC but also take over responsibility from the DHSS for the national education programme on AIDS, with an extra £20 million budget earmarked for that purpose.

There was a very mixed reception to this announcement. Some saw it as a logical step identifying health education firmly as a priority and also as a direct responsibility of the NHS, with the new body more likely to be responsive to the needs of the various health authorities within the service. However, grave doubts were expressed in other quarters, voiced most strongly by the medical press and Labour and Alliance MPs. There were fears that this move was another attempt to subdue independent criticism of official policies voiced by bodies like the HEC in the 1980s. Professional and consumer disquiet would have smaller influence and the commercial interests of big business, entrenched among parliamentary and ministerial representatives, would tend to dominate.

Alliance MPs suggested to the Health Minister that 'the termination of the HEC had far more to do than Ministers admitted with its high-profile campaigning on issues such as smoking, drinking, and diet, which had offended great interests the government preferred to keep sweet' (*Lancet*, 1987a).

The expected election, of course, heightened sensitivity to any report likely to pose difficult questions about the government's handling of policy.

History repeats itself

It was against this background that *The Health Divide* was launched on Tuesday, 24 March. Pre-publication copies were sent to Regional and District Health Authorities and Community Health Councils. The Academic and popular press were also circulated with the report over the previous weekend and were invited to a briefing on the afternoon of the 24th. A panel of distinguished experts in the field, some of whom had acted as scientific advisers in the preparation of the report, had agreed to take part and answer questions on aspects of their research featured in *The Health Divide*. The panel consisted of two of the original members of the Working Group for the Black Report – Sir Douglas Black and Professor Peter Townsend, together with Professor John Fox, Professor Michael Marmot, Dr David Player and Dr Alex Scott-Samuel, as well as the report's author.

Television, radio and national press representatives were already showing great interest and arranging interviews when the Chairman of the HEC, Sir Brian Bailey, decided to cancel the press briefing at the Council offices an hour before it was due to begin. Media interest was thereby heightened. Sir Brian was quoted by the *Independent* as saying the report was 'political dynamite in an election year', and he issued a statement explaining that it was necessary to postpone the briefing until the full Council was able to consider this 'important and possibly controversial document'.

Members of the panel, who had already assembled, decided to proceed with the press briefing at the nearby offices of the Disability Alliance. The Director General of the HEC and his staff, however, were instructed by Sir Brian not to attend. During the briefing some journalists who had also been present at the Black Report's alternative conference nearly seven years earlier admitted to experiencing a distinct feeling of *déjà vu* – in the event, both reports had been similarly treated. This helps to explain the huge media coverage. The report and the manner of its launch provided the leading story that evening on Channel 4 news and it was featured prominently on ITV and BBC television and radio news programmes. By the next morning the story was on the front pages of *The Times*, the *Guardian*, the *Independent* and the *Daily Mirror*, and virtually all the other national papers carried features or leaders on the report. The *Independent* even started a series of daily extracts from it. In the weeks that followed a wide range of regional newspapers took up the story, as did the medical and nursing journals and a variety of discussion and phone-in programmes from the BBC World Service to the Jimmy Young Show. But what exactly were they saying? The majority presented the cancellation of the press conference as an attempted cover-up of unpalatable information about the nation's health and duly brought the information to the attention of readers. Others, like *The Times*, saw the report more as a devastating 'final salvo' from David Player to the government as the HEC was about to be disbanded. The *News of the World* saw more sinister undertones in it and went so far as to suggest that the whole affair was part of a plot by an anti-government group to 'hijack' the HEC!

More controversy was generated when it was discovered that an official from the DHSS had been in touch with the Chairman of the HEC about the report the night before the conference was cancelled. Attention was turned to possible intervention from the DHSS or even government Ministers. The Prime Minister was challenged in the House of Commons and denied any involvement by Ministers or officials. The Department agreed that there had been contact but 'there was no pressure'. Others argued that even if Sir Brian had acted entirely of his own accord, he could be accused of trying to blunt the report's political impact (*Lancet*, 1987b).

By 30 March all available copies of *The Health Divide* had been distributed and an uncharacteristic row broke out in the House of Lords because Members of the House could not obtain copies for a major debate on the NHS scheduled for 1 April. Baroness Seear argued that 'unless this report is published, we are all bound to assume that there are things that the government do not wish the public to see' (Seear, 1987). Viscount Whitelaw calmed the peers by promising to look into the whole matter of publication. A rush reprint was ordered and copies were also made available to the Lords for their debate. In the House of Commons a debate on 6 April on social and economic inequalities gave a great deal of prominence to health inequalities.

Political reaction

Because of the uproar created upon its publication, *The Health Divide* was read by a much wider audience than would otherwise have been expected, and the Black Report's findings were examined once again. Although there was much misquoting of the evidence, concern about the inequalities in health was expressed in many quarters. Twenty-six MPs put down a Commons motion calling for a programme recognizing the relationship between poverty and poor health.

In the House of Lords it was obvious that some peers had understood fully the fundamental issues involved. A common response of the government Ministers questioned about the action to be taken on inequalities in health was to divert attention to improvements in overall health in the United Kingdom, with rising life expectancy and falling infant mortality. These improvements were in fact acknowledged in both reports (pp. 57–62 and 256–60), but that is not the point at issue. Improvements in the health of the poor have failed to keep up with improvements enjoyed by the prosperous – a detail which is hidden when only overall health trends are quoted. Lord Kilmarnock seized on the significance of this and expressed it eloquently in the House of Lords debate:

'Just as the gap between the richest and the poorest has increased within an overall increased national income and the plight of the homeless has become worse within an overall pattern of increased home-ownership, so health inequalities have increased ... It is all part of the same pattern.' (Kilmarnock, 1987)

We would argue that the improved health of the nation as a whole should not be used as an excuse for inaction on the health problems affecting substantial sections of, indeed many millions within, the population.

In the House of Commons attempts were made to discredit the reports by suggesting that they were biased and did not reflect mainstream scientific opinion. A former Under-Secretary of State for Health, Mr Ray Whitney, observed:

'These issues can be approached from a class bias, a fascination with a class division of society which is basically a Marxist approach ... Marxism is entirely based on this class approach and is carefully reflected in the Black Report and *The Health Divide* ... the answer is not to impose on society the socialism that everyone else has rejected, and seemingly only the few authors of these reports and a few left-behind diehards on the Opposition Benches still believe in.' (Whitney, 1987a)

Other MPs reminded this former Minister that the Archbishop of Canterbury's commission on 'Faith in the City' had likewise been labelled Marxist when it raised the issues of poverty and deprivation in the cities.

Two points should be made in response to the former Minister's remarks. Firstly, against the charge of bias can be set testimonies to the unbiased nature of the reports. In the Lords debate, for instance, much was made of the fairness of *The Health Divide*, referred to as 'scrupulously fair' (Lord Kilmarnock); 'a worthy successor to the Black Report, an objective account' (Lord Rea). A *Lancet* leader stressed that *The Health Divide* was not mere polemic but 'a critical scientific review ... properly careful when inferring causation' (*Lancet*, 1987c). Secondly, against the suggestion that the reports are out of touch with scientific opinion can be set the hundreds of studies listed on pages 357–81 testifying to the upsurge of interest in the research field concerning the issue of health inequalities. As we shall emphasize later, recommendations stemming from the two reports are not exceptional or unrepresentative but very much in line with the strategies running through many other recent reports from a large number of independent sources, including those from the British Medical Association, the Faculty of Community Medicine and the World Health Organization, not to mention several stemming from the DHSS itself. Many of the recommendations could be said to reflect the general consensus among specialists in the field of health promotion.

Another common response from Ministers was to accept that health differences exist but to suggest that these differences were due to individual behaviour patterns, like smoking, heavy drinking and lack of exercise, rather than to poverty or other forms of deprivation – an approach commonly referred to as 'victim-blaming' in the literature. For example, the former Under-Secretary of State for Health, Ray Whitney, suggested that both reports ignored the evidence on life-styles and concentrated on poverty. 'Those rates do not mean that those diseases are a function of poverty. Other reasons and issues are neglected by those who write these reports and those who pounce on them and seek to benefit politically from them' (Whitney, 1987b). Such a criticism requires detailed refutation.

First, inspection of pp. 110–15 of the Black Report and pp. 289–96 of *The Health Divide* will show that life-style factors are discussed in both reports. The evidence is illustrated in various tables and the influence of behaviour acknowledged: 'the evidence outlined above suggests that differences in life-style could indeed account for some of the class differential in health' (p. 295). However, the point is also made in both reports (which some politicians seem to have missed) that life-style factors, while explaining some of the health differences observed, cannot adequately explain them all. Attention is drawn to all the causes of death showing a marked class gradient which do not appear to be linked to smoking, alcohol abuse or any other known risk factor. Studies are also quoted which control for life-style factors, yet the gradient in health remains marked. In the Whitehall study (p. 295), for example, the difference in mortality from coronary heart disease between grades of the Civil Service was reduced by less than a third when known risk factors were controlled for. The Alameda County study (p. 295) also showed a small reduction in the difference in the survival chances of rich and poor when thirteen risk factors were controlled for, yet most of the differential remained. While some of the links between deprivation and ill-health are still very poorly understood, life-style is clearly far from being the whole answer. Even where life-style is implicated it cannot be assumed that choice of life-style is completely voluntary in the way ordinarily believed. Groups and upbringing, but also commercial advertising and interventionist policies of the state, exert a major hold over individual behaviour. Evidence from in-depth studies (pp. 297–302) also suggests that some people have more freedom than others by virtue of their individual situation and circumstances to choose a healthy life-style, the unlucky ones being restrained from adopting a healthier life, even when they would wish to do so, by income, housing, work and other social constraints. Such evidence has led some observers to criticize certain health education campaigns for putting all the emphasis on individual responsibility while neglecting the government's responsibility to develop policies to support the desired life-style changes. For example, on the 1987 'Look after your Heart' campaign Dr Tim Lang of the London Food Commission was quoted as saying, 'instead of exhorting people to eat better, smoke less and exercise more, Ministers should make it easier for them to improve their health – that means tackling poverty by improving welfare benefits, improving the quality of food and making the industry tell people what it puts in their food' (*Guardian*, 22 April 1987).

Individual and state accountability

The problem of distinguishing between individual and corporate or government responsibility for health can be illustrated by one event in 1986. The publication by the Northern Regional Health Authority of a report about inequalities of health in the North (Townsend, Phillimore and Beattie, 1986) happened to coincide with a visit to Newcastle by a newly appointed junior Health Minister, Mrs Edwina Currie, who was quoted by the *Daily Telegraph*, the *Guardian* and other newspapers as having 'dismissed' or 'rejected' the report's link between ill-health and material deprivation or poverty: 'I honestly don't think it has anything to do with poverty. The problem very often for many people is just ignorance ... and failing to realize they do have some control over their own lives.' Her comments provoked widespread controversy, and the prevalence of unhealthy dietary practices and heavy smoking and drinking in the North were at the centre of that controversy for several weeks. Mrs Currie subsequently had second thoughts, but these attracted rather less attention. In an article in the *Evening Chronicle* (10 October 1986) she wrote: 'Nor would I ever deny the links between poverty, unemployment and ill-health ... What bothers me is that this is too simple an explanation. We may be ignoring the possibilities of improving people's health ... by encouraging a greater awareness of other links between smoking, heavy drinking and illness.' That is plainly a very different position, and equally carries profound implications for government interpretations of the problems of the nation's health and its sponsorship of scientific research.

No one would deny that individual options in life-style substantially affect outcomes in health – though they can of course be influenced in turn by education, family, the press, commerce and other institutions. The question is whether the scientific and political establishment may be said to be taking sufficiently seriously the evidence that material deprivation accounts for much the largest part of variations in health outcomes. The Working Group under Sir Douglas Black had concluded that, while genetic and cultural or behavioural explanations played their part, the predominant or governing explanation for inequalities in health lay in material deprivation. For statisticians perhaps the most impressive finding of the study of 678 wards in the North was that 65 per cent of the variation in ill-health, as measured not only by deaths but also permanent sickness and low-weight births, could be 'explained' (in regression analyses) by indicators of material deprivation. That finding needs to be followed up in depth, using research strategies very different from those of the laboratory and the symptomatology of the individual, to pin down both the factors within 'material deprivation' which are most at issue for different forms of ill-health, and the specific policies which can reduce particular effects of deprivation. Nonetheless, the finding helps to confirm what should be the government's first priority in any strategy designed to improve health, and puts into proportion the scope for complementary individual action with the same aim.

Confused messages

In contrast to the hostile reception from government, the health professions and the research community have taken the findings of the two reports seriously. There is widespread agreement on three main premises in the reports: that in absolute terms the standards of health of the population as a whole have improved since the Second World War; that despite that improvement serious social inequalities in health have persisted; and that socio-economic factors have played an important part in maintaining and even increasing these differentials.

However, a few social scientists have questioned the finding that the health gap between the rich and poor has widened since the war. They have expressed to an undue extent reservations about the usefulness of occupational class as a social indicator when making comparisons of health over long time-spans. They have minimized the findings about the class differentials in health or the trends in those differentials on a variety of grounds and have put forward an alternative measure not of differences of ill-health or mortality between classes or rich and poor but of differences in the age of death of people dying in different years (LeGrand, 1985; LeGrand and Rabin, 1986; Illsley, 1986, 1987a, 1987b; Illsley and LeGrand, 1986; Le-Grand, 1987). The problems of using occupational class in studies of health trends are widely appreciated and are set out in the Black Report (pp. 39–41) and *The Health Divide* (pp. 256–8). However, as there has recently been much confusion in reporting this issue, even in professional journals, some of the main arguments will be examined again here.

Occupational class has been used for many years as a convenient indicator of the standards of living and way of life of different groups and has been used to represent 'social' class. A person's named occupation is basically a pragmatic guide to that person's social position and his or her likely command over resources, and as such has its limitations. It is only an approximate indicator of family living standards or social position. Some objections to its use for measuring trends are related to the changes successive Registrars General have made in allocating occupations to different classes. Others are related to structural shifts in the pattern of employment over the past fifty years, which have led to more non-manual and fewer manual jobs. But these changes can be monitored and, by applying strict estimation procedures, generalizations about quantitative trends can reliably be made. Doubts have been raised particularly about studies which only compare classes I and V, the two extremes of the social range, covering a small proportion of the population. In the latest report on mortality, for example, by the Registrar General, attention was called to the uncertain classification of some occupations in class V. But, like some of the residual problems in measuring the national income, such problems have to be put into proportion, and can be controlled. These are legitimate reasons for concern, and *The Health Divide* specifies recent studies which have re-examined the figures with these problems in mind. The studies assess inequalities across all classes, not just between the extremes, and weight each according to its share of the population. To compensate for classification changes the analyses were also checked by following only those occupations which could be consistently traced throughout the time-span. Using such techniques, health inequality was found to have increased for adults of working age over the years from 1931 to 1971, confirming the original observations of the Black Report. A further study (Marmot and McDowall, 1986, quoted on p. 261) which reported a widening health gap between manual and non-manual classes from 1971–2 to 1979–83 also noted the measurement problems and re-evaluated the results accordingly. The authors concluded that neither changes in classification nor the 4 per cent shift in the population from manual to non-manual occupations during the decade could account for the widening of the health gap which they observed.

Illsley and LeGrand have also raised objections to studies based only on people aged under 65, partly because the proportion of deaths in this age range has changed over the past fifty years, making comparisons difficult, and partly because a large proportion of deaths now take place over the age of 65 and the results found in the under-65s may not apply to the older age-groups. Two responses have been made to this objection. Firstly, it is still very important to consider deaths under the age of 65. Even though they are a minority they are premature deaths, and in many cases they can also be regarded as the most preventable. It is customary in many areas of preventive medicine and health promotion to focus on premature deaths for this very reason. Secondly, new evidence available on the health of people aged over 65 tends to confirm the pattern of inequality found among younger people.

The familiar occupational class gradient in mortality has now been established securely for those aged 65–75 and even for those aged 75 plus (see p. 230). Rates of chronic sickness are higher in manual than in non-manual socio-economic groups at ages over 65 and the gap between the two widened significantly over the years 1974 to 1984. The 1986 Health and Life-Style Survey confirmed the social pattern of chronic disease and disability in older people in different socio-economic and income groups. Such evidence is in line with the findings at younger ages. There is certainly no evidence to suggest that the social pattern of health suddenly reverses after age 65.

Most confusion has arisen over the statistical methods for studying the health of populations. The method of measuring trends in the distribution of age at death which, following their critique of occupational class, Illsley and LeGrand have put forward has been widely misinterpreted in the press as an alternative way of measuring social inequalities in health. This statistical patterning of deaths by age appears to show a steady decrease in inequality since the 1920s, in contrast to the prevailing social or occupational class evidence. In fact it does not measure differences between social classes or between rich and poor at all. It measures only the variation in the age of death of individuals in the population. LeGrand makes it quite clear that he considers his approach to be complementary to that taken by the Black Working Group, rather than a competing or conflicting approach. Latterly the two authors have diverged in their interpretation of the 'age-at-death' methodology. Illsley still believes it challenges the thesis of a widening inequality in health (Illsley, 1987). However, LeGrand concludes that the techniques of measuring inequalities in age of death 'do not answer the same kinds of questions' as comparisons between social classes 'and therefore should be viewed as complements to them, not as substitutes'. Although this method shows that the variation in the age of death is decreasing over the population as a whole, it cannot help us with the question of whether social inequalities in death are changing too. As the British Medical Association comments, 'it makes no distinction between random variations in life-span and variations that are due to different people's experience of deprivation or social inequality' (BMA, 1987). Some social scientists have countered the conclusions drawn from the 'age-at-death' methodology in specific terms (see, in particular, Wilkinson, 1986, 1987; Hart, 1987).

What has been happening since the 1920s is a dramatic decrease in the infectious and respiratory diseases which caused high mortality in childhood and fell most heavily on the poor. The variation in the age of death would be expected to decrease as a result. But the diseases which predominate today, the degenerative diseases of middle and old age, still affect the poor sections of society more than the rich, and some of them to an even greater extent proportionately than they did, though Illsley and LeGrand's calculations would not be able to detect this situation. In theory it would be possible for the variation in the age of death of *individuals* to decrease over the same period as *social* inequalities in death increased. In short, the research on life-span changes should not be regarded as challenging the conclusions of the Black Report and *The Health Divide* but treated on its own merits in addressing a limited and different set of questions.

Action at the grass roots

A leader in the *British Medical Journal* has likened the Black Report to the Bible: 'much quoted, occasionally read and largely ignored when it comes to action' (*British Medical Journal*, 1986).

The treatment of the report at a national level would indeed fit this description. In *The Health Divide* the progress made on the thirty-seven recommendations of the Black Report is assessed (see pp. 306–50) and a distinct lack of action at national and central level is apparent. However, what is remarkable in the assessment is the amount of activity stimulated at the grass-roots level and in research as a result of the Black Report. Major initiatives have been taken by people in the health services, local government, voluntary agencies and research units around the country in response to the deeply disturbing situation documented in the report. The professional bodies representing members in the health and social services have also taken substantial initiatives, as the account on pp. 341–3 shows. Nevertheless, without a national commitment all this activity has, understandably, been piecemeal and largely unco-ordinated.

With the publication of *The Health Divide*, inequalities in health were once again put firmly on the agenda. As a result the topic has featured prominently as the theme of numerous professional conferences, and in meetings and seminars sponsored by community health councils throughout the country. The correspondence columns of the medical journals include many references, briefing papers on the issue have been prepared by many of the agencies concerned with health, and health education officers have expressed support for the publication in the form of petitions to the new Health Education Authority.

Most discussion centres not on the evidence, which by and large is accepted, but on what kind of action can and should be taken to remedy matters. This is plainly of crucial importance and the rest of this Introduction will be devoted to a review of the most realistic options.

A broad strategy

In any public debate on health policy there still tends to be a preoccupation with the provision of traditional health services, with hospital closures and the reduction of operation waiting-lists, equating better health with more and better medical services. It was striking that exchanges in the 1987 General Election campaign were almost exclusively of this nature. But many concerned to reduce health inequalities, and indeed to promote the health of the population in general, are convinced that a new kind of health policy is required which takes account of the many and varied factors which influence health far beyond the domain of the health services. Just as the NHS should not take all the blame for the present state of health inequalities in this country, neither should it be expected to reduce the problem single-handedly in the future. (Those who suggest that the evidence on widening health inequalities undermines the achievements of the NHS have totally misunderstood this fundamental point.)

A wide strategy encompassing co-ordinated action at local and national government level is required in addition to health service activity. This point is stressed time and time again throughout discussions in the Black Report and *The Health Divide*. Nowhere is this premise more evident than in the World Health Organization's 'Targets for Health for All by the Year 2000', with the theme of reducing inequalities in health by broadly based strategy running right through the thirty-eight detailed targets. To save repetition here, attention is drawn to pp. 347–9 of *The Health Divide* which review some of the most recent policy developments on the issue and ask what this country's commitment to the WHO programme would entail if adopted wholeheartedly. This is seen not only as a realistic policy option but also as an essential re-orientation if the current health problems of the nation are to be tackled.

Turning to a consideration of the economic arguments, although they are central to any discussion on health policy they are often treated in a very superficial way. The following sections offer the opportunity to air the arguments more fully.

The economic argument for more resources for health

Successive governments have argued that the country cannot afford to implement the Black Report's recommendations. But to a large extent this is a question of what the nation chooses to spend on health and welfare. The fundamental point in a wealthy country like Britain is that money for health is only not there if it is being spent on something else – like defence, roads or the marketing of consumer goods. Underlying the Working Group's judgement of the measures which might be possible in the current political and economic climate there runs a powerful argument: that a positive health strategy depends on political and economic priorities. The choice of those priorities is partly a question of arguing that health deserves to have a higher place in the claims that can be made on a nation's resources, partly that this in turn will necessarily involve spreading wealth around more equally than has been customary in Britain, and partly that expenditure on health has a lot to do with national production and hence with wealth *and* with welfare. Substantial expenditure on a programme for health represents a necessary part of wise national investment in a thriving economy.

This point about investment in health deserves to be explained more clearly, because successive governments seem disinclined to accept it as a necessary assumption of planning. Much public discussion about social objectives is distorted by the rigid division invariably made between the public and private sector and the assumption that the former is financed by the latter. Part of the conventional wisdom is that expenditure on the welfare state, including health, is 'unproductive', and that the amounts available for welfare depend on the prosperity of the private sector – which tends to be equated with the prosperity of the national economy as a whole. On these assumptions governments have no choice but to reduce welfare spending during periods of recession. Both these assumptions can be questioned.

The welfare state was born at a time when public expenditure was seen as an aid or adjunct to economic growth and the pioneers of the welfare state, in making a case for spending some public money on welfare, did so without any doubt that welfare expenditure was conditional on that growth taking place; a desirable spin-off. It was not seen, except in the most incidental sense, as contributing in its own right to that growth. Welfare expenditure came to be regarded as something different from economic growth and efficiency; at best neutral, at worst a potential 'burden' on growth.

Since then governments of all political persuasions have repeated the same message, over and over again. Yet it is a distortion of reality. To understand this we need to understand what is usually meant by economic growth. To simplify, economic growth is a measure of the increase in the value of the sum total of goods and services that are sold by either a company or a national economy. And that is all. Consider an example. Every extra unit produced and sold from a factory is a contribution to the growth of that factory and, in as much as that factory is part of the national economy, to the growth of the national economy. But suppose that in increasing the number of units sold safety standards are reduced, thereby increasing the number of industrial injuries and also raising the levels of stress among the workforce and reducing work satisfaction. This 'hidden cost', known as an 'externality' in mainstream economics, is not deducted or in any way connected with the increased 'wealth' generated by that factory. Yet the community as a whole will have to meet the cost of treating and caring for the casualties, which must imply some decrease in overall well-being. The apparent wealth generated by an industrial unit and the actual wealth taking into account such externalities are therefore two very different measures. To get a real sense of the increased wealth and prosperity of the community we have to take the formal figure for economic growth and then deduct the externalities. It is not, of course, a calculation that is evident or, indeed, one which can easily be done. It is hard enough to quantify the costs of injury, still less treatment given free in the home and the lowered levels of positive health which represent a by-product. Yet, as Richard Titmuss has argued, social costs, 'if allowed to lie where they fall, may result in larger costs in the shape of physical or psychological handicaps, destitution, deprived children, ill-educated workers unable or unwilling to acquire new skills and a general slackening in the sense of social involvement'. When either economic growth or economic loss is considered in range or depth, it cannot be distinguished from social growth or social loss.

Economic and social development are intertwined in ways which still require analysis. Whether we consider the urban riots in the summer of 1981 or the millions of people who are unemployed, social costs can be very real costs, even if not easily measurable in pounds and pence. To quote Richard Titmuss again: 'We need to find ways of seeing economic growth and social growth as interdependent in the sense that lagging behind in one has, necessarily, negative consequences on the other.' To see welfare merely as a potential by-product from economic growth, and as having no contribution to make to that growth, is at best shortsighted and at worst profoundly misguided. What requires at least as much consideration is the possibility that by according priority to the pursuit of social objectives there may be beneficial by-products for the economy.

The problem is in quantifying the money costs and gains of social policy. Cost-benefit analysis and output budgeting cannot be taken very far. It is hard, and perhaps at the moment impossible, to demonstrate and quantify social costs; to turn intangibles into tangibles. The technical wizardry of accountants, actuaries, statisticians and econometricians is hard to apply to even a fraction of the daunting problems, particularly health problems, of an entire population. It is difficult to put a cost on injury, pain, discomfort or dissatisfaction, and to measure matters pertinent to 'positive' health like range of physical and mental activity, degree of social integration or extent of personal fulfilment. There is a sense in which the amount a nation can afford to spend on the pursuit of health is what it chooses to spend. Qualitative judgements as well as quantitative measures of health have to be combined. Certainly there is an impressive case to be made – whether by comparison with other equally rich societies, the demonstrated need in our

Table A: *Resources available for services (1980/81 to 1985/6)*

	1980–81	1981–2	1982–3	1983–4	1984–5	1985–6
Hospital and Community						
Health Services, current						
Total spending (£m)	6,963	7,681	8,244	8,667	9,161	9,678
Increase (%)		10.3	7.3	5.1	5.7	5.6
Inflation etc. (%)		8.2	6.5	5.1	5.8	5.2
Change after inflation						
(%)		2.0	0.8	0.0	−0.1	0.4
Family Practitioner						
Services, current						
Total spending (£m)	2,173	2,504	2,894	3,110	3,419	3,649
Increase (%)		15.2	15.6	7.4	9.9	6.7
Inflation etc. (%)		12.9	11.6	5.4	6.9	6.5
Change after						
inflation (%)		2.0	3.6	2.0	2.8	0.2
*NHS total**						
Total spending (£m)	9,971	11,183	12,197	12,921	13,874	14,724
Increase (%)		12.1	9.1	5.9	7.4	6.1
Inflation etc. (%)		9.0	7.4	5.0	5.9	5.5
Change after						
inflation (%)		2.9	1.5	0.9	1.4	0.6

* The figures for NHS total spending include both capital expenditure on Central Health and Miscellaneous Service, therefore these figures will not equal the sum of HCHS and FPS expenditure.

Source: Social Services Committee, *Public Expenditure on the Social Services* (1985–6), quoted in the NAHA *NHS Economic Review* (1986).

own society, or the health benefits which accrue from lessening inequality – for a more generous national commitment of resources to lessening inequality.

These arguments, however, are not in favour today. Recent governments have reiterated their belief in giving priority to economic growth as a pre-requisite for spending anything more on health and welfare. As a result, funding for health and welfare services has continued to be tight. While successive governments have continued to insist that funding of the NHS is well ahead of inflation, a closer examination of the figures reveals a mixed story. A study by the National Association of Health Authorities, an independent research organization which lobbies on behalf of health authorities, reveals the following picture of NHS funds. 'During the 1980s, expenditure on the NHS has risen at a higher rate than in many other areas of the public sector. Nevertheless . . . after inflationary pressures in the NHS have been taken into account, the annual increases in expenditure have been small.' The table on page 20 provides an outline.

This table reveals that the gross figures for NHS funding as a whole hide the fact that the bulk of the increase in real terms has been absorbed by the Family Practitioner Service, that is to say services run on behalf of and by GPs. Expenditure by the hospital and community health services has been virtually stationary throughout the early and mid 1980s. As the NAHA report explains:

> By the beginning of the financial year 1986/7 it was evident that very little centrally financed growth for the hospital and community health service would be available. The bulk of the increase in FPC expenditure, which remains the only part of the NHS not cash limited, can be accounted for by the rising drug bill.

The second point that needs to be made is that the gross figures for hospital and community services ignore the fact that funds are unevenly distributed across the country. Since the mid 1970s, the DHSS has been engaged in an exercise designed to foster greater equality in health resources in the different regions of the country. This had its origins in the recommendations of the Resource Allocation Working Party (or RAWP for short) which were designed to channel extra resources to those parts of the country which have been historically neglected, primarily the North and the Midlands. But in a period of virtually static growth the only way this redistribution can take place is if some areas gain *at the expense of others*. This is what has happened. The Thames regions in particular have suffered net falls in their budgets in order that the historically poorer regions, like Trent and Northern, can continue to grow. NAHA, in a profile of one of the Thames regions, recorded:

> The RAWP allocation process has led to planned reductions in real resources of up to 0.3 per cent per year. However, by far the largest proportion of reductions in resources came from unplanned and therefore unanticipated factors. These unplanned reductions stemmed from the consequences of pay award shortfalls and the recurring loss of the 1983/4 public expenditure cuts. Therefore during the period 1982/3 to 1985/6, the real reduction in resources amounted to approximately 3 per cent of total resources.

One result of this extremely tight funding is that all health authorities, but particularly those on the losing end of the RAWP reallocation, have come to rely heavily on efficiency savings to balance their books. The NAHA survey is one of several which has suggested that up to 40 per cent of health authorities are now using efficiency savings as the only way of making up for shortfalls in the money allocated to them for new, nationally agreed, pay awards and some are also looking to them as the only mechanism for funding new services. Indeed in some health districts there is an explicit recognition that the only growth money they can expect to receive will come from rationalizations of existing services. There are those who have questioned the longer-term implications of this. Nicholas Bosanquet (1985), in a survey of NHS expenditure, has written: 'The general picture is of a service finding that the available resources cannot stretch to meet all policy commitments.'

The long history of under-funding

The critical interpretation of government funding of the NHS which we are developing here becomes even more critical if a further qualification is attached to the figures in Table A. If that qualification is accepted the overall result is to make much more understandable the growing volume of complaints by staff, including large numbers of consultants and nurses within the service, about the deterioration in facilities and conditions. For many years government Ministers, backed up by the Royal Commission on the National Health Service in the late 1970s, have conceded that a margin of real growth has to be allowed for the NHS in public expenditure planning for demographic change – largely because of the ageing of the population and the disproportionate demands on health care services made by the oldest members of the population. The figure has been put at 2 per cent. Each year, it is implied, 2 per cent more has to be spent, *even after adjusting for inflation*, simply to maintain standards of service for the changing population. Some planning specialists have argued that this figure should be higher than 2 per cent (though there is no consensus about the amount) to reflect the increased cost of new forms of drugs, examination and surgery which are replacing the older forms sinking into obsolescence. This line of thinking makes the bottom line of the table look pretty sick.

The problem of under-investment is not new. For many years the United Kingdom has devoted a smaller fraction of her Gross Domestic Product to health than countries at a comparable stage of economic development. We spend about 25 per cent below the average spent by the fifteen OECD member countries for which reliable information exists – in fact, the smallest expenditure of any of those countries. Sweden, the Federal Republic of Germany, France, the Netherlands, the United States and Denmark spend between a third and half as much again, proportionate to their income (OECD, 1985).

Relative to some other health care systems – for instance, that of the United States – it is arguable nonetheless that the NHS has been consistently more efficient, but this cannot explain or make up for all the under-spending. For long periods different categories of long-stay patients in hospital and living at home have found it hard to get the services they need.

For many years health centres were slow to develop. As long ago as 1956 the Guillebaud Committee exposed the scaremongering about the alleged runaway costs of the NHS and showed that in fact health care was economical in the UK. In 1974 the House of Commons Public Expenditure Committee declared that 'it is the opinion of this committee that no government has ever provided sufficient money to allow the health service to function and react to growing needs effectively'. Much evidence could be quoted along these lines.

Judged on the basis of history and the available quantitative evidence for the UK and other countries it is hard to believe that funding for the NHS as a whole, as distinct from certain parts of it, has ever been more than just adequate. Even the days of bare sufficiency seem now long gone. Extra money for mentally and physically handicapped people, for the mentally ill and for large numbers of the elderly would make an enormous difference to their lives. Many long-stay hospitals need to be transformed in their amenities and their conditions. NHS waiting-lists for many routine but important operations are too long. Large numbers of hospitals and clinics have outlived their useful life. The wages and conditions of many low-paid staff need to be greatly improved. Only with a steady increase in available resources can the inequalities between different arms of the service, as well as between regions, be eliminated and the deficiencies in parts of the service everywhere made good.

One area of conspicuous neglect in national policy is any commitment to positive discrimination in favour of communities or sections of the population suffering greater health disadvantage. Despite much grass-roots activity and enthusiasm flowing from the original Black Report recommendations, and steps taken by some local councils and District Health Authorities set out below (pp. 322–47), the government has still to develop a 'small areas' strategy to complement the RAWP strategy.

These problems have been exacerbated by unduly severe financial restrictions on other welfare agencies, notably local authority social service departments, which contribute to the wider welfare support system. Many councils have been rate-capped or face the prospect of it; voluntary and charitable agencies are finding it extremely difficult to make ends meet. In many areas community support services like home-helps, meals-on-wheels and community services for the mentally ill and handicapped are woefully inadequate and overstretched. The House of Commons Social Services Select Committee examined community provision and reported an 'approaching crisis in the community'. They argued that 'the stage has now been reached where the rhetoric of community care has to be matched by action'. The displacement of patients into the community has not led to any rational redirection or augmentation of resources to meet their needs.

The difficult mix of private market and public service

Above all, the prospects for doing something about inequalities in health have been affected by the government's ideology in favour of a private market and cutting public expenditure. This takes different forms. One of these is a very significant shift in the climate now governing the thinking of many NHS staff and administrators. Since the early 1980s, the NHS has been increasingly dominated by the values inherent in cost-benefit analysis. And that is part of a broader incursion of business values into the NHS.

The year 1979 saw the election of a Conservative government strongly committed to the values of the market-place and private enterprise. It was simultaneously impressed and embarrassed by reports at the time which suggested that the public services in general, and the NHS in particular, were 'out of control'. The House of Commons Public Accounts Committee, for instance, published a highly critical report of the management and administration of the health service which questioned whether the service was susceptible to normal managerial controls.

As on other occasions the government turned to the private sector and the business community for advice, and invited Roy Griffiths, Managing Director of the Sainsbury supermarket chain, to review the entire administration of the NHS. The Griffiths team was struck by what it saw as an apparent lack of clearly identified leaders and lines of management authority. In a frequently quoted passage they wrote: 'If Florence Nightingale were carrying her lamp through the corridors of the NHS today, she would almost certainly be searching for the people in charge.'

They argued that the absence of overall general managers meant that 'there is no driving force seeking and accepting direct and personal responsibility for developing management plans, securing their implementation and monitoring actual achievement'. They said that, coming from a business environment, they were surprised to find that 'rarely are precise management objectives set; there is little measurement of health output; clinical evaluation of particular practices is by no means common and economic evaluation of these practices is extremely rare'.

The result was a series of recommendations, the most important of which were the adoption of a management structure and management techniques common in the business and commercial world. The existing system of 'consensus management', whereby administrators and health care professionals shared the task of running the health service, would be replaced by a service of professional general managers who would not only assume overall control of the service, but whose task it would be to introduce clearer planning guidelines and performance targets and regular monitoring of progress towards these targets. The proposals were rapidly accepted by the government.

But perhaps more important than the detailed proposals themselves, the Griffiths Report represented the triumph of a set of beliefs about what was important and how things should be done. It thrust management and management preoccupations to the very centre of NHS thinking, pushing aside, or at least subordinating, the arguably less clearly formulated collection of ideas about service and the public good which had hitherto provided the dominant ethos.

The results are still working their way through the service, but already it is possible to discern a distinct shift in thinking. Modern management is about establishing procedures in which activity can be measured against clearly defined objectives. It involves breaking down an activity into inputs and outputs and developing procedures for monitoring the achievement of one against the other. But to do this it becomes essential to be able to measure activity, and in something as complex as health care this cannot be done without ignoring key aspects of treatment and recovery and oversimplifying measures of outcome. In an attempt to come to grips with the problems, the NHS has developed a series of indicators of its performance: how many people pass through a hospital bed in a year; how many operations are performed; and how much it costs to keep a patient in hospital for a day. There are now several thousand of these performance indicators, as they are called, covering almost every area of activity. They have been put on to computer disks so that a health authority can look up its own performance and, more importantly, can compare this with other districts. Very rapidly an informal 'league table' has been established, with those districts with the best performance indicators at the top and those at the bottom setting out to emulate them.

But what exactly is being measured and what is being left out in this attempt to create a 'scientific' management ethos for the health service? The difficulty revolves around the fact that performance indicators as management tools have been developed in a business environment where inputs and outputs can be readily quantified and measured. It is by no means clear that they are so easily extended to something like health provision which, as much as anything else, is also about qualitative issues. It is of limited use to know how many patients are passing through a hospital bed each year if we don't also know the outcome of their treatment. Activity, in the case of health care, does not necessarily equal beneficial activity, and performance indicators put us in the difficult position of being unable to say whether an increase in activity is actually improving the nation's health.

It is easy to forget, in all the management jargon, what is implied. The significance of the new scientific, business, ethos is that it has shifted attention away from a concern with the overall quantity and quality of the service being provided to a preoccupation with how resources can best (most productively) be used. The objectives are changing. What counts are service outputs – so many extra operations, so many extra patients treated. In other words, as inputs become virtually static, the focus of attention has shifted from the adequacy of what's going into the NHS to how much can be squeezed out. Good management, business management, holds out the promise that the NHS can still flourish even when its budget is falling.

But the shift in attention is not just from inputs to outputs. Inputs raise questions of need. Outputs merely raise questions of efficiency – how productively are health authorities using their resources as judged by their comparative performance indicators. Even this is a very narrow scientific criterion on which to decide resources.

The worry must be that in substituting efficiency for need, the health service is turning in on itself and away from the social context within which it is operating. The new management ethos is fostering an inward-looking, narrow and self-preoccupied administration which has neither the inclination nor the tools to look beyond its own immediate problems, and has very little interest in the broader issues raised by reports like the Black Report and *The Health Divide*. It is no longer concerned with the common good, citizenship rights and outstanding public service. It is impossible simultaneously to pursue privatization, with different standards of care, and a high common standard of public service, with equal access irrespective of income. This narrowing of managerial horizons puts great responsibility on the lay members of health authorities to ensure that the broader issues are not lost. Yet it is generally accepted that lay members have very little power or influence over health authority policy today. Cost-benefit analysis and its associated disciplines which serve the ideology of the containment or reduction of public expenditure have come to dominate our thinking.

An unequal conception of service

The internal changes taking place in the management of the NHS have to be recognized as forming only one part of the realignment of the service with the private market. Thus expenditure generally on public services has been cut or held back, parts of the NHS have been or are being privatized, competing forms of external private service have been and are being subsidized, and the entire structure of the NHS is being encouraged to conform with the private sector model. The government understands that there is more than one way of skinning a cat.

The process began before 1979, though it has greatly accelerated since then. There were moves in the 1970s by multinational companies to build private hospitals and extend private medical insurance. The Health Services Act of 1976 was intended to control the private sector of health care but ended up by having little effect on the existing number of pay-beds and opened the way to an expansion of the private medical sector.

During the 1980s a long struggle has gone on to contain expenditure. Prescription and other charges have been increased several times. In 1980 the Health Service Bill was passed to stop the enforced withdrawal of pay-beds from NHS hospitals, to change the control over private practice and to abolish the Health Service Board, which had been created by the Labour government to supervise private hospitals. Full-time consultants were permitted to gain an additional 10 per cent of their gross earnings from private practice. The Conservative Minister of State for Health said that he would like at least 25 per cent of treatment to be carried out in the private sector. Hospital cleaning and other ancillary services have been privatized. The competitive tendering system for NHS ancillary services has not in fact led to the substantial decline in state services expected, because the majority of contracts have been won by the NHS itself. In 1985 the Social Services Select Committee of the House of Commons concluded that the system 'has failed to bring home the bacon after four years despite the waste of much management time and the engendering of industrial conflict'. The virtues of running health care as a comprehensive public service, and acknowledging that there is an alternative morality of service to the song and dance about private management, have not been voiced.

Behind the present government's approach to medicine and health care is a tenacious set of market values; a belief in the virtue of individualism – that people should have the 'freedom' to buy the best medical care they can afford and that those who are able and willing to pay more should get more. Against this, those of all political colours who have for four decades favoured a very strong NHS have emphasized the importance of collective responsibility and equal access to medical attention regardless of individual financial, social or cultural constraints. These are two different visions of society. It is this difference which, more than anything else, seems to underlie the government's rejection of 'inequalities in health'. But fundamentally these two views have to be thought through and worked out in relationship to the achievement of health and the organization and future development of health services. In affirming belief in the basic principles of the NHS many people in Britain must accept the challenge to develop a better theory about health and translate such theory into an effective programme for health.

List of Abbreviations and Definitions

GHS: General Household Survey. Carried out annually by the Office of Population Censuses and Surveys. Based on a sample of 15,000 households in the United Kingdom, it provides data on a range of topics including health, education, employment, housing and migration. It has been running annually since 1970.

HIPE: Hospital Inpatient Enquiry. An annual survey carried out jointly by the Department of Health and Social Security, the OPCS and the Welsh Office and designed to find out how fully hospitals are used and what for.

MRC: Medical Research Council.

Neonatal mortality: Deaths during the first four weeks of life.

OPCS: Office of Population Censuses and Surveys. A governmental department which is in charge of the national census and many other recurrent and occasional surveys and collections of statistics.

Perinatal mortality: Still-births and deaths in the first week of life.

Post-neonatal mortality: Deaths after the first month but before the end of the first year of life.

Registrar General: The head of the OPCS responsible for the collection of official statistics by that department.

Registrar General's Decennial Supplements: The OPCS gathers mortality and morbidity data annually. Every ten years it supplements these annual data with extra information from the ten-year census and publishes it as decennial supplements, one on occupational mortality and the other on area mortality.

SMR: Standardized Mortality Ratio. A method of comparing death rates between different sections of the population, holding other variables constant; e.g. comparing one area with another holding age, sex and occupation constant. Thus Merseyside has a higher SMR than East Anglia, even allowing for the different population structures of the two areas.

WHO: World Health Organization.

The Black Report

Foreword by Patrick Jenkin

The Working Group on Inequalities in Health was set up in 1977, on the initiative of my predecessor as Secretary of State, under the Chairmanship of Sir Douglas Black, to review information about differences in health status between the social classes; to consider possible causes and the implications for policy; and to suggest further research.

The Group was given a formidable task, and Sir Douglas and his colleagues deserve thanks for seeing the work through, and for the thoroughness with which they have surveyed the considerable literature on the subject. As they make clear, the influences at work in explaining the relative health experience of different parts of our society are many and interrelated; and, while it is disappointing that the Group were unable to make greater progress in disentangling the various causes of inequalities in health, the difficulties they experienced are perhaps no surprise given current measurement techniques.

It will come as a disappointment to many that over long periods since the inception of the NHS there is generally little sign of health inequalities in Britain actually diminishing and, in some cases, they may be increasing. It will be seen that the Group has reached the view that the causes of health inequalities are so deep-rooted that only a major and wide-ranging programme of public expenditure is capable of altering the pattern. I must make it clear that additional expenditure on the scale which could result from the report's recommendations – the amount involved could be upwards of £2 billion a year – is quite unrealistic in present or any foreseeable economic circumstances, quite apart from any judgement that may be formed of the effectiveness of such expenditure in dealing with the problems identified. I cannot, therefore, endorse the Group's recommendations. I am making the report available for discussion, but without any commitment by the government to its proposals.

PATRICK JENKIN
Secretary of State for
Social Services

August 1980

Chapter 1

Concepts of Health and Inequality

Throughout history different meanings have been given to the idea of 'health'. One is freedom from clinically ascertainable disease, which has been central to the development of medicine. In ancient Greece the followers of Asclepius believed that the chief role of the physician was to 'treat disease, to restore health by correcting any imperfections caused by the accidents of birth or life' (Dubos, 1960, p. 109). Beginning with primitive surgical intervention and herbal treatment, a tradition was established which was to prove extraordinarily powerful, accelerating in the eighteenth century with the rise of science and again in the twentieth century as a consequence of the massive resources provided for research and innovation in medical technologies. The Cartesian philosophy of the body conceived as a machine and the body controlled as a machine provided an impetus for scientific experiment and a stream of practical outcomes which for an increasing proportion of the population seemed to validate a mechanistic perspective.

There can be no doubt about the success with which such an 'engineering' approach in medicine has been applied. Medical education became concerned with the structure and functions of the body and with disease processes, and medical science became represented predominantly by the acute hospital with its concentration of technological resources (Abel-Smith, 1964). The relatively restricted and familiar use of the word 'health' is therefore associated with the belief systems and the practice of a medicine from which its origins can be traced. Health, which derives from a word meaning whole, is the object of the healing process. To heal is literally to make whole or to restore health. The structure of medicine and of the health services helps to sustain this meaning. Some (for example, McKeown, 1976) have argued however that this development in medicine has distorted our understanding of the problems of human health and well-being and that there are alternative or complementary approaches which it is increasingly important to clarify and properly finance.

Much wider meanings have been given to the word 'health', which hold major implications for the organization of society and the pattern upon which personal life may be modelled. To the followers of the ideas symbolized in ancient Greece by the goddess Hygeia, rational social organization and rational individual behaviour were all-important to the promotion of human health. It was an attribute to which men were entitled if they governed their lives wisely and is echoed in today's 'life-style' approaches to good health. According to them, 'the most important function of medicine is to discover and teach the natural laws which will ensure a man a healthy mind in a healthy body' (Dubos, 1960, p. 109). Implicit also are ideas of the good life: not just freedom from pain, discomfort, stress and boredom, which themselves extend beyond the competence of clinicians to diagnose or treat, but positive expression of vigour, well-being and engagement with one's environment or community. In some respects this more comprehensive approach reached its apogee in the definition of health adopted at the foundation of the World Health Organization at the end of the Second World War as a 'state of complete physical, mental and social well-being and not merely the absence of disease or infirmity'. Adherents of this more comprehensive approach, which is usually called 'social', have worked both within and outside medicine. In most countries there are movements for physical fitness and good diet. Immunization is a standard public health practice. And through direct and indirect 'health education' and counselling, higher standards of health are encouraged. In the case of children this wider conception of health directs concern not only to the presence or absence of disease, but to growth and development, physical, cognitive and emotional. (There is, anyway, abundant evidence for the interaction of disease and development in infants. Low-birth-weight babies show a higher mortality and also incidence of neurological and physical disorder (Birch and Gussow, 1970, p. 52) and, later in life, there is evidence for the aetiological significance of even mild under-nutrition in inhibiting growth (Marshall, 1977, p. 118).) It becomes relevant to look at evidence relating to acuity of hearing and vision in children, and at heights, weights and age at the onset of puberty, even though none of these things is in any sense an aspect of 'disease'. Given the significance of this kind of thinking, we consider that the different meanings of 'health' and hence of national objectives in maintaining and promoting health are often not given as much attention as they might be, a point we shall return to. Plainly for our purposes the 'social model' of health is more relevant than the 'medical' and we have therefore in the main followed it.

The two models are not, of course, either exclusive or exhaustive. (Discussions based essentially on the 'medical model' are given by Black (1979) and by Dollery (1978).) Conceptions of health and illness vary among different groups within a single society and between societies, as well as in any single society over time (Morris, 1975). It is in part for this reason that 'illness behaviour' – the response to symptoms and the tendency or reluctance to define any symptom as a health problem and to seek medical care – varies between cultural and social groups (Mechanic, 1968). Conceptions are moreover in constant process of adaptation or revision. Changes occur by virtue of scientific discovery and innovation, and developments in professional judgements of needs and the status of different diseases and treatments. They also occur in response to the pressure of established interests, and the extent of public anxiety about illness or safety, as well as the current level of demand for health, environmental and social services. Thus one result of research on the elderly and disabled, and the heightening of public interest and concern about their problems, has been that pain, discomfort, debility and different forms of incapacity have come to play a more prominent part in social and medical conceptions. If we consider mental illness or mental handicap, or the history of 'fringe' medicine, to take very diverse examples, we can see how conceptions of health and illness have changed. And just as conceptions themselves may gradually change, elements within them are accorded different weight or priority. We make this point for two reasons. The first is that our understanding of 'health' will always be evolving, and we must be prepared to absorb new knowledge about changes in health and social conditions. The second is to make better judgements about the strengths and weaknesses of the present health care services.

Within for instance any general approach to the meaning of 'health', views are reached about the seriousness of certain states of health. The construction of the health care services and the priorities which are identified in their development reflect those views. To the extent that a mechanistic model of health holds sway, the health care services will give priority to such matters as surgery, the immunological response to transplanted organs, chemo-therapy and the molecular basis of inheritance. Medicine comes to be structured according to a scale of values associated with such a model. The most sought-after posts will be those at the heart of the model, and medical education and medical careers are similarly influenced. Medicine is not, we know, monolithic, as developments in paediatrics, obstetrics, psychiatry and rehabilitation, and research in the social aspects and in prevention, indicate. However, once a conception of disease finds embodiment in the structure of a service, major changes become more difficult to introduce. All professions tend to become over-committed to existing practice and their receptivity to the need for change is liable to become weak. The medical, nursing and other professions are no different in this respect. We have to face the uncomfortable fact that society cannot look to the professions working within the health services for an account of illness and health which is always as detached or as full as it might be. Indeed, particularized conceptions of health and illness (including their stages and severity) are already institutionalized in medical practice and the organization, sub-divisions and administration of services.

Therefore, while the knowledge, experience and views of the health care professions are bound to play a predominant part in the debate, the extension of knowledge about the problems of human health and illness depends also on sources outside the health professions. Under the auspices of the medical and social sciences there needs to be a determined search for evidence of a wide variety of health conditions and their social, environmental and psychological as well as physiological significance.

In the last hundred and fifty years it could be said that the pursuit of health has increasingly been acknowledged to be a social and not merely a technical enterprise. In part this is due to the success of medical science in reducing mortality from infectious disease and thus directing attention towards chronic diseases of complex aetiology, but it is also due to the development of public health services, statistical studies of health, the work of epidemiologists in demonstrating the importance of living standards, protection from hazards and population limitation in improving health, and latterly the work of sociologists on the complex effects of the economy and different forms of social organization, including the family, upon levels of health. (See for example Susser and Watson, 1971; Morris, 1975; McKeown, 1976; Tuckett, 1976.)

Nevertheless the shift in emphasis from a medical to a social model still has some way to go. Although bio-medical research will continue to be vital, there is, in the words of one commentator, a 'need for a shift in the balance of effort, from laboratory to epidemiology in recognition that improvement in health is likely to come in future, as in the past, from modification of the conditions which led to disease rather than from intervention in the mechanism of disease after it has occurred' (McKeown, 1976, p 179). The sociological contribution is recognized to be, in part, to increase understanding of the social and socio-economic factors which play a part in the promotion of health and the causation of disease and in part to take the natural next step and relate these factors themselves to the broader social structure (see Brown and Harris, 1978).

Some working in medical sociology would emphasize a different perspective. They would argue that their contribution is not only like that of social medicine, to contribute to the understanding of the origins of health and disease in the way people live together in society. 'Disease', they would argue, is a medical, not a sociological concept. Sociology is concerned with the social production of understanding, meanings, knowledge; with social structure and process; and with the behaviour of people. Sociologists will try to understand the failure to seek medical attention for what to the physician is a serious disease episode not in terms of simple irrationality, but in terms of the individual's own (learned) coping mechanisms, social situation, and the meaning which he attaches to his symptoms. Hence there is a lot of interest in the social production of conceptions of health, in inconsistencies between lay and professional conceptions, and in conditions which are generated by different forms of social organization.

While the perspectives adopted in the three fields – medicine, epidemiology and sociology – tend to be different, they are subject to mutual influence and some of the most creative practitioners acknowledge the need to absorb or combine their strengths. Thus, nearly forty years ago Sigerist, a famous American medical historian (following Virchow, a German pathologist, long before), argued that 'The task of medicine is to promote health, to prevent disease, to treat the sick when prevention is broken down and to rehabilitate the people after they have been cured. These are highly social functions and we must look at medicine as basically a social science' (Sigerist, 1943, p. 241).

Choice of indicators of health and ill-health

Conceptions of health may vary in time and according to place, but science demands precision, and different aspects of the meaning of health and ill-health have to be translated into operational terms and applied systematically.

Measures of the 'health' of populations can take many different forms. Among the most familiar are mortality rates, prevalence or incidence of morbidity rates, sickness-absence rates and restricted-activity rates. Each of these indicators poses problems of measurement and has its limitations. For example, undue dependence on mortality rates can induce comparative indifference towards problems of chronic illness. Undue dependence on morbidity rates can discourage interest in congenital and other permanently incapacitating conditions, as well as conditions affecting human well-being which fall outside the conventional classification of 'morbidity'.

Partly because of the problems of measurement, but also because of the need for time-series statistics, we have given precedence to mortality rates. But we wish to call attention to the need for measures of health which combine several factors and which allow the real experiences among the population to be captured. For instance a combined indicator of pain and restricted activity has been proposed (Culyer *et al.*, 1972) and in current Canadian work indicators reflecting social, emotional and physical functioning are being developed (Sackett *et al.*, 1977). Again, the need to relate rather complex indicators of depression to the measure of life events was felt to apply to the community generally and not just those selected for psychiatric treatment (Brown and Harris, 1978).

A distinction is often drawn between acute and chronic sickness, and attempts have been made to relate the utilization of health services to these conditions. But it is clear from GHS reports over the years that the choice of terminology in 'indicator' questions can considerably affect the percentage of the population identifying themselves as having 'short-term' or 'chronic' health problems. Moreover, whatever method is adopted for distinguishing acute from chronic sickness we would also want to call attention to the dangers of treating any two sets of people so identified as distinct (Morris, 1975). Acute and chronic conditions in some patients are difficult to distinguish. Since the evidence suggests that the poorer groups are at greater risk of chronic sickness and disablement, there are dangers of distorting conclusions being reached about the characteristics of the 'acute' sick if all those with chronic sickness are first excluded from any analysis.

Disablement is also an important related concept. While interpretation of the concept of disability varies, it has been identified increasingly in recent years (as in the GHS surveys) with restriction of activity, which includes self-care, household management, and occupational and social activities. Parallel with this trend has been a greater emphasis on treating severity of disablement irrespective of cause or sex or age. Most local authorities have made returns since 1975 which have sought to distinguish the numbers of the physically handicapped according to severity of handicap. Non-statutory bodies are pressing for even wider application of this principle. 'All disabled people: the old, young adults and children; the mentally and physically handicapped, those disabled at home as well as at work or in war; and those disabled from birth, after an accident, or a long illness must be treated alike. It is not the origins or type of disablement or age which should count.' This statement is made on behalf of a large number of organizations of and for disabled people (*Disability Rights Handbook for 1980*, 1979, p. 48) which are concerned to call public attention to the consequences for individuals of the effects of disablement rather than its origins or type. Surveys of public opinion seem to endorse such statements (*Help for the Disabled*, 1974).

Concepts of inequality

The distribution of health or ill-health among and between populations has for many years been expressed most forcefully in terms of ideas on 'inequality'. These ideas are not just 'differences'. There may be differences between species, races, the sexes and people of different age, but the focus of interest is not so much natural physiological constitution or process as outcomes which have been socially or economically determined. This may seem to be straightforward, but the lengthy literature, and widespread public interest in the subject of inequality, show that factors which are recognizably or discernibly man-made are not so easy to disentangle from the complex physical and social structure in which man finds himself. Differences between people are accepted all too readily as eternal and unalterable. The institutions of society are very complex and exert their influence indirectly and subtly as well as directly and self-evidently. For some the concept of inequality also carries a moral reinforcement, as a fact which is undesirable or avoidable. For others the moral issue is relatively inconsequential. For them differences in riches or work conditions are an inevitable and hence 'natural' outcome of the history of attempts by man to build society, and they conclude that the scope for modification is small and, besides other matters, of little importance.

Central to the development of work on inequality has been the development of concepts of 'social class': that is *segments of the population sharing broadly similar types and levels of resources, with broadly similar styles of living and* (for some sociologists) *some shared perception of their collective condition*. This too has been controversial and there remains considerable controversy within sociology about the origins and relative importance of class in relation to social inequalities and social change.

The problems of choosing indicators of inequality

Traditionally inequalities have been portrayed through a characterization of class obtained by ranking occupations according to their social status or prestige. Of course, a variety of other factors may be said to play a part in determining class: income, wealth, type of housing tenure, education, style of consumption, mode of behaviour, social origins and family and local connections. They are interrelated and none of them should be regarded as sufficient in itself. But historically occupation has been selected as the principal indicator, partly because it has been regarded as more potent than some alternatives, but partly because it was the most convenient for statistical measurement and analysis. Occupation not simply designates type of work but tends also to show broadly how strenuous or unhealthy it is, what are the likely working conditions – for example whether it is indoors or outdoors and whether there is exposure to noise, dust or vibration – and what amenities and facilities are available, as well as level of remuneration and likely access to various fringe benefits. Pay will also determine family living standards and, while members of a family will not be exposed to some features of the working conditions experienced, there are others which may affect them indirectly, like the risk of intermittent unemployment, or the stress of disablement and of shift work.

Throughout this report we shall employ occupation as a basis of class because of its convenience. In particular we shall use the Registrar General's categories as follows:

I. Professional (for example accountant, doctor, lawyer) (5 per cent)*

II. Intermediate (for example manager, nurse, schoolteacher) (18 per cent)

IIIN. Skilled non-manual (for example clerical worker, secretary, shop assistant) (12 per cent)

IIIM. Skilled manual (for example bus driver, butcher, carpenter, coal face worker) (38 per cent)

IV. Partly skilled (for example agricultural worker, bus conductor, postman) (18 per cent)

V. Unskilled (for example cleaner, dock worker, labourer) (9 per cent).

But in doing this we should also be aware of its limitations. *We believe an effort should be made to make this classification in the rankings of occupations as objective as possible, by taking into account current and lifetime earnings, fringe benefits, security, working conditions and amenities.* Our intention is to shift attention from the more elusive subjective rating of 'prestige' or 'general standing' of occupations that have been traditionally used, to their material or environmental (and more measurable) properties. *Second, it would be desirable for the term 'occupational class' to be used rather than 'social class' when the current occupation of the individual is used as the basis of the classification* (and we shall do this throughout the report when we use this definition of class). *Third, it will become increasingly important to use the married man's occupation in combination with the married woman's occupation in analysing various health conditions and experiences,* for example infant and child mortality. *Fourth, the need for a 'social class' measure for analysis of the health of the family unit as a whole or of individual members of the family unit will become increasingly important.* One possibility is using the current occupations of both parents, together with information, where it can be obtained, about the main occupations of the husband's father and the wife's father. We return to these possibilities in Chapter 7.

* The percentages are of the total number of economically active and retired males

Finally, use of occupation as an indicator of social class has become so widespread in Britain in recent decades that the pre-occupations of some pioneer health statisticians have been forgotten. Some, however, were particularly concerned to relate health experience to riches or poverty (for example, Stevenson, 1928). Efforts should be made to restore this tradition, and not only because of the difficulties of taking occupation as a reliable indicator of a family's social class. The growth of absolute levels of resources, the spread of employer welfare benefits in kind and of social service benefits, and the increase of owner-occupation among the working classes makes a measure of 'resources' all the more important. The term 'resources' seems to be more appropriate than 'income' because of the present-day impact of wealth and both employer welfare and social service benefits-in-kind upon living standards. Considerable sums are spent each year on official annual surveys – including the Family Expenditure Survey (FES), the General Household Survey (GHS) and the National Food Survey. The FES provides the best measure of income, and although some information is collected about employer welfare and social service benefits it is incomplete and rather rough. Valuable data about the distribution of health are collected in the GHS, and although the information collected about income has, since 1979, been the same as in the FES, it is not supplemented by information on other resources. The development of a more adequate measure will not be easy, and the Royal Commission on the Distribution of Income and Wealth took a very cautious view in some of its reports about the possibilities of linking income and wealth in surveys (see especially Reports Nos. 1, 4 and 5). However, its Seventh Report took a more positive view about the need to develop joint distributions of income and wealth as a priority (p. 160) and about the desirability of sample surveys of personal wealth holdings.

We recommend that in the General Household Survey steps should be taken (not necessarily in every year) to develop a more comprehensive measure of income, or command over resources, through either (a) a means of modifying such a measure with estimates of total wealth or at least some of the most prevalent forms of wealth, such as housing and savings, or (b) the integration of income and wealth, employing a method of, for example, annuitization. (Questions of improvements in our knowledge about health in relation to inequalities are also taken up in Chapter 7.)

Summary

In examining the state of health of a population it is necessary to remember there are different meanings of 'health' which have different implications for action to improve health. On the one hand 'health' can be conceived as the outcome of freeing man from disease or disorder, as identified throughout history by medicine. On the other hand, it can be conceived as man's vigorous, creative and even joyous involvement in environment and community, of which presence or absence of disease is only a part. While there are many indicators of health and ill-health, including mortality rates, morbidity rates, sickness-absence rates and restricted activity rates, we concentrate most attention in this report, mainly for practical reasons, on mortality rates.

Different meanings are also given to the term 'inequality'. Interest tends to be concentrated on those (substantial) differences in condition or experience among populations which have been brought about by social or industrial organization and which tend to be regarded as undesirable or of doubtful validity by groups in society. Inequality is difficult to measure and trends in inequalities in the distribution of income and wealth, for example, cannot yet be related to indicators of health, except indirectly. Partly for reasons of convenience, therefore, occupational status or class (which is correlated closely with various other measures of inequality) is used as the principal indicator of social inequality in this report.

Chapter 2

The Pattern of Present Health Inequalities

Inequalities in health take a number of distinctive forms in Britain today. This chapter examines the pattern of inequalities according to a number of criteria: the relationships between gender and mortality, race and mortality, regional background and mortality, plus a range of measures of ill-health. But undoubtedly the clearest and most unequivocal – if only because there is more evidence to go on – is the relationship between occupational class and mortality. This will be the main theme of the next chapter.

Occupational class and mortality

Every death in Britain is a registered and certified event in which both the cause and the occupation of the deceased or his or her next of kin are recorded. By taking the actual incidence of death among members of the Registrar General's occupational classes and dividing this by the total in each occupational class it is possible to derive an estimate of class differences in mortality. This shows that on the basis of figures drawn from the early 1970s, when the most recent decennial survey was conducted, men and women in occupational class V had a two-and-a-half times greater chance of dying before reaching retirement age than their professional counterparts in occupational class I (Table 1, p. 49). Even when allowance is made for the fact that there are more older people in unskilled than professional work, the probability of death before retirement is still double.

What lies behind this gross statistic? Where do we begin to look for an explanation? If we break it down by age we find that class differences in mortality are a constant feature of the entire human life-span (see Fig. 1). They are found at birth, during the first year of life, in childhood, adolescence and adult life. At *any* age people in occupational class V have a higher rate of death than their better-off counterparts. This is not to say that the differences are uniform; in general they are more marked at the start of life and, less obviously, in early adulthood.

At birth and during the first month of life the risk of death in families of unskilled workers is double that of professional families. Children of

Figure 1. *Mortality by occupational class and age. Relative mortality (%) is the ratio of rates for the occupational class to the rate for all males (or females). (Source:* Occupational Mortality 1970–72, *H M S O, 1978, p. 196)*

skilled manual fathers (occupational class III M) run a 1.5 times greater risk.

For the next eleven months of a child's life this ratio widens still further. For the death of every one male infant of professional parents, we can expect almost two among children of skilled manual workers and three among children of unskilled manual workers. Among females the ratios are even greater.

If we measure this against different causes of death – Fig. 2 – we find that the most marked class gradients are for deaths from accidents and respiratory disease, two causes which we will show later to be closely related to the socio-economic environment (see Chapter 6). Other causes, associated

Figure 2. *Infant mortality by sex, occupational class and cause of death. (Source:* Occupational Mortality 1970–72, *H M S O, 1978, p. 158.)*

with birth itself and with congenital disabilities, have significantly less steep class gradients.

Between the ages of 1 and 14 relative class death rates narrow, but are still clearly visible. Among boys the ratio of mortality in occupational class V as compared with I is of the order of 2 to 1, while among girls it varies between 1.5 and 1.9 to 1.

Once again the causes of these differences can be traced largely to environmental factors. Accidents, which are by far the biggest single cause of childhood deaths (30 per cent of the total), continue to show the sharpest class gradient. Boys in class V have a ten times greater chance of dying from fire, falls or drowning than those in class I. The corresponding ratio of deaths caused to youthful pedestrians by motor vehicles is more than 7 to 1. Trailing somewhere behind this, but also with a marked class gradient, are infectious and parasitic diseases, responsible for 5 per cent of all childhood deaths, and pneumonia, responsible for 8 per cent of the total. Most other causes of death show less clear evidence of class disadvantage (Fig. 3).

Figure 3. *Class and mortality in childhood (males and females 0–14)*. (*Source:* Occupational Mortality 1970–72, *H M S O, 1978, p. 160.*)

Figure 4. *Occupational class and mortality in adult life (men and married women 15–64), by husband's occupation. (Source: Occupational Mortality 1970–72, HMSO, 1978.)*

Among adults, taken in this context to be people aged between 15 and 64, class differences appear to narrow further, but the overall statistic conceals a large difference for those in their twenties and thirties and a relatively small one for adults nearer pension age.

As in childhood the rates of death from accidents and infectious disease show steep class gradients, but equally an extraordinary variety of non-infectious diseases like cancer, heart and respiratory disease also show marked class differences (Fig. 4). This will be discussed further in the next chapter when we come to describe *trends* in the pattern of death rates.

Finally, as pension age is reached, class differences in mortality diminish still further, but by this age classification by occupational class becomes less meaningful. Information about occupation and cause of death recorded on death certificates for people over 75 is sometimes imprecise or inaccurate, particularly in the case of widows who, dying in their seventies or later, may still be classified according to the last occupation of husbands who may have died many years earlier. Again, there is some movement late in working life from skilled to unskilled occupations which is not reflected in the occupation reported at death. A minority of men, dying in their sixties, are recorded with the skilled occupation held for most of their working life rather than the unskilled occupation they may have had in the last five or ten years of that life.

Occupational class may therefore be a weak indicator of life-style and life chances over lengthy periods. Bearing this in mind, data about the mortality of men aged 65 to 74 in 1970/72 showed that there were very large differences between some groups of manual and non-manual workers. For example, the mortality ratio for former miners and quarrymen was 149, gas, coke and chemical makers 150, and furnace, forge, foundry and rolling mill workers 162, compared with administrators and managers with a ratio of 88 and professional, technical workers and artists with a ratio of 89 (OPCS, 1978, p. 107).

Now let us look at some other criteria for dividing the population which have a bearing on any attempt to describe the 'structure' of health among the population.

Sex differences in mortality

The gap in life expectancy between men and women is one of the most distinctive features of human health in the advanced societies. As Table 1 indicates, the risk of death for men in each occupational class is almost twice that of women, the cumulative product of health inequalities between the sexes during the whole lifetime. It suggests that gender and class exert

Table 1: *Death rates by sex and social (occupational) class (15–64 years) (rates per 1,000 population, England and Wales, 1971)*

Social (occupational) class	Males	Females*	Ratio M/F
I (Professional)	3.98	2.15	1.85
II (Intermediate)	5.54	2.85	1.94
IIIN (Skilled non-manual)	5.80	2.76	1.96
IIIM (Skilled manual)	6.08	3.41	1.78
IV (Partly skilled)	7.96	4.27	1.87
V (Unskilled)	9.88	5.31	1.86
Ratio V/I	2.5	2.5	

*In this table women with husbands have been classified by their husband's occupation, women of other marital statuses are attributed to their *own* occupational class.
Source: *Occupational Mortality 1970–72* (microfiches and 1978, p. 37).

highly significant but different influences on the quality and duration of life in modern society.

It is also a gap in life expectancy which carries important implications for all spheres of social policy, but especially health, since old age is a time when demand for health care is at its greatest and the dominant pattern of premature male mortality adds the exacerbating problem of isolation for many women.

Although attempts have been made to explain the differences between the sexes, comparatively little systematic work exists on the aetiology of the mortality and morbidity differences between men and women and much remains to be disentangled. Women suffer uniquely from some diseases and it would be wrong, for example, to assume too readily that all wives share the same living conditions or even standards as their husbands. Some men have the advantage, for instance, not only of a preferential diet at home but subsidized meals at work. Where both husband and wife are in paid employment, the meals they get in the day, as well as working conditions and the nature of the work, may be radically different. There is a great deal more research to be undertaken to sort out these various influences.

Regional differences in mortality

Mortality rates also vary considerably between the regions which make up the United Kingdom. Using them as an indicator of health, the healthiest part of Britain appears to be the southern belt below a line drawn across

Table 2: *Regional variations in mortality*

Standard region	SMR: standardized for	
	Age	Age and class
Northern, Yorkshire and Humberside	113	113
North-west	106	105
East Midlands	116	116
West Midlands	96	94
East Anglia	105	104
South-east	90	90
South-west	93	93
Wales I (South)	114	117
Wales II (North and West)	110	113
England and Wales	100	100

Source: *Occupational Mortality 1970–72*, p. 180

the country from the Wash to the Bristol Channel (see Table 2). This has not always been true. In the middle of the nineteenth century, the south-east of England recorded comparatively high rates of death, while other regions like Wales and the far north had a rather healthier profile.

Race, ethnicity and health

Another important dimension of inequality in contemporary Britain is race. Immigrants to this country from the so-called New Commonwealth, whose ethnic identity is clearly visible in the colour of their skin, are known to experience greater difficulty in finding work and adequate housing (Smith, 1976). Given these disabilities it is to be expected that they might also record rather higher than average rates of mortality and morbidity.

This hypothesis is difficult to test from official statistics, since 'race' has rarely been assessed in official censuses and surveys. Moreover it is far from clear what indicator should be utilized in any such assessment – skin colour, place of birth, nationality – and the most significant may depend on the precise issue of interest.

The pattern of social and economic disadvantage experienced by black Britons is connected with occupational class and is reflected in the working of the labour market. But other factors may also be important, and at least amongst adult males the variables of occupational class and race do not compound one another in a linear fashion as far as health is concerned, when place of birth is used as a means of measuring race. The age standardized mortality ratios of immigrant males compares favourably with their British-born equivalents in occupational classes IV and V, but less so higher up the scale in classes I and II (see Table 3). The interpretation of these ratios is made difficult at the higher end of the occupational scale because they are based on small numbers.

In the poorer occupational classes, where the standardized mortality ratio is based on larger numbers of deaths, men born in India, Pakistan or the West Indies seem to live longer than their British-born counterparts. It should be remembered, however, that the percentage of workers in class V among the British-born is less than 7 while the equivalent percentage of those born in, for example, India and Pakistan is 16. In addition, of course, the average British-born male classified as an unskilled manual worker is likely to be older than his foreign-born counterpart and is more likely to have acquired this low occupational status after a process of downward social mobility associated with failing health.

This rather favourable comparison between immigrant and British-born males may also reflect the underlying tendency for migrants to select themselves on the grounds of health and fitness. Men and women prepared to cross oceans and continents in order to seek new occupational opportunities or a new way of life do not represent a random cross-section of humanity. A better comparison for exploring health inequality would ideally involve second- or third-generation immigrants, but these are the very groups that are difficult to trace for statistical purposes. What little evidence that has

Table 3: *Mortality by country of birth and occupational class (SMR) (males 15–64)*

Country of birth	I	II	IIIN	IIIM	IV	V	All
India and Pakistan	122	127	114	105	93	73	98
West Indies	267	163	135	87	71	75	84
Europe (including UK and Eire)	121	109	98	83	81	82	89
UK and Eire (including England and Wales)	118	112	111	118	115	110	114
England and Wales	97	99	99	99	99	100	100
All birth places	100	100	100	100	100	100	100

Source: *Occupational Mortality, 1970–72*, pp. 186–7.

been accumulated, however, does suggest that the children of immigrants do suffer from certain specific health disabilities related to cultural factors such as diet or to their lack of natural immunity to certain infectious diseases (Thomas, 1968; Oppé, 1967; Gans, 1966). Studies based on small samples of immigrant children have pointed to the possibility of higher-than-average morbidity associated with material deprivation, but the evidence is scarce and somewhat inconclusive and needs to be augmented by further research (Hood *et al.*, 1970).

Housing tenure and mortality

Because of its bearing on our discussion in Chapter 6 of explanations for inequalities in health, it should also be noted that when the population is divided into housing tenure groups – owner-occupiers, private tenants and local-authority tenants – class gradients vary considerably (Table 4). People who live in houses which they own have lower rates of mortality than those who rent their homes from private landlords who in turn have lower rates than those who are tenants of local authorities. Housing tenure is, of course, one possible measure of the accumulation by an individual or family of fixed property or assets; it also says something about familial attitudes and priorities. Here it can be shown that this variable shows a very close relationship with the risk of premature death.

Table 4: *Mortality by tenure and class (S M R) (males 15–64 years)*

Class	Tenure		
	Owner-occupied	*Privately rented*	*Local-authority tenancy*
I	79	93	99
II	74	104	99
IIIN	79	112	121
IIIM	83	99	104
IV	83	100	106
V	98	126	123

Source: Unpublished data, Medical Statistics Division, OPCS, preliminary results of the LS 1970–75.

Illness and class

Morbidity data provide a second way of looking at the pattern of class inequalities in health. Moreover there is a sense in which the extent of ill-health in a social group is a better indicator of its health vis-à-vis another group than is the relative mortality rate. Morbidity data are available from a variety of studies and *ad hoc* surveys and are of two kinds, though both are scant at the national level. The first is based on examination of, or symptom identification in, the social group as a whole or in a properly selected sample. An approach of this kind has sometimes been used in the attempt to assess the prevalence of specific diseases within research studies. Social or occupational class is sometimes noted.

The second kind of data derives from analysis of medical consultation and hospital admission rates. But not only do we have few data of this kind by occupational class, there is the disadvantage that rates reflect not only the incidence of disease but also the process by which an individual defines himself (or herself) as ill, seeks medical attention and has his (or her) definition confirmed or legitimated by medical authority. Since we know that there are class-related differences in the propensity of an individual with a given set of symptoms to go for treatment or attention, as well as in the subsequent medical response (Chapter 4), we recognize that data of this kind cannot be interpreted clearly.

Nevertheless data from both these sources confirms, broadly speaking, the picture which mortality data has already indicated.

An example of the first sort of morbidity data is provided by a survey of the prevalence of chronic bronchitis in Great Britain. Ninety-two GPs, distributed throughout the country, were asked to select similarly sized age/sex-stratified random samples from their practice lists. All were to be aged between 40 and 64. In terms of GP diagnosis, the percentage suffering from chronic bronchitis rose with descending class from 6 per cent in class I to 26 per cent in class V. Bronchitis is diagnosed from symptoms and these can vary from doctor to doctor, but even when a more rigorous 'standard diagnosis' was used, the picture was broadly the same.

GPs have also recorded details of consultations. Results from one study showed that consultation rates for each of a wide range of conditions for males, females and children, classified according to occupational class, are of considerable interest though not easy to interpret (Logan and Cushion, 1960, p. 21). The findings were summarized in the following scheme, where + indicates morbidity above and − below average.

	agricultural occupations	*non-manual occupations*	*manual occupations*
psychoneurotic disorders	–	+	–
cardio-vascular disorders	–	+	–
respiratory disorders	–	–	+
gastric disorders	–	–	+
arthritis/rheumatism	–	–	+
injuries	–	–	+

Table 5: *Comparison of distribution of standardized patient consultation ratios (males 15–64, May 1955–April 1956) and standardized mortality ratios (males 20–64, 1949–53) by class: selected conditions*

	SPCR class					SMR class				
	I	II	III	IV	V	I	II	III	IV	V
Respiratory tuberculosis	102	85	105	102	91	58	63	102	95	143
Malignant neoplasms	75	111	94	91	111	94	86	104	95	113
Diabetes mellitus	89	123	100	108	74	134	100	99	85	105
Coronary disease/angina	89	108	102	89	93	147	110	105	79	89
Hypertension	120	127	99	70	89	123	106	103	83	101
Influenza	83	82	103	113	107	58	70	97	102	139
Pneumonia	70	87	90	121	132	53	64	92	105	150
Bronchitis	49	70	99	118	146	34	53	98	101	171
Gastric and duodenal ulcer	48	78	99	88	116	68	76	101	99	134

Source: Logan and Cushion, 1960, p. 16.

Another way of looking at the results is by comparing mortality ratios (by class and disease) with consultation ratios, as in Table 5. If we compare the class gradients on the left-hand side of the table with those on the right-hand side we find that with some exceptions (for instance coronary disease and diabetes) the gradients on the right-hand side are steeper. This suggests more severe sickness or smaller likelihood of treatment with declining class.

This tends to be brought out too in more recent national studies of self-reported illness, like the General Household Survey. Thus, the rates of 'limiting long-standing illness' (as defined in the GHS) rise with falling socio-economic status and are three times as high among unskilled manual males and females as they are among their professional counterparts (see Table 6). Further details are given on pp. 64–5 and 69–71. It will be

Table 6: *Sickness and medical consultation in early adulthood (average rates per 1,000 population 1971–1976)**

Socio-economic group	Limiting long-standing illness		Restricted activity (in two-week period)		Consultations	
	males	females	males	females	males	females†
Professional	79	81	78	89	105	134
Managerial	119	115	74	83	113	137
Intermediate	143	140	83	95	116	155
Skilled manual	141	135	87	86	123	147
Semi-skilled manual	168	203	87	102	131	160
Unskilled manual	236	257	101	103	153	158
Ratio unskilled manual to professional	3.0	3.2	1.3	1.2	1.5	1.2

* England and Wales for 1971–2.
† 1972–6.

Source: *General Household Survey, 1976*, HMSO, 1978

seen however that the comparable ratios for 'restricted activity or acute illness are much smaller, and generally resemble the ratios for consultation rates. However, inequalities are smaller in childhood and larger in middle age. Rates of sickness absence from work are also widely unequal. Thus, a special inquiry into the incidence of incapacity for work found marked class gradients for a number of diseases. When the number of employed males beginning a spell of incapacity was expressed per 1,000 in each occupational class, standardized for age, there were, for disease of the respiratory system, 91 in combined classes I and II and 177 in class V For influenza the figures were 39 and 70, bronchitis 15 and 57 and arthritis and rheumatism 7 and 40 (Ministry of Pensions, 1965).

Summary

There are marked inequalities in health between the social classes in Britain. In this chapter mortality rates are taken as the best available indicator of the health of different social, or more strictly occupational classes and socio-economic groups. Mortality tends to rise inversely with falling occupational rank or status, for both sexes and at all ages. At birth and in the first month of life twice as many babies of unskilled manual parents as of professional parents die, and in the next eleven months of life nearly three times as many boys and more than three times as many girls, respectively, die. In later years of childhood the ratio of deaths in the poorest class falls to between one and a half and two times that of the wealthiest class, but increases again in early adulthood before falling again in middle and old age.

A class 'gradient' can be observed for most causes of death and is particularly steep for both sexes in the case of diseases of the respiratory system and infective and parasitic diseases.

Other aspects of class than merely occupational category have an impact on health, although few data relating mortality to education and income, for example, are available. This is however illustrated by evidence that in all classes owner-occupiers have lighter mortality than those paying rent.

Available data on (self-reported) morbidity tend to reflect those on mortality, though inequalities between occupational classes are more pronounced, and the gradients more uniform, in the case of chronic sickness than in the case of acute or short-term ill-health.

Chapter 3

Trends in Inequality of Health

For about 100 years mortality rates for both sexes, taken one decade with the next, have declined, even after discounting changes that have taken place in the age structure of the population (Fig. 5). At the same time rates for males have remained markedly higher than for females, and in recent decades the difference has become relatively greater (Fig. 6). In fact since 1946 the excess of male over female deaths has increased at all ages and

Figure 5. *Death rates, standardized to 1901 population (England and Wales). (Source: T. McKeown, The Role of Medicine. Nuffield Provincial Hospitals Trust, 1976, p. 30.)*

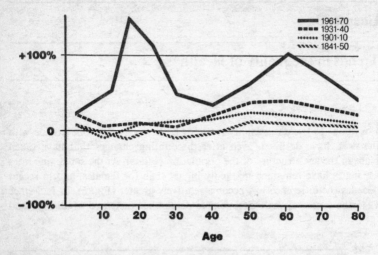

Figure 6. *Percentage excess of male over female death rates by age, 1841–1970.*
(*Source: OPCS*, Trends in Mortality, *1978.*)

especially between the ages of 10 and 30. For most of this chapter we shall
concentrate on the last thirty years.

The trend among men

After a long decline in the death rates of men in different occupational
classes, a sharp change took place in the 1950s which persisted into the 1970s
(see Table 7). The trend can be examined during two recent decades,
approximately the 1950s and 1960s. Between 1949/53 and 1959/63 inequalities between the highest- and lowest-ranking occupational classes in
mortality experience appear to have widened. Some of this is due to changes
in classification, but in his 1961 *Decennial Supplement* the Registrar General
concluded: 'The most disturbing feature of the present results when compared with earlier analyses is the apparent deterioration in social class V ...
Even when the rates are adjusted to the 1950 classification it is clear that
class V men fared worse than average.'

The next *Decennial Supplement*, covering occupational mortality during
1970/72, shows little or no change in the mortality 'advantage' of classes I
and II, but although there was an improvement in the mortality of social
class V relative to other classes, this improvement fell short of restoring the
position the class had reached in 1949/53 (OPCS, *Occupational Mortality,*

Table 7: *Mortality of men by occupational class (1930s–1970s) (standardized mortality ratios)*

Occupational class			Men aged 15–64			
			1959–63 unadjusted		1970–72 unadjusted	
	1930–32	1949–53*		adjusted †		adjusted
I Professional	90	86	76	75	77	75
II Managerial	94	92	81	—	81	—
III Skilled manual and non-manual	97	101	100	–	104	—
IV Partly skilled	102	104	103	—	114	—
V Unskilled	111	118	143	127	137	121

* Corrected figures as published in *Registrar General's Decennial Supplement England and Wales, 1961: Occupational Mortality Tables,* London, HMSO, 1971, p. 22.

† Occupations in 1959–63 and 1970–72 have been reclassified according to the 1950 classification.

Source: *Registrar General's Decennial Supplement* and *Occupational Mortality Tables* (see above).

Decennial Supplement, 1970–72, England and Wales, 1978, p. 174), and compared with 1959/63 the mortality of class IV relative to other classes had deteriorated.

Behind these relative changes in position (and those looked at in Chapter 2) lie absolute changes in mortality rates for the different classes. If we break the trends down by age group (Table 8) we see that mortality rates for younger men of all occupational classes declined throughout the 1950s and 1960s, but that for men in different ten-year age groups between 35 and 65 in occupational classes III, IV and V, the mortality rate actually increased or stood still, while rates for men in occupational class I and II continued to fall. The inequality between the classes was therefore greater by the beginning of the 1970s, as the bottom half of Table 8 demonstrates, by virtue of changes in the pattern of mortality rates for older men. (The trends among married women revealed by the table are discussed below.)

As before, one way of trying to understand this is to look at the changing causes of death. In 1959/63 more class V men died at every age than in 1949/53 from cancer of the lung, vascular lesions of the central nervous system, arteriosclerotic and degenerative heart disease and motor vehicle

Table 8: *Mortality rates per 100,000 and as percentage of rates for occupational classes I and II (1951–71, England and Wales, men and married women)*

Occupational class	Age	Men: rates per 100,000			Married women: rates per 100,000		
		1949–53	1959–63	1970–72	1949–53	1959–63	1970–72
I and II	25–34	124	81	72	85	51	42
III		148	100	90	114	64	51
IV and V		180	143	141	141	77	68
I and II	35–44	226	175	169	170	123	118
III		276	234	256	201	160	154
IV and V		331	300	305	226	186	193
I and II	45–54	712	544	554	427	323	337
III		812	708	733	480	402	431
IV and V		895	842	894	513	455	510
I and II	55–64	2,097	1,804	1,710	1,098	818	837
III		2,396	2,218	2,213	1,202	1,001	1,059
IV and V		2,339	2,433	2,409	1,226	1,129	1,131
		as per cent I and II			*as per cent I and II*		
I and II	25–34	100	100	100	100	100	100
III		119	123	125	134	125	121
IV and V		145	177	196	166	151	162
I and II	35–44	100	100	100	100	100	100
III		122	134	151	118	130	131
IV and V		146	171	180	133	151	164
I and II	45–54	100	100	100	100	100	100
III		114	130	132	112	124	128
IV and V		126	155	161	120	141	151
I and II	55–64	100	100	100	100	100	100
III		114	123	129	109	122	127
IV and V		112	135	141	112	138	135

Source: OPCS.

and other accidents. Some diseases, like lung cancer and duodenal ulcer, which forty to fifty years ago showed no trend with social class or, like coronary disease, an inverse trend, were by the 1960s producing higher mortality among social class IV and V than I and II. Indeed by 1959/63, forty-nine of the eighty-five observed causes of male death showed higher SMRs for classes IV and V than I and II. (And fifty-four out of eighty-seven applying to women.) For only four causes of death among men, and four among married women, was the class gradient reversed. (See *Registrar General's Decennial Supplement*, 1959/63, op. cit.)

By 1970/72 this position had grown still more marked. For ninety-two causes of death which were picked out for men aged 15 to 64 in the latest OPCS report, the mortality ratios for both classes IV and V were higher than for I and II in as many as sixty-eight, a proportionate increase compared with ten years earlier. For only four causes were mortality ratios for I and II higher than IV and V: accidents to motor vehicle drivers, malignant neoplasm of the skin, malignant neoplasm of the brain and polyarteritis nodosa and allied conditions (OPCS, 1978, op. cit., Table 4A). The question of course is why should there have been this proportionate increase in the number of causes of death showing a class gradient, a question we shall return to in Chapter 6.

The trend among women

With the exception of the youngest group, the 'spread' of inequality among women has been narrower than for men, as an examination of the lower half of Table 8 illustrates. But between 1949/53 and 1970/72, the 'spread' increased among married women aged 35 to 64, as Table 8 also illustrates. The trend for single and married women aged 15 to 64 in the second of the two decades is given for each occupational class in Table 9. The numbers in class I are small and the figures in the table have been placed in brackets on that account. There are also relatively small numbers of women, especially married women, in class V. With these reservations, it can be seen that the relative mortality of both married and single women in class IV, and of single women at least in class V, deteriorated between 1959/63 and 1970/72.

When causes of death are divided into thirteen broad groups for women aged 15 to 64, there is markedly higher mortality among the partly skilled and unskilled classes (whether defined by their own or a husband's occupation) in the case of infective and parasitic diseases, circulatory diseases, respiratory diseases, diseases of the genito-urinary sytem and, though less markedly, congenital anomalies, diseases of the blood, endocrine and nutritional diseases and diseases of the digestive system.

Table 9: *Mortality of women by occupational class (1961–71) (England and Wales) (standardized mortality ratios)*

| | Women aged 15–64 | | | |
| | Married | | Single | |
	1959–63	1970–72	1959–63	1970–72
I	(77)	(82)	(83)	(110)
II	83	87	88	79
III non-manual	} 103 {	92	} 90 {	92
III manual		115		108
IV	105	119	108	114
V	141	135	121	138

Sources: *Registrar General's Decennial Supplement: 1961*, pp. 91, 503; OPCS, *Decennial Supplement*, 1970–72, p. 211.

In the case of benign neoplasms there is no trend by class, but in mental disorders, diseases of the nervous system, malignant neoplasms and accidents, and poisoning and violence, there was a higher mortality in 1970/72 among classes I and II.

Throughout the 1960s maternal mortality fell by more than a third, but mortality among women in class V was still nearly double that of class I and II.

Infants and childhood mortality

Inequalities in mortality among infants reflect those among adults. Since the 1930s deaths per 1,000 live births have diminished among all classes, but in 1975 inequality was still marked. As the Court Committee (appointed by the government to examine the development of child health services) commented in its report in 1977, between 1950 and 1973 the perinatal mortality rate declined by 45 per cent for those of professional and 49 per cent for those of managerial class, but by only 34 per cent for those of unskilled manual class (Table 10).

Among children (1 year old and above) trends during the 1960s and early 1970s varied with age. There was a small reduction in the class difference between 1 and 4 years of age, especially for girls, little or no change between the ages of 5 to 9 and an increase in the difference between the ages of 10 and 14. For boys aged 1 to 14, mortality ratios for classes IV and V

Table 10: *Trends in infant mortality by occupational class (England and Wales)*

	Ratios of actual to expected deaths of infants			
	1930–32	*1949–53*	*1959–63**	*1970–72†*
I	53	63 ⎫	73	74 ⎰ 66
II	73	73 ⎭		⎱ 77
III	94	97	98	94
IV	108	114 ⎫	119	128 ⎰ 111
V	125	138 ⎭		⎱ 175

	Infant deaths per 1,000 legitimate live births			
I	32	19	—	12
II	46	22	—	14
III	59	28	—	16
IV	63	35	—	20
V	80	42	—	31

* For 1959–63, estimates calculated from C. C. Spicer, and L. Lipworth, *Regional and Social Factors in Infant Mortality*, GRO, Studies on Medical and Population Subjects No. 19, London, HMSO, 1966, by J. Tudor Hart, 'Data on Occupational Mortality 1959–63', *Lancet*, 22 January 1972, p. 192.

† For 1970–72, estimated from OPCS, *Occupational Mortality, Decennial Supplement*, 1970–72, England and Wales, pp. 168 and 216.

in 1970/72 were both higher than for classes I and II for twenty-three of thirty-eight observed causes of death, compared with only one cause (asthma) where the ratios were lower. For girls the corresponding figures were twenty-two and nought respectively (OPCS, 1978, op. cit., Table 7E).

The elderly

By 1970/72 the mortality ratios for several groups of manual occupations, including former miners and quarrymen, gas, coke and chemical makers and furnace, forge, foundry and rolling mill workers, had deteriorated relative to the death rate for all men. But we should bear in mind the qualification made in Chapter 2 about the value of occupational class as an indicator of life chances among older people.

Morbidity

It is difficult to trace morbidity data by class for any span of years. The General Household Survey has now been running since 1971, but it is still too early to distinguish reliable trends in health from that source. For example, Table 11, drawn from GHS data, shows that absence from work because of sickness or injury is sharply related to class, but that the precise rates are liable to fluctuation from year to year. The average number of days lost through illness or accident among unskilled manual men was 4.5 times that among professional men in 1971 and 1972 (the data are not given for 1977).

Table 12 is also drawn from GHS data and also shows a class gradient during the 1970s for restricted activity, this time measured in terms of acute sickness, long-stay (chronic) sickness and GP consultations, but the rates are even more uneven from year to year and in some years, for some age groups, there is no perceptible gradient. (However, information published since the report was submitted shows that in 1979 the gradient was marked.)

Table 11: *Working males absent from work owing to illness or injury* (*England and Wales 1971*)

Socio-economic group	Absent from work due to illness or injury in a two week reference period – rate per 1,000			Average number of work days lost per person per year	
	1971	*1972*	*1977**	*1971*	*1972*
Professional	37	21	20	3.9	3.1
Employers and managers	37	39	20	7.2	6.2
Intermediate and junior non-manual	44	48	50	7.6	6.0
Skilled manual	57	56	60	9.3	9.4
Semi-skilled manual	56	68	70	11.5	10.5
Unskilled manual	88	99	60	18.4	17.6
All groups	52	54	40	9.1	8.4

* Rate given only to nearest 10.

Sources: OPCS, *The General Household Survey, Introductory Report*, HMSO, 1973, p. 304; OPCS, *The General Household Survey, 1972*, HMSO, 1975, p. 207; OPCS, *General Household Survey, 1977*, HMSO, 1979, p. 65.

The figures illustrate the problem of drawing conclusions about trends

Table 12: *Rates of long-standing and acute illness and consultations per 1,000 of occupational classes IV and V, as a percentage of class I (1971–6, Britain)*

Sex/class/health indicator	1971	1972	1973	1974	1975	1976
Males class IV						
Long-standing illness	—	158	163	157	160	157
acute sickness	126	133	110	134	102	80
GP consultations	133	132	125	146	129	91
Males class V						
Long-standing illness	—	196	213	218	197	196
acute sickness	155	181	129	150	85	102
GP consultations	143	175	164	147	121	125
Females class IV						
Long-standing illness	—	274	214	182	197	176
acute sickness	105	128	115	115	134	95
GP consultations	—	108	150	110	123	114
Females class V						
Long-standing illness	—	320	276	204	253	246
acute sickness	107	141	113	122	128	94
GP consultations	—	117	150	120	107	102

Source: Reports of the General Household Survey.

in self-reported sickness for some major sex/age groups, if not for the population as a whole, during a short span of years.

Conclusion

When examining indicators of health for different occupational or socio-economic classes for a span of years, any changes that may be taking place in the relative size of particular classes may be as important as any changes in the inequality between classes in assessing trends in the overall health of the population. Some commentators have pointed out that while inequalities in health between the unskilled manual class and other classes may not have diminished, or may even have increased, that class has become smaller and therefore there has still been an 'improvement' in the distribution of health. This change has been regarded as compensation for the lack of any closing of the gap *between* classes.

Two comments should be made. The first is that changes in occupational classification have caused commentators to believe that the reduction of class V since 1931 has been greater than it has. (See Appendix, Tables 1 and 2.) In fact, as attempts to adjust census findings show, the fall in the proportion of men in class V has been small since 1961 and in absolute numbers has not fallen at all.

The second is that relatively poor health experience applies to other manual classes and especially class IV and that though this class too has fallen in proportion to the population, it continues to make up, together with class V, more than a quarter of the economically active male population. Mortality indicators for class IV, relative to other classes, have shown some deterioration between the early 1960s and the early 1970s, but perhaps the most important general finding is the lack of improvement, and in some respects deterioration, of the health experience of *both* class V and IV relative to class I, as judged by mortality indicators, during the 1960s and early 1970s.

The more specific conclusions, underlying this finding, are as follows. (These conclusions apply to England and Wales. Scottish experience has been rather similar, though certain differences are noted in the text.)

1. Mortality rates of males are higher at every age than of females and in recent decades the difference between the sexes has become relatively greater.

2. For men of economically active age there was greater inequality of mortality between occupational classes I and V both in 1970–72 and 1959–63 than in 1949–53.

3. For economically active men the mortality rates of occupational class III and combined classes IV and V for age groups over 35 either deteriorated or showed little or no improvement between 1959–63 and 1970–72. Relative to the mortality rates of occupational classes I and II they worsened.

4. For women aged 15–64 the standardized mortality ratios of combined classes IV and V deteriorated. For married and single women in class IV (the most numerous class) they deteriorated at all ages.

5. Although deaths per thousand live births in England and Wales have diminished among all classes, the relative excess in combined classes IV and V over I and II increased between 1959–63 and 1970–72.

6. During a period of less than a decade maternal mortality fell by more than a third. Although that of class I fell less sharply than other classes inequality between the more numerous class II and classes IV and V remained about the same.

7. Among children between 1 and 4 years of age, there has been a small reduction in the class differential (especially for girls), for children aged 5 to 9 little or no change, but for children aged 10 to 14 an increase in the differential. For boys aged 1–14, mortality ratios for classes IV and V in 1970–72 were *both* higher than for classes I and II for twenty-three of thirty-eight causes of death, compared with only one cause (asthma) where the ratios were lower. For girls the corresponding figures were twenty-two and nought respectively. There is evidence that as rates of child death from a specific condition decline to very low levels class gradients do disappear. The gradual elimination of death from rheumatic heart disease over the post-war period provides evidence of this (Morris, 1959).

Chapter 4

Inequality in the Availability and Use of the Health Service

One of the fundamental principles of the NHS is to 'divorce the care of health from questions of personal means or other factors irrelevant to it' (Cartwright and O'Brien, 1976). Yet a number of studies have revealed significant social inequalities in the availability and use of health services. In 1968 Richard Titmuss argued, on the basis of evidence then available, that: 'Higher income groups know how to make better use of the Service: they tend to receive more specialist attention; occupy more of the beds in better equipped and staffed hospitals...' Subsequent studies, many of which we shall refer to, have cast further light on the issue and added to the evidence.

Unequal usage will never be more than a partial explanation of the overall inequalities in standards of health. Several commentators have shown, and we shall go on to show this later, that differences in health between sections of the population may be far more a function of 'variations in the socio-demographic circumstances of the population than the amount and type of medical care provided and/or available' (Martini, Allan, Davison and Backett, 1977). Nevertheless, any inequality in the availability and use of health services in relation to need is in itself socially unjust and requires alleviation. This remains true whatever the relative importance of health care in comparison with other areas of social policy.

Moreover, since equal access has always been a fundamental principle of the NHS, the extent to which it has been achieved is a matter of considerable interest. In sorting out the evidence we have found it useful to look separately at GP consultation rates, hospital care, preventive services and services for the disabled and infirm. This is partly because such a distinction reflects the availability of information and the foci of research, and also because, as we shall show, while some uncertainty remains as to the existence of inequalities in the first two cases, there are no grounds for doubt in the case of preventive services in particular.

GP consultations

There is no simple interpretation of the evidence linking class with rates of consultation with general practitioners. The GHS is the best source of information, but the trend, while clear enough for the sample of males and females in general, does not apply to males aged 0 to 14 or females aged 0 to 14, and is uneven for some other age groups. GHS results have fluctuated from year to year and the consulting rate (and even more the average number of consultations) has not generally shown as marked a class gradient, as have the measures of morbidity discussed in earlier chapters. (See table on p. 55 above.)

For most years covered by the GHS the number of people consulting a doctor, and the average number of consultations, has tended to increase with falling class. However, for some years the figures are uneven and the rate for classes III, IV and V is lower than for classes I and II. This may partially miss the point. It may be that the proper basis for comparing rates of consultation is not one of simple population but of the *need* for care. One study, for example, using the GHS data, divided the number of GP consultations by the number of restricted activity days, each in a two-week reference period, for each occupational group (defined a little differently from the occupational classification referred to earlier). The 'use/need ratios' clearly declined in going from socio-economic class I to class V (Brotherston, 1976). Table 13 shows use/need ratios calculated on the basis of the GHS for 1974/6 which similarly show an overall pattern of decline from socio-economic group 1 to group 6. The table shows that the observation that the poor use GP services more is reversed once 'usage' is corrected for 'need'.

Another study used aggregated 1971 and 1972 GHS data and also found statistically significant trends in consultation rates/morbidity, where the 'morbidity' measure was rate of chronic sickness or rate of sickness absence

Table 13: *'Use/need ratios' by social group (Great Britain, 1974–6)*

Socio-economic group	Males	Females
1	0.23	0.23
2	0.21	0.24
3	0.20	0.22
4	0.18	0.22
5	0.20	0.20
6	0.17	0.19
All	0.19	0.22

from work or school, but a non-significant trend in the case of acute sickness (Forester, 1976). The study showed that in proportion to reported sickness and sickness absence from work, the semi-skilled and unskilled in fact made less use of GP services than did other groups.

A weakness of this method of relating use to need derives from the fact that many of those with restricted activity may not visit a GP but may visit a hospital out-patients' department, whereas others may visit a GP for reasons different from restricted activity. In other words, comparison of these rates may be purely indicative of differences in receipt of care when sick.

At the same time, comparison of *rates* of consultation, even when related to need as shown by mortality or morbidity data, is not a wholly adequate conceptualization of inequality in care. Several studies have shown that middle-class patients tend to have longer consultations than working-class

Table 14: *Morbidity and GP attendance indicators for socio-economic groups: semi-skilled and unskilled as a percentage of professional*

	Males					
	1971	1972	1973	1974	1975	1976
Long-standing illness						
semi-skilled	—	158	163	157	160	157
unskilled	—	196	213	218	197	196
Limiting long-standing illness						
semi-skilled	272	203	233	179	174	222
unskilled	,371	290	333	274	244	292
Acute sickness (restricted activity)						
semi-skilled	126	133	110—	134—	102—	80—
unskilled	155	181	129—	150	85—	102—
Acute sickness (days per person)						
semi-skilled	—	169	168	169	130	122
unskilled	—	268	206	215	121	196
GP consultations: persons consulting (rate per 1,000)						
semi-skilled	122	132	121	146	122	91
unskilled	128	157	145	141	111	111
GP consultations (rate per 1,000)						
semi-skilled	133	132	125	146	129	91
unskilled	143	175	164	147	121	125

	Females					
Long-standing illness						
semi-skilled	—	274	214	182	197	176
unskilled	—	320	276	204	253	246
Limiting long-standing illness						
semi-skilled	245	303	257	213	259	248
unskilled	298	355	332	246	346	348
Acute sickness (restricted activity)						
semi-skilled	105	128	115—	115	134	95—
unskilled	107	141	113—	122	128	94—
Acute sickness (days per person)						
semi-skilled	—	205	137—	117	136	127
unskilled	—	238	148	122	129	133
GP consultations:						
persons consulting (rate per 1,000)						
semi-skilled	—	113	147	110	118	116
unskilled	-	112	141	123	111	115
GP consultations (rate per 1,000)						
semi-skilled	—	108	150	110	123	114
unskilled	—	117	150	120	107	102

Source: Reports of the GHS 1971–6.

patients and that more problems are discussed during this period. One study also found that middle-class patients were able to make better use of the consultation time, as measured by the number of items of information communicated and the number of questions asked (Cartwright and O'Brien, 1976). Moreover, even though working-class patients tended to have been with the same practice for longer, the doctors seemed to have more knowledge of the personal and domestic circumstances of their middle-class patients. An earlier study found, for example, that middle-class patients were more likely to be visited by their GP when in hospital than were working-class patients (Cartwright, 1964). For cultural reasons, then, and also because there is a tendency for the 'better' doctors to work in middle-class areas (as we shall see), the suggestion must be that middle-class patients appear to receive a better service when they do present themselves than their working-class contemporaries.

The data are limited and further analyses remain to be carried out, but what is available suggests that the level of consultation among partly skilled and unskilled manual workers does not appear to match their need for health care (see Table 14). With certain exceptions,* the socio-economic or class differences in ill-health are larger than the corresponding class differences in GP attendance (rates for persons consulting and total number of consultations). If we were to combine different measures of chronic and acute ill-health and compare 'need' with 'care received' (on the basis of some principle of weighting), there would be no exceptions for any year.

Hospital services

There is no regular source of class-related information on use of hospital services comparable with that obtained on GP consultation rates, even though questions on hospital attendance are asked in the GHS. In the case of hospital in-patients, the percentage concerned (about 2 per cent) is too small for any class breakdown of GHS data to be statistically meaningful. Attendance at out-patients is higher, and although since 1972 these rates have not been published on a class basis, some information is available. This suggests that there are no systematic class gradients in out-patient attendance for either males or females.

Data given in the 1972 GHS report does however seem to suggest that men in occupational class V aged 15–64 do have particularly high rates of attendance, which drop off after retirement. Referring to this 'relatively much greater use of "out-patients" by unskilled males than by males of other groups', the report indicated that it did not distinguish between attendance at out-patient casualty departments and other ancillary services. But the decline in rate at retirement at least suggests that 'the higher rates amongst unskilled males of working age than amongst males of other groups may reflect a rather particular use of out-patient facilities related to their greater risk of exposure to accident or injury compared with other groups'. Though later data do not show this discontinuity at retirement, the possibility of this special use of hospital out-patients is a matter of interest.

Such little evidence as is available on hospital in-patient care describes not the proportions of various social groups spending time in hospital but the social composition of the groups admitted. For England and Wales admission rates on an occupational basis are available only prior to 1963 (from HIPE), after which date they ceased to be centrally collected (mainly owing to doubts about their quality). The older data, however, suggest that the rate of usage of hospital beds rises with declining class. In Scotland, an analysis of hospital admission rates and duration of stay found clear

---

* The relative consultation rates of semi-skilled and unskilled groups exceed the relative rates of restricted activity in the cases in the table marked with a dash, though in most of those instances they no longer do so when *days* of restricted activity are taken.

upwards trends in both with declining class. Moreover SHIPS (Scottish Hospitals In-Patient Survey) does continue to code social class and more recent figures confirm this class gradient, both in admission rates (given by SDR in Table 15) and length of stay (given by SBDR).

Table 15: *Hospital standardized discharge ratios (SDR) and standardized bed-day ratios (SBDR) by occupational class (Scotland, 1971)*

	SDR		SBDR	
Class	Males	Females	Males	Females
I	79.5	95.9	63.7	92.5
II	80.9	98.0	73.3	93.6
III	94.0	90.4	93.9	91.0
IV	115.1	107.4	116.4	106.7
V	141.4	161.1	151.7	153.9

Source: Scottish Hospitals In-Patient Survey.

Preventive and promotive services

Although neither administrative returns nor the GHS provide information on the utilization of community health and preventive services by social or occupational class, there is a substantial body of research on which to draw, and it is well established that those in the manual classes make considerably less use of them than do those higher up the occupational scale. Moreover, the ambiguity which surrounds the relation of utilization to 'need' in the case of GP consultations is not encountered here. Assessment of morbidity, or need for care, is not at issue in comparing rates of attendance for ante-natal care (though this may be more essential for those put at risk by social factors), cervical screening, radiography or immunization of children.

In the case of family planning and maternity services substantial evidence shows that those social groups in greatest need make least use of services and (in the case of ante-natal care) are least likely to come early to the notice of the service. A study published in 1970 found clear class gradients in the proportion of mothers having an ante-natal examination, attending a family planning clinic and discussing birth control with their GP (Cartwright, 1970). Unintended pregnancies were also more common among working-class women. A second study, in 1973, appears to confirm these findings (Bone, 1973). It found that women from the non-manual classes make more use of family planning services than those from the manual classes. This is true both for married and unmarried women. Scottish data also show that late ante-natal booking is more common in poorer social groups, although the situation seems to be improving in all classes (Table 16). (They further suggest that late attendance for ante-natal care is an effective predictor of subsequent infant morbidity and mortality within families (Brotherston, 1976).)

Table 16: *Late ante-natal booking. Percentage of married women in each occupational class making an ante-natal booking after more than twenty weeks of gestation (Scotland 1971–3)*

Occupational class	1971	1972	1973
I	28.4	27.2	27.0
II	35.3	32.3	29.8
III	36.3	33.4	30.6
IV	39.3	37.8	35.3
V	47.1	44.2	40.5

Source: Brotherston, 1976. Data from Scottish Information Services Division.

Similar class differences have been found in attendance at post-natal examinations (Douglas and Rowntree, 1949), and immunization, ante-natal and post-natal supervision and uptake of vitamin foods (Gordon, 1951). Among slightly older children the National Child Development Study (1958 birth cohort) found substantial differences in immunization rates in children aged 7, as well as in attendance at the dentist (Table 17).

These patterns are further confirmed in studies of screening for cervical cancer, even though working-class women are much more likely to die from it. A study in Greater Manchester, for instance, showed that while women from classes IV and V accounted for over one third of all women living in the study area, they made up only about one sixth of women who had a smear test done.

Further studies show that working-class people make less use of dental services (Gray *et al.*, 1970; Bulman *et al.*, 1968) and of chiropody (Clarke, 1969) and receive inferior dental care (Sheiham and Hobdell, 1969). Many of these studies are admittedly old, and their findings cannot necessarily be accepted as still valid. Nevertheless, taken together, and in the absence of later evidence to the contrary, a clear relationship between social class and use of preventive services seems to have been demonstrated.

Table 17: *Use of health services by children under 7 by occupational class of father* (*Great Britain, 1965*).

	I	II	IIIN	IIIM	IV	V
Per cent who had never visited a dentist	16	20	19	24	27	31
Per cent not immunized against						
smallpox	6	14	16	25	29	33
polio	1	3	3	4	6	10
diphtheria	1	3	3	6	8	11

Source: Second Report of the NCDS.

Table 18: *Percentage of old persons of different occupational class who receive or feel the need for chiropody treatment* (*Great Britain, 1962*)

Source of chiropody treatment	Occupational class					
	I	II	IIIN	IIIM	IV	V
	%	%	%	%	%	%
Public or voluntary service	2	6	6	9	8	8
Privately paid	20	18	14	8	9	8
Non-professional or none, need felt	6	8	13	11	13	10
Non-professional or none, no need felt	72	68	67	72	71	74
Total	100	100	100	100	100	100
Number	82	557	396	1,193	1,040	457

Note: A further 42 persons were classed in armed services occupations, 10 had no occupation and 290 were unclassifiable.

Source: Townsend and Wedderburn, 1965.

Care of the infirm and disabled

There is little information on class inequalities in the care received by the infirm and disabled, though we now enter that awkward and neglected area where health care shades into the variety of other forms of social service provision. That is, to make comparisons of the care or services received by those who are disabled or infirm (including the aged infirm and the long-term chronic sick) would necessarily be to consider not only health care in the strict sense, but social work support, delivery of meals, home help, sheltered housing, mobility aids, sheltered work and rehabilitation etc., all or many of which may be crucial to the well-being of an infirm or disabled person.

But the slight, and unfortunately somewhat old, empirical evidence available does indicate that class inequalities are to be found here. A study of the elderly in residential homes and in geriatric and psychiatric hospitals carried out some years ago found not only that the manual and non-manual elderly were likely to be in different kinds of institution (the latter less commonly in hospital), but a gap in the standard of living and care available in institutions catering principally for one or the other group (Townsend, 1962). A second national study of people aged 65 and over found disparities

Table 19: *Percentage of old persons of different occupational class who were receiving public or private domestic help, or who said help was needed (Great Britain, 1962)*

Source of domestic help	Occupational class					
	I	II	IIIN	IIIM	IV	V
	%	%	%	%	%	%
Local authority	1	2	4	6	4	4
Privately paid	42	27	12	5	3	2
Other (e.g. family) or none, but need felt	10	7	6	6	6	4
Other (e.g. family) or none, no need felt	47	64	78	83	87	90
Total	100	100	100	100	100	100
Number	81	555	396	1,188	1,033	447

Source: Townsend and Wedderburn, 1965.

in receipt of a number of services. Both publicly provided chiropody services and domestic help, for instance, fail fully to compensate for unequal ability to purchase such services (Townsend and Wedderburn, 1965). (See Tables 18 and 19.)

Of equal concern is the difference in attitude between old people of different social classes. Table 19 shows that 90 per cent of those in class V neither receive domestic help (from outside their family) nor feel the need of it. Among the elderly who are incapacitated 'nearly half those in Social Classes I and II ... already had privately paid or local authority domestic help, and nearly half the others said they needed help. But only a sixth of those in Social Class V who were severely incapacitated had such help already and only a fifth of the remainder felt the need for it' (Townsend and Wedderburn, 1965, p. 46). While we cannot tell if these differences still exist, the study shows all too clearly the way in which norms and values associated with class may influence subjective perceptions of need.

In considering the needs of the disabled, aged infirm and chronic sick, not only is it difficult clearly to distinguish needs for strictly medical services from needs for other supportive services, but it is similarly difficult to distinguish needs related to the condition 'itself' (i.e. medically defined) from those relating to its social and economic consequences. In this context it may be helpful to look at the circumstances of the long-term sick, that is those receiving sickness, invalidity and industrial injury benefits for periods of between a month and a year (Martin and Morgan, 1975). This shows not only that the sample of benefit recipients as a whole contained a much higher proportion of semi-skilled and unskilled manual workers, which is to have been expected, but that the longer the spell of sickness, the higher the proportion of unskilled workers. Moreover, the longer the period of incapacity the less likely the sick person is to be able to return to the same type of work with the same employer as before, though skilled manual workers are more likely to have their jobs kept open for them than are semi-skilled or unskilled workers. Unsurprisingly also, receipt of sick pay from the employer is also related to duration of invalidity and to level of job (defined by occupational group).

Clearly therefore in considering the needs of the disabled, long-term sick and aged infirm, financial problems and (in some cases) problems of subsequent re-employment are both pertinent and class-related. The implication of this for policy (which we take up in Chapter 9) is that the equalization of provision of health and social services is not justifiably separable from the equalization of the social and economic consequences of long-term invalidity or sickness.

The interaction of geographic and social disparities

It has been known for a long time that there are differences in the health services available in well-to-do and poor areas. In 1957 a study of the social aspects of prescribing found that the average total cost of drugs per prescription was higher in wealthier areas (Martin, 1957). More recently an analysis of health expenditure at the regional level also found a positive correlation between the percentage of the population in professional and managerial socio-economic groups and both community health expenditure and hospital revenue expenditure, and a negative correlation between expenditure and proportion of population in unskilled and semi-skilled occupations (Noyce, Snaith and Trickey, 1974). The authors concluded: 'There are no regions of above-average spending which are not also high socio-economic status regions. Indeed, if one knew no other facts it would be possible to explain two thirds of the variation in community health expenditure by a knowledge of what proportion of the population in each region were managers, employers, or professional workers.'

In 1971 Tudor Hart (a general practitioner working in a poor area of Wales) contrasted the availability of medical care in poor industrial areas of high need and affluent salubrious areas of lower need in memorable terms. He wrote:

In areas with most sickness and death, general practitioners have more work, larger lists, less hospital support and inherit more clinically ineffective traditions of consultation than in the healthiest areas; and hospital doctors shoulder heavier caseloads with less staff and equipment, more obsolete buildings and suffer recurrent crises in the availability of beds and replacement staff. These trends can be summed up as the inverse care law: that the availability of good medical care tends to vary inversely with the need of the population served. (Tudor Hart, 1971)

An analysis of data in 1976 on need for and provision of child health services for each of the fifteen pre-1974 hospital board regions of England and Wales showed how, in particular, regional provision of GPs and health visitors is negatively correlated with a number of indicators of need (including still-birth rate, level of infant mortality and birth rate to teenage mothers) (West and Lowe, 1976). There are indeed very few positive correlations; midwives alone seemed to be relatively well distributed throughout the regions. The authors go on to suggest: 'When data becomes available for area health authorities even greater differences between need and provision will probably be uncovered between areas than between regions' (cf. Morris, 1975, pp. 53, 77). In the meantime it has at least been established that *variations* in expenditure (Rickard, 1976) and in the provision of services

(Buxton and Klein, 1975; Jones and Masterman, 1976) are greater at the sub-regional than at the regional level. This, of course, is the level at which it matters to people. It is extremely difficult to know for sure what this means for small typically working-class areas in comparison with typically middle-class areas. One recent study does give some indications though. It looked at three areas of council housing, one in Newham (east London) and two in the Midlands, one solidly middle class, the other a council estate with a history of social problems. Unlike Newham, which has long suffered from severe deprivation of the environment, both Midlands areas were situated in 'a socially mixed county, with a teaching hospital, and an attractive environment: a highly desirable county in which to work, with no reputation for recruitment problems in general practice.' Questions covered morbidity (GHS questions were used) and experiences in seeking help from the GP. Although much was found to be common to the two working-class areas, differentiating their inhabitants from the middle-class residents of the third area, this was not the whole picture. Indeed, the principal conclusion of the study is as follows:

The provision of health care and the subjective experience of seeking that care are all partly determined by the socio-economic structure of society on an area basis, so that *a working-class person is at a greater disadvantage if he lives in a predominantly working-class area than if he lives in a socially mixed area.* The data ... are consistent with a theory of structural determination of need and demand for health care from an area, operating both through environmental and social conditions on the level of health, and through the social pressures and life experiences that further affect demand, particularly in the case of childhood illness. The level and quality of available medical manpower, relative to need and demand, is likely also to be strongly affected by the environment and social class composition of an area through the operation of the market for recruitment. (Skrimshire, 1978)

It is likely that similar conclusions would follow from a consideration of race or ethnicity. However, information on use of services by ethnic groups is sparse. One study has referred to hesitation in seeking ante-natal care among immigrants and their difficulties in securing adequate dietary information (Coombe, 1976), and there is evidence of some lack of appreciation among health services staff of the special needs of some immigrant groups, as well as a clear lack of adequate facilities in some of the areas in which they have been obliged to concentrate.

Conclusion

Generalization about inequality of utilization is made difficult partly because of sampling errors in the case of national surveys and of partial information in the case of local studies, and because of the (as yet unresolved) problem of relating utilization to need.

Inequalities appear to be greatest (and most worrying) in the case of the preventive services. Severe under-utilization by the working classes is a complex result of under-provision, of costs (financial, psychological) of attendance, and perhaps of a life-style which profoundly inhibits any attempt at rational action in the interests of *future* well-being. Such factors are not, in this case, outweighed by the costs of present disruption of normal social functioning. We have also seen, however, how services provided on an 'outreach' basis can serve to reduce at least some of the costs of attendance, with beneficial results.

The situation is not clear-cut in the case of GP attendance, partly because attendance rates cannot be compared with any precise measure of need. Excepting, for some years, children, more of those in lower than in higher socio-economic groups consult a doctor, and their total consultations are, relatively, greater. But on most of the health indicators their need for care is greater still. It is hard not to conclude that poorer groups make relatively low use of GP services, irrespective of the separate question of the *adequacy* of the services to which they typically have access.

Middle-class parents are, however, more likely than working-class parents to seek medical attention for their children. Since the (direct) costs of attendance may be presumed similar, this may imply that working-class *adults* are likely to be typically *more* sick than are middle-class ones before help is sought. Moreover, we have seen also that middle-class patients typically receive better care from their GP – a consequence, once more, of both interpersonal and ecological factors.

Hospital out-patient departments are used more by the working class than by the middle class. In the case of Accident and Emergency departments there is evidence of some use in place of the GP, access (as to the GP) being on the basis of self- (or 'lay') referral. It has been suggested that this preferred use of out-patients in treatment of 'traumatic' conditions (suffered at work or in the home) is principally a result of their greater availability: they are open twenty-four hours a day, no appointment is needed and availability of diagnostic aids is certain.

In the case of in-patient departments too, evidence suggests greater use by the working class. It may be noted that, since admission is generally on the basis of GP referral, a higher proportion of working-class patients than of middle-class patients consulting a GP must be subsequently admitted to hospital. This in turn must imply that more working-class patients have illnesses requiring hospital admission, or that the working-class patient seeing his GP is *typically* sicker and/or that he or she is seen as less likely to receive adequate care at home. And indeed, evidence from a survey of the elderly suggests that this is so: public provision of domiciliary services seems not fully to compensate for differential ability to purchase such services.

It is hard to resist the conclusion that this pattern of unequal use is explicable not in terms of non-rational response to sickness by working-class people, but of a rational weighting of the perceived costs and benefits to them of attendance and compliance with the prescribed regime. These costs and benefits differ between the social classes both on account of differences in way of life, constraints and resources, and of the fact that costs to the working class are actually increased by the lower levels and perhaps poorer quality of provision to which many have access.

Class differentials in the use of the various services which we have considered derive from the interaction of social and ecological factors. Differences in sheer availability and, at least to some extent, in the quality of care available in different *localities* provide one channel by which social inequality permeates the NHS. Reduced provision implied greater journeys, longer waiting lists, longer waiting times, difficulties in obtaining an appointment, shortage of space and so on. A second channel is provided by the structuring of health care *institutions* in accordance with the values, assumptions and preferences of the sophisticated middle-class 'consumer'. Inadequate attention may be paid to the different problems and needs of those who are less able to express themselves in acceptable terms and who suffer from lack of command over resources both of time and of money. In all cases, for an individual to seek medical care, his (or her) perception of his (or her) need for care will have to outweigh the perceived costs (financial and other) both of seeking care and of the regime which may be prescribed. These costs are class-related.

It is the interaction of these two sets of factors which produces the inequalities documented in this chapter

Chapter 5

International Comparisons

The success or otherwise of comparable developed countries in altering patterns of health inequality is an inevitable yardstick against which to measure the British performance and is also a possible pointer to what should or should not be done here. Accordingly we shall now attempt to set the British experience in an international context and in a limited way to explore what has been happening elsewhere. We start by looking at overall national levels and trends and go on to look at the different experiences of inequalities in health. Inevitably there are cultural and social (structural) variables which make any such comparisons complex and subject to a variety of interpretations. Nevertheless the success of some countries in raising health standards makes it an essential input into our analysis of the British experience. Once again mortality data are the most available indicator of relative levels of health, and in particular infant mortality, because infancy remains one of the most vulnerable periods of human life and infant mortality has long-term consequences, has been accepted as an important index of a country's achievements in the health field.

Levels of health and changes over time

International comparisons over the last two decades highlight a number of points about the relative success or otherwise of British health policy (see Tables 20 and 21).

1. In 1975 England, Wales and Scotland (in particular) experienced significantly higher perinatal mortality rates than those of the four Nordic countries and the Netherlands. France and Germany had broadly similar rates to the British.*

2. The overall decreases in perinatal mortality rates between 1960 and 1975

---

*More recent data show that by 1978 Scotland had caught up with England but that the conclusion otherwise holds. Rates of perinatal mortality in 1978: England 15.4; Wales 16.8; Scotland 15.4; Sweden (1977) 10.1; Norway (1977) 13.2; Denmark (1977) 10.6; Finland (1977) 11.0; Netherlands (1977 provisional) 12.9; France (provisional) 14.7; W. Germany (1977) 14.9.

Table 20: Perinatal and infant mortality in Europe

	Perinatal mortality per 1,000 live births				Infant mortality per 1,000 live births			
	1960	1975	% Decrease 1960–75	Annual % decrease 1971–5	1960	1975	% Decrease 1960–75	Annual % decrease 1972–5
England & Wales	33.5	17.9*	46.5†	4.1	21.8	14.2*	34.3‡	4.5
Scotland	38.1	18.5*	51.3‡	5.1	26.4	14.8*	44.0‡	5.4
Sweden	26.2	11.1	57.7	7.3	16.6	8.3	50.0	7.7
Norway	24.0	14.2	40.8	5.1	18.9	11.1	41.3	2.0
Denmark	26.5	12.7*	52.1‡	5.5	21.5	10.3*	52.0‡	3.9
Finland	25.3	13.9†	45.0§	5.9	21.0	11.0†	47.6§	1.4
Netherlands	25.6	14.0	45.3	4.3	16.5	10.6	35.7	3.1
France	31.8	19.5†	38.7§	4.8	27.4	11.1	59.8	10.2
W. Germany	36.3	19.4	46.5	4.8	33.8	19.7	41.6	4.5
(E. Germany)	—	(17.6)	—	—	—	(15.9)	—	(3.4)
USA	29.4	20.7	29.2	—	26.0	16.1	38.1	4.3

* 1976 † 1974 ‡ 1960–76 § 1960–74

Sources: 1960–72 data: *Health Care – the Growing Dilemma*; 1975 data: WHO and *World Health Statistics, 1978*, Vol. 1; 1975, France: *Eurohealth Handbook*, 1978.

Table 21: *Adult mortality in Europe: deaths per million*

	Men				Women			
	35–44		45–54		35–44		45–54	
	1964	1975	1964	1975	1964	1975	1964	1975
England and Wales	2,471	2,095*	7,330	6,985*	1,778	1,468*	4,382	4,298*
Scotland	3,245	2,817*	9,322	8,876*	2,029	1,896*	5,473	5,412
Sweden	2,205	2,343*	5,223	5,736*	1,444	1,372*	3,546	3,056*
Norway	2,327	2,012*	5,664	6,009*	1,299	947*	2,938	2,955*
Denmark	2,128	2,420*	6,126	6,865*	1,695	1,579*	4,000	4,529*
Finland	4,427	4,171†	?	10,748†	1,746	1,430†	4,413	3,537†
Netherlands	2,043	1,859*	5,811	5,897*	1,336	1,159*	3,421	3,159*
France	3,400	3,388†	8,200	8,288†	1,830	1,552†	4,145	3,681†
W. Germany	2,919	3,016	7,724	7,504	1,942	1,601	4,461	4,164
USA	3,836	3,469	9,643	8,563	2,315	1,908	5,227	4,563

* 1976 † 1974

Sources: 1966–9 data: McKinsey, *Health Care*; 1975 data: *World Health Statistics*, 1978, Vol. 1.

show that as a percentage of the 1960 rate, England and Wales, and Scotland in particular, performed more than averagely well. However, if we then look at the annual percentage decrease over the more recent period (1971–5) it appears that the result for England and Wales at least was no longer satisfactory, and improvements were not up to those being achieved in any of the other countries.*

3. Infant mortality rates (deaths in the first year of life) reflect socio-environmental factors to a greater degree than perinatal rates. In 1975 the Nordic countries and the Netherlands once again showed the lowest rates, but France had also joined them. There is then a significant jump to England, Wales, Scotland, Germany (East and West, the former being substantially lower than the latter) and the USA.

4. The decreases in infant mortality recorded between 1960 and 1975, as a percentage of the 1960 rates, show England and Wales to have done sub-stantially less well than Scotland and, indeed, than any other country. By far the highest rate of improvement was obtained in France. In contrast to the perinatal rates, however, the relative performance of England and Wales, and Scotland in particular, was more creditable in the more recent period. Between 1972 and 1975 only France and Sweden recorded higher average annual rates of decrease.

5. The picture for adult mortality is somewhat less clear. Certainly so far as younger men are concerned, the 1975 rate for England and Wales com-pares favourably with several other countries and even with three of the four Nordic ones. Moreover the general improvement recorded over the period 1964 to 1975 (or 1976) was not paralleled in some of the countries with the lowest rates (Sweden, for example, showing rising mortality among men). In the case particularly of women aged 45–54, however, the data offer little comfort.

How are we to explain the differences? One way is through comparison of the relative importance of causes of death. If Sweden is compared with England and Wales, taking rates of infant death for a number of major causes, it becomes apparent that perinatal factors and respiratory conditions are major contributors to the poorer British rate.

If the difference between the two national rates is 5.9 per 1,000 live births, 2.8 of these are accounted for by various perinatal factors and 1.4 by respiratory conditions and pneumonia (Table 22). In other words it is not

---

*This conclusion does not hold for the most recent period. Rates of improvement since 1975 have been similar to those of, for example, Finland, France and W. Germany.

difficult to see how both factors impacting before and during birth *and* those which relate principally to the environment and care of the infant have their effect. The difference in death due to congenital abnormality is relatively slight and the fact that in Sweden, with its excellent record in perinatal and infant death, the congenital abnormality death rate remains comparable with the situation in England and Wales has led some commentators to the view that there may here be an 'irreducible minimum' beyond which progress is, given present knowledge, unlikely on this particular front (see for example Pharaoh and Morris, 1979).

Table 22: *Mortality rates under 1 year per 1,000 live births, for selected causes* (*1976*)

	Sweden	England and Wales	difference
Infections	0.26	0.43	0.17
Acute respiratory conditions	0.04	0.57	0.53
Pneumonia	0.13	1.02	0.89
Accidents	0.08	0.35	0.27
Various anoxic and hypoxic conditions of pregnancy	1.43	2.96	1.53
Other causes of perinatal mortality	1.07	2.30	1.23
Congenital abnormality	3.03	3.45	0.42

Another approach to an explanation might be through a comparison of levels of provision of health care in different countries (Table 23). Differences in numbers of doctors per head of population are not, however, extreme, and West Germany, which throughout the 1960s and early 1970s was the most generously endowed, shows up relatively poorly in the mortality tables. The supply of nurses accords a little better with mortality. But the importance of medical care provision, however expressed, has to be considered in relation to socio-environmental variables which are the principal determinants of relative levels of, and changes in, the health of nations.

For instance a comparison of health services in England, Sweden and the USA found that although Sweden put greater emphasis on child health and the USA on the health of old people (both spent similar proportions of GNP on health care) and that there were differences in access between income groups, the main conclusion was that: 'The dominant reason why

Table 23: *Availability of health care: physicians, nurses and hospital beds in Europe per 10,000 population*

	Physicians			Nurses		General (non-psychiatric) hospital beds	
	1960	1971	1975	1960	1975*	1960	1971
England and Wales	10.5	12.7⎫	11.0	20.8†	37.5	46.0	40.7
Scotland	11.8	15.6⎭		22.0	48.2	47.8	49.4
Sweden	9.5	13.9	16.2§	28.6	71.1	—	69.4
Norway	11.8	14.6	18.3¶	28.1	73.6	55.8	46.1
Denmark	12.3	—	17.9‡	37.7	80.4	59.7†	60.1
Finland	6.4	11.1	13.3§	33.8	81.9	41.9	46.8
Netherlands	11.2	13.2	15.9¶	—	32.2	45.0†	53.6
France	10.0	13.9	14.6	18.6	50.2	55.5†	60.5
W. Germany	14.9	17.8	19.2	22.0	35.9	65.3	66.8
USA	13.4	15.4	—	27.9	63.7	41.4	46.7

* breaks in series: data not comparable around break † 1959 ‡ 1968 § 1974 ¶ 1976

Sources: McKinsey, *Health – The Growing Dilemma*, New York, 1974; 1975 physicians' data: *Eurohealth Handbook*; 1975 nurses' data: WHO *World Health Statistics*, 1978, Vol. III.

the Swedish mortality rates are lower than in any state in the United States is a high minimum standard of living for everyone and a cultural homogeneity ... Health services are, of course, also a factor in the low mortality rates, but the elimination of poverty in the United States in the sense true for Sweden would be more likely to bring mortality rates closer to Sweden than a policy limited to health services only' (Anderson, 1972, p. 158).

One factor which can probably be eliminated as an explanation of the relatively poor British showing is the degree of regional disparity in medical services. Indeed, in so far as broadly aggregated data give an accurate picture, the regional disparity of physicians is more equitable in England (Table 24).

Inequalities in health: the international experience

While in the UK mortality and morbidity statistics are routinely presented by social class, the same is not true of other countries. It may be that social class is a less politically salient dimension of social stratification than in

Table 24: Regional variations in number of physicians per thousand population: highest and lowest areas

	England		France		Germany		Netherlands	
Average	1.06		1.47		1.74		1.36	
Highest (H)	1.31	(N.W. Thames)	2.18	(Paris)	2.97	(W. Berlin)	2.10	(Utrecht)
Lowest (L)	0.91	(Trent)	0.98	(Basse Normandie)	1.41	(Nieder-Sachsen)	0.92	(Friesland)
Ratio H/L	1.4		2.2		2.1		2.3	

Sources: England, France, Germany: A. Maynard in *Social and Economic Administration*, 12, 1, 1978; Netherlands: Compendium Gezondheitsstatistiek Nederland, Centraal Bureau voor de Statistiek, 1974.

the UK and other dimensions are more important, but whatever the reason, health inequality data are more commonly presented on a geographic or, as in the USA, ethnic basis. Certainly in those Nordic countries made up of industrialized densely populated southern regions and cold rural northern regions with sparse and declining populations this is not surprising. One result, though, is that international data expressing the extent of health inequalities are not readily presented on a comparable basis. Moreover, where social or occupational groupings are used these are not strictly comparable with the groupings used in Britain by the Registrar General. Additionally, the overall social class compositions of countries are far from identical. Nevertheless, though the data we have collected relate variously to regional, industrial, occupational or income groups, they do permit some attempt at answering the question: are the health inequalities in England and Wales which we have illustrated encountered also in Europe and the USA? The best way of dealing with our somewhat disparate data is to make country-by-country comparisons with England and Wales.

Denmark

Denmark has lower perinatal and infant mortality rates than England and Wales and has succeeded in reducing the latter but not the former by more than we have. Their rate is also more evenly divided among the social groups. While in England and Wales neonatal mortality rates in class V are twice those in class I, with regular class increments in between, in Denmark the difference is significantly less: 5.7 neonatal deaths per 1,000 live births in 1974 in the top social group against 9 per 1,000 in the bottom (Table 25). The neonatal mortality rate for unskilled workers in Denmark has also fallen by the same percentage as for the country as a whole, which it has not in Britain.

Table 25: *Denmark: neonatal mortality rate by occupation per 1,000 live births*

	1970	1972	1974
Self-employed	10.9	8.1	5.7
Salaried employee	9.9	9.8	7.5
Skilled worker	10.1	8.9	8.1
Unskilled worker	13.5	11.3	9.0
Other/unknown	11.1	10.2	8.8
All	11.0	9.7	8.0

Source: *Medicinisk Fødselsstatistisk*, Copenhagen, 1974.

Table 26: *Finland: age-adjusted mortality indices (1970) by social group per 10,000 adults*

	Male	Female
I Higher administrative or clerical employees, comparable employers, and people with academic degrees	78	95
II Lower administrative or clerical employees, and comparable employers	95	100
III Skilled and specialized workers	92	102
IV Unskilled workers	148	103
V Farmers	87	96

Source: S. Naytia, 'Social Group and Mortality in Finland', *British Journal of Preventive and Social Medicine*, 31, 4, 1977, p. 23.

Table 27: *France: rates of infant, neonatal and post-neonatal death by socio-professional group of father (per 1,000 legitimate live births)*

	1956–60			1970–72		
	Infant	Neo-natal	Post-neonatal	Infant	Neo-natal	Post-neonatal
Liberal professions; higher and middle cadres	17.0	12.4	4.6	11.6	8.7	2.9
Employees	24.9	19.7	8.2	14.7	10.8	3.9
Industrial and commercial proprietors	25.4	17.4	8.0	15.0	11.2	3.8
Skilled workers	28.1	17.7	10.4	26.2	11.4	4.8
Farmers	31.2	20.8	10.4	15.2	11.4	3.8
Specialized workers	32.9	19.6	13.3	19.0	13.2	5.8
Agricultural workers	35.3	21.0	14.3	19.8	14.0	5.8
Labourers	44.8	23.1	21.7	25.7	16.5	9.2
All	29.6	18.4	11.2	15.9	11.4	4.6

Note: Certain categories of workers, which fall within the range shown, are not given.

Source: Dinh Quang Chï and S. Hemery, 'Disparités régionales de la mortalité infantile', *Économie et statistique*, 1977, 85, pp. 3–12.

Finland

Finland is a country which, though enjoying low rates of perinatal and infant mortality, suffers from very high rates of adult mortality, far above those of England and Wales. The existence of regional disparities in adult Finnish mortality is well known, but there are also differences between social groups (Table 26).

France

The classification system in France suggests at first glance greater inequalities than in Britain, but in fact it seems the relativities are broadly comparable. There are pronounced differences in infant mortality rates both between social groups and regions. During the period 1956/60 and 1970/72,

Table 28: *France 1968: mortality rates among economically active men aged 45–64 (unstandardized) (per 100,000)*

I	Higher cadres (administrators etc.)	699
II	Industrialists, liberal professions, large commercial proprietors	919
III	Middle cadres (including teachers, medical/social service personnel, army, police)	928
IV	Artisans and small shopkeepers	1,225
V	Farmers	1,117
VI	Employees (including service workers, clergy)	1,392
VII	Qualified workers	1,589
VIII	Agricultural workers	1,520
IX	Other workers (including miners)	1,169
	All	1,189

Note: The French data shown in Table 28 refer to men aged 45–64 (unstandardized for age), excluding those classified in the census as 'inactive' (16 per cent of the total, and with a very much higher mortality rate) and excluding three regions of France in which a very high proportion of deaths are attributed to unspecified or inadequately specified causes. If those classified as 'inactive' are included, the overall rate rises from 1,189 to 1,443. Thus, though the classifications within I, II and III on the one hand and VII, VIII and IX on the other do not correspond to those in Great Britain, the picture of distinctly higher mortality rates in the latter group is comparable with the British.

Source: Derrienic *et al.*, 1977.

the ratio between infant mortality in the most favoured group (liberal professions) and the least favoured (labourers) fell slightly from 2.6 to 2.2 (Table 27). There was no change in the ratio of neonatal rates (first month), which remained at about 1.9. In the case of post-neonatal death rates, however, the least favoured social group has improved its relative standing very strikingly, the ratio falling from 4.7 to 3.2. This latter change is in marked contrast to Britain and seems to imply a greater levelling of socio-environmental factors closely implicated in post-neonatal death than has taken place here.

Among adults the difference between the most and least favoured social groups in terms of mortality is slightly more than a factor of two, a figure roughly comparable with the UK (Table 28).

From a regional point of view a factor of two separated the area of France enjoying the lowest infant mortality rates in 1970/72 from the highest. While Île de France, including Paris, had a figure of 13 per 1,000 legitimate live births, Corsica had a figure of 24.6 per 1,000. In 1956/60 these two regions also ran first and last and in the intervening years there has been no change in the ratios separating them.

The interaction between socio-economic and regional disparities can be shown by the cross-tabulation of infant mortality rates by occupation and region simultaneously. One study showed that for the group 'liberal professions and higher and middle cadres', the infant mortality rate in 1970–72 ranged from 10.2 in Haute-Normandie and Rhône-Alpes, to 17.6 in Corsica; but that in two areas (Franche-Comté, Languedoc-Roussillon) 'industrial and commercial proprietors' actually had lower rates. Similarly, for 'labourers', the range was from 18.3 (Pays de la Loire) to 33.4 (Franche-Comté); but once more in two areas (Corsica and Aquitaine) the group 'specialized workers' showed up less well. In terms of the ratio mortality rates between 'labourers' and 'liberal professions ...' there was also a considerable range, from 1.4 (Corsica and Aquitaine) to 2.7 (Brittany).

West Germany

In the German case it is necessary to use regional disparities as an indicator of the existence of health inequalities. On this basis, and using infant and neonatal mortality as an indicator, the German experience shows up as being less favourable than that in England and Wales (Table 29).

Both rates, but particularly the infant mortality rate, show substantial variation. The same is true for England and Wales. The range in infant mortality rates for the German *Länder* is from 17.9 (Baden-Württemberg) to 25.9 (Bremen): a difference of 8.0 or 40 per cent of the lower figure. The comparison may be made with the RHAs of England and Wales. The lowest infant mortality rate here (1975) is Oxford (12.68 per 1,000 live births), the highest Yorkshire (17.93) – a difference of 5.2 or about 40 per cent of the lower figure (OPCS, DH3, no. 2, 1977).

Table 29: *West Germany 1974: infant mortality and early neonatal mortality rates, by Land*

Land	Infant mortality rate	Early neonatal mortality rate
	per 1,000 live births	
Schleswig-Holstein	18.0	10.5
Hamburg	19.0	11.2
Niedersachsen	21.9	13.5
Bremen	25.9	12.1
Nordrhein-Westfalen	23.2	14.3
Hessen	21.5	13.3
Rheinland-Pfalz	22.3	12.6
Baden-Württemberg	17.9	11.4
Bayern	20.4	13.2
Saarland	25.6	15.7
W. Berlin	18.7	9.3
All	21.1	13.0

Source: Statistisches Bundesamt, 1974.

Netherlands

Here too social class or occupation categories do not seem to be employed in analyses of inequalities in health: provincial differences are, however, available. Table 30 shows variation in adult mortality rates between the Dutch provinces, standardized for age.

Once more, comparison may be made with OPCS statistics giving SMRs by English and Welsh RHAs (OPCS, DH5, no. 2, 1977). The range in SMRs among males is from 87 (Oxford), 88 (East Anglia) to 113 (North-West) and 111 (Northern); for females the range is distinctly smaller, from 92 (Wessex) and 93 (East Anglia) to 108 (Northern) and 110 (North-West). Allowing for the different bases on which the two sets of figures are given, the ranges from lowest to highest do not seem very different. The superior performance of the Netherlands seems, rather, to be reflected in the distribution of provinces within this range. There are more nearer the lower end than the higher.

Table 30: *Netherlands 1971: age-standardized adult mortality per 10,000 population*

Province	Males	Females
Groningen	88.8	71.6
Friesland	84.9	71.9
Drenthe	88.0	76.8
Overjssel	89.7	73.1
Gelderland	93.6	77.4
Utrecht	93.8	70.5
Noord Holland	94.5	73.0
Zuid Holland	92.4	71.4
Zeeland	80.9	68.5
Noord Brabant	95.5	79.4
Limburg	101.4	82.7
All Netherlands	92.8	74.3

Source: Centraal Bureau voor de Statistiek, 1974.

Norway

Like the Netherlands, Norway distinctly surpasses England and Wales in its rates of perinatal, infant and adult mortality. Norwegian statistics give standardized mortality rates for the twenty Norwegian counties, in relation to the national average, for adult males and females. The picture differs somewhat between the two groups. In both cases, however, the highest rates are found in Finnmark (the most northerly and very sparsely populated part of the country): 122 for men and 118 for women (1969–72). In the case of men the next highest rate is found in the Oslo area (the industrialized capital in which over 10 per cent of the population live); whereas in the case of women it is in Troms (a county also many hundreds of miles into the Arctic circle). These rates are 111 and 110 respectively. The southern regions of more moderate climate which are not industrialized have much lower mortality rates. Leaving aside Finnmark, the range for men is 85–111 and for women 95–110. However, if Troms also is omitted, the range for women falls to 95–104, the figure for Oslo being 99 (less than the national average). Clearly, in the case of Norway climatic factors render such comparisons of uncertain value.

Also available are morbidity data, more or less comparable with those given in the GHS, on an income basis. These data suggest something of an income gradient in morbidity among single persons and among the older members of multi-person households, though not among 16–49-year-olds.

Table 31: *Norway 1975: morbidity* by age and income: percentage of all in each group*

annual income	persons in multi-person households						single persons, ages over 16
			Age				
	0–6	*7–15*	*16–30*	*30–49*	*50–66*	*67+*	
under 15,000 kr	35	31	36	52	74	80	78
15,000–29,999 kr	29	30	44	54	76	78	75
30,000–49,999 kr	33	36	45	54	72	78	58
50,000–79,999 kr	31	34	42	52	65	77	58
over 80,000 kr	24	32	39	48	60	67	—

* 'Morbidity' is defined as persons sick on 1 October and/or at least one day of restricted activity in the period 1–15 October.

Source: Central Bureau of Statistics, Oslo, 1977.

Sweden

Sweden has the lowest perinatal and infant mortality rates in the world and, moreover, is succeeding in continuing to reduce them. The Swedish situation in this respect is of particular interest.

Early in the century Sweden suffered from substantial differentials in infant death rates, on both a geographical and an income basis. Thus, among legitimate infants born in Stockholm between 1918 and 1922, the infant mortality rate in families with an income over 10,000 S Kr was 14.3 per 1,000, in families with an income of less than 4,000 S Kr it was 48.9 per 1,000.* Professor Sjolin of Uppsala University writes of this differential: 'Today the difference is probably completely erased, but there are no recent studies to confirm it' (Sjolin, 1975). The decline in regional differentials is shown by Fig. 7, which compares rates for the three most northern and relatively poor counties with two southern counties (Uppsala, Göteborg). By 1971, Sjolin writes, the northern county of Vasternorrland had the lowest rate of infant mortality among all the Swedish counties (8.2).

Moreover, Sweden seems also to have eliminated socio-economic differ-

* Rietz Acta Paediat, **9**, quoted by Sjolin.

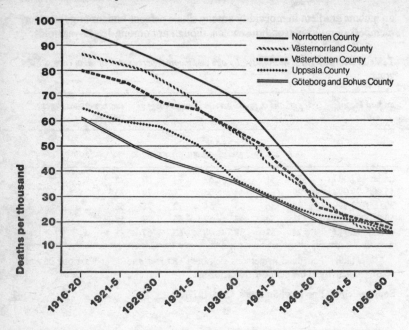

Figure 7. *Infant mortality in five Swedish counties, 1916–60.* (*Source: Sjolin, 1975.*)

ences in height and age of maturity among children. A study in 1976 found no such differences in a sample of 740 Swedish urban school children followed from age 9–17 (Lindgren, 1976). (By contrast, Rona, Swan and Altman (1978) found that social class remains an important determinant of children's height – between ages 5 and 11.5 years – in England and Scotland. Moreover, within each of the class-groups children with *unemployed* fathers were shorter.)

The reduction of inequalities

Several recent studies in the USA have attempted to focus on the question of *changing* inequalities. In particular there have been attempts to assess the effect of the poverty programmes of the 1960s on health inequalities, measured by adult and infant mortality rates and morbidity/utilization of the health services rates (Lerner and Stutz, 1977; Chase, 1977; and Wilson and White, 1977).

Taken together they indicate that the medico-social programmes of that period were associated (since causality cannot be assumed) with reductions in infant mortality differentials, though not adult mortality differentials, and with improved utilization of medical services by the poor relative to the non-poor, but again not with reductions in differentials in morbidity. In so far as this is an accurate picture, it might conceivably be seen as indicative of the feasibility of influencing the various indicators of 'health inequality' with which we are concerned.

So far as policies designed specifically to reduce the overall incidence of perinatal and infant mortality (and the associated morbidity among survivors) are concerned, the experience of France and Finland is particularly significant.

A study in France has attempted an analysis of the effect of laws promulgated in 1970/71 requiring all pregnant women to attend at least four pre-natal consultations (at three, six, eight and nine months) and requiring examination of all newborn infants by a doctor in the first week of life. The law also recommended pre-natal consultation with a doctor qualified in obstetrics and additional consultations for those assessed as 'at risk' (Rumeau-Rouquette *et al.*, 1977). The study took a representative sample of about 1,000 pregnancies in the Rhône-Alpes region in July 1972 and in June 1975, and looked at both the effect on the patterns of usage of services and the outcome. Overall, the proportion of women having less than four consultations fell from 14.4 per cent to 10.6 per cent, and the number with an obstetrician responsible for pre-natal surveillance rose from 56.6 per cent to 69.3 per cent. At the same time, however, there was a rise in the average educational level of the mothers, in the standard of housing, in the use of contraception and in the percentage of mothers working, and a fall in the percentage of mothers who already had two or more children. So far as outcome was concerned, it was found that the distribution of birth-weights was unchanged, but the rate of 'anomalies or pathologies at birth' fell from 23.8 to 15.6 per cent.

The adequacy of pre-natal surveillance as a function of various 'class' factors showed a complex pattern of change. In 1972 inadequate surveillance (a total of less than four consultations or first consultation after three months) was associated with immigrant status (mother or father), no post-primary education (mother or father), number of children and manual employment of father. By 1975 the association with educational level of mother and number of children had both fallen considerably. There was no clear change on the basis of manual/non-manual employment of the father.

In Finland success in reducing perinatal and infant mortality rates has been attributed in particular to a reduction in the hazards of child-birth for larger babies (over 2,500g birth-weight) and a reduction in the proportion of babies born at below 2,500g, even though there has been no improvement in the survival chances of the reduced number of fragile babies (Wynn and Wynn, 1974). A study of perinatal mortality in Sweden reaches similar conclusions (Geijerstam, 1969). In reducing the incidence of low birth-weight, nutrition seems to be crucial, and it is perhaps worth noting that ante-natal clinics in Finland typically recommend the consumption of 1–1½ litres of milk per day by the pregnant woman – considerably more than is recommended in England. There is, of course, a typically large difference in the consumption of dairy products between England and Finland – among all income groups – a fact which may show up both in perinatal and adult mortality rates (though in opposite senses).

High rates of attendance for ante-natal care are also characteristic of the Nordic countries and are generally agreed to be importantly related to low rates of mortality and morbidity. In Finland, a 1944 law required the establishment of at least one maternal health centre in each local authority area. At that time, according to the Wynns, 31.3 per cent of pregnant women who subsequently gave birth were registered: by 1968, 99.3 per cent were registered at one of the health centres. (The figure for Sweden is also over 95 per cent.) Moreover, by 1968 91.2 per cent were attending for first examination by the end of the fourth month of pregnancy. By contrast, it seems likely that only about 50 per cent of women have registered by this stage in England and Wales, and in some areas the figure is undoubtedly very much lower.

In addition in Finland all women deemed to be at risk by virtue of, for example, a previous failed pregnancy or hypertension are referred from the health centre to the ante-natal department of a major central hospital, for either one or more consultations. This accounts for about one quarter of all the women. It is part of a broader policy of disbanding domestic deliveries and concentrating child-birth in major specialized centres.

In emphasizing the importance of surveillance from an early stage of pregnancy, both Finland and France have made use of financial incentives to improve ante-natal take-up.

In Finland, only mothers who go for examination to a doctor, midwife or maternal health centre within the first four months of their pregnancy can receive the maternity grant. In 1974 this could be taken as a cash grant of 80 FMK (£10) or in the form of a baby 'kit' (which the Wynns estimated to be worth double) which most took. The view is that this relatively modest grant served as the necessary inducement at times and among groups of low income. Attendance now is simply taken for granted by all. It might also be noted that travel to the health centres is subsidized.

In France, maternity grants were initially seen as an instrument of population policy. Between 1946 and 1975 they were paid only where (1) a baby was conceived within two years of marriage, or (2) the mother was less than 25 years old, or (3) the interval between births was not more than three years (Doguet, 1978). Today, the grants, which form part of a rather complex French 'family policy', are seen specifically as a means of reducing perinatal mortality and birth handicap. To this end the total grant of 1,620 francs (£190) is paid in three instalments: at the end of three, six months and eight months of pregnancy, dates judged to be of significance for the detection of anomalies, and with proof of attendance at ante-natal examinations necessary. A fourth examination, in the ninth month, is also required according to a law of 1971.

A recent secondary analysis of survey data relating to 11,000 1972 births shows that among French-born mothers (where the father also was born in France) 14 per cent had three or less ante-natal examinations and 9 per cent attended for their first examination after three months of pregnancy. These figures rose to 27 per cent and 16 per cent for non-French (migrants) (and to 35 per cent and 16 per cent for the North African-born in the migrant group). However when those mothers who were French-born but were *also* both married to a manual worker and had received no post-primary education were considered alone, they also rose to 20 per cent and 12 per cent (Kaminski *et al.*, 1978). Thus, although there are both class and ethnic differences in this respect in France, like those in Britain, the overall rate of attendance seems to be distinctly better.

In both France and Finland financial incentives also play a part in ensuring post-natal medical examination. In Finland, the maternity health centres are informed of all births to mothers registered with them. Within forty-eight hours of returning home, the mother is visited by a midwife, who has the duty of ensuring that the child is registered at a child health centre. Today, over 90 per cent of children are registered within one month of birth. The proportion of those registered within the first year rose from 84.7 per cent in 1957 to 94.2 per cent in 1969.* Each child is seen ten to eleven times in the first year (twice by a doctor), and then twice a year between the ages of one and six by health centre staff. The Wynns point to the important contribution made by these staff beyond the assessment of purely medical well-being. They teach parents about nutrition, the care of minor ailments,

---

* This is higher than in Britain, where the National Child Development Survey found a figure of about 80 per cent. Official statistics show that of children born in England in 1974 90.1 per cent attended a child health clinic in 1976. However, in some AHAs the figure is very much lower: for example, Birmingham 71.2 per cent, Camden/Islington 70.6 per cent, Salford 68.2 per cent, Cornwall 62.4 per cent.

dealing with behaviour problems and the importance of mental stimulation of the child. It appears that parents increasingly go there for advice on all aspects of child behaviour. The third maternity allowance instalment is only paid after attendance at the post-natal medical examination.

In France, there exists a post-natal allowance of 2,130 francs (about £240), paid in three instalments. For the first, the child must be examined within the first week of life, for the second within the ninth month and for the third within the twenty-fourth month.

As well as these incentives, it is important to note that in Finland, when an appointment at the health centre is missed, a midwife or health visitor visits the home. This is felt to be very important and is, of course, made possible by very much more generous staffing levels. Also regarded as important to Finnish practice is the accountability for coverage required of Finnish public health services.

Today it is clear from the experience of both of these countries that a deliberate policy of attempting to ensure that ante-natal and child health services have a 100 per cent take-up yields major benefits for perinatal and infant mortality rates. It is not possible unambiguously to conclude that the financial incentives used in Finland and France are themselves directly responsible for the improved rates of attendance and consequent reduction in death and, inevitably, in perinatal morbidity. But irrespective of this, the 'outreach' capacity of the Finnish system (following up all missed appointments, etc.) must be stressed. So too, in our view, must the importance of adapting the functioning of these health centres to the needs and the difficulties of those whose attendance must be secured.

It is worth noting, also, that the obligations upon women in France to attend ante-natal care in force since 1971, intended to increase coverage, form part of a broader attack on handicap of perinatal origin (Wynn and Wynn, 1976). Other measures include the improvement in equipment and staffing of major obstetric departments; the establishment of more ICUs for newborn infants; and the regulation of minimum standards of equipment, staffing, size etc. binding on all establishments with maternity units, whether public or private. This latter has led to the closure and amalgamation of many small units. Moreover, it now appears that concern in France is not with coverage of ante-natal care (which is adequate) but with the poor quality, and often perfunctory nature, of the examinations given. Also, the striking reduction in 'class' differential in post-neonatal mortality rates suggests some levelling in social, economic and environmental conditions. It is noteworthy that, between 1956–60 and 1970–72, this reduction has been much greater than the (negligible) reduction in the class differential in neonatal rate – implying a greater relative levelling of environmental conditions than in obstetric care.

Conclusions and summary

Comparison of the British experience with that of other industrialized Western countries, on the basis of commonly used overall mortality rates, shows that British perinatal and infant mortality rates are distinctly higher than those of the four Nordic countries and of the Netherlands, and comparable with those of Western Germany. The rate of improvement in perinatal mortality enjoyed by Britain over the period 1960–75 was as good as that of most other countries, though the rate of gain is *now* poor. Moreover in the case of infant mortality all comparable countries have done better, especially France. Adult mortality patterns, especially in the younger age groups, compare reasonably with other countries.*

Why, then, might it be that infant mortality in particular presents so dismal a picture? Analyses quoted earlier suggest that infant death rates are associated with a number of characteristics of socio-economic and health systems. Low infant death rate seems clearly to be associated with per capita GDP, and there is some evidence for an association with an egalitarian income distribution. (In other words distributional aspects of society – and the extent of income inequalities – may be related to national performance in the infant mortality rankings.) So far as health policy is concerned, it seems that extent of provision of nurses and midwives, and of hospital beds, are more important than provision of physicians. Not unrelated, it seems that a relative emphasis upon preventive, ante-natal and child health services within health policy is required. International comparison here may thus have implications for policy.

It is possible, of course, that the superior performance of Sweden, Netherlands etc. might be attributed to difference principally in the extent of internal inequalities. Thus, if the perinatal mortality rate for all England and Wales were equal to that of social classes I and II, or the infant death rate equal to that obtaining in Oxford RHA, there would be little difference between these countries and ours. The second question, then, is whether the inequalities in health between social classes and regions, found in Britain, also exist elsewhere.

---

* It has, however, recently been noted that whereas the death rates among men aged 45–54 from coronary heart disease in Australia, Canada, Finland and America are now *declining*, those in England and Wales have merely *stopped rising*. The reasons for decline remain to be explained (Morris, 1979).

Briefly, the evidence – although disparate and not permitting comprehensive comparison – suggests that they do. The evidence relating to France and Germany (in the first case on an occupational basis, in the second on a regional basis) indicates disparities broadly corresponding to those of Britain. Finland also seemed comparable. So too did the Netherlands, at least in terms of the total range of regional inequality noted. Only in the cases of Norway and Sweden did a significantly smaller inequality appear to obtain. Moreover, in both these cases the extent of regional inequality (at least on the index of adult male mortality rate) seems to have fallen consistently over the years. American evidence on changing inequalities suggests an improvement in the case of infants and access to medical services, but not in adult mortality or morbidity.

If the evidence for changes in the extent of inequalities is slight (and in the American case ambiguous), that for the success of specific policies designed to reduce inequalities is slighter still. Clearly, as the study by Rumeau-Rouquette *et al.* showed, various dimensions of comparison can produce discrepant results, and changes in extraneous variables may often interfere. Of course, this study also suggested that reductions in inequality of access to, or utilization of, pre-natal care can come about.

None of the results quoted enables us to deal with the question of the relative importance of inequalities in provision or utilization of health services on the one hand and other forms of inequality on the other in determining inequalities of outcome. (Although it is noteworthy that provision of physicians is more equal on a regional basis in England than even in the Netherlands.) An aspect of this question is that of the intervention of social class or related factors between morbidity and use of health services. Is it *commonly* the case that working-class or low-income individuals or families have less recourse to the health services when they are sick? There are relatively few studies to draw upon.

One important study was carried out by Purola *et al.* in Finland in 1964, just prior to the introduction of much expanded health insurance (Sickness Insurance Act), which for the first time covered primary medical care. Methodologically this study, like the General Household Survey, was based on a questionnaire administered to a representative sample of non-institutionalized families (not households). Questions covered self-reported morbidity, use of health services, income etc. The most important conclusion for our present purposes was that the number of consultations with a GP in a given period of time was proportional to income, when number of days of reported sickness was held constant. A similar relationship obtained in the case of the chronic sick. On the other hand, the number of days spent in hospital was not a function of income. Moreover, since it was known that incomes in rural areas were lower than in urban areas, and it had been established that distances to physicians were greater in rural areas and that consultation rates were inversely proportional to distance, the effects of income were examined holding both morbidity and distance constant. The effects of income on GP consultation rates and those of distance were independent of each other (Purola *et al*, 1968).

The Finnish Sickness Insurance Act was designed to reduce the financial disincentive to making use of physicians' services. It does not appear however that organizational or financial arrangements can wholly compensate for income inequalities in bringing about parity of usage.

An analysis by Salkever of data collected in five countries with very different health systems (Liverpool, Helsinki, Lodz, Baltimore and north west Vermont, and an area of Saskatchewan) – in the context of a WHO study – throws some light on this (Salkever, 1975). Relating probability of contacting a physician to an index of ill-health (perceived seriousness of condition; days restricted activity; days in bed), according to income Salkever found first that in all cases except Saskatchewan low-income children fared worse. That is, their reduced utilization was independent of the organization and costs of health care. Among adults, it appeared that the clearest association of low income with low utilization was found in Liverpool. If American and French experiences are any guide, this is one aspect of the cause of health inequality which can be corrected.

Chapter 6

Towards an Explanation of Health Inequalities

Death rates in present-day Europe have reached what appear to be their lowest points in the history of human society. The twentieth century has witnessed a dramatic decline in the rate of infectious disease, as well as the introduction of powerful therapies for its treatment. Common causes of death like TB and diphtheria, often linked with poverty and material deprivation, have greatly diminished, though they have been replaced by new diseases, some of which have been linked in particular studies with affluence and material abundance. On that account inequalities in health might have been expected to diminish. But the evidence which we have presented in earlier chapters suggests that this has not been the case. In this chapter we ask why occupational class continues to exert so significant an influence on health in Britain.

There are a number of approaches to an explanation, though none in our view provides a wholly satisfactory answer. Indeed, the variable of occupational class is in itself multifaceted, and its influence probably varies according to age or stage in the life-cycle and according to the natural history of disease.

Theoretical approaches

Theoretical explanations of the relationship between health and inequality might be roughly divided into four categories:

1. Artefact explanations.
2. Theories of natural or social selection.
3. Materialist or structuralist explanations.
4. Cultural/behavioural explanations.

In some respect each one of these approaches sheds light on the observed relationships between class and health in present-day Britain. We shall first describe and discuss in general terms the four approaches and then go on, by reference to the problems of different age groups, to show that any satisfactory explanation must build essentially on the ideas of the cumulative dispositions and experience of the lifetime, and of multiple causation

The artefact explanation

This approach suggests that both health and class are artificial variables thrown up by attempts to measure social phenomena and that the relationship between them may itself be an artefact of little causal significance. Accordingly, the failure of health inequalities to diminish in recent decades is believed to be explained to a greater or lesser extent by the reduction in the proportion of the population in the poorest occupational classes. It is believed that the failure to reduce the gap *between* classes has been counterbalanced by the shrinkage in the relative size of the poorer classes themselves. The implication is that the upwardly mobile are found to have better health than those who remain, or that their health subsequently improves relative to the health of those they join. We would make two comments. One is that informed examination of successive census reports shows that the poorer occupational classes have contracted less sharply than often supposed (see Appendix, Tables 1 and 2). The other is that indicators of relatively poor progress in health apply to much larger sections of the manual occupational classes than just those who are 'unskilled' (see p. 60, for example).

Natural and social selection

Occupational class is here relegated to the state of dependent variable and health acquires the greater degree of causal significance. The occupational class structure is seen as a filter or sorter of human beings and one of the major bases of selection is health, that is, physical strength, vigour or agility. It is inferred that the Registrar General's class I has the lowest rate of premature mortality because it is made up of the strongest and most robust men and women in the population. Class V by contrast contains the weakest and most frail people. Put another way, this explanation suggests that physical weakness or poor health carries low social worth as well as low economic reward, but that these factors play no causal role in the event of high mortality. Their relationship is strictly reflective. Those men and women who by virtue of innate physical characteristics are destined to live the shortest lives also reap the most meagre rewards. This type of explanation has been invoked to explain the preponderance of individuals with severe mental disorders in social class V (a thesis which was reviewed critically in, for example, Goldberg and Morrison, 1963). It is postulated that affected people *drift* to the bottom rung of the Registrar General's occupational scale

Similar selective processes are thought to occur with other forms of disease even though the extent of drift may not be so great and there is little actual evidence of it.

Materialist or structuralist explanations

The third type of explanation emphasizes the role of economic and associated socio-structural factors in the distribution of health and well-being, and, because it is frequently misunderstood, requires fuller exposition. There are several separate strands of reasoning within it which can be ordered more or less according to the extent to which the primary causal significance is assigned directly or indirectly to the role of economic deprivation. Amongst explanations which focus on the *direct* influence of poverty or economic deprivation in the production of variation in rates of mortality is the radical Marxian critique. With the benefit of a century's hind-sight the validity of much of this nineteenth-century theory of the relationship between health and material inequality has been accepted today, especially for the earlier phase of competitive industrial capitalism (Stedman-Jones, 1971; Thompson, 1976). Exploitation, poverty and disease have virtually become synonymous for describing conditions of life in the urban slums of Victorian and Edwardian cities, as they are today for the shanty towns of the under-developed world.

But can it be so readily applied to contemporary health experience? Can the premature mortality of the working class still be directly attributed to subsistence poverty and exploitation? It is true that a relationship between material deprivation and certain causes of disease and death is now well established, but then so is the capacity of the capitalist mode of production to expand the level of human productivity and to raise the living standards of working people. Economic growth of the kind most readily associated with the European style of industrialization has in itself been credited with the decline in mortality from infectious disease during the nineteenth and twentieth centuries (cf. McKeown, 1976; Powles, 1975). Today death rates for all age groups in Britain are a fraction of what they were a century ago and many of the virulent infectious diseases have largely disappeared (cf. Morris, 1975; OPCS, 1978), and the 'killer' diseases of modern society – accidents, cancer and heart disease – seem less obviously linked to poverty. Against this background, the language of economic exploitation no longer seems to provide the appropriate epithet for describing 'Life and Labour' in the last two decades of the twentieth century. Through trade-union organization and wages council machinery it is now argued that labour is paid its price and, since health tends to be conceptualized in optimum terms as a fixed condition of material welfare which, if anything, is put at risk by affluent living standards, it is assumed by many that economic class on its own is no longer the powerful determinant of health that it once was.

The flaw in this line of reasoning is the assumption that material subsistence needs can be uniquely and unambiguously defined in terms independent of the overall level of economic development in a society. People may still have too little for their basic *physiological* as well as social needs. Poverty is also a relative concept, and those who are unable to share the amenities or facilities provided within a rich society, or who are unable to fulfil the social and occupational obligations placed upon them by virtue of their limited resources, can properly be regarded as poor. They may also be relatively disadvantaged in relation to the risks of illness or accident or the factors positively promoting health.

It is worth illustrating how this can happen. New types of industrial process can introduce entirely new risks for the workforce or the population in the area. Certain forms of building or construction or town planning can introduce new hazards for adults as well as children. Changes in distances from work, type of participation in the local community and in leisure can alter the balance for many people in their access to health services as well as their knowledge about health. People living alone who have a fall, or people who have a heart attack, face different problems in different communities. Warnings about undesirable food and other products (inflammable clothing and furniture, for instance), as well as the latest information about the means of obtaining a healthy diet, may or may not be communicated, depending on the social circumstances. Many other examples of how new problems of health arise in a changing society might be given. The material deprivation of some sections of the population can paradoxically grow even when their income increases, relative to changing structures and amenities.

How far might differences in access to resources help to explain this? How unequal is the distribution of wealth in Britain? Historically the structure of living standards has been slow to change. Personal wealth is still concentrated in the hands of a small minority of the population, as reports of the Royal Commission on the Distribution of Income and Wealth have shown.

The question whether the richest men and women in Britain have maintained their economic position at the expense of less well-endowed citizens eludes a categorical answer. The Royal Commission has referred to the 'remarkable' stability of the unequal distribution of income over the past two decades (see also Appendix, Table 4). Moreover there is no doubt that the proportion as well as number of the population dependent on a subsistence or near-subsistence income from the state has grown. For some groups, and especially manual groups, relative lifetime resources will have been reduced. Earlier retirement, unemployment and redundancies, single-parent status and disablement, as well as the proportionate increase in the elderly population, all play some part in this development. For recent years Table 32 shows the tendency for those at the lowest relative income standards to increase in number and proportion.

Table 32: *Numbers of persons in poverty and on the margins of poverty (Family Expenditure Survey)*

Income relative to supplementary benefit	Britain (000s)			
	1960*	1975	1976	1977
Under supplementary benefit standard	1,260	1,840	2,280	2,020
Receiving supplementary benefit	2,670	3,710†	4,090†	4,160†
At or not more than 40 per cent above standard	3,510	6,990	8,500	7,840
Total	7,740	12,540	14,870	14,020
Per cent of population	14.2	23.7	28.1	26.6

*From B. Abel-Smith and P. Townsend, *The Poor and the Poorest*, Bell, 1965, pp. 40 and 44. The data are for the UK and are on a household rather than an income unit basis. It should be noted that this column is based on national assistance scales, not supplementary benefit scales.

† Drawn separately from a supplementary benefit sample inquiry with people drawing benefit for less than three months excluded. In the FES, such people are categorized according to their normal income and employment.

Sources: For 1960, Abel-Smith and Townsend, 1965, pp. 40 and 44. For 1975–7, DHSS (SR3), Analyses of the FES.

There is therefore a paradox: while we would not wish to assert that the evidence is consistent and complete, the proportion of the population with relatively low lifetime incomes (in the widest sense of 'income') seems to have increased in recent decades, just as the proportion assigned to classes IV and V seems to have decreased, though the latter continue to comprise more than a quarter of the population. While economic growth has improved the access of both groups to income and other resources, other groups have gained in proportion, and since neither facilities nor knowledge is a finite commodity, those with relatively low incomes (in increasing numbers) have remained relatively disadvantaged.

So it has been with health. Occupational classes IV and V may in time catch up with the contemporary levels achieved by I and II but by that time the latter groups will have forged even further ahead. There is nothing fixed about levels of physical well-being. They have improved in the past and there is every likelihood that they will improve in the future. But class inequalities persist in the distribution of health as in the distribution of income or wealth, and they persist as a form of relative deprivation.

Unfortunately the opportunity for examining the association between income and health is restricted by lack of information and the role played by material factors in creating the pattern of health and ill-health which can be found in the population is complex. Occupational class is multifaceted in 'advanced' societies, and apart from the variables most readily associated with socio-economic position – income, savings, property and housing – there are many other dimensions which can be expected to exert an active causal influence on health. People at work, for instance, encounter different material conditions and amenities, levels of danger and risk, degree of security and stability, association with other workers, levels of self-fulfilment and job satisfaction and physical or mental strain. These dimensions of material inequality are also closely articulated with another determinant of health – education.

Two other related theoretical approaches should be mentioned. Each is concerned with the effect of macro-economic variables – levels of production, unemployment etc. – on health. First an American social scientist, Harvey Brenner, making use of time-series data trends in the US economy and fluctuations in rates of mortality, purports to show that recessions and wide-scale economic distress have an impact on a number of health indicators, including foetal, infant and maternal mortality, the national mortality rate – especially of death ascribed to cardio-vascular disease, cirrhosis of the liver, suicide and homicide rates – and on rates of first admission to mental hospitals (Brenner, 1973, 1976 and 1977).*

In fitting the data on economic trends, essentially unemployment, to health indicators, Brenner suggests there is a delayed effect of between two and five years, choosing the lag to obtain the best fit. By doing this he purports to be able to estimate both the initial impact of recession on the dependent variable as well as the cumulative impact over the space of several years. He also posits time lags of varying numbers of years between economic changes and changes in various health indicators (on a purely empirical basis) and in doing so claims to establish the direction of causality in a temporal sequence as well as suggesting the length of time involved. A major

---

*Studies of this kind were actually carried out by Morris and Titmuss in the 1940s, in an attempt to examine the effects of the violent economic fluctuations of the 1920s and 1930s upon a variety of health and mortality indicators (see, for example, Morris and Titmuss, 1944a, 1944b).

problem with such research, even if validated, is, of course, the causal mechanism. *How* does unemployment increase mortality? Brenner makes use of the somewhat ill-defined concept of 'stress' to link the two.

The second approach, in opposition to Brenner's, is concerned to disprove the common assumption that economic growth leads to an increase in general levels of health. In advanced capitalist societies, it is argued, profit is realized through hazardous, punishing and physically stressful work. Time-series data on employment and death rates are here presented in such a way that high rates of mortality appear to follow on from low rates of unemployment and high levels of prosperity (Eyer, 1975, 1977a, 1977b). In periods of high unemployment this is supposed to be the combined result of weakened institutionalized pressures to consume, relief of workers from stressful work routines, an increase of social solidarity (unlikely as this may seem), the added stimulation of supportive relationships and networks, and in general a more varied and more elevated meaning for human existence.

Cultural/behavioural explanations

A fourth approach is that of cultural or behavioural explanations of the distribution of health in modern industrial society. These are recognizable by the independent and autonomous causal role which they assign to ideas and behaviour in the onset of disease and the event of death. Such explanations, when applied to modern industrial societies, often focus on the individual as a unit of analysis emphasizing unthinking, reckless or irresponsible behaviour or incautious life-style as the moving determinant of poor health status (cf. Fuchs, 1974). What is implied is that people harm themselves or their children by the excessive consumption of harmful commodities, refined foods, tobacco and alcohol, or by lack of exercise, or by their under-utilization of preventive health care, vaccination, ante-natal surveillance or contraception. Some would argue that such systematic behaviour within certain social groups is a consequence only of lack of education, or individual waywardness or thoughtlessness. Explanation takes an individual form. What is critical, it is implied, are the personal characteristics of individuals, whether innate or acquired – their basic intelligence, their skills obtained through education and training, their physical and mental qualities, and their personal styles and dispositions. Others see behaviour which is conducive to good or bad health as embedded more within social structures – as illustrative of socially distinguishable styles of life, associated with, and reinforced by, class.

Tables 33, 34 and 35 provide the kind of data sometimes used to illustrate a cultural/behavioural type of explanation. Certain styles of living, like a diet strong in carbohydrates, cigarette-smoking and lack of participation in sporting activities, are known to cut across class. It is implied that there are individual or, at most, sub-cultural life-styles, rooted in personal characteristics and level of education, which govern behaviour and which are therefore open to change through changes in personal activities or educational inputs. However, data of the kind illustrated in these tables are not easy to interpret. For one thing, the observations are themselves only indicators which are subject to qualification if their meaning is to be put into context.

Table 33: *Household food consumption by income group* (*oz./person/week*) (*Great Britain, 1979*)

Income group	Food				
	white bread	brown, including wholemeal bread	sugar and preserves	potatoes	fresh fruit
A	17	5.3	11	39	25
B	22	4.5	12	40	20
C	26	4.3	13	48	16
D	29	4.3	15	48	15

Gross weekly income of head of household: A = £145+; D = less than £56 per week.

Source: Adapted from *Household Food Consumption and Expenditure*, HMSO (see Morris, 1979).

Table 34: *Cigarette-smoking by socio-economic group* (*males and females aged 16 +*) (*1980*)

SEG	Current smokers %	
	Men	Women
Professional	21	21
Managerial	35	33
Intermediate non-manual	35	34
Intermediate manual	48	43
Semi-skilled manual	49	39
Unskilled manual	57	41
All	42	37

Source: *General Household Survey*: OPCS Monitor, 28 July 1981.

Table 35: *Active leisure pursuits by males: ratio of participation rates, non-manual to manual workers, by age (males aged 16 or over engaging in each activity in the four weeks before interview) (Great Britain, 1977)*

	Age group		
	16–29	*30–59*	*60+*
Squash/fives	4.4	6.9	*
Athletics (incl. jogging)	3.3	3.3	*
Rugby	2.9	*	*
Golf	2.8	3.2	4.9
Badminton	2.8	2.8	*
Cricket	2.4	1.7	*
Tennis	2.4	4.1	*
Table-tennis	1.7	3.1	*
Swimming outdoors	1.6	2.1	*
Walking (more than 2 miles)	1.6	1.8	1.7
Bowls (indoor)	1.4	1.3	1.1
Bowls (outdoor)	1.4	1.4	1.6
Playing football	1.1	1.6	*
Swimming (indoor)	1.1	2.2	*
Dancing	0.9	1.1	1.2
Gymnastics/yoga/keep fit	0.9	2.1	*

*Ten or fewer participants in either manual or non-manual group.

Source: *General Household Survey*, 1977.

Thus, a balanced diet, or balanced physical activity, to promote health is easy neither to define nor measure. People who eat one type of food to excess may make up for that disadvantage in some other respect. And manual workers who are spectators rather than active sportsmen include those who have to exert physical strength and agility in their everyday jobs.

Again, the data can be interpreted in other ways than in relation to level of knowledge or education, or personal responsibility. Commercial advertisements are planned to 'educate' tastes, and the education provided in schools is not always calculated to prepare young people to ward off influences upon their consumption and behaviour which may be undesirable for health. Moreover, access to good food and sports facilities depends also on the area in which people live and the resources they can command, and not only their personal characteristics or behaviour, or education. But, in emphasizing these reservations we must also call attention to the *cumulative* importance of those contributions to personal behaviour made by genetic endowment of attributes, the influence of family upbringing and practices and the evolution of modes of self-management which contribute to wide differences in health achieved by different members of the same occupational or socio-economic class.

The interpretation of level of personal knowledge or education as a causal factor in health illustrates our theoretical problem. It is on the basis of success or the lack of it at school that children are selected for manual and non-manual work and, as we have seen, this occupational distinction plays an important part in measured health status differentials. But we can go further. Bernstein has argued that distinctive patterns of child rearing and socialization, such as those which tended to differentiate between working-class and middle-class families, produce quite different linguistic capacities which are in turn correlated with quite different intellectual approaches to the social world (Bernstein, 1971). The working-class child is rendered at a particular disadvantage on account of these differences because of the *fit* which exists between middle-class norms of socialization and the dominant structure of the educational system. The outcome of this is that children from middle-class homes enter the school system already equipped with the appropriate mode of communication and, as a result, they have more successful educational careers and leave school with a greater facility to manipulate their social and economic environment (which of course includes health services) to personal advantage. These ideas carry the variable of education far beyond the simple idea of the transmission of know-ledge and skills. They imply that the educational system tends to be substan-tially developed and maintained in conformity with the class system or with that pattern of differential material advantages or disadvantages, and social opportunities or obstacles, which govern both the place taken in the system by the individual child and the chances of that child having a successful career within the system. On this reasoning, level of education becomes difficult to treat as intrinsically independent of class.

More theoretically developed as the basis for cultural/behavioural explanations is the 'culture of poverty' thesis – which has much in common with the idea of 'transmitted deprivation'. As originally proposed by Oscar Lewis, an anthropologist who studied poor communities in Central America and, later, migrant groups in New York, the 'culture of poverty' was intended to apply only to market-organized social structures with poorly developed public systems of health, welfare and income maintenance (cf. Lewis, 1967). Starting from a distinct cultural anthropological perspective, Lewis argued that human existence in any given environment involves a process of biological and social adaptation which gives rise to the elaboration of a structure of norms, ideas and behaviours. This culture over time acquires an integrity and a stability because of the supportive role it plays in helping individuals to understand and cope with their environment but, through its influence on socialization practices and the like, it also comes to have an important autonomous influence in the social consciousness of individuals. The integrity of the culture ensures its autonomous survival even when the material base from which it emerged has changed or been modified. It is for this reason that people cling on to outmoded ideas or old-fashioned practices which do not seem to accord with the changed material realities of modern existence. The 'culture of poverty' thesis has been widely criticized by British social scientists (Holman, 1978, Chapter 3; Rutter and Madge, 1976; Townsend, 1979, pp. 65–71).

Consider, for example, the diffusion of the acceptance of the idea of family planning, which is generally agreed to have been first adopted by the professional classes (Banks and Banks, 1964), from whence it diffused to poorer classes. On the basis of the 'culture of poverty' thesis this should not have happened or, at least, there should have been more evidence of stiff resistance to the adoption of the practice. However, the fact that family planning has spread rapidly to all classes is one strand of historical evidence which is felt to cast doubt on the 'culture of poverty' thesis. The implication of that example is that the beliefs and values of poorer sections of the population are less autonomous, and more dependent upon conventional or orthodox beliefs and values, than has been assumed by proponents of the thesis. Instead social scientists have felt it right to place emphasis on the material circumstances of families and their access to the means of contraception in explaining class variations in the readiness or otherwise to adopt new methods of family planning. While recognizing the force of many of their criticisms we believe it is difficult to settle questions of interpretation like that of family planning one way or the other. We are aware that even if it is difficult to make a case for separately identifiable sub-cultures that does not dispose of the possible role of cultural variations in contributing to any overall explanation of variations in health.

Choosing between such complex and sometimes competing approaches, when applied to evidence as complex as that which we have assembled, is a daunting task. We must make clear our belief that it is in some form or forms of the 'materialist' approach that the best answer lies. But there can be little doubt that amongst all the evidence there is much that is convincingly explained in alternative terms: cultural, social selection and so on. Moreover, it may well be that different kinds of factors, or forms of explanation, apply more strongly, or more appropriately, to different stages of the life-cycle. This possibility has guided the presentation of our data.

Birth and infancy

Today the greatest risk at child-birth is among mothers who are older and who have already had several children. Such cases, of course, were more prevalent in Victorian society, where knowledge about birth control was scanty and where rather different ideologies about family size existed. In recent years the percentage of mothers in classes IV and V having a fourth or fifth child has decreased, but remains higher than in classes II and III. It could therefore be that higher rates of still-birth or perinatal death are a consequence of differences in maternal age and 'parity' (family size) between the classes. But class inequalities in rates of death at birth and throughout the first year of life are found even when parity and maternal age are held constant (Morris and Heady, 1955; Morris, 1975). While age and parity exert an important influence on the risk of all still-births, the significance of these variables is much more evident among the wives of semi-skilled and unskilled manual workers. The risk of still-birth for the wives in professional and managerial households is lower no matter what their age or their previous record of pregnancies. (Similarly for perinatal death rates: at all ages and parities, the class differential remains.)

Rates of post-neonatal mortality differ somewhat – class differences are generally greater among young mothers under the age of 25 – but overall the broad pattern remains the same. The inescapable conclusion is that occupational class differences are *real* sources of difference in the risk of infant mortality.

Equally importantly, there are similar differences in the class incidence of low birth-weight which, as we shall see, can have, except under the most advantageous conditions, long-term implications for the health and development of the young child.

There are a number of explanations for this situation. Several studies have pointed to the importance of the mother's health, and the quality of obstetric care received, and there can be no doubt, on the basis of the evidence we have presented so far, that these are class-related (Hellier, 1977; Doll, Hill and Sakula, 1960).

Other explanations tend to be more complex. Studies over the last twenty years suggest that genetic factors play a 'predisposing' role in giving rise to congenital defects, with adverse environmental factors acting as a trigger (Lawrence, Carter and David, 1968; Janerich, 1972).

Work in the 1950s ascribed class differences in infant mortality to selective processes in mating and marriage (Illsley, 1955). Tall women married above their father's occupational class, short women below it, and these physical characteristics of women were then associated with different rates of infant mortality, the taller mothers having lower rates of infant death. The study concluded that higher-class men appeared to be recruiting as wives the most effective child-bearing women.

'Transmitted nutritional deprivation' offers another variant on the theme of selection (Baird, 1974). It suggests the existence of a vicious cycle of nutritional deprivation which leads to low birth-weight and congenital malformation. This cycle is difficult to break because, the evidence suggests, it originates in the nutritional deprivation of the mother not at the time of giving birth but *at the time of her own birth.* By this account, perinatal death and low birth-weight are seen as caused, in part, by the effects of nutritional deprivation upon the reproductive capacity of the mothers of the infants. These explanations are based upon data accumulated on the childbearing population of Aberdeen over many years, and they offer valuable insights into the mechanisms and processes whereby social class differences in mortality are produced and perpetuated.

If the relative importance of factors such as these in determining rates of perinatal death, and of handicap among survivors, is controversial, the situation is somewhat clearer in the *post-neonatal period.* When we look at causes of death in infancy which exhibit the steepest class gradients, there is much evidence to suggest that the important causal variables are contained within the socio-economic environment. The causes of death which are most likely to be associated with the nutritional status of the mother have the shallowest of gradients, while respiratory disease and accidents show steep class gradients. These observations lead us directly to consider the role of material deprivation on the life chances of the infants, and to the hypothesis that any factors which increase the parental capacity to provide adequate care for an infant will, when present, increase the chance of survival, while their absence will increase the risk of premature death. The most obvious of such factors fall within the sphere of material resources: sufficient household income, a safe, uncrowded and unpolluted home, warmth and hygiene, a means of rapid communication with the outside world, for example a telephone or car, and an adequate level of manpower – or womanpower (two parents would normally provide more continuous care and protection than one). In addition to these basic material needs must be added other cognitive and motivational factors which are not independent of the distribution of material advantage. Those factors would include knowledge, certain skills and resources in verbal communication and a high level of motivation to provide continuous and loving care. When all these factors are present the infant's chance of survival is very good indeed. When some or even many of these are absent, the outlook is less propitious. Moreover, it should not be forgotten that these very same factors play a part in determining the development of the infant's own cognitive/linguistic and other skills. Competences acquired at this stage of life can profoundly influence later intellectual (and hence educational) achievement.

Table 36: *Causes of death from accidents of children aged 1–14 years* (*1968–74*)

Type of accident (or violence)	Total age 1–14 years	
	Number	%
Total accidents and violence	10,877	100.0
All accidents	10,204	93.8
Motor vehicle collision with pedestrian	3,656	33.6
Other motor vehicle collisions	1,199	11.0
Other transport accidents	619	5.7
Accidental poisoning	276	2.5
Falls	625	5.7
Fires	904	8.3
Drowning	1,401	12.9
Inhalation of food or other object	343	3.2
Accidental suffocation	375	3.4
Blows, cuts, explosions etc.	460	4.2
Accidents caused by electric current	150	1.4
Other accidents	196	1.7
Total violence	673	6.2
Suicide	33	0.3
Homicide	417	3.8
Injury undetermined whether accidentally or purposely inflicted	223	2.1

Source: OPCS.

Childhood: 1–14 years

The most important causes of death amongst all children aged 1 to 14 are, in descending order, accidents (with a small number of deaths also due to poisoning and violence – see Table 36), respiratory disease, neoplasms, congenital abnormalities and infections. Among 1- to 14-year-olds, and this we wish to stress, *almost all* the differences in mortality between occupational classes I and V are due to accidents, respiratory disease (bronchitis and pneumonia) and to a much lesser extent congenital abnormality. Among older children, deaths from accidents remain highly class-related, though deaths from respiratory disease become less so.

It follows that one approach to explaining this situation is to unravel those aspects of the social situations responsible for respiratory disease and for accidents. There are a number of epidemiological studies which help us to do this.

A study in 1966, for instance, found that the principal correlate of respiratory symptoms was the extent of air pollution in the child's area of residence (Douglas and Waller, 1966). But there was no tendency for working-class children to be more concentrated in high-pollution areas and social class had a small independent effect.

A more recent study in the mid-seventies took 2,000 children living in Harrow (which consequently did not permit consideration of a range of air pollution levels) and concluded: 'Illnesses occurred much more commonly in infants born to families which had several other children already, and in those families where the parents had respiratory disability or were smokers' (Leeder, Corkhill, Irwig, Holland and Colley, 1976). When all variables were taken together the most important proved to be: (i) bronchitis/pneumonia in siblings; (ii) parent smoking (affecting air inhaled by children); (iii) number of siblings (and likelihood of infection); (iv) parental history of asthma/wheeze. Class had no effect independently of these factors; but both smoking and family size are clearly related to class.

A third study of over 11,000 children aged 6 to 10 in a number of urban environments looked more directly at the interplay of social class and physical environment (Colley and Reid, 1970). It concluded that at the equivalent levels of air pollution children of occupational classes IV and V were much more likely to suffer from respiratory diseases than their counterparts in occupational classes I, II and III. Air pollution in short was an exacerbating factor. More directly, it reaffirmed that a past family history of respiratory disease is closely associated with a chronic cough in the 6- to 10-year-olds. It also once more found a clear class gradient in respiratory disease.

The general implication seems to be that the class gradient in bronchitis is largely a consequence of parental smoking, family size (and the increasing likelihood of infection by siblings), and a parental history of lung disease (which may also to some degree genetically place the child at risk). Parental history of lung disease is, of course, as shown independently, a function of type and severity of occupation. Environmental pollution is also implicated, and may be a particular danger for those children made vulnerable through other factors.

The second condition responsible for much of the gradient in child mortality is accidents. Among child pedestrians, for example, the risk of death from being hit by a motor vehicle is multiplied by five to seven times in passing from class I to class IV; for accidental death caused by fires, falls and drowning, the gap between the classes is even greater. These substantial differences demonstrate the non-random nature of these events. While the death of an individual child may appear as a random misfortune, the overall distribution clearly indicates the *social* nature of the phenomena. How is it to be explained?

Accidents have two primary causes: either environmental hazard, or dangerous behaviour reflecting carelessness, adventure or irresponsibility. These primary causes involve both material and cultural factors and indeed a full explanation of inequalities in the risk of death in childhood implicates each of them.

To begin with, the class pattern of accidents has to be seen in the light of the great differences in the material resources of parents, which may place significant constraints on the routine level of care and protection that they are able to provide for their children. Children of parents in occupational classes IV and V are amongst the poorest members of their age group in the population. Their opportunities to play safely within sight or earshot of their parents are less than those of their better endowed peers higher up the social scale. Furnishings, including forms of heating in the home, are likely to be less safe, as are the other domestic appliances which they encounter.

Differences in the material resources of the household also mean that the children of semi-skilled and unskilled workers are more likely to be thrown on to their own devices during holidays and out of school hours, which alone would be sufficient to increase the probability of their being involved in an accident.

It is impossible to escape the conclusion that in the context of childhood the most straightforward of material explanations is capable of providing a simple chain of causation by which the pattern of health inequality is illuminated. Households in occupational classes IV and V simply lack the means to provide their children with as high a level of protection as that which is found in the average middle-class home. This can mean both material and non-material resources. A study in Camberwell in south London, for example, concluded that one of the reasons for the greater prevalence of accidents in working-class homes is the higher incidence of stressful life events experienced by mothers. Such women lack the means to resolve the recurrent setbacks which dominate their domestic lives and are less well equipped to provide continuous and vigilant protection: 'The mother's psychiatric state and the presence of a serious long-term difficulty or a threatening life event were related to increased accident risk to children under 16. These factors were more common among working-class children, and in so far as they are causal, they go a long way to explain the much greater risk of accidents to working-class children' (Brown and Harris, 1978).

One recent study, valuable because it reports a field survey, focused on a sample of boys of 6 to 7 and 10 to 11 years old from severely deprived large families in Birmingham known to the social services department. Children were compared with a control group of similarly aged children, living in the same area but not under social service department supervision. The study was published in two parts.

In the first Brennan (1973) focused on medical characteristics. She found that both groups of children were below national age norms in height but that the sample children were more so. There was a high degree of visual impairment among both groups but again it was more marked among the sample children. (Moreover of the forty-six sample children who suffered visual impairment only one wore spectacles.) There was a higher degree of hearing loss among the sample children. Finally 78.2 per cent of sample children as against 58.9 per cent of control children were diagnosed as having some illness on clinical examination, far higher than indicated for the city as a whole from school health records, the most important being respiratory disorders, orthopaedic defects, speech defects, skin disorders and chest complaints.

The second study, with a cultural approach (Wilson and Herbert, 1978), also considered the 3–4-year-old siblings of those older brothers, and made extensive use of interviews, observation over a long period and psychological test data. This study vividly illustrates the nature and the effects of severe poverty on family life and on child development. It suggests that ill-health, inhibited cognitive development and behaviour problems are associated in a general 'poverty syndrome'.

Accidents to the children were common: thirty-four out of fifty-six families had experienced severe accidents (one child had lost an eye, sixteen suffered burns or scalding needing skin grafts).

Particularly striking was the extent to which ill-health was found to cluster in families. Of the fifty-six families studied: 'In forty families all, or most, members of the family were reported as having had much illness, or as suffering from defects or conditions which affected their activities. Respiratory diseases were most frequently mentioned, followed by gastric conditions and skin conditions.' Moreover, 'only four among the sixteen fitter families can be truly said to be healthy and obstetric problems were frequently mentioned'.

The authors concluded:

The children, in the process of growing up, have many shared experiences. They live in overcrowded conditions, being members of large families; their homes are inadequate by current standards; the neighbourhoods are rough and disliked by most who have to live in them. They experience poverty, by which we mean that they go short of things considered essential or normal by others around them. Most, if not all, the children have first-hand knowledge of illness, disability, accidents and mental stress expressed in a variety of symptoms. (p. 104)

The objective is survival, the operative unit is the family. The needs of individuals must take second place. Decisions were made at family level and related to the main wage earner or recipient of benefit rather than to the needs of individual children. (p. 186)

Finally there is considerable evidence that material deprivation affects physical development in young children and that ill-health contracted in childhood can dog an individual for life. Several studies, for example, have pointed to the effect of nutritional deprivation not only on physical growth, but also on the brain and nervous system. Some of the evidence is circumstantial, but laboratory experiments on animals suggest that malnutrition during the period of rapid brain growth – the first six months after birth – can affect the size and number of brain cells in several ways that can never later be compensated for (Birch and Gussow, 1970; Eichenwald and Fry, 1969). The implications for children from poor families in modern Britain who have a meagre diet are unclear, but few would disagree with the view expressed in an official publication that 'a hungry child is unlikely to be alert during lessons' (DHSS, *Eating for Health*, 1978).

Poor physical development also renders children susceptible to illness, and several reports have suggested that this may then persist. A study of 1,000 Newcastle families illustrates how repeated respiratory infections in the first five years, if inadequately treated, can lead to some degree of disability at the age of 15 (Miller, Court, Knox and Brandon, 1974).

Studies such as this – there are many more – suggest, as one government inquiry put it, that inadequately treated bouts of childhood illness 'cast long shadows forward' (the Court Report). Working-class children are more likely to suffer from them and less likely to be adequately treated for them.

Adult life

Among adults, as we have already seen, health differences between occupational classes have remained or have even widened. The phenomenon is principally one of relative deprivation – the maintenance of big differences in life chances against the dynamic background of a growing economy.

Explanations for this continued inequality have taken a number of forms. The twentieth century has witnessed and will continue to witness a series of revolutionary changes in the structure of occupations. To date these changes have resulted in some contraction of the size of the semi- and unskilled manual labour force and an expansion in non-manual occupations (see Appendix, Table 1). These changes have given rise to alterations in the age composition of each occupational class, older workers tending to be found in the contracting areas – though not as emphatically as some people suppose – and younger and more recent recruits to the workforce in the expanding area. Besides making comparisons between the occupational classes over time somewhat difficult, these shifts in the occupational structure in themselves offer an analytical solution to the continuing pattern of health inequality, for it is argued that the higher death rates of social class IV and V are, at least in part, a reflection of the older age structure of these occupational groups. The same argument has been used conversely to explain, to a small extent, the relatively low death rates of social class I.

In any event, Fig. 8, on the relationship between age and occupation for some of the major causes of death, shows that for all causes except malignant neoplasms class gradients are steepest in early adulthood and most shallow in the decade before retirement. The artefact explanation does not throw light on these observed patterns of fatal disease incidence amongst younger men.

These same distinctive trends also highlight the limitations of the thesis that the health gap is caused by age-related processes of social mobility. Occupational drift throughout the span of working life may help to contribute to class differences among the over-fifties but it cannot be said to be the cause of class inequalities between the ages of 15 and 45 years.

The limitations of these explanations especially among the male workforce of 45 years and under leads to a consideration of the direct role of material life on the production of health differentials. The most obvious starting point is the division between manual and non-manual occupations. Men engaged in manual occupations routinely confront a much higher degree of risk to

Figure 8. *Mortality ratios by occupational class, age and cause of death (men 15–64, England and Wales). (Source:* Occupational Mortality 1970–72, *H M S O, 1978, pp. 44–5.)*

health and physical well-being in their work than their non-manual counterparts. These risks are manifold. They may result in direct loss of life either suddenly in the form of accidents or in an attenuated manner through long-term exposure to dust or poisonous substances in the workplace. The same eventualities may also entail, antecedently, physical injury, disability and chronic illness. (This is why in Chapter 9 we pay attention to the importance of improving working conditions.)

But significant as occupation is, it is not a sufficient explanation. The influence of material deprivation in the aetiology of modern degenerative diseases is poorly understood, especially when applied to adults below the age of 45. In the past, poverty was an obvious antecedent in mortality, but its influence in deaths traced to cancer or circulatory disease, for example, is less clear-cut. It is thought these causes of death have their origins in over-indulgence rather than poverty and in behaviour which abuses and misuses the human body. The modern diet, rich in fats and with its emphasis on highly refined foods, and the modern sedentary patterns of work and leisure, are prime targets in the search for causes, as is, at a rather more specific level, the mass consumption of tobacco products.

Let us consider one of these. Smoking is becoming more class-related. Tobacco and the tobacco industry are part of the material and cultural life of Britain – an important source of tax income for the government, still freely permitted in public places and backed up by a multi-million pound advertising campaign which includes sports sponsorship. This is changing, and there is a slow swing against smoking, but not surprisingly the avant garde of cultural change are drawn from the higher occupational classes. If cigarette smoking is a major contributory cause of deaths due to cancer or heart disease, then the uneven response in the population to the news that it is dangerous is likely, in future years, to make class differentials in health even wider than they are at present. This raises questions, of course, about the social and economic factors whioh explain the fact and the prevalence of smoking in the first place and whether these, independent of individual education or counselling, have to be given priority in reducing the differentials.

Old age

After retirement the appropriateness of mortality rates as a proxy measure of standards of health is increased by the fact that health may literally become a matter of life and death for the over-65s. The bodies of men seem to exhibit the effects of wear and tear sooner than those of women and those of manual workers sooner than those of non-manual, and the manifestations of degeneration in disease become more frequent. What has to be remembered is that these outcomes are the end product of inequalities in the use made of, and the demands upon, the human body earlier in the lifetime and the kind of environment in which human beings have been placed.

This interpretation suggests that inequalities in health are the direct reflection of inequalities in the social division of labour. In the collective effort of social production, some workers' bodies wear out first. But inequalities in health at the end of the lifetime also emanate from the distribution of rewards associated with the social division of labour. Old age is a time of poverty, albeit poverty expressed in the form of relative deprivation, which among Britain's aged can mean material scarcity in very real terms, as deaths from hypothermia among the old reveal in severe winters. A recent DHSS report estimated malnutrition at 7 per cent among a sample of the elderly who were studied (DHSS, 1980, p. 3). In old age the relationship between income and the capacity to protect personal health is stronger perhaps than at any other time in the life-cycle, and in general it is likely that individuals who are well endowed through generous or index-linked pension schemes will lead the healthiest, the most comfortable and the longest lives after retirement. These material fortunes or misfortunes of old age are closely linked with occupational class during the working life. To have secure employment and an above-average income when one is at work is to be better able to provide for one's retirement. It is in this way that continuity in the distribution of material welfare is sustained, and inequalities in health perpetuated, from the cradle to the grave.

Conclusions

Several conclusions can be drawn from this look at different stages in the human life-cycle. First, while cultural and genetic explanations have some relevance – the latter is particularly important in early childhood – more of the evidence is explained by what we call 'materialist' or 'structural' explanations than by any other.

Secondly, some of the evidence on class inequalities in health can be understood in terms of specific features of the socio-economic environment: features such as accidents at work, overcrowding and smoking, which are strongly class-related in Britain. Since such features are recognized objectives of various areas of social policy we feel it sensible to offer them as contributory factors, to be dealt with in their own right, and not to discuss their incidence further in social-structural terms. The same is true of other aspects of the evidence which we feel show the importance of health services themselves. Ante-natal care, for example, is important in preventing peri-natal death, and the international evidence presented in Chapter 5 suggests that much can be done through improvement of ante-natal care and of its uptake. The international evidence also suggests the importance of preventive health within health policy, despite studies, to which we alluded earlier, which suggest that few of the differences in mortality either between nations, or between British regions, can be explained in terms of health care provision. But beyond this there is undoubtedly much which cannot be understood in terms of the impact of such specific factors. Much, we feel, can only be understood in terms of the more diffuse consequences of the class structure: poverty, work conditions (and what we termed the social division of labour) and deprivation in its various forms in the home and immediate environment, at work, in education and the upbringing of children and more generally in family and social life.

It is this acknowledgement of the complex nature of the explanation of health inequalities – involving access to and use of the health services; specific issues in other areas of social policy; and more general features of class, material inequality and deprivation – which informs and structures the recommendations we make in Chapters 8 and 9.

Chapter 7

The Need for More Information and Research

The scope and quality of national statistics relating to health and mortality in Britain are exceptionally good. Our task in compiling this report would have been much more difficult in most, if not all, other European countries. We have drawn on routine birth and death statistics, statistical returns collected for administrative and management purposes such as the hospital in-patient enquiry (HIPE), annual surveys like the GHS and the National Food Survey, the three national birth cohort studies and specific research projects.

Nevertheless there are gaps and imperfections which we feel necessitate either the initiation of further research or modification of the regular instruments of data collection.

There is a real need for continuing assessment of the development of children from birth to at least through primary school. It needs to be undertaken in relation to occupational class and must include surveillance of the nutrition of children. Studies of the kind we have in mind were in fact initiated in 1971, when the availability of school milk was reduced and the price of school meals raised, under the auspices of the Committee on Medical Aspects of Food Policy (COMA), and are still being carried out. Some of the findings of this work are discussed in Chapter 9, where we present our recommendations for policy relating to school meals and milk. The feasibility of surveillance of this kind has now been demonstrated, and the assessment of children's growth in relation to class and nutrition should become a matter of routine.

We recommend that school health statistics should routinely provide the results of tests of hearing, vision, and measures of height and weight, in relation to occupational class. Authorities might also be requested to report separately on schools in inner city areas, or to differentiate between a wide range of urban/rural locations. *As a first step we recommend that local health authorities, in consultation with education authorities, select a representative sample of schools in which assessments on a routine basis be initiated.* We should also like to see progress towards routine collection and reporting of accidents to children. Such reporting should ultimately distinguish not only between occupational classes and age groups, but also locations of accident

– on the road, at home, in school or elsewhere – and when appropriate the articles or building design features involved in accidents. At present the only national source of information is the HIPE. However, not only does HIPE fail to record occupational class, it also omits the vast bulk of accidents not requiring in-patient admission.

We recognize there are difficulties in working towards a national system of child-accident reporting, which may require the co-operation not only of hospital accident and emergency departments, and the police in the case of traffic accidents, but conceivably of health visitors also. In view of the importance of the topic, *we recommend that representatives of appropriate government departments (Health and Social Security, Education and Science, Environment, Trade, Transport, and the Home Office), as well as of the NHS and of the police, should consider how progress might rapidly be made in improving the information on accidents to children, nationally and locally.*

A further area where a concept of health broader than acute sickness has to be employed is in relation to the distribution of impairment and disability. We would like to see local authorities reporting systematically on numbers of disabled as well as, however crudely, on assessments of the severity of disablement. In the late 1970s local authorities began to classify handicapped people by the self-care criteria (whether they could wash and dress, and look after themselves in an elemental way), but that classification is not yet comprehensive, even for the physically handicapped, and needs to be extended, above all to the mentally handicapped. Social service departments and local officers of the Department of Employment should seek to introduce categorizations of severity, preferably on the basis of limitation of activity. This would permit comparison of priorities between services, as well as between authorities.

We would also like to draw attention to the importance of the National Food Survey, for which the Ministry of Agriculture, Fisheries and Food has responsibility. This annual survey is the principal source of information on the food purchased and consumed and hence the diet of the population, and is therefore of great importance. There are, however, problems relating to the low response rate of the survey. We feel that much could be done, through greater recourse to epidemiological expertise, to transform the survey into a more effective instrument of nutritional surveillance in relation to health.

We recommend that consideration be given to the development of the National Food Survey into a more effective instrument of nutritional surveillance in relation to health, through which various 'at risk' groups could also be identified and studied. We fully recognize that such a development may raise questions about proper responsibility for the survey.

Finally, *the importance of the problem of inequalities in health and their causes, as an area for further research needs to be emphatically stated. We recommend that it be adopted as a research priority by the DHSS and steps taken to enlist the expertise of the Medical Research Council (MRC), as well as the Social Science Research Council (SSRC), in the initiation of a programme of research. Such research represents a particularly appropriate area for departmental commissioning of research from the MRC.*

A strategy for advance

In our view, the six areas in which further research – leading, it should be said, in some instances to improved or augmented administrative statistics – is essential are:

a. surveillance of the development of children, especially in relation to nutrition and accidents;

b. better understanding of the health effects of such aspects of what can be regarded as individual behaviour as smoking, diet, alcohol consumption and exercise;

c. the development of area social condition and health indicators for use in resource allocation;

d. health hazards in relation to occupational conditions and work;

e. better measures of the prevalence and course of disability, and the degree of its severity.

f. study of the interaction of the social factors implicated in ill-health over time, and within small areas.

The importance of each of these derives from its relevance to our overall strategy of developing new policy.

In order to study the dynamics of child health – the process by which ill-health and educational under-achievement (whether a consequence of handicapping conditions, absence from school or cultural factors) develop together and so perpetuate the link between health and social class – it is necessary to turn to longitudinal studies.

In our view three issues upon which research needs to be brought to bear are:

i. the *interaction* of processes leading to physical and mental disadvantage, handicap and ill-health;

ii. the role which services related to child health play, and might play, in inhibiting the cumulation of disadvantage;

iii. the routes by which some children escape what is for most born into similar conditions an unenviable fate.

Conclusions and recommendations

We have made various recommendations which will improve and extend the quality of class-related health and health service utilization data on a regular basis and enhance knowledge of their interrelationships.

It is argued, in relation to health, that the monitoring of ill-health (itself still so imperfect) should evolve into a system also of monitoring health in relation to social and environmental conditions. Two areas where progress could be made are (i) in relation to the development of children, and (ii) in relation to disability. Certain modifications to community health statistics are proposed:

We recommend that school health statistics routinely provide locally and nationally, in relation to occupational class, the results of tests of hearing, vision, and measures of height and weight. As a first step we recommend that local health authorities, in consultation with education authorities, each select a representative sample of schools in which assessments on a routine basis be initiated.

We should also like to see progress towards the routine collection and reporting of accidents to children, ultimately distinguishing the age and occupational class of the parents as well as the location and circumstances of accidents. In relation to traffic accidents there should be better liaison between the NHS and the police, both centrally and locally.

We recommend that representatives of appropriate government departments (Health and Social Security, Education and Science, Environment, Trade, Transport and the Home Office), as well as the NHS and the police, should consider how progress might rapidly be made. The Child Accident Prevention Committee, if suitably constituted and supported, might be a suitable forum for such discussions, to be followed by appropriate action by government departments.

In relation to the disabled, we should like to see local authorities reporting systematically on numbers of disabled as well as (however crudely) on assessments of severity of disablement applying to mentally handicapped people, elderly people in residential homes and other groups of handicapped people, as well as the general classes of the handicapped, as at present.

In our view it is the extent to which need is unmet, rather than pressure upon existing services, which should form the basis for planning, and it is this view which has underpinned our recommendations. Turning, then, to the health services themselves, it is clear that systematic knowledge of the use made of the various services by different social groups is extremely scanty. We recognize that the collection and central reporting of occupational data within the context of the various administrative returns pose problems of feasibility and accuracy. Nevertheless we feel that the desirability of such information is such that further thought should be given to how these problems might be overcome, within the context of the current review of health service statistics.

Further, we draw attention to the importance of the National Food Survey as the major source of regular information on the food purchase (and hence nutrition) of the population. *We recommend however, that consideration be given (drawing upon epidemiological expertise within the OPCS and elsewhere) to development of the National Food Survey into a more effective instrument of nutritional surveillance in relation to health, through which various 'at risk' groups could also be identified and studied.*

Beyond this, we feel that the six areas in which further research is needed are:

– surveillance of the development of children, especially in relation to nutrition and accidents;
– better understanding of the health effects of such aspects of behaviour as smoking, diet, alcohol consumption and exercise;
– the development of area social conditions and health indicators for use in resource allocation;
– health hazards in relation to occupational conditions and work;
– better measures of the prevalence and course of disability, and the degree of its severity;
– study of the interaction of social factors implicated in ill-health over time, and within small areas.

Though these issues are in an obvious sense quite distinct, yet they can also be seen as aspects of an overall strategy, and it is this strategy which we particularly wish to commend. Our concern is with the interaction of variables traditionally seen as directly implicated in ill-health (such as smoking behaviour and work conditions) with social variables. It will be necessary to examine the effects upon the health of social groups of a wide range of social and behavioural variables, implying further work both on the development of health indicators and upon the way in which disadvantageous social and environmental conditions may give rise to or exacerbate the effects of patterns of dietary behaviour, leisure behaviour etc.

The importance of the problem of social inequalities in health and their causes, as an area for further research, needs to be emphatically stated. *We recommend that it be adopted as a research priority by the DHSS, and steps taken to enlist the expertise of the Medical Research Council, as well as the*

Social Science Research Council, in the initiation of a programme of research.
Such research represents a particularly appropriate area for departmental
commissioning of research from the MRC.

While we ourselves have not attempted to develop a research strategy in
detail within this report, it is our view that two types of study are needed.
First, a study of the interaction of social and environmental variables over
time, and their relationship to the (healthy) development of children. The
longitudinal approach, as in the existing cohort studies, is appropriate here.
Second, a study carried out in a small number of carefully selected places.
Such a study would concern itself with the whole range of social conditions
relevant for health, as well as patterns of behaviour which may in some senses
be damaging to health. Crucial for further progress in the elimination of
health inequalities is greater understanding of the interactions of this complex set of variables: social and individual. Such interactions will necessarily
have both diachronic and locational dimensions, and the studies we have in
mind will be sensitive to, and permit elucidation of, both.

Chapter 8

Planning the Health and Personal Social Services

Any strategy for improving health inevitably involves both the health care system and a range of social policies not immediately related to that system. In this chapter we look at those services which fall under the general administration of the Department of Health and Social Security, while in the next we outline some of the major changes which need to be made in other areas of social policy.

Objectives and principles

We believe the health and social services should adopt a three-fold scheme of priorities:
* Priority for children to have a better start in life.
* Priority for disabled people bearing the brunt of cumulative ill-health and deprivation to improve their quality of life and reduce the need for institutional care.
* Priority for preventive and educational action to encourage good health.
    We shall look at each of these in turn.

1. Priority for children at the start of life

The wide gap in life prospects between babies born of members of different occupational classes – amongst the widest we have found in society – together with the likelihood that the beneficial effects of any reduction in that gap will be carried over into adult life and may lead to savings in health expenditure, demands that action be taken at this stage.

It would be wrong to suppose that improvements in infant and child care could be fully effective without paying heed to the need for improvements in the living standards of their families and the physical constitution and access to health services of their parents. Nevertheless some specific action aimed at this age group is possible. The great majority of 'excess' infant deaths in classes IV and V are attributable to congenital abnormalities and other complications of birth and the period immediately afterwards, and in later infancy and childhood to accidents, respiratory diseases and gastro-intestinal infections. As we shall go on later to show, this means that special measures need to be taken to improve the quality of community health services, especially those devoting resources predominantly to children and those which reduce risks of ill-health, injury and accidents.

2. Priority for disabled people bearing the brunt of cumulative ill-health and deprivation

It cannot be sufficient to plan only for the next generation or to take steps to prevent certain health problems arising in the future. The cumulative deprivations of a lifetime are a potent source of class inequality in health. Those who are the worst victims of past and current industrial and social practices, who have been exposed for prolonged periods to bad housing, poor working and environmental conditions and low incomes, also deserve services to improve their health and to enable them to cope with disabilities. As with our first priority area, a marked shift of resources to community health and welfare services is called for.

3. Priority for the preventive services

Greater equality in health depends upon a high national standard of knowledge about self-care, the care of children and other dependants, and the pursuit of activities conducive to health which themselves depend on such factors as high standards of home-keeping, good education and widely diffused recreational and sporting activities. This suggests a coherent national programme of enormous scope and we can only hope to give illustrations in this and the next chapter of some of the most important parts of such a programme. They will include an expansion of health education, selective screening and strong anti-smoking measures. It is important, however, to convey at once the relative inexpensiveness of such measures. At the same time we are deeply conscious not only of the preposterously small part of NHS resources committed to 'preventive health', but also the lack of understanding by health authorities (and education authorities) of what is good health practice and how they might contribute to strengthening and supplementing such practice.

Planning

We know these concerns are not new, and indeed they are very much within the spirit of much recent government thinking. At least in theory, the whole period of the middle and late 1970s saw an emphasis on greater care in the community, as well as a higher priority for children, families with children, for the elderly and for preventive health measures.

Nevertheless at least two disconcerting observations need to be made about government priorities. First, objectives are not clearly defined. A good example is that of 'community care'. The DHSS itself seems to mean different things by this concept at different times. In one overall review of planning the department defined a primary objective for the elderly to be to develop domiciliary provision and encourage 'measures designed to prevent or postpone the need for long-term care in hospital and residential homes' (DHSS, *Social Care Research*, 1978, p. 13). But in the planning document *The Way Forward* in 1977 community care was defined as covering a whole range of provision, including community hospitals, hostels, day hospitals, residential homes, day centres and domiciliary support. Again the 1976 Priorities Document which represented new directions in government policy called for relatively higher growth rates for some services but gave no rationale for the percentage growth rates chosen. This laid them open to charges of arbitrariness.

We believe that a clear statement of what is planned and intended produces a better educated and more understanding public, a more democratic and accountable public service, and above all offers an opportunity to question and clarify any shortcomings there may be in the initial thinking.

There is certainly no mathematically precise or exact way of determining the relative priority of different services, but there is room for the development of more precise analytical tools. Although, for instance, there are problems in conceptualizing and measuring 'need' (Lind and Wiseman, 1978; Smith, 1980) *we consider there is no better alternative conceptual basis for developing a coherent rationale for the allocation of health care resources, and we recommend accordingly*. We shall return later to a discussion of 'need'.

Secondly, some of the changes recommended in the various priority documents are simply not materializing or are materializing so slowly as to be difficult to discern. The latest trends in spending on the personal social services, for instance, give little or no sign of the planned decline in spending on *residential* care, with the corresponding expected increase in *community* care. A summary of local authority planning returns does not bear out the change in emphasis recommended by the DHSS (*Local Authority Personal Social Services Summary of Planning Returns 1976–77 to 1979–80*, 1978).* Even though the planned changes in the emphasis of spending were modest

*Later information shows that this statement still applies.

(extremely modest in some cases) the inability to fulfil even these limited objectives is disturbing.

We recommend a shift of resources within the national health service and the personal social services on a larger and more determined scale than so far accomplished towards community care and particularly towards the increased availability of care for young children. We see this as an important part of a strategy to break the links between social class or poverty and health.

What does this mean in practice? Table 37 illustrates what we have in mind. Column one shows actual expenditure on the various components of the health and social services in 1976/7. Column two is a projection of expenditure to 1981/2 and shows how modest the shift in resources sought by the last Labour government was. Column three (alternative 1) illustrates our idea of a more determined shift in emphasis assuming current planned levels of expenditure. This shows savings of £200 million in 1981/2 set against additional expenditure of £200 million (plus £30 million for an experimental action programme we shall explain further on). It doesn't imply a reduction in current levels of expenditure for any services but rather cuts in the anticipated growth (admittedly very small) in some areas. In our view the largest scope for reductions in rates of growth, if not in absolute costs, is in the pharmaceutical services.

Column four (alternative 2) is based on the belief that in fact current planned levels of expenditure, taking into account inflation and demographic changes, are inadequate and will do no more than permit an overall maintenance of existing levels. It follows that any reduction, even in anticipated growth, could end up as a real cut. Column four illustrates therefore how the shift in resources should be brought about on the more optimistic assumption that no service should be financed at a level below that previously forecast for 1981/2 and that additional resources could be made available. On this basis our proposals would require an additional £287 million, plus the £30 million mentioned before.

The setting-out of alternatives in Table 37 reflects a clear division of opinion within the Working Group. While we were completely in agreement on the importance of strengthening community and preventive services, two of us (DB and JNM) were opposed to obtaining the necessary resources by reducing expenditure on the hospital services, believing that these are already straitened by inflation and cash-limits; the others, on what may well be a sound appreciation of the financial outlook, were not so opposed to this. Naturally, all of us would wish to see additional resources.

These recommendations should, however, be thought of as money-saving in two senses. First, by reducing inequality and laying a better basis for the maintenance of health, the incidence of ill-health (and hence the need for

Table 37: *Planned and recommended revenue expenditure on selected services (£m.; November 1976 prices)*

Services to be given higher priority than at present	1976–7 actual	1981–2 DHSS projection (1978)	1981–2 Alternative 1	1981–2 Alternative 2
1. *Health and Welfare of mothers and pre-school and school children*				
Midwives	24	24	26	28
Family planning	12	15	20	21
Health visiting	47	63	66	70
Day nurseries	33	37	60	63
School health	51	51	60	65
Welfare food	18	19	40	43
Boarding out	20	26	28	30
Sub-total	205	235	300	320
2. *Family practitioner (other than pharmaceutical)*	440	494	514	547
3. *Care of disabled in their own homes*				
Home nursing	81	108	116	124
Chiropody	11	13	13	14
Home help	105	131	160	170
Meals	12	15	20	21
Day care	57	76	90	96
Aids, adaptations	13	14	30	32
Services for disabled	42	40	50	53
Sub-total	321	397	479	510
4. *Other specific preventive measures*	14	17	50	53
Total selected 'higher priority' services	980	1143	1343	1430
Recommended increases (Total 1, 2, 3 and 4)	—	—	+200	+287

Table 37: *Cont.*

Services to be given smaller priority than at present	1976–7 actual	1981–2 DHSS projection (1978)	1981–2 Alternative 1	1981–2 Alternative 2
5. *Acute in-patients and out-patients*				
6. *Mental handicap in-patients and out-patients* *Mental illness in-patients and out-patients* *Residential care for elderly*				
7. *Pharmaceutical services*				
Total selected 'lesser priority' services (5 + 6 + 7)	2992	3295	3095	3295
Recommended decrease 'lesser priority' services (5 + 6 + 7)	—	—	−200	0
Experimental ten-area programme			(30)	30

health care treatment) could be diminished. Second, by precautionary and supportive action the need for more expensive types of treatment will be reduced. While it may be true that many of those in hospital require additional resources, yet if fewer patients need be admitted or if the duration of stay can be safely reduced, there can still be scope for savings.

Resource allocation

The mid-seventies also saw a commitment to redistributing resources geographically across the country in a more appropriate fashion. There is abundant evidence that some parts of the country have historically had much higher health budgets and consequently more adequate facilities. Since these tend to be the better-off regions, health inequalities are reinforced.

In 1975 the government commissioned a DHSS Resource Allocation Working Party to investigate ways of establishing a formula for distributing resources that corresponded more closely to 'need' rather than historical practice. The working party interpreted its objectives as being to secure through resource allocation equal opportunities of access to health care for people at equal risk. We wish to endorse this objective.

Unlike the parallel priority document (1976) it did seek to establish a mathematically quantifiable definition of need as a basis for determining future resource distribution. This rested primarily on mortality rates, which were taken as a proxy for morbidity rates. The procedure was, essentially, to take the age and sex structure of a population together with the average death rates for people of different sexes at different ages and then to 'weight' a region's population according to its need for various services – hospital, GP, ambulance etc. These services were costed and target revenues set accordingly. The RAWP proposal was that those regions furthest from their targets should have relatively larger growth budgets than those nearer, or, in the case of regions in the south-east of England (the so-called rich regions), already well past it. The more difficult questions of exactly how to redistribute resources more fairly at area and district level were largely ignored.

The RAWP formula was complicated and we were unable to get a complete picture of how its method was being applied around the country. Between 1976 and 1979 at least nine of the fourteen health regions had only partially implemented it. Four had not yet analysed their populations according to average death rates and five had not done this in relation to the particular need for general hospital care. Even among the remaining five, progress appeared to be cautious in moving towards targets for particular services.

We believe there are several points which deserve further attention. First, neither RAWP principles nor RAWP methodology has been consistently applied at area or district level and some of the misunderstandings about it have arisen because of the lack of precise illustrations at health district level of the actual and desirable operation of different services. This leads us to recommend that health authorities should consider increasing the volume of information collected and published regularly for each health district about: (a) health experience (indicators of morbidity, mortality and positive health); (b) rates of usage of health and health-related services (including GP consultations, out-patient attendance, home nursing and health visits and in-patient and residential care); and (c) social and environmental conditions.

Secondly, there has been insufficient thought given to how the concept of need could be enhanced by additional indicators. Are there, for instance, indicators of social deprivation which might be used independently or to supplement death rates in developing a formula for resource allocation?

There is in Britain a long tradition of study of the relationship between social conditions and death rates. While surveys like the General Household Survey do not break down information into sufficiently small areas, census data, although biased towards housing information and quickly out of date, does offer material on a range of deprivation-related factors at local authority and ward level.

One study in 1961 used a variety of census indicators, plus climatic and air pollution indicators, in the attempt to explain differences in adult mortality rates between the larger county boroughs of England and Wales. Multiple regression techniques allowed these authors to show, for example, that 'social conditions' (an indicator combining amount of overcrowding, social class, average educational level etc. was used), air pollution levels and inclement climate were independently associated with mortality rates from bronchitis (Gardner, Crawford and Morris, 1969).

More recently a second study, using 1971 census data together with 1971 mortality rates for children aged 0 to 4 and 5 to 14, sought to relate the death rates for children to social need variables, also at county or metropolitan borough level (Brennan and Lancashire, 1978). It found significant correlations between mortality rates, especially for the younger children, and extent of overcrowding, lack of basic amenities, extent of unemployment among male working population and extent of council house occupancy.

A significant correlation was also obtained with the proportion of unskilled workers, and the authors then examined whether or not social class composition (understood in the restricted sense of the percentage of population in class V), housing variables (density, possession of amenities) and unemployment rate are *independently* related to mortality rates. Calculation of partial correlations (housing variables and unemployment rate held constant) showed that the effects were independent of each other in the case of the under-5s.

Although this kind of analysis cannot be extrapolated to causes of mortality at the individual level, it is important here in suggesting that areas having high unemployment rates, *or* bad housing, *or* a high proportion of unskilled workers, or worse, all three, are likely to have high rates of child mortality especially in the first five years of life. The authors also conclude that the percentage of population in social class V *alone* will inadequately

Table 38: Highest-ranking local authority areas on each of eight 1971 census and mortality indicators (England)

1 Households with more than one person per room (per 1,000 households)	2 No. unemployed per 1,000 persons	3 No. unskilled workers per 1,000 economically active	4 Married couples with four or more children per 1,000 families	5 Perinatal mortality rate (average 1974–6)	6 Infant mortality rate (average 1974–6)	7 Adjusted mortality ratio (1976)
Knowsley	Knowsley	Tower Hamlets*	Knowsley	Wolverhampton	Rochdale	Salford*
Islington*	Liverpool*	Southwark*	Liverpool*	Sandwell	Oldham	Tameside
Hackney*	S. Tyneside	Newham*	Manchester*	Liverpool*	Salford*	Gateshead*
Tower Hamlets*	Sunderland	Knowsley	Birmingham*	Gateshead*	Wolverhampton	Liverpool
Lambeth*	Manchester*	Liverpool*	Cleveland	Salford*	Manchester*	S. Tyneside
Kensington/Chelsea	Newcastle*	Cleveland	Sefton	Rochdale	Bradford	Tower Hamlets*
Hammersmith	Cleveland	Humberside	Hackney*	Bolton	Calderdale	Durham
Southwark*	Gateshead*	Salford*	Lambeth*	Manchester*	Kirklees	Bolton
Brent	Hammersmith	Newcastle*	Newham*	Walsall	Walsall	Wirral
Camden*	Tower Hamlets*	Islington*	Salford*	Knowsley		N. Tyneside
			Wirral			
			S. Tyneside			
			Sunderland			
			Lewisham*			

* indicates Inner City Partnership Scheme area

Note: Adjusted Mortality Ratio (AMR) is the local death rate standardized for population age/sex structure and divided by the national rate.

Sources: Columns 1–4 Imber, 1977; 5–6 DHSS/OPCS (unpublished); 7 OPCS Local Authority Vital Statistics 1976.

reflect the extent to which social factors pre-disposing to high infant mortality are present in an area. Of course more 'inclusive' measures of class composition remain to be examined in relation to mortality. Table 38 shows which metropolitan districts and non-metropolitan counties show up worst on each of four census social indicators, and three indicators of mortality (using recent mortality data). The frequent appearance of certain areas notably in the north-west and the north-east is apparent. Further work on relationships between indicators of social disadvantage and of mortality is needed.

Third, we do not believe that a more equitable distribution of resources alone, without parallel attention to *how* these resources are to be used, will greatly serve to reduce inequalities in health care, still less in health. In the debate on the RAWP recommendations too much attention has been concentrated on criteria of the need for health care and too little on the effects upon health of allocating resources to one type of service rather than another. We believe that 'need' for health care must govern the definition of priorities and that at the present time the definition of such need shows the case for making a more pronounced shift of resources towards community and preventive health care. This leads us to suggest a possible modification to the implementation of the RAWP philosophy.

At present, the proposal is that weighted populations for each kind of health service are combined on the basis of the share of total revenue which each of these services currently represents, that is 8.8 per cent for community health, 55.9 per cent for non-psychiatric in-patients etc. We believe that this process should reflect not *current* distribution of expenditure but that which is *aimed* at in the planning of services. That is, if community health is a *priority* (and is intended to absorb, say, 10 per cent of total resources, excluding those for family practitioner services, within 5 years' time) then it is this figure which should be used in the combining of weighted populations. *We therefore recommend that the resources to be allocated should be based on the future planned share for different services, including a higher share for community health.*

In saying this we reiterate the Royal Commission's endorsement of the Expenditure Committee's view that: 'the expenditure planning and priority setting of DHSS should be synchronized so as to enable Parliament to examine the relationship between the two' (*Ninth Report from the Expenditure Committee.* Session 1976–7, 1977, p. lvi; and see also *Report of the Royal Commission on the NHS*, 1979, p. 56).

A district action programme

To ensure the vigorous implementation of the three-fold priority programme we outlined at the beginning (p. 133) we also propose the establishment of what we have called a *district action programme*. It would be adopted nation-wide and would involve additional modifications to the present structure of care not so far seriously pursued by government policies. It is a four-point programme.

1. The health and welfare of mothers, pre-school and school children

The under-utilization of the community and preventive health services by poorer groups is well documented. While we cannot assess the *extent* to which this is a consequence of the inequitable provision of services – so that, for example, working-class women might have longer journey times and waiting times in visiting child health clinics – we have known for a long time that under-utilization is associated with organizational and cultural aspects of services. One authority puts the problem as follows:

> Under-utilization of ante-natal and child-health services results from inadequacies in the services themselves and particularly from their insensitivity to the uncertainty and conflict of responsibility mothers feel regarding the question of their baby's health. Two particular areas of inadequacy are highlighted by recent research: firstly, inadequacies as regards the organization of ante-natal clinics (timing of clinics and length of waiting, location of clinics, facilities for children and other relatives, etc.) and secondly, inadequacies as regards the actual content of the check-up (lack of individual attention and advice tailored to the individual's needs, lack of privacy, etc.). (Graham, 1978)

We recommend that areas and districts should review the accessibility and facilities of all the ante-natal and child-health clinics in their areas, and develop plans to increase utilization by mothers. On the basis of our own experience this must include such reforms as experimenting with evening and weekend opening, the dispersion of ante-natal sessions from hospitals covering large catchment areas to new centres in small areas, and the humanization of ante-natal procedures and settings, especially in clinics in hospitals. One clinic which we visited was described, not unfairly it seemed, as a 'cattle market'.

The DHSS should furthermore publicize factors which explain high utilization in some areas, like Liverpool, and low utilization in others, like Salford. Wherever possible clinics should be established in conjunction with group practice and health centres, in partial fulfilment of the recommendations of the Court Committee. As some commentators have pointed out, relatively few general practitioners are keen to devote more time to practising preventive medicine, and a change in outlook will take a long time to bring about (Alberman, Morris and Pharaoh, 1977, p. 394), but it might be encouraged if more health visiting staff were seconded full-time or part-time to group practice. There is room for experiment, and it is possible for some health visitors to combine territorial and team responsibilities. There is an even more powerful case to be made out for the secondment of social work staff, but in this case knowledge of welfare rights would be a very necessary part of their skills. Ease of access, good facilities, respect for the individual and availability of care and advice throughout infancy and childhood might be the watch-words of any planned development of services.

We should perhaps, at this point, mention the experiments in France and Finland (see Chapter 5), where ante-natal care is supported by financial inducements. We have examined these but we are not convinced that reluctance on the part of mothers to attend clinics is the real key to their under-utilization in Britain. In Finland the establishment of a national network of clinics in 1945 preceded the introduction of payments and may have been the key factor in encouraging high rates of attendance. In France ante-natal payments were introduced many years before the dramatic improvements in the French perinatal mortality rate.

One of the problems we face in Britain is that with the huge proportion of hospital births it can be difficult securing the involvement of GPs at an early stage in the life of a child. There are a number of possible solutions to this. One, already mentioned, is the association of more ancillary staff with primary care teams. We would then urge that the teams should generally be constructed on the basis of two and at most three general practitioners so that some contribution might be made to the vitality and integration of the local community. Another is immunization, where GPs have a much better knowledge of family history and the health and development of a child and are in a much stronger position to know about untoward reactions. In principle we advocate such a policy, though we recognize that for some time to come there will have to be back-up provisions in the community where the medical service is inadequate.

Unfortunately this inadequacy is disturbingly widespread and we were very concerned about the standard of GP service in some poor areas with high mortality. There are single-handed general practitioners who live at a considerable distance from the areas in which their patients reside, have little knowledge of or interest in local culture – which leads them to prescribe or otherwise treat patients inappropriately – who rely for a disproportionately large part of the year, the week or the day on the deputizing services, and take little or no interest in the possibilities of new health centres, group practice or other forms of collaboration among and between health service and social service professional personnel.

Some are considerably older than 65 and others are new to practice in this country and include those who are virtually in transit to other career destinations. There are some who have resorted to work in these areas because they have been unsuccessful elsewhere and are exposed here to less criticism. As the Royal Commission said of declining urban areas, 'Many health professionals are coping courageously and effectively in these areas, but there is evidence in some places that services are inadequate. The GPs tend to be older and to have large lists. The accepted view today is that a GP will work most efficiently in a group practice or partnership with several other GPs and there may be some connection between the extent of single-handed practice and low quality of care, although there are many excellent single-handed GPs. More single-handed practices are found in the inner city areas' (*Report*, 1979, p. 88). For the inner London area, these problems have been well documented in the Acheson Report (London Health Planning Consortium, 1981).

We are aware that some of the best and most dedicated members of the medical profession also work in these areas and that the problems of quantifying the problem are immense. Nevertheless we are in no doubt that the problem is sufficiently serious to demand action. The Royal Commission took a similar view and recommended, among other things, close supervision of deputizing services, a review of controls on the appointment of GPs, the offer of an assisted voluntary retirement scheme to GPs, a study of the feasibility of introducing a compulsory retirement age, the introduction of audit or peer review of standards of care and treatment and the development of health centres as a priority in inner city areas.

We accept this, but we would want to go further. *We recommend that the professional associations as well as the Secretary of State and the health authorities should accept responsibility for making improvements in the quality and geographical coverage of general practice, especially in areas of high prevalence of ill-health and poor social conditions. Where the number or scope of work of general practitioners is inadequate in such areas we recommend health authorities to deploy or redeploy an above-average number of community nurses attached where possible to family practices.* The review of coverage must include definitions of desirable standards of practice and keeping abreast of modern methods of practice as well as advancement in medical knowledge, and not only questions of remuneration and inducement. *We further recommend that the distribution of general practitioners should be related not only to population but to medical need, as indicated by SMRs, supplemented by other indicators, and that the per capita basis of remuneration be modified accordingly.*

One possibility deserving careful consideration is the attachment of additional, newly qualified GPs to existing group practices and health centres for periods of, say, two to five years. Every effort should be made to provide housing temporarily or permanently within the areas. One problem of the poor areas is that health centres are not yet the main form of medical organization. In Gateshead only a fifth and in Tower Hamlets fewer than a tenth of GPs are in health centres. Previous studies have demonstrated that a more effective policy deserves to be adopted. 'The NHS has not brought about any dramatic shift in the location of GPs ... Areas which are currently facing the most serious shortages seem to have a fairly long history of man-power difficulties, while those which are today relatively well supplied with family doctors have generally had no difficulty in past years in attracting and keeping an adequate number of practitioners...' (Butler, Bevan and Taylor, 1973). A separate study of mortality and GP statistics in 1972 and 1973 found a significant lack of correlation between measures of illness and death and the number of GPs, suggesting that the supply of GPs is not matched to health care need (Forster, Frost, Francis and Heath).

We believe the evidence suggests that it is precisely those areas most in need of good medical facilities – judged on the basis of rates of mortality and morbidity – which are often least likely to have them.

Education facilities are another area that causes us concern. With the relative increase in number of one-parent families and increased employment of young mothers with children, the problem of facilities for those without relatives living nearby is considerable. Present plans for the expansion of day nurseries are meagre, and the rate of expansion needs to be larger. Within the proposed Health Development Programme at national level *we recommend the financing of new services for children under 5 from the savings that are being made as a result of the decline in the school population.* This proposal is further elaborated below (Chapter 9, pp. 172–5).

School health services are another neglected but valuable resource. They make it possible, for instance, to monitor the health of children in certain types of family more frequently, and there are possibilities of relating health surveillance to teaching about health and the health service. At the same time there have been a number of suggestions that all health services for children should be more tightly integrated. A Scottish working party expected that 'in the course of time much routine school health work will be carried out by primary care teams but the more specialized aspects such as the assessment of handicapped children will be the responsibility of paediatricians working closely with other professional colleagues' (*Towards an Integrated Child*

Health Service, 1973, p. 101). Like the working party, we recognize that there will have to be different systems of provision of school health care for some time to come, but *recommend that every opportunity should be taken to link revitalized school health care with general practice, and to intensify surveillance and follow-up both in areas of special need and for certain types of family*. For this purpose we take the view that certain assessments can be undertaken by health visitors and social workers, especially where they are already working in association with group practice. Much of this has already been accepted, at least in principle, by Ministers.

One area of school health which requires separate attention is the child guidance system. This has traditionally provided psychiatric care for a relatively small number of maladjusted children on an intensive basis. There is evidence of long waiting lists, misunderstood systems of queueing, and a negative image of the work among parents (Fitzherbert, 1977, pp. 85-96). At the same time there is evidence from surveys in the Isle of Wight and in London (Rutter *et al.*, 1970, 1975) of a very much higher prevalence of maladjustment among children than had been thought, or than could be helped by traditional psychiatric methods. Consequently there is a growing view, which we share, that the emphasis must increasingly be upon preventive methods and upon increasing co-operation between psychiatrists, educational psychologists and teachers. For example, the so-called 'nurture group' pioneered by Marjorie Boxall provides a special therapeutic environment to compensate for inadequate early experience *within* the school from which children are gradually returned to normal classes. Such experiments should be encouraged and evaluated.

For handicapped children Ministers have already accepted in principle the establishment of District Handicap Teams. The teams can help to provide careful diagnosis and continuing help and advice and support to handicapped children and their parents. *We recommend that an assessment which determines severity of disablement should be adopted as a guide to health service priorities, and that this should be related to the limitation of activities rather than loss of faculty or type of handicap*. This procedure would help to equate the provision of services for mentally handicapped as well as physically handicapped children.

2. The care of disabled and elderly people in their own homes

When disablement is understood in terms of functional limitation it becomes possible to rank severity and provide a better guide to the selection of priorities. For example, conventions about the division of clients according to type of handicap, or the conventional categorization of patients as requiring hospitalization, residential care, sheltered housing or domiciliary support, may need to be re-examined. Many people seem to find themselves in a particular category more by chance than for any specific medical reason. Moreover the quality of care provided by the different types of institution, judged by costs, manpower, amenities etc., may bear little relation to need.

We believe disabled people suffer two distinct forms of inequality. One is inequality of opportunity for treatment for those in different types of hospital. *We recommend a review of the distribution of facilities and services between acute and long-stay units and also of the distribution of elderly patients in geriatric, psychiatric and general hospitals.*

The second form of inequality is in opportunities for care, rehabilitation, occupation, privacy and social relations between hospital patients and residents of local authority, voluntary and private homes on the one hand and disabled people living in their own homes on the other. These inequalities have attracted rather less attention than inequalities in services for people in different areas.

Both these forms of inequality require attention. However, we believe the first step in doing this is to clarify the meaning of community care and give much greater emphasis to the tendencies towards that objective favoured in government planning documents.

For instance the Jay Committee, which reported on mental handicap nursing and care in 1979, identified three broad sets of principles which should govern community care: (i) Mentally handicapped people have a right to enjoy normal patterns of life within the community; (ii) Mentally handicapped people have a right to be treated as individuals; (iii) Mentally handicapped people will require additional help from the communities in which they live and from professional services if they are to develop to their maximum potential as individuals.

The Committee concluded:

The mentally handicapped person should have access to the full range of services and facilities available to the general public and specialist services should be provided only where the general services cannot cope with a special need. But where special provisions are required they should offer a wide range of options in the three spheres of day, domiciliary and residential services. Mentally handicapped people in residential care should not be isolated from their neighbourhood or, more importantly, from their families. The staff who care for mentally handicapped residents should be compassionate and caring, but also professionally trained; their role should be to help each mentally handicapped person to develop mentally, physically and emotionally. Residents should live in small family-type groups sharing experiences informally with the staff, making their own decisions and taking necessary risks. (DHSS, Jay Committee, March 1979, p. 140)

In realizing such aims one obstacle in the development of services for mentally handicapped people, as for other groups of disabled people, is that responsibility for sheltered housing, as distinct from residential accommodation, is not the responsibility of the personal social services. As a result residential care is sometimes offered when sheltered housing would be the more rational choice. *We recommend that a Working Group, to include representatives of voluntary organizations concerned with relevant client groups, should be set up to review whether sheltered housing should be a responsibility of social service or housing departments and make recommendations.*

The elderly have also continued to have a poor deal from 'community care'. It has certainly not developed as rapidly as the general policy aims would suggest. The 1976 Priority Document argued:

The general aim of policy is to help the elderly maintain independent lives in their own homes for as long as possible. The main emphasis is thus on the development of the domiciliary services and on the promotion of a more active approach towards the treatment of the elderly in hospital. But old people who can no longer continue to live independently in the community even with the support of all available health and social services will need long-term residential or hospital care. (DHSS, 1976, p. 38)

In practice, evidence of capacities among residents and their subjective preferences is not always given the attention it deserves. *We recommend that clear criteria for admission to, and for continuing residence in, residential care should be agreed between the DHSS and the local authority associations, and steps taken to encourage rehabilitation, and in particular to prevent homeless elderly people from being offered accommodation only in residential homes. Priority should be given to expansion of domiciliary care for those who are severely disabled in their own homes.*

It may even be that, in the light of evidence which emerges, numbers in residential care could be frozen and even reduced, thus freeing additional resources. At times the DHSS has seemed to favour such a policy (for example, DHSS, *Social Care Research*, 1978, p. 13). It is true that in the 1970s the population of residential homes became older. This does of course suggest a rising number who are likely to be substantially incapacitated – though that correspondence needs to be demonstrated – but there still remains considerable evidence that a large fraction of residents, perhaps two fifths or even more, do not require continuous or even substantial 'care and attention' in a residential setting (Table 39). This may not mean that it would be right or practicable to attempt to find alternative accommodation for many present residents, but it does suggest that alternative accommodation must be found in future for those who would otherwise be admitted unnecessarily.

Table 39: *Evidence of capacity of elderly residents in homes for self-care*

Date of study	Scope of study	Percent of residents with capacity for self-care (*local authority residents only unless otherwise specified*)	
(i) 1958–9	National sample survey of homes in England & Wales	72%	neither bedfast nor requiring help dressing
		59%	mobile outside home without assistance
		52%	(new residents only) with 'little or no incapacity for self-care'
(ii) 1963	National sample survey of homes in Britain	37%	little or no incapacity for self-care
		21%	little or no incapacity for self-care *and* household management
(iii) 1969	National survey of homes in Scotland	67%	complete capacity for self-care (i.e. able to wash, dress and use toilet)
		48%	'fit', i.e. having complete capacity for self-care plus no impairment or only mild impairment of mobility, mental state and continence
(iv) 1970	National census of homes in England	45%	minimally dependent (i.e. continent, mobile without assistance, able to eat and drink without assistance, *and* mentally alert)
(v) 1972	Survey of council homes in eight London boroughs	55%	high or very high capacity for self-care
(vi) 1973	64 homes in Cheshire	63%	able to wash, dress, feed and go to toilet unaided
		42%	no mobility problems, no assistance of any kind required *and* no behavioural problems

Sources: (i) and (ii) Townsend, 1962 and 1973; (iii) Carstairs and Morrison, 1972; (iv) DHSS, 1975; (v) Plank, 1977; (vi) Kimbell and Townsend, 1975.

Moreover we believe the tendency of the residential population to grow and become older reflects in part the social difficulties of elderly people, not just the fact that more of them are 75 and over. Factors such as lagging real incomes, displacement at younger ages from occupations and housing and especially the tendency for women increasingly to outlive men and to live alone all make life more difficult, and services have not developed fast enough to compensate.

Ironically another explanation is to be found in the reduction of the percentage of elderly cared for within the hospital system. For reasons of cost or professional definitions of medical or nursing need fewer elderly are to be found in hospital at any particular date, and the elderly residential population has grown at the same time as the hospital population has diminished. We are not sure this change-over has been entirely beneficial. The most severely disabled sector of the elderly population may now have *less* access to medical and nursing expertise than they used to and there may be less effort put into their rehabilitation.

Residential care is by far the most costly element in the personal social services and deserves a thorough review. In planning an efficient system of care for the elderly we may need to ensure that the minority of people in residential accommodation who are very frail and require close and continuous medical and nursing supervision and treatment for long-term conditions receive it in very small residential nursing hospitals, annexes and even day centres under local geriatricians. On the other hand, sheltered housing may be the best environment for that large fraction of people in residential accommodation whose disabilities are slight or at least not substantial, and perhaps in some instances also of residents whose disabilities are severe. *We therefore recommend that the present functions and structure of hospital, residential and domiciliary care for the disabled elderly should be reviewed in relation to their needs, in order to determine the best and most economical balance of future services.* We believe that such a review is likely to demonstrate the accelerated relative priority that deserves to be accorded to the development of domiciliary services. Strictly, the responses to the consultative document *A Happier Old Age* (DHSS, 1978) provide in some respects the material for just such a review. However, the issue deserves more sustained expert examination and research, especially into the subjective attitudes of elderly patients and consumers of residential and community services, than it appears to have attracted.

Overall, the care of disabled people, many of whom are *elderly* disabled people, requires more co-ordinated action by health and social service authorities than currently exists. The introduction of joint funding has encouraged more collaborative planning. *We recommend that this initiative should be developed and that there should be further central government funding of a more specific kind to encourage joint care programmes.* Within the general category of severely disabled people, sub-categories should be more clearly defined so that both types of authority can comprehend their individual but also joint responsibilities at different stages of chronic illness or disablement. *We further recommend that sums within the joint finance allocation should be reserved for payment to authorities putting forward joint programmes to give continuing care to disabled people – for example, post-hospital follow-up schemes, pre-hospital support programmes for families, and support programmes for the severely incapacitated and terminally ill.* Funding might be based on a percentage or per capita grant. Health and local authorities may be involved in broader types of in-service training and acknowledgement of the need to interchange staff between hospital and day centre, or hospital and home.

Like many policies, a more vigorous community care policy on behalf of disabled people in their own homes will encounter difficulties. Risks are involved in encouraging some people to continue living alone when disabled. Attempts to increase the pattern of social contacts in supplementation of support services for some elderly people living alone have not always met with success, and traditions of individual privacy, quite apart from the constraints of poverty and bad housing, do not make any easier the patterns of supportive social interaction which would better suit disablement in old age. In the long run a choice has to be made between the encouragement of further dependency on the part of disabled people in the hands of different professionals, and the ready availability in the community of support, including greater diffusion of information and expertise, reciprocation of services within the community, self-help, and all the risks of depending on spontaneous and other expressions of good-will among neighbours and generally in the community. This latter option is, of course, a form of 'prevention', for it would help people to deal with their own problems in their own homes and preserve for them the dignity of the status of responsible actors.

Finally, there has been a rapid expansion of the home help service. *In practice many home helps undertake a wide range of responsibilities on behalf of disabled people and we recommend that this should be formally encouraged, with short courses of training, specialization of some functions and with access to mini-bus transport, especially to day centres.*

3. Prevention: the role of government

A consultative document on prevention and health was published in 1976 and reprinted three times within the space of a year. This suggests widespread public interest. As Ministers stated in a foreword to the document, 'the preventive approach should permeate and inform all aspects of the health services'.

This will involve a change of outlook in the DHSS and more determined changes in organization and the allocation of resources. For the attainment of national objectives the distribution of information and knowledge about health and management of illness needs to be less hierarchical and more widely shared. In part this means taking a new view of health education We have already called for the resurgence of the school health service and the introduction of special forms of teaching in the schools. But the issue is not simply the better instruction of individuals at key periods of their lives As those concerned with health education are aware, there are at least three distinguishable sets of reasons for health education: (1) 'to produce changes in beliefs and behaviour in order to reduce mortality and morbidity; (2) to influence norms and values governing the use of health services; (3) to produce a general understanding of certain more diffuse "health" issues in order to obtain a population who have a general understanding of health issues and to avoid certain forms of "undesirable" or not directly definable "unhealthy" behaviour' (Tuckett, 1979, p. 4). A balance has to be struck between creating better and safer conditions of work, safer travel, well-regulated manufacture of food products and other goods and the creation of social and occupational conditions minimizing stress, as well as the conventional individual 'do-it-yourself' approach to health education.

While laying stress on the importance of designing and regulating appropriate occupational environmental and social structures, *we recommend that a greatly enlarged programme of health education, with a particular focus on schools, should be sponsored by the government. The DHSS and the DES, as well as other departments, would be involved, and at the local level health education in schools should be the joint responsibility of AHAs and LEAs.* Such a programme of health education would include new initiatives to use the media for publicity, a drive to involve young parents in a programme of health education arranged in conjunction with local clinics, and corresponding programmes for those caring for disabled people at home.

However, as we have seen, it is not sufficient to regard preventive medicine as a question of individual initiative and responsibility based upon more information, important though this is. We explained in Chapter 6 (pp. 110–125) how the very possibilities for such initiative and responsibility are themselves a function of social circumstances. We accept, for example, the importance of publicity for, and advice on, the importance of adequate diet and of exercise, for health. Yet, it is not always possible for people to act in what they know to be their own best interest, and there are strong occupational class trends of the familiar kind in recreation and exercise (Morris, 1979, 1980). While the value of exercise must be made clear through the media, *facilities* for exercise are also required. We therefore endorse the view of the House of Commons Expenditure Committee in 1977 (HC 169–i,

1977) that 'The Department of the Environment and local authorities [should] be required to make more adequate provision for physical recreation in any future major developments or redevelopments both public and private, particularly in inner city areas.' We consider also that additional grants for the establishment of facilities for physical recreation should be made available.

Vaccination and immunization are not used as much as they should be and in some cases, polio for instance, the rate of immunization has actually declined. Doctors and others in the NHS must convince members of the public of the importance of these preventive measures. Tougher measures against both smoking and alcoholism are also required. In general we would note that the government's response to the Expenditure Committee report (*Preventive Medicine*) contained in the White Paper *Prevention and Health* (Cmnd 7047, 1977) failed to provide the positive measures we believe necessary. *We recommend that national health goals should be established and stated by government after wide consultation and debate. Measures that might encourage the desirable changes in people's diet, exercise and smoking and drinking behaviour should be agreed among relevant agencies.*

In the case of smoking these measures are clear, and cannot rest upon exhortation alone. An anti-smoking policy must involve new forms of education and counselling but also preventive and stringent control measures. During recent years there has been disturbing evidence of a growing inequality in cigarette-smoking between rich and poor sections of the population. Between 1961 and 1980 men in professional occupations reduced their smoking by well over half, whereas unskilled workers reduced their consumption by much less. We take the view that unequal access to information about the effects of smoking has contributed powerfully to this trend. We recommend the adoption of the following measures, which should be seen not only as priorities in themselves, but as illustrative of the determined action which needs to be taken by government in relation to all necessary elements of a strategy for prevention:

i. *Legislation should be rapidly implemented to phase out all advertising of tobacco and sales promotion of tobacco products (except at place of purchase).*

ii. *Sponsorship of sporting and artistic activities by tobacco companies should be banned over a period of a few years, and meanwhile there should be stricter control of advertisement through sponsorship.*

iii. *Regular annual increases in duty on cigarettes in line with rises in income should be imposed, to ensure lower consumption.*

iv. *Tobacco companies should be required, in consultation with the trades* unions, to submit plans for the diversification of their products over a period of ten years with a view to the eventual phasing out of sales of harmful tobacco products at home and abroad.

v. *The provision of non-smoking areas in public places should steadily be extended.*

vi. *A counselling service should be made available in all health districts, and experiments in methods to help people reduce smoking should be encouraged.*

vii. *A stronger, well-presented health warning should appear on all cigarette packets and such advertisements as remain, together with information on the harmful constituents of cigarettes.*

We appreciate that cigarette-smoking has a very strong hold on a large section of the population and that no government can appear to be excessively authoritarian in its measures to eradicate it. None the less, international comparisons have shown that Britain is particularly weak in the policies it has pursued. For example, in 1976 Britain was seventeenth among twenty European countries in provision of non-smoking facilities and bans on smoking in public places (ASH, 1976; and see also House of Commons Expenditure Committee report, *Preventive Medicine*, 1977). We wish to stress the relevance of an anti-smoking campaign to any measures at district or national level to reduce inequalities in health.

4. Screening programmes

In this country, general screening programmes have usually been offered to, and accepted by, special high-income groups such as business executives, in whom compliance tends to be higher than average. The question naturally arises whether extension of such programmes to other groups would carry a high priority. On balance, the cost of population screening and the possible production of anxiety might well outweigh any likely benefits, even where there is a known higher incidence of disease in lower-income groups. A similar view on unselected screening is expressed by the Royal Commission on the National Health Service in para. 5.7 of their report.

Screening for particular disorders suffers from similar weaknesses. However there are exceptions. One is ante-natal screening, and we recommend that steps should be taken to educate women of child-bearing age in the importance of reporting suspected pregnancy at the earliest possible stage so that ante-natal care can be provided early in pregnancy. With early attendance at ante-natal clinics there are practicable programmes for screening for Down's syndrome and neural tube defects in the foetus.

The other exception is screening for hypertension in adults, which is both relatively simple and also becoming a more common practice.

In the light of the present state of knowledge we recommend that ante-natal screening for Down's syndrome and for neural tube defects (especially in high-risk areas) on the one hand, and in relation to adult disease for serious hypertension on the other, should be made generally available.

Before leaving this topic we should make it clear that this action programme is not complete and there is plenty of scope for local and voluntary initiatives. In particular we hope that Community Health Councils might be invited to monitor developments in their areas. What is most important is that standards of health, and knowledge about health, should be raised through face-to-face contacts and local group practices, clinics, day centres and schools.

A programme for ten special areas

What might be called an 'area deprivation' strategy has not so far been formally adopted in health policies although it has been followed up in the policies of other central departments, the Department of Education, the Home Office and the Department of the Environment, in the last twelve years. The concepts of 'Educational Priority Area', 'Community Development Project', 'Housing Action Areas' and 'Inner Cities' have become well known and the idea of 'positive discrimination' has been pursued with enthusiasm though with some loss of clarity and coherence.

We are conscious of both the advantages and disadvantages of different forms of 'positive discrimination'. The term itself can be misleading. It implies or rather tends to be taken to mean that individuals, groups or populations are singled out for preferential or above-average treatment to redress their deprivation. In practice, close examination suggests that new programmes are attempting only to bring services in a small number of places closer to the national standard by exceptional, supplementary action. There have been difficulties in selecting areas of deprivation because of lack of certain kinds of information. And the programmes have rarely been related either to the possibility of putting experimental schemes subsequently into wider practice or integrating them fully into the administration of services in their areas. On the other hand, when money is tight there is some advantage from developing demonstration, experimental and compensatory projects.

The argument is three-fold: (i) *for purposes of demonstration.* When resources are scarce the beneficial effects of adopting additional measures generally can be demonstrated for a few places; (ii) *for purposes of experiment.* When there are doubts about the best methods of developing certain features of services – for example early ante-natal attendance or collaboration in assessment and visiting of disabled or elderly people by the statutory and voluntary services – alternatives need to be tried and evaluated; (iii) *for purposes of developing reasoned priorities.* Comparatively little is known about the relationship between health service inputs and outputs and it is becoming more and more important to discover what additional developments, and rearrangements of service, are most economically related to high standards of health in a population and the reduction of inequalities in health.

We therefore recommend that the government should finance a special health and social development programme in a small number of selected areas, costing about £30 m. in 1981–2 (the figure given in Table 37). The following ten areas have the highest death rate, standardized for population and age/sex structure (see also Table 38, p. 141):

Salford
Tameside
Gateshead
Liverpool
South Tyneside
Tower Hamlets
Durham
Bolton
Wirral
North Tyneside

It should be pointed out that *within* these areas wide variations in mortality rates are to be found. In Gateshead, for example, the ratio of infant mortality in some wards to that in others in the mid-1970s was 3:1, but the wards with highest mortality were also wards with the smallest proportions of population in classes I and II.

We propose that in each of the ten areas experimental programmes within the three priority spheres should be introduced. We envisage that a proportion (say at least £2 m.) of the £30 m. should be reserved for evaluative research and statistical and information units, and that the remaining sum should be divided among the ten areas for development of the types of services listed below.

In order to gain a better sense of the problems to be found in these areas, two, Tower Hamlets and Gateshead, were visited by members of the Working Group. Gateshead is in fact already one of the three beneficiaries of the Comprehensive Community Programme. There is no doubt that the health and personal social services, and especially the community health services, in such areas of high mortality where there are also other indicators of severe health and social problems deserve additional government aid.

It is perfectly true of course that many innovations in service provision on a local basis, such as mobile clinics, are already being attempted in areas like the ten listed above. Many of these may indeed be proving successful in reaching those in particular need (the mobile clinic may well be an example), but these innovations are rarely (if ever) the subject of rigorous experimental assessment. It is this essential element of experimental assessment, the equivalent of the randomized clinical trial of clinical procedures, that we wish to stress, certainly in relation to child health, but also in relation to disabled people. Without this not only can change be on no more than an intuitive basis, but learning by one area from another is inhibited. Although the precise form of the proposals will need to take specific aspects of the local situation into account, and there is inevitably an element of overlap among our three spheres of activity, the following would appear to be among the candidates for action:

Making clinics more responsive to needs

i. Developing clinics in group practice and dispensing with hospital clinics dealing with large populations;

ii. Providing child play facilities;

iii. Combining child welfare and ante-natal clinics;

iv. Providing evening and weekend clinics;

v. Setting up counselling services for mothers, covering pregnancy, infant and child care and family health;

vi. Provision of detailed nutritional counselling to pregnant women by trained nutritionists;

vii. Additional or special clinics for (1) lone and/or young mothers (2) handicapped children.

viii. Experiments to enable mothers to keep in touch with each other independently of ante-natal and post-natal appointments by such developments as Young Family Centres and the provision of facilities to enable mothers and babies to meet together regularly.

Domiciliary services

i. More health visitors to (a) follow up all missed clinic appointments; (b) undergo special training in helping ethnic minorities; (c) provide better services at home for severely disabled people.

ii. Liaison between GPs and health visitors: GPs should notify health visitors of all pregnancies promptly, and all pregnant women should be visited. GPs can be encouraged either in existing partnerships or health centres, or, if single-handed, collaboratively, to set up special maternity and infant care groups (possibly, through notification of first births, for first-time mothers and, through child benefit registrations or schools, for mothers of four or more children).

iii. Active development of community nursing services so that nurses are trained to work in the community as well as hospital and prevent certain hospital admissions as well as provide services for disabled or chronically sick people when discharged;

iv. Planned joint services with: (a) social service departments; (b) voluntary bodies. Schemes should include attachment of social workers to primary care teams and use of voluntary visitors on a 'preventive' basis for the disabled.

v. Special counselling services (including services on income rights, heating and housing problems) for severely disabled (especially elderly and mentally handicapped) people and their relatives.

School health

i. Special programme of assessment of health of school children;

ii. Special health education programme in schools as an integral part of the curriculum.

Food

i. Special welfare food provision on greatly increased scale;

ii. Enhanced (free) school meals programme.

Smoking

Experimental anti-smoking programmes (educational and therapeutic).

Screening

Experimental services aimed specifically at older mothers and middle-aged people.

It should not be supposed that an additional area programme would simply add to existing resource allocation. It would contribute to a better balance between necessary and less necessary services and hence would contribute to the more economical satisfaction of the aims of the health and personal social services.

Conclusion and summary

We have identified three objectives for the administration of health and personal social services and recommend their adoption by the Secretary of State. They are:

i. To give children a better start in life.

ii. For disabled people, to reduce the risks of early death, to improve the quality of life whether in the community or in institutions, and as far as possible to reduce the need for the latter.

iii. To encourage good health among a larger proportion of the population by preventive and educational action.

We believe that if these three objectives are pursued vigorously inequalities in health can be reduced. To fulfil them we recommend a shift in the allocation of resources (Table 37). However, this in itself is not enough. It must be combined with an imaginative, and in part necessarily experimental, approach to the nature and delivery of care. District action programmes, by which we mean general programmes for the health and personal social services to be adopted nationwide and involving necessary modifications to the structure of care, should be developed in each area; and an additional experimental programme should be funded in ten areas of high mortality and adverse social conditions.

We have argued for changes in the planning of the development of health services and especially resource allocation. We believe that allocation of resources should be based on need. We recognize that there are difficulties in assessing need, but we agree that standardized mortality ratios (SM Rs) are a useful basis for broad allocation at regional level. At district level, further indicators of health care and social needs are called for. These should be developed as a matter of urgency, and appropriately to reinforce, supplement or modify allocation according to SM Rs.

Resources within the National Health Service and the personal social services should be shifted more sharply than so far accomplished towards community care, particularly towards ante-natal, post-natal and child health services, and home help and nursing services for disabled people. We see this as an important part of a strategy to break the links between social class or poverty and health.

In building up revenue targets it is not the current distribution of expenditure between services which should be used, but that which is aimed at in the planning of services. In particular, this process should reflect a higher share of resources for community care.

While we are aware of the problems of conceptualizing and measuring 'need', we consider there is no better alternative conceptual basis for developing a coherent rationale for the allocating of health care and resources, and recommend accordingly.

Our main recommendations for a district action programme can be listed under the three objectives set out above.

(A) *Health and welfare of mothers, pre-school and school children*

i. A non-means-tested scheme for free milk should now be introduced, beginning with couples with their first infant child and infant children in large families.

ii. Areas and districts should review the accessibility and facilities of all ante-natal and child health clinics in their areas and develop plans to increase utilization by mothers, particularly in the early months of pregnancy.

iii. Savings from the current decline in the school population should be used to finance new services for children under 5. A statutory obligation should be placed on local authorities to ensure adequate day care in their area for children under 5, and a minimum number of places (the number being raised after regular intervals) should be laid down centrally. Further steps should be taken to reorganize day nurseries and nursery schools so that both meet the needs of children for education *and* care.

iv. Every opportunity should be taken to link revitalized school health care with general practice, and intensify surveillance and follow-up both in areas of special need and for certain types of family.

Some necessary developments apply to other groups as well as children and mothers.

v. The professional associations as well as the Secretary of State and the health authorities should accept responsibility for making improvements in the quality and geographical coverage of general practice, especially in areas of high prevalence of ill-health and poor social conditions. Where the number or scope of work of general practitioners is inadequate in such areas we recommend health authorities to deploy or re-deploy an above-average number of community nurses, attached where possible to family practices. The distribution of general practitioners should be related not only to population but to medical need as indicated by SMRs, supplemented by other indicators, and the per capita basis of remuneration should be modified accordingly.

vi. An assessment which determines severity of disablement should be adopted as a guide to health service priorities, and this should be related to the limitation of activities rather than loss of faculty or type of handicap.

Although we attach priority to the implementation of this recommendation in the case of disabled children we believe that it must ultimately apply to all disabled people. We are aware that since 1977 most local councils have adopted classification of severity of disablement of people on their registers of the handicapped. We hope that this can be extended to people with all types of handicap and to patients in the health services.

(B) *The care of disabled people in their own homes*

i. A Working Group, to include representatives of voluntary organizations concerned with relevant client groups, should be set up to review: (a) whether sheltered housing should be a responsibility of social service or housing departments, and to make recommendations; and (b) the present functions and structure of hospital, residential and domiciliary care for the disabled elderly in relation to their needs, and to decide the best and most economical balance of future services.

ii. Joint funding should be developed and further funding of a more specific kind should be introduced, if necessary within the existing NHS budget, to encourage joint care programmes. A further sum should be reserved for payment to authorities putting forward joint programmes to give continuing care to disabled people – for example post-hospital follow-up schemes, pre-hospital support programmes for families, and support programmes for the severely incapacitated and terminally ill.

iii. Clear criteria for admission to, and continuing residence in, residential care should be agreed between the DHSS and the local authority associations, and steps taken to encourage rehabilitation and in particular to prevent homeless elderly people from being offered accommodation only in residential homes. Priority should be given to expansion of domiciliary care for those who are severely disabled in their own homes.

iv. The functions of home helps should be extended to permit a lot more work on behalf of disabled people; short courses of training, specialization of functions and the availability of mini-bus transport, especially to day centres, should be encouraged.

(C) *Prevention: the role of government*

i. An enlarged programme of *health education* should be sponsored by the government, and necessary arrangements made for optimal use of the mass media, especially television. Health education in schools should become the joint responsibility of LEAs and health authorities. However, we do not believe that an effective programme of preventive health can be a matter entirely for personal initiative and responsibilities. Commitment on the part of government is required, and has not so far been demonstrated, especially in so far as it involves (as it must) departments other than the DHSS. For example, there has been no major attempt at making more adequate provision for physical recreation in inner city area developments, as recommended by the Expenditure Committee in 1977. Additionally, the decline in recourse to vaccination and immunization (as in the case of polio) is worrying. Doctors and others in the NHS must be encouraged to convince members of the public of the importance of these preventive measures.

ii. *National health goals* should be established and stated by government after wide consultation and debate. Measures that might encourage the desirable changes in people's diet, exercise, and smoking and drinking behaviour should be agreed among relevant agencies.

Legislation, and fiscal and other financial measures, may be required and a wide range of social and economic policies involved. We see the time as now opportune for a major step forwards in the field of health and prevention.

iii. Stronger measures to *reduce cigarette smoking* must be adopted. Our recommendations here should be seen not only as a priority in themselves, but as illustrative of the determined action by government necessary in relation to all essential elements of a strategy for prevention. Measures should include those listed on pp. 154–5.

We have already recommended that steps be taken to increase utilization of ante-natal clinics, especially in the early months of pregnancy. Given early attendance there are practical programmes for screening for Down's syndrome and for neural tube defects in the foetus. In relation to adults screening for severe hypertension is practicable, and effective treatment is available.

iv. In the light of the present state of knowledge we recommend that ante-natal screening for neural tube defects (especially in high-risk areas) and Down's syndrome on the one hand, and in relation to adult disease for severe hypertension on the other, should be made generally available.

Additional funding for ten special areas

We recommend that the government should finance a special health and social development programme in a small number of selected areas, costing about £30m. in 1981–2. At least £2m. of this sum should be reserved for evaluation research and statistical and information units. The object would be both to provide special help to redress the undeniable disadvantages of people living in those areas, and also to permit special experiments to reduce ill-health and mortality, and provide better support for disabled people. Some possibilities have been illustrated particularly in connection with the development of more effective ante-natal services.

Chapter 9

The Wider Strategy

While the health care service can play a significant part in reducing inequalities in health, measures to reduce differences in material standards of living at work, in the home and in everyday social and community life are of even greater importance. We have in mind not simply a general reduction of inequalities in living standards, but a marked relative improvement in the living standards of the poorest people, together with measures to prevent new technologies, new working procedures, changes in styles of urban and rural living and the emergence of new social and political associations from undermining the existing living standards of some groups. Like the strategy we proposed for the health care system, the strategy to be adopted outside that system needs to be comprehensive and interlinked.

We therefore outline how a broad strategy might be made up and make certain specific proposals for inclusion in it. Specifically, we shall first indicate the general need for an anti-poverty strategy and then discuss and recommend selected measures, especially for families with children and disabled people.

A comprehensive anti-poverty strategy

Despite increases in GNP during the 1960s and 1970s successive governments have recognized the wide extent of poverty in the United Kingdom. In 1966 the report of a government survey of retirement pensioners estimated that up to 750,000 elderly people were living below national assistance standards – most of whom were eligible to draw national assistance and were not claiming it (Ministry of Pensions and National Insurance, 1966, p. 20). In 1967 a further report on a survey of families with children estimated that there were 160,000 families with half a million children who were living under the new supplementary benefit scale rates (Ministry of Social Security, 1967, p. iv). Further reports from the DHSS in the early 1970s tended to confirm the large numbers of people with incomes below the scale rates and yet who were in, or were dependants of people who were in, full-time employment.

(See for example, Howe, DHSS, 1971.) In Table 32 (p. 108) we showed, on the basis of DHSS estimates, that in 1977 over 14 million people (or 26.6 per cent of the population) had incomes of below or not more than 40 per cent above the supplementary benefit level (a cut-off chosen in recent government and independent studies). About a third were employed, or were dependants of people who were employed, and about two fifths were on retirement pensions. (Because of the under-representation of elderly, sick and disabled people, the use of a measure of 'normal' instead of 'current' income for people who have been sick or unemployed for less than three months, and the exclusion of those receiving supplementary benefit from the data, numbers with incomes below SB level are underestimated (Townsend, 1979, pp. 275–276 and 908–9).) At these levels of income there is evidence of multiple deprivation in diet, housing and environmental amenities, leisure activities and at work. Because of changes in earnings and numbers of dependants, the movement of people into and out of poverty is considerable, and while there is no hard evidence covering a long span of individual life it may be inferred, from survey or cross-sectional data, data about incomes currently and for the previous year, and New Earnings Survey data followed through for several years, that a very high proportion of manual workers experience poverty, or exceptionally low living standards, for a substantial part of the life-cycle.

There are differences of view about what in fact constitutes poverty. The main question is how far a definition acceptable to the government should depend on needs as assessed in contemporary society and how far on needs as measured by some historical bench-mark. Today's poor in Britain have more purchasing power than the poor of the depression years of the 1930s because of the growth of national prosperity. But they are living in a different kind of society, in which they have, and are held to have, different and often *additional* obligations as workers, parents, householders, friends and citizens. We therefore take the view that any historical standard of need becomes more and more unreal with the passage of time in a changing and especially growing economy even when it is repriced in accordance with rises in the cost of living. An effort has to be made every few years to redefine the standard itself in accordance with changing social conditions. As long ago as 1812 Adam Smith recognized the need for such redefinition, declaring that 'by necessities I understand, not only the commodities which are indispensably necessary for the support of life, but whatever the custom of the country renders it indecent for creditable people even of the lowest order to be without'. One of the last reports from the Supplementary Benefits Commission (*Annual Report for 1978*, 1979) expresses the point as follows: 'Poverty in urban industrial countries like Britain is a standard of living so low that it excludes and isolates people from the rest of the community. To keep out of poverty they must have an income which enables them to participate in the life of the community.'

We believe a comprehensive anti-poverty strategy must fall into two parts. The first is a fairer distribution of resources. Successive governments have supposed that they did not so much have to intervene in the initial production and determination of the structures of wealth and of gross incomes in the first place, as redistribute through taxation a slice of gross income to make up minimum subsistence incomes for the poor. But attempts to raise the relative living standards of the poor have been largely frustrated by growing opposition to progressive taxation as well as the diminution of its practical effects, and the steady growth relative to the employed population, of a dependent population. Different examples might be given of this growth. Between 1951 and 1976 the number of social security beneficiaries, excluding those receiving family allowances, grew from just over 7.5 million to 14.25 million, or by 88 per cent, while the total population increased from 51 million to 56 million, or by only 10 per cent. The government expects the number of social security beneficiaries to grow to over 15.5 million by 1982/3, even on an assumption of no growth in unemployment (*Social Trends*, 1979).

Governments have tried to meet this developing problem by lowering the tax threshold, so that people start paying tax on lower incomes, and shifting the balance from direct to indirect taxation. They have also tried to reduce the growing costs of categories already defined as dependent, as well as meeting the additional costs of new categories, by relying increasingly on the supplementary benefit and other means-tested schemes.

Even this solution, however, has now reached a dead end. In the 1980s either the living standards of the poor will not be maintained relative to the rest of the population as their numbers grow, or if living standards are maintained or efforts are made even to improve them, then radically new methods of financing them from the prosperous sections of the population will have to be devised.

We believe that a new approach to the fairer distribution of resources needs to be developed on the following basis. It starts with a recognition that the dispersion of resources *is* very unequal, and that the long-term objective of reducing by a moderate amount the proportionate share of, say, the top 30 per cent of income recipients would substantially augment the sum redistributed at present to the poor. If the share of disposable income of the top 30 per cent, as given in Report No. 5 (p. 75) of the Royal Commission on the Distribution of Income and Wealth, were only moderately reduced, the sum available for distribution in social security benefits, for example, could be doubled.

It follows that although it will be politically difficult, we shall need to develop greater restrictions on the amount of wealth which may be inherited and accumulated, together with more effective measures to inhibit the growth of top incomes and reduce present differentials in incomes. Quite how this might be done and how it might be democratically agreed and enforced is not something we can cope with here. But we believe it may be desirable to establish national minimum *and* maximum earnings (and family income) as indispensable elements of a nationally approved framework of incomes. Within statutory limits local and industrial or occupational wage-levels might be negotiated. Below we shall recommend certain measures to be included in such a strategy.

The second part of a comprehensive anti-poverty strategy is to encourage self-dependence and a high level of individual skill and autonomy as a basis for creating a more integrated society. We believe that this is possible only by raising the standards and broadening the content of education so that the need for advice or supervision from professionally trained personnel in medicine, nursing, law, housing, child care or administration is less marked and the capacity to undertake a range of skills is greater. This includes improving individual access to information about, and control over, what goes on in the immediate community as well as society generally, and conferring rights to employment and occupation and creating corresponding opportunities for such employment. There are of course possibilities of augmenting formal education and of introducing into the curriculum more studies of such subjects as health and nutrition, and (some believe) political education. Methods of enabling adults to have better access to knowledge, theoretical and practical, are equally important.

Most important, of course, is the right to fulfilling employment. Among a variety of possible measures there are two which deserve special mention. One is the energetic sponsorship of new industrial enterprise, based upon newly emerging technologies. In the face of a world recession in trade and severe foreign competition the nation cannot afford to be timid. The other measure is to expand employment within different branches of community service. Up to the present time the youth opportunities programme and similar schemes have done little more than provide some people who would otherwise count as unemployed with temporary, and ill-paid, employment. There are thousands of other men and women who have been unemployed for many months and whom it costs the state nearly as much to support as it would to employ in useful work.

Within this broad outline there are a number of specific measures which need to be picked out and given priority. In the rest of this chapter we shall develop certain priorities outside the health service which correspond with those picked out for the health care system.

A major concern must be families and children. Top priority must be given to measures which will enhance family living standards and reduce the high risk of children suffering those forms of deprivation and poverty which inhibit healthy development. In drawing this conclusion we are conscious in particular of two facts of the utmost importance:

i. There is evidence of substantial deprivation among young children (for example, Wilson and Herbert, 1978; Bone, 1977) and, after people of advanced age, they run the highest risk of all age groups of being in poverty (Townsend, 1979, p. 285);

ii. Those in middle and late middle life (mostly couples without dependants) have a standard of living, measured in relation to supplementary benefit scale rates, far higher than that of families in which there are young children (Townsend, 1979, Figure 7.1, p. 288). This difference between the young and the middle-aged appears to have grown more marked in recent years, partly because the rearing of children has been completed after the first twenty or twenty-five years of adult life by more married couples in each succeeding cohort, but partly because more married women have re-entered employment, non-manual occupations with strongly defined incremental pay scales have grown disproportionately, and more of the middle-aged have had access to cheap housing, through the completion of mortgage repayments or a relative fall in the real value of repayments, because of inflation. The implication for policy is therefore both that a need exists to direct more resources towards children and that checks might be placed on the tendencies for people in middle life without dependants to attract an undue share of additional national resources, so that adequate measures for young children might with less difficulty be financed. A complex programme covering financial well-being, education, nutrition and housing must be developed. In this chapter we have selected some principal measures to give effect to such a programme.

A policy for families and children

It is our view that *the abolition of child poverty should be adopted as a national goal for the 1980s.* We recognize that this requires a redistribution of financial resources far beyond anything achieved by past programmes, and is likely to be very costly. We recognize also that with the growth in national income it will become easier to find the resources for such an anti-poverty strategy.

The recommendations which we make below are presented as a modest *first step* which might now be taken towards such an objective.

1. Child benefit

The history of child benefit has proceeded through two stages and is now entering a third. The first was the campaign to establish family allowances, culminating in the Family Allowances Act 1945. History demonstrates the different motives of the participants in the campaign.

Family allowances were supported in the early days as a means of reducing inequalities between rich and poor, and between men and women. To socialists and feminists these were worthy ends in themselves but were not regarded as legitimate ends for government social policy until the Second World War. Broader support from Liberals and Conservatives was forthcoming only when family allowances became linked with other problems: a declining birth rate, poverty and malnutrition among children, the maintenance of work incentives and the need to curb inflation. These problems were established concerns of government and thus, by association, the legitimacy of family allowances was enhanced. (Land, 1975, p. 227)

The government agreed to pay 25p (less than the 40p recommended by Beveridge) per week for every dependent child excluding the first.

The second was the re-kindling, in the mid 1960s, of a campaign to extend family allowances to the first child in the family and simultaneously increase the real value of all family allowances, partly in exchange for the phasing-out of child tax allowances. This stage culminated not so much in the Child Benefit Act of 1975 as the completion of its phasing-in during the two years from April 1977 up to the budget of 1979.

Yet throughout this entire period government support for family allowances was never more than luke-warm. (For the recent history see *The Great Child Benefit Robbery*, 1977; Land, 1978; Field, 1978.) Between 1946 and 1978 pensions and other major social security benefits were increased on seventeen occasions: family allowances were increased only six times. This poor record must have some bearing on the relatively large numbers of wage-earning families found in national surveys and by statistical comparison with other countries to be living in poverty or on its margins, and on such indicators as the failure of infant mortality rates to decline as rapidly as those in some other countries.

Over the last half-decade the position has not substantially altered. Improvements introduced in the last years of the 1970s have done little more than restore the levels of the late 1960s, and inflation continues to eat into these 'improved' rates.

The importance of a properly endowed child benefit programme to the future health of the children of this country cannot be exaggerated. In its report for 1973 the Supplementary Benefits Commission stated: 'The adequacy of family benefits in general, and the new child benefits in particular, seems to us to be the most urgent concern of the whole field of social security' (Cmnd 6615, p. 17). This was reiterated in the next report, and in its response to the review which preceded the reorganization in 1979–80 of supplementary benefits, the Commission went on to affirm: 'Further improvements in child benefit and help for the unemployed – particularly in the form of better opportunities for work – are the most urgent of our proposals' (*Response of the SBC*, 1979, p. 40). From our different remit we endorse those priorities. *We recommend as an immediate goal the raising of the level of child benefit to 5.5 per cent of average gross male industrial earnings – in November 1979 equivalent to the rate for a dependent child of a sick or unemployed person (£5.70 including child benefit).* [The latter sum would have to be increased to about £7.00 by April 1981 to keep pace with earnings.] In the longer term, we recommend that larger child benefits be paid for older children, perhaps with age bands corresponding to those used by the SBC. Also in the longer term we should like to see age-related child benefit rates index-linked to average gross male industrial earnings, or, because an increasing number of women are entering employment and because in many cases both husband and wife have earnings, to some other perhaps more appropriate standard (such as average net disposable personal income). Otherwise it will be difficult to maintain the 'tax equity' as well as the 'need-serving' functions of child benefit. One-parent families present special problems, and in our view their financial needs too would be better met through an increase in child benefit.

2. Infant care allowance

A re-grouping of resources on behalf of young mothers with infants is required. In principle, needs at child-birth are met through the maternity benefit and maternity grant. But the grant has not been maintained during inflation and would need to be raised to *about £100* from the present £25.00, which has not been changed since 1969, to restore its value to that equivalent to the payment when first introduced. We recommend that *the grant should be increased to £100 to acknowledge the high cost to parents of child-birth.*

The special responsibilities of caring for young children, other than through the married man's tax allowance, are, however, not yet recognized in Britain. Some countries – Hungary is one example – have introduced infant care allowances in addition to child benefit. The case for the introduction of a home responsibility payment has been made in Britain:

The benefit would be paid to all families in which there were children or other dependants needing home care, except those where the social insurance benefit included a dependant's allowance for the wife. In the case of children such a benefit could presumably be paid simply by paying an addition to the child benefit payable for the eldest dependent child in the family, and it might be better presented in this way. The payment for the care of adult dependants would then be a separate benefit, a development of the present invalid care allowance. (Meade Report, p. 287. See also pp. 498–9)

The Child Poverty Action Group has proposed a more differentiated scheme, whereby women with children under 5 would receive twice as much as those with dependent children of school age (Select Committee on Tax Credit, Vol. II, pp. 325–30). The allowance could be phased in, beginning with all births after a particular date. *We recommend the introduction of an infant care allowance of approximately the same level as of child benefit, to be paid to mothers of children under 5 years of age, to be phased in over a period of five years.* As suggested later (p. 182), the cost might be met not so much from new resources as by restricting the scope of the married man's tax allowance to wives with dependants.

Beyond these initial elements of an anti-poverty strategy, a number of other steps need to be taken.

3. Pre-school education and day care

In Chapter 8 we recommended that local authorities should be under a statutory obligation to ensure an adequate provision of day care facilities (taking this term to include not only places in day nurseries but also in nursery classes, and with trained and registered childminders). To emphasize the importance we attach to this recommendation as well as its central place in any policy devoted to meeting the developmental needs of the under-5s, we further elaborate on it at this point.

It is well known that the desire for day provision on the part of parents of under-5s greatly exceeds what is currently available. A survey in 1977 found that 'provision was wanted for twice as many children as were receiving it, so that whilst 32 per cent of children were using facilities, they were desired for 64 per cent (Bone, 1977). The survey also found that this unmet need was class related (see Table 40) and that cost was a significant factor in inhibiting usage of such facilities by the children of working-class parents.

The same survey also looked at the demand for facilities judged on the basis of the number of 'disadvantaged' children who might benefit from them. The need criteria used, which more or less correspond to those leading to priority admission to day nursery, were as follows:

Need Group A	Need Group B
Child had only one parent	Child already allocated to need group A
or	or
Child had two parents but father's income was less than 150 per cent of long-term SB level	Child's mother was worried he might be handicapped (no definite diagnosis)
or	or
Child's household accommodation was two or more bedrooms less than standard	Child was 3 or 4 years old and soiled himself more than twice a week
or	or
Child's household accommodation was inadequate in four ways	Child's mother classified as 'depressed' or 'anxious'
or	or
Child was definitely handicapped (definite diagnosis)	Child had behaviour difficulties (on standard scaling)

On this basis, 15 per cent of all pre-school children fell into need group A and 36 per cent into need group B (which includes A). In fact only 28

Table 40: *Desire for day provisions for under-5s by occupational class**

	Occupational class				
	I	II	IIINM and IVNM	IIIM	IVM and V
Day provisions used	40	40	32	29	24
Not used but desired	22	26	36	33	39
Day provisions not desired	37	33	31	36	33
Total percentage†	100	100	100	100	100

*This survey used a different social class breakdown including a 'semi-skilled non-manual' (IVNM) category.
† Includes a few instances of 'not known'.

Source: Bone, 1977, Table 3.2.

per cent of all children in need group A were making use of any facilities for day provision and 30 per cent in need group B. All these figures are, perhaps, rather crude and we were unable to make a more detailed calculation of the need for day provision, but clearly the unmet need is substantial. What has to be remembered is that although the poorest children experience multiple forms of deprivation a very large proportion of children can be said to experience one or more forms of it. It is difficult to distinguish between deprived and non-deprived children and there are degrees of gradation, but by any calculation the unmet need is very substantial indeed. On the most conservative of estimates, the difference between the 36 per cent of children whose health and cognitive and psychological development (or financial circumstances, with the risks that might ultimately be entailed) make their need for day care overwhelming, and the 27 per cent of all under-5s who currently receive some provision (9 per cent of some 3¼ million under-5s in England and Wales), amounts to a minimum need of some 300,000 places. (This of course is based on the impossible assumption that all current places are taken up by children in need.) If the criterion of parental *desire* for some day provision were to be adopted, then the number of places available would have to be doubled, according to Bone's survey. This implies the creation of some 900,000 extra places in England and Wales.

The health and developmental needs of children, especially children rendered at risk by their environments, lead us to emphasize the importance of day facilities for under-5s catering for *both* these needs, and provided on an adequate scale. The precise pattern of such provision will necessarily vary with local conditions. It is clear that all available resources in the community must be used to their utmost: childminders, voluntary organizations and parents. More efficient use of existing facilities, such as nursery schools and classes, is also required. We are eager to see local authorities sponsoring collaborative arrangements between parents and others in the local community to complement the extended statutory services for the under-5s. This represents the principle of prevention at the local level. To reiterate the recommendation we have already made in Chapter 8: *We recommend that a statutory obligation should be placed on local authorities to ensure adequate day care in their area for children under 5, and that a minimum number of places (the number being raised after regular intervals) should be laid down centrally.*

Before leaving this topic it should also be made clear that different forms of provision – day care, nursery classes, playgroups, childminders etc. – cater for different needs. Local authority day nursery places are largely restricted to children regarded by social workers as 'at risk', or living in poor housing, or where a single parent is anxious to go to work. Staffed by nursery nurses they are less specifically concerned with the child's cognitive development than are nursery schools or classes. Our own view of the close relationship between health, social well-being and cognitive development in children leads us to argue for much greater integration between these forms of provision. This is of course widely acknowledged (as in the joint DES/DHSS circular *Co-ordination of Provision for the Under-Fives* of January 1978). So too is the need for more flexible provision of nursery education which caters better for the needs of working mothers (CPRS, 1978). It must be borne in mind that not only is the proportion of under-5s with mothers in paid employment rising (25 per cent in 1976) but that empty school places (due to the decline in the population of school age) represent an inefficient use of resources.

4. Nutrition: School milk and meals

In Chapter 6 we drew attention to the importance of the nutrition of children for their development. The DHSS booklet *Eating for Health* stated:

If all were to enjoy the best possible diet, the variation in average height and weight of different socio-economic groups in the United Kingdom would probably be less marked. The attained height of adults depends to some extent on nutrition during growth as children and in particular during the most rapid period of growth as babies. Any persistent restriction of diet in a young child may impair growth to such an extent that the affected child never reaches its full hereditary endowment of height. (DHSS, 1978, pp. 12–13)

This booklet goes on to point out the remarkable gains, notably in perinatal mortality, which followed wartime food rationing, despite the overall short-ages of food, and the introduction of such welfare foods as cod-liver oil and welfare orange juice: 'The unequal distribution of food, which had restricted the diet of families with low incomes, was made equitable by this system which included food subsidies on and control of the price of meat, bread, sugar, milk, potatoes, butter, margarine, cheese' (p. 16). The wartime scarcities which led to these policies fortunately no longer exist. It nevertheless remains important to *ensure* that all children are adequately nourished, if all are to achieve their potential for healthy growth.

In 1967 the Committee on Medical Aspects of Food Policy commissioned a nutritional survey of pre-school children, which was carried out in 1967–8 and eventually published in 1975. The acknowledged under-representation of large families, poor families and immigrant families in this survey must to some degree reduce the confidence which can be placed in the assessment of the adequacy of nutrition among these 'at risk' groups. The study nevertheless showed a clear decline in vitamin intake (A, C, D) with rising family size, and declining occupational class and income. Protein consumption rose with income though there was no trend with family size or occupational class. Calcium intake showed no trend. Total energy consumption actually rose with increasing family size, declining social class and falling income (except among the poorest families) – but some of this trend was certainly due to extra consumption of 'added sugar' – sweets, biscuits, soft drinks etc. – in poorer, larger working-class families (DHSS, *Reports on Health and Social Subjects*, No. 10, 1975).

Although the report concluded that there is 'no evidence that our pre-school children were underfed', it was hard to reconcile this with some of the statistics revealing under-nutrition and deprivation among some poor minorities. The proportions of children found to have intakes below 80 per cent of the recommended levels of specific nutrients varied from 20 to 30 per cent in some cases of energy, total protein and iron and around half were below that level for vitamin C (p. 27). The survey also showed the importance of milk in the diet of children. Although this was age-related, even at the age of $3\frac{1}{2}$ to $4\frac{1}{2}$ milk continued to provide, on average, 16 per cent of total energy intake, 26 per cent total protein and 62 per cent calcium and 42 per cent riboflavin.

A study of a sample of about 1,000 children resident in Kent aged 8–11 and 13–15, carried out between September 1968 and March 1970, throws some light on the nutritional status of older children. The sample was weighted to include larger numbers of children from occupational classes IV and V, large families, and families lacking fathers, and included a dietary assessment over a one-week period. Important conclusions were that: there was no clinical evidence of nutritional deficiency, and significant differences in average daily nutrient intake were not associated with class, number of siblings, or whether or not the mother worked. However, the *quality* of the child's diet (expressed in nutrients per 1,000 kcals) was class-related, falling with declining occupational class (Cook *et al.*, 1973). The study also showed that differences in nutrient intake and quality of diet were not explained by income differences when other class-related factors were held constant (Jacoby *et al.*, 1975).

Few today would therefore dissent from the view that given the importance of adequate nutrition for a child's development, and in the absence of a comprehensive food policy, attention quite properly focuses on school milk and meals. Between 1946 and 1968, one third of a pint of milk was available free every school day to all school children. From 1968 it ceased to be provided to secondary school pupils. In 1971 it was stopped for all children after the end of the school year of their seventh birthday, except where the school doctor recommended otherwise. Late in 1978 local authorities were once more permitted, though not obliged, to provide milk for 7–11-year-olds. In 1971, when the reduced availability of school milk was accompanied also by an increase in the price of school meals, the Committee on Medical Aspects of Food Policy (COMA) was asked to monitor the effects of these changes. Its Sub-Committee on Nutritional Surveillance issued an interim report in 1973 in which it indicated the dimensions on which effects would be monitored: height, obesity and dental caries were central.

So far as provision of milk to primary school children aged 7+ is concerned, the evidence, though not clear-cut, does not indicate a significant effect on growth. The earlier study of Kent children to which we referred above, conducted in 1968–70, found that, among 8–11-year-olds, those who regularly drank school milk had significantly higher intakes of energy, calcium and animal protein, but that this was not associated with height or other measures of nutritional status (Cook *et al.*, 1975a). The same research group, conducting a national surveillance study of a longitudinal kind under COMA auspices, found that between 1972 and 1973 the *growth* of 6–7-year-olds was not influenced by availability of school milk. The same held true of a special sample of children from occupational classes IV and V (formed by aggregation of successive age cohorts) (Cook *et al.*, in press). A study of 7–8-year-olds in South Wales, employing a sample deliberately weighted in favour of large families and occupational classes IV and V, also found that growth over twenty-one months was unaffected by provision of school milk (Baker *et al.*, 1978). Cook *et al.* summarize by stating 'the availability of school milk has no real effect on group well-being where drinking milk at home is almost universal'. It has however been suggested that linear growth may not be a wholly adequate measure of the benefits of milk consumption. Reed, for example, has referred to the need also to take account of bone status (Reed, 1978).

Moreover, current policy towards provision of school milk has to be judged, and developed, in the light of the continuing fall in household consumption of liquid milk revealed by the National Food Survey. In 1977 this average household consumption was 4.54 pints per person per week, compared with 4.71 pints in 1976 and 4.76 pints in 1975 (*National Food Survey*, 1977, p. 7). Moreover, the survey shows that in 1977 of 7–9-year-olds in lower-income families with three or more children, 12 per cent consumed less than 2 pints per week in the home, and over 25 per cent less than 3 pints.

It is clear that current policy must therefore be kept continuously under review, in the light of these trends, and also in the light of further research on growth and development.

The evidence in relation to provision of schools meals is more clear-cut. School meals are intended to provide about one third of the daily allowance of nutrients and energy for a child, and are recommended to contain, on average, 29g total protein, 880 kcals energy, and 32g fat. We have no evidence on the range in nutritional quality of the meals in practice provided. We have no doubt that this meal is the principal source of essential nutrients for many low-income children. Many may be offered a poor-quality evening meal, and many come to school without breakfast. (This sixteen hour 'fast' may well affect the child's powers of concentration, and hence his ability to profit from his schooling.) It should be regarded as a matter of importance – on education *and* health grounds – to ensure that all children receive a school meal or an adequate substitute at least during term time. To leave school children, especially young school children, to make their own free choices of what food is to be purchased would be wrong. Children will frequently prefer to consume foods high only in sugar and other sources of energy. As an inadequate substitute for a nutritious meal, this is likely to lead to increases in obesity and in dental caries.

Certainly, great importance has been attached to the nutritional variety and adequacy of school meals by a number of official committees. For example, the Working Party on the Nutritional Aspects of School Meals has commented: 'We do not think it is safe to assume that all children necessarily receive a satisfactory diet at home. We are especially concerned that all children should receive enough protein at school since any shortfall in the midday meal might easily not be made up in other meals or snacks and drinks consumed outside school' (DES, 1975, p. 8).

The survey of Kent children aged 8–11 and 13–15 offers some support to these views (Cook *et al.*, 1957b). Consumption of school meals (about 80 per cent overall) proved to be higher among children without fathers, with working mothers, etc. Distinguishing children who had all five, or no, school meals in the test week, the study found that younger children who had school meals had higher lunchtime intakes of nearly all nutrients (and more nutrients per 1,000 kcals) than those who did not. It also found that children from classes IV and V taking school meals obtained a very much higher proportion of their total weekday nutrient intake from their lunches than did children from the same classes who did not. The same was not consistently true of class I/II children.

Taking these findings together with known biases in the information, it is possible to conclude, with the authors, that

families without a father, those in lower social classes, and with large numbers of children relied to a greater extent than others on the intake of nutrients important for growth from school meals. This reliance may or may not depend on a conscious decision. The present study took place before recent large increases in the cost of protein-rich foods and such families may now rely even more on the food intake from school meals.

Yet the percentage of pupils receiving school meals (whether free or paid for) is falling: from 70 per cent in 1975 to 62 per cent in 1977. There are a number of explanations for this, partly cost, partly poor quality and partly administrative inertia.

At present local authorities administer a government scheme making school meals free for children of parents receiving supplementary benefit or parents whose income is below certain limits laid down in national regulations. In May 1978 about 15 per cent of school children were getting it. The limits are revised regularly, normally when supplementary benefit scales are increased. In recent years the Department of Education has estimated that about three quarters or four fifths of children eligible to receive school meals free are in fact receiving them. Others consider the right figure may be no higher than 60 per cent. Part of the problem arises in fluctuating incomes and frequent assessments or reassessments, but also in the fluctuation in standards of living brought about by changing household dependencies. Experimental campaigns by the government, especially in 1967 and 1968, have shown that take-up can be increased substantially through letters addressed directly to parents and through advertisements. But because of the numbers of children passing through the schools and fluctuations in family living standards, quite apart from the effect of inflation, higher take-up rates do not endure. Twice in 1977 and again in 1978 the Secretary of State for Education was asked to renew the approach adopted in 1967 and 1968 and issue a simple letter to all parents advising them about free school meals. Although an estimated half a million children were not obtaining free dinners although entitled to them, this invitation was not accepted. Whatever the exact short-fall, there is no doubt that it is substantial and there have been a large number of research studies demonstrating that means-tested exemption from charges for school meals is not a satisfactory way of helping poor families (Field, 1975; Field and Townsend, 1975; Townsend, 1979). A recent study has shown that there are even wide variations among areas with similar characteristics. 'This type of analysis can help to identify areas where there may be low take-up to inadequate efforts by local authorities and central Government' (Bradshaw and Weale, November 1978, p. 22).

In our view any reduction in the provision of school meals, or in eligibility for free meals, would mean putting further at risk the development of significant numbers of children. A study carried out by a team from St

Thomas's hospital showed that children receiving free school meals are significantly shorter than those who do not. Though the study was not designed to assess the value of school meals in terms of growth, the indicators are 'that free school meals are going to the right group of children and that withdrawal might well prejudice their future development' (Rona *et al.*, 1979).

Moreover from the perspective of this report it is clear to us that expansion in such provision, elimination of inequalities in provision, and elimination of the barrier to take-up which means-testing represents, are essential aspects of a policy designed to break the continuing association between social class and health in its broad sense. We are aware that much of what we have said about school meals is very different from current government policy and much orthodox opinion in the teaching profession. Nevertheless, in our view the evidence strongly supports a change of direction.

We believe that the number of schools with facilities for providing meals for all or most of their pupils can be increased, and that more consultation with parents about the organization and administration of meals would be an important element in raising quality. Children from families living in poverty sometimes attend schools lacking facilities for meals, and although others go home at mid-day for meals because their parents believe they can provide a more nutritious meal for them, there is no doubt that some would get meals at school if they were an automatic right.

At the same time the attitude of a school does seem to influence the consumption of school meals and the eating habits of children generally. It is therefore important that teachers should understand the importance of adequate nutrition for a child's physical development and concentration in school. Moreover meals are also a social occasion when some of the intentions of an education can be consolidated. School staff are apt to underestimate the value of social relationships that can be developed.

We accordingly recommend:

i. *That the provision of nutritionally adequate meals at all schools should be required of local authorities and that the service should be extended in areas where there is under-provision;*

ii. *That there should be regular consultations between local authority representatives, community dietitians, and parents and teachers from each school in turn, over the provision and quality of school meals;*

iii. *That meals be provided in schools without charge.*

5. Accidents to children

In Chapter 2 we drew attention to the fact that the steepest gradients in childhood mortality are found with accidents, a fact all the more disturbing now that accidents account for one third of deaths of children. Moreover there has been little improvement in this class differential over the period 1959–63 to 1970–72. It is remarkable, given these facts and given that there is a known course of action which could be put into effect rapidly without great cost to the public, that so little has been done.

Although accidents in the home are not the largest single group of accidents to children it is probably in the home that major progress could be made most quickly. Regulations could be introduced immediately to produce a safer home environment, and these could be applied stringently to public housing. Risks of falls from roofs and staircases can be reduced without great cost by safer design, and the positioning of windows could make a substantial difference. Much could also be done to reduce the dangers from household equipment, especially the dangers from fire and burning. There is still a great deal which can be done to reduce the risks of poisoning by the clearer packaging of dangerous substances. Although important work has been done by RoSPA and the Health Education Council in educating the public, it is likely that 'safety devices built in as a constant feature of the environment are more effective than attempts to alter people's behaviour'.

The problem, as elsewhere in preventive health, is that there is no focus for government action, and although the new voluntary Joint Committee on Accident Prevention may help, a clear initiative is needed from a powerful Minister if adequate co-operation is to be forthcoming from the Department of Environment, the Department of Trade and the local authorities.

Outside the home, traffic accidents are the single most serious factor. Despite the laudable attempts of town planners to separate traffic from pedestrian ways there are still over 700 children killed on the roads each year. Although it is important to give due recognition to the accident prevention campaign in schools and elsewhere, the only reliable long-term answer is to give children safe areas in which to play. Moreover, if there is a need to step up safety education it is the motorists, especially young drivers, who should be the target. Motorists need to be made more sensitive to the presence of children in the areas they drive through, and conscious of the way in which children behave on the roads.

Apart from the specific dangers of road traffic it is likely that the working-class child lives in a more dangerous physical environment than middle-class children. Derelict slum housing about to be cleared, deserted canals, mineshafts and factories, railway lines, rubbish tips; all these present potential dangers to the child in the urban-industrial area. Given the ingenuity and sense of adventure of children it is difficult to conceive of such areas ever being made danger-free, but more could be done by environmental health authorities to monitor the risks and keep the owners of such properties up to the required standards of safety protection.

When accidents happen there is no lack of concern for the child to see he gets the best treatment possible, but unfortunately public attitudes soon return to their normal complacency. If childhood accidents are to be reduced and the gradients between social classes minimized, the issues must be kept before the public gaze. The voluntary organizations both local and national have the important role here in stimulating the political will for action.

We recommend that the Health Education Council should be provided with sufficient funds to mount child accident prevention programmes in conjunction with the Royal Society for the Prevention of Accidents. These programmes should be particularly directed at local authority planners, engineers and architects.

6. Paying for the programme

The annual cost of our proposals might be roughly as follows:

1. increase in child benefit from £4 to £5.70 for each child	£970 m.
2. infant care allowance (on assumption that there are 600,000 births per annum)	£180 m. in first full year (rising to £870 m. after five years)
3. expansion of day provision	£150 m.
4. free school meals	£200 m.

We do not regard it as our function, nor are we technically equipped, to make specific recommendations as to how the costs of our proposals might best be met. We would suggest, however, that the additional tax allowance now made to married couples without dependants be considered as a source of savings to be set against the proposals we have made for increasing the well-being of families and children.

The wider community

1. A comprehensive disability allowance

Evidence suggests that disabled people are more likely than their able-bodied contemporaries to be living below or on the poverty line (Table 41). There are also indications that among disabled people income is inversely related to severity of disability (Townsend, 1979, Chapter 20; Harris *et al.*, Vol. III, 1972).

As a result of such findings, a strong case developed in the late 1960s and early 1970s for the introduction of a comprehensive allowance scheme for all disabled people. It was felt that equally disabled people were very unequally treated under different income security schemes. While there were fairly elaborate provisions for the war-disabled and those disabled in industry, those who were injured in home accidents, people who were congenitally handicapped, disabled housewives and disabled elderly people had little or no entitlement to additional income. But in 1974, while adopting different positive proposals for improvement of income benefit, both major political parties failed to commit themselves in principle to the phased introduction of a comprehensive scheme. Today major anomalies still exist and have been documented at length (Royal Commission on the Distribution of Income and Wealth, Report No. 6 (1978), Chapter 4, pp. 115–19, 152). The Snowdon Working Party stated (1976): 'The evidence clearly demonstrates the need for the fundamental methodical reforms advocated (by DIG and the Disability Alliance) to rectify the anomalous structure of disablement benefits whereby two people with equal handicaps and needs may end up with widely differing financial help to meet them' (p. 9).

After allowing for savings because of existing schemes, the introduction of a disablement allowance by stages has been costed at a little under £500 m. (Disability Alliance, 1978). Included in this estimate of costs are disabled elderly people. We believe that the establishment of such an allowance represents a major means of reducing inequalities of health and restoring equity between disabled and non-disabled people and we recommend accordingly that *a comprehensive disablement allowance for people of all ages should be introduced by stages at the earliest possible date*. There are of course other supporting measures, especially in improving the employment and wage rates of disabled people, which are important. We believe that the first step must be to establish equity for the most severely disabled people of all. At the present time there is a choice between introducing an allowance at a low rate, say £6, for all severely disabled children and adults in sup-

Table 41: *Numbers and percentage of total and disabled population living in poverty or on the margins of poverty (1977)*

Level of income	Total population		All ages (000s)	Disabled over pensionable age (000s)	Sick and disabled under pensionable age (000s)	Disabled of all ages (000s)
	Over pensionable age (000s)	Under pensionable age (000s)				
Below supplementary benefit level	760	1,270	2,020	250	70	320
Receiving supplementary benefit	2,000	2,160	4,160	790	240	1,030
At or up to 40 per cent above supplementary benefit level	3,010	4,830	7,840	860	400	1,260
More than 40 per cent above supplementary benefit level	2,750	35,960	38,720	690	1,380	2,070
Total	8,520	44,220	52,740	2,590	2,090	4,680
Below supplementary benefit level	8.9	2.9	3.8	9.7	3.3	6.8
Receiving supplementary benefit	23.5	4.9	7.9	30.5	11.5	22.0
At or up to 40 per cent above supplementary benefit level	35.3	10.9	14.9	33.2	19.1	26.9
More than 40 per cent above supplementary benefit level	32.3	81.3	73.4	26.6	66.0	44.2
Total	100	100	100	100	100	100

Note: The estimate of sick and disabled persons under pension age applies to those sick or disabled for three months or more and includes dependants in the income unit.

Source: DHSS (SR3), Analysis of FES 1977 for columns 1, 2, 3 and 5. The distribution of column 4 is based on evidence about those of pensionable age 'appreciably or severely incapacitated' in Townsend, 1979, p. 712 (and survey printout).

plementation of other income benefits and developing a scheme parallel to the main features of the war pensions and industrial injuries disablement pension schemes (into which the mobility allowance might be merged), introducing first a 100 per cent rate of payment (equivalent to the rate of £38 per week payable from November 1979 under the war and industrial injury disablement pension schemes). Even if the aggregate national sum available under either option were the same we believe the latter would be the right option. The net cost of establishing an allowance for 100 per cent disablement (the first stage) for people of all ages and causes of disablement would be approximately £24 m. at November 1979. (At November 1978 the cost was estimated by the Disability Alliance at £20 m.)

2. Improving working conditions

In our studies of inequalities in health we have been struck by the ill-developed nature of conceptions of deprivation at work. Although the hazards of working in particular industries have been carefully documented in the past, and detailed studies made of hours of work and conditions in which strikes and other conflicts between management and labour have occurred, generalizations of working conditions or work situations across industries have not been pursued very far. The point can be made by analogy. Generalization about diets, clothing, leisure-time pursuits, housing conditions and even environmental conditions are readily made, and standards of overcrowding, facilities and amenities are defined nationally for housing and are commonly understood and discussed. As a consequence, discussion about remedial measures is based upon statistics about the members who live in overcrowded or slum housing and lack particular amenities. Such standards do not exist for the world of work. There are no measures of the number in employment who have bad or deprived conditions of work, the industries or areas in which they are to be found and the degree to which they also experience bad housing conditions and low incomes.

So far as health is concerned the emphasis has been on safety and specific identifiable risks of accident or of contamination by toxic substances. For example, the Robens Committee, set up by the government in 1972 to look at health and safety at work, did not attempt to collect evidence about safety and health in relation to general working conditions. Neither did it attempt to pursue the interrelationship between fatal accidents, deaths and injuries arising from prescribed industrial diseases and occupational mortality and morbidity, for each of which independent sets of statistics exist. The importance of reports on occupational mortality to a better understanding of the work situation as well as to the circumstances outside work remains to be plumbed.

In Table 42 the wide differences between some occupations are illustrated. The marked gradient from sedentary non-manual to heavy unskilled manual work, which with some exceptions the table shows, is accompanied by wide variations between the mortality rates for specific occupations within each occupational class.

Table 42: *Mortality by occupation unit: men aged 15–64 (selected examples)*

Occupations units	Direct age-standardized death rate (per 100,000)	SMR
Relatively low death rate		
University teachers	287	49
Physiotherapists	297	55
Paper products' makers	302	50
Managers in building and contracting	319	54
Local authority senior officers	342	57
Company secretaries and registrars	362	60
Ministers of the Crown, MPs, senior government officials	371	61
Office managers	377	64
Primary and secondary school teachers	396	66
Sales managers	421	70
Architects, town planners	443	74
Civil service executive officers	467	78
Postmen	484	81
Medical practitioners	494	81
Relatively high death rate		
Coalminers (underground)	822	141
Leather products' makers	895	147
Shoemakers and shoe repairers	898	156
Machine-tool operators	934	156
Watch repairers	946	154
Coalminers (above ground)	972	160
Steel erectors, riggers	992	164
Fishermen	1028	171
Deck, engineering officers and pilots, ship	1040	175
Labourers and unskilled workers, all industries	1247	201
Policemen	1270	109
Deck and engine-room ratings	1385	233
Bricklayers' labourers	1644	274

Specific and well-known work hazards, characteristic of many manual occupations and differing from one to another, are one factor. But in the light of the analysis of this report, we consider that in addition to these hazards, and associated risks of accidents and of certain occupational injuries and diseases, a wider variety of job characteristics may be implicated. These would include security and material rewards of employment, patterns of work (such as shift-work), conditions of work and welfare and other amenities. However, the *extent* to which work conditions, interpreted in this broad fashion, are responsible for differences in rates of occupational mortality remains uncertain and requires further research (although the work of Fox and Adelstein, 1978, suggests that other and more general elements of the 'class' factor may also be important).

Nevertheless, reduction in inequalities between occupations in their work conditions may be of importance in reducing inequalities in health. *We recommend that representatives of the DHSS, the Department of Employment, the Health and Safety Commission, together with representatives of the trade unions and CBI, should draw up minimally acceptable and desirable standards of work; security; conditions and amenities; pay; and welfare or fringe benefits.*

A national study found that in 1968, 20 per cent of the employed population, representing over 4½ million people, had poor conditions of work (Townsend, 1979, p. 453) and a list of individual examples from a random sample called attention 'both to the diverse hazards and frequent poor conditions of manual work'. They also suggested uncertainty or ignorance on the part of many about the hazards involved with dust, noise and chemicals. Doctors, for whatever motives, as well as employers, may withhold information, and the importance of the role of union safety representatives (the legal right to which workers have enjoyed since October 1978) is clear. There is still a tendency to accept poor working conditions as an inevitable accompaniment of particular jobs, and attention needs to be devoted to the question of enlightened standards which *can* be introduced, as in public housing and town planning. Among the matters which we hope will attract more attention are facilities for meals, warmth and shelter from bad weather, a dry and secure place for outer clothes and other belongings, access to a telephone, availability of first aid and first aid equipment, 'unsocial' hours, warmth, humidity, light, noise, availability of machinery to avoid or reduce the physical stress of the work, washing and toilet facilities, and facilities for changing clothes. In many of these instances regulations under current legislation are non-existent, or partial, or complex and confused (TUC, 1978).

What we are calling for is more preventive work by government departments, employers and unions and would hope to see a shift of emphasis in the work and functions (as defined by legislation) of the Health and Safety Commission and Executive, and the Employment Medical Advisory Service. It is fair to say that although there are provisions for both bodies to follow positive policies they are at present restricting their activities to specific hazards and general questions of safety. The need for legislation defining acceptable working conditions and basic employer welfare benefits is urgent.

3. Housing

Housing conditions are associated with health status in a variety of ways. Inadequate heating (or a form of heating which is too expensive for a resident) can give rise to hypothermia in old people (Wicks, 1978). Over-crowding can produce respiratory and other diseases (some of the studies are reviewed by Benjamin, 1965, who, however, pointed out that class explained more of the inter-area variance than housing). It can also produce adverse psychological responses and may give rise to mental illness.

High-rise living is known to have deleterious consequences for children. In some areas (such as Tower Hamlets) TB is common among the homeless vagrants and represents a real problem for the health authorities.

It is families with children, and especially large poor families with many children, who are most likely to be living in overcrowded conditions. Over-crowding adds to the health risk under which working-class children labour, and the extent to which such children, and especially those born into larger families, are being brought up in overcrowded conditions is unacceptable. Bone's survey of pre-school children found that 10 per cent of them inhabited dwellings inadequate on at least one of four criteria: overcrowding; no separate unshared bathroom; shared WC; no sole use of permanent fixed water supply (Bone, 1977, p. 26). But this percentage was highly class-related: 3 per cent in class 1 increasing to 29 per cent in classes IVM and V. For some of these children there is a risk of ill-health throughout life, because chronic respiratory disorder (for example) in childhood is an all too effective predictor of adult suffering. Such considerations tend not to weigh as heavily with housing departments as they should.

We showed in Chapter 2 (on the basis of the new OPCS longitudinal study) that there is an association between tenure and SMR, independent of the occupational class of the household head. Of course, this does not demonstrate that being a tenant *causes* ill-health. But we wish to stress that the rights and privileges which are so unequally associated with housing tenures *are* associated with health both in the negative sense of freedom from ascertainable clinical disease and in the positive sense of welfare. Fear of eviction is the sort of situation which has been related to clinical depression in women (Brown and Harris, 1978). Security in housing does have health benefits and should be equally available for all. Accessible play areas for young children are vital and owner-occupation often meets this need, by virtue of garden space available. Gardening is one of the most popular outdoor leisure pursuits for people in Britain who have access to a garden, and we have already indicated the health benefits attaching to active outdoor recreation. We believe that there must be a much greater extension of the rights and privileges associated with owner-occupation to the tenants both of local authorities and private landlords. Health considerations are certainly among the factors which justify such extension.

In order to allow good housing policy to play its part in promoting health we consider the *most essential step is to co-ordinate policies in the council and owner-occupied sectors*. The changing pattern of housing tenure has been leading to problems of access to housing for the poor and mobile, which have gradually become more acute in recent years. Only in part has that been due to the decline of the privately tenanted sector. In part it has been due to rigidities in the management of council housing, together with a very uneven flow of new housing. There needs to be a more vigorous programme of rehabilitating rented housing which is obsolescent. This includes many thousands of council housing units. Comparisons need to be made between the tenures so that priorities in improvement policies and the allocation of resources, but also new standards of space, amenities and access to play areas, including gardens, can be determined. *We therefore recommend a substantial increase in local authority improvement spending under the 1974 Housing Act*.

But broad equity between the sectors must be achieved in other ways as well. The previous administration tended over-optimistically to reiterate the view that there was no longer any overall shortage of housing, while allowing local authorities to refuse housing to such groups as homeless single and childless couples. Secondly, the rights and opportunities of tenants need to be reviewed in the light of conditions enjoyed by owner-occupiers. The previous administration experimented with a 'Tenants Charter', but in some respects this was half-hearted, and among the most important measures to be introduced are freedom of movement, freedom to carry out minor improvements and repairs (and benefit from them in the terms under which the tenancy may be passed on subsequently), greater freedom in the rules of residence and more effective representation in the management of housing estates.

A number of housing charities believe that local authorities have been interpreting their obligations under the 1977 Housing Act rather too loosely. Some councils are exploiting the loop-hole of 'intentional' homelessness while others have taken advantage of the fact that the Act does not impose any standard for homeless accommodation. Moreover the Act allows local authorities to refuse accommodation to single homeless and childless couples.

We believe the legislation on homelessness deserves strengthening along the lines recommended by the housing charities. With the dwindling of the private rented sector, local authorities must provide rented accommodation for a wider range of households, including the single and childless, who are unable to enter owner-occupation. *We recommend, therefore, that local councils should increasingly be encouraged to widen their responsibilities to provide for all types of housing need which arise in their localities.*

We also believe that the sale of council houses badly needs to be placed in the changing context of the relationship between the different housing sectors. If, in the long run, a better balance could be struck in the conditions enjoyed in the two sectors, objections in principle to interchange of stock could be minimized. But indiscriminate sales may worsen housing opportunities for families needing to rent; they may reduce the quality and attractiveness of the council housing stock; and, by introducing a new basis to the relationships in many estates, they may affect the cohesion of existing communities.

Finally, a further aspect of the relationship of housing to health concerns the housing of the disabled. If the institutionalization of disabled people is to be avoided, as we have recommended, there must be sufficient provision of sheltered and adapted housing. This implies a much better working relationship than is frequently the case today between social service and health authorities and housing departments, so that necessary adaptations to dwellings can be obtained easily. We have elsewhere recommended that serious consideration should be given to the possibility that social service departments assume responsibility for the management of sheltered housing. A second aspect of such collaboration concerns policy over the re-housing of disabled people, which seems generally to be inadequate. The Working Party on Housing of the Central Council for the Disabled wrote in its (1976) report, of local authority policy:

... unless the disabled person *also* happens to be living in overcrowded accommodation with few amenities, his position on the waiting list is likely to be low indeed, even if he has the maximum medical points possible ... But the housing difficulties that are peculiarly associated with disability ... require a separate type of solution ... the priority given to disabled people should not be decided at an individual level – as tends to happen at present – but should be decided within an overall strategy of priorities within the housing policies of the authority as a whole.

... [T]he existing system means that a disabled person may not be rehoused until the situation has reached a desperate pitch. By that time the move may really be too late: his physical condition may have deteriorated too rapidly – possibly aggravated by his inadequate housing – so that he is not in a position to settle into a new environment ... Where a disabled child is concerned, to move the family to suitable housing when the child is grown and the situation has reached breaking point may work against the educational development of the child and his ability to learn to cope independently ... (Working Party on Housing of the Central Council for the Disabled, *Towards a Housing Policy for Disabled People*, 1976, pp. 58–60)

We therefore recommend that special funding on the lines of joint funding for health and local authorities should be developed by the government to encourage better planning and management of housing, including adaptations and provisions of necessary facilities and services for disabled people of all ages by social service and housing departments. This recommendation is on the same lines as that made by the Snowdon Working Party, which argued that one immediate priority was 'to develop a real choice of life-style for the severely disabled through joint planning and financing by the Department of Environment and the Department of Health and Social Security'. We also endorse that Working Party's plea for the 'urgent establishment of schemes for non-institutional accommodation for severely disabled people living in every area of the country' (Report of the Snowdon Working Party, 1976, p. 32).

Towards a co-ordinated government policy

We believe that an improvement in the nation's health should be a priority for government. The evidence of various indicators of mortality shows that in this respect Britain's record in recent years has not compared well with other countries. We should like to see drastic reduction in rates not only of perinatal and infant death, but of the extent of chronic and acute sickness and of physical and mental handicap, much of which develops in the period around birth, as well as promotion of health in its positive sense of 'well-being' and functional capacities.

The costs of sickness – the direct costs of the National Health Service, of supporting care, and of sickness benefits, as well as the indirect costs of sickness for productivity – though not easily calculated *in toto*, are very great. Acute care provided in hospitals demands an increasing share of national resources. The financial costs of bouts of ill-health, chronic sickness and handicap to individuals and families – especially poor families – are frequently immense. These private costs are not fully captured in financial terms. The alarming prevalence of depressive illness, especially among working-class women, cannot be without profound effect on family life and child-rearing, irrespective of the misery the women themselves suffer.

It is also our view that the attempt to reduce, and ultimately eliminate, the social inequalities in health which we have documented offers the greatest opportunity for achieving this overall improvement. It is surely no accident that, as we showed in Chapter 5, those countries such as Sweden and Norway which have particularly low mortality rates also seem to have greatly reduced inequalities in health. This argument is quite separate from the argument – to which we also attach great weight – that simple justice demands that this attempt be made.

Part of what is required involves attention to those regions and small areas, for example in the inner cities, where concentrations of sickness are high and levels of service provision low. Another part involves attention to improvements that can be made and new measures that can be introduced for families in all areas of the country. A third part involves attention to the vicious cycle by which, through a variety of mechanisms, poor families are locked into material, educational, environmental and social disadvantage for a lifetime and even sometimes for generations, with all that this implies for their health.

Our analysis has shown that inequalities in health have complex, multi-causal explanations. They seem to be rooted in the general nature and conditions of activity, both in work and outside work, and in the styles and standards of living of different occupational classes. Some factors have a clear causal association with ill-health: inadequate access to and use of (particularly preventive) health services; the hazards attaching to certain occupations; overcrowded and damp housing, and smoking. But there remains much that is probably not explicable in any direct fashion and meanwhile must be attributed to the pervasive effects of the class structure.

It follows, and our recommendations reflect this fact, that a reduction in health inequalities depends upon contributions from within many policy areas. Our recommendations have involved reference to community and preventive health services, to the personal social services, to health education in a very broad sense including the promotion of physical recreation, to social security measures, to uptake of school meals, to improvement in working conditions, to housing and to measures directed specifically at minority groups and notably in inner city areas. Clearly such a range of services and policies involves many departments of central government: DHSS, DOE, DES, DE (and the Health and Safety Executive), MAFF, the Department of Transport and the Home Office, as well as the Welsh

Office and the Scottish and Northern Ireland Offices. Our objectives will be achieved *only* if each department makes its appropriate contribution and this in turn, we believe, requires a better degree of co-ordination than presently exists. The fact is of course that housing, leisure, education and other relevant policies have important objectives traditionally associated with them: there is always the danger that this potential contribution to the reduction of health inequalities will receive little attention in departmental decision-making.

Machinery of government

For this reason, *we propose recourse to Cabinet Office machinery*, in order to ensure that this does not happen. A broadly based programme of work needs to be explicitly adopted, and seen to be adopted. Our analysis is very much within the spirit of the Joint Approach to Social Policy (JASP), and we envisage that a Ministerial and, secondly, an Officials Committee, corresponding to those established under JASP, would provide appropriate fora: we would certainly wish the Central Policy Review Staff to be involved. It would then be for these committees regularly to consider developments and to propose developments in relevant policies from the perspective of health inequalities. Major initiatory responsibility would be vested in the Department of Health and Social Security, and we envisage the two committees being chaired respectively by a Minister and by a senior DHSS official having major responsibilities for health and prevention. They should have before them relevant statistical material, provided by government statisticians, and relating to changes in uptake and provision of services, changes in relevant distributional aspects, and evaluation of policies. New methods of transmitting the information reviewed would have to be adopted, not least because it would need to reach a wider, public audience.

There would have to be local counterparts of national co-ordinating machinery, and a joint approach to health policies would be necessary at local level to a greater extent than at present. This might take a number of forms – inter-departmental action, for example, to reduce environmental pollution and squalor and redistribute skilled manpower to communities where the risk to health was high, acceleration of joint funding schemes, and the establishment of joint committees for planning and for the monitoring and supervision of hazards to health.

The need for a joint framework for social policies has been increasingly acknowledged in recent years. Of course, a co-ordinated approach could achieve a variety of objectives. One would be simply to warn central departments earlier than at present of forthcoming plans of individual departments.

Another would be to work out more smoothly than at present the over-lapping functions of two or more departments (a good example is nursery education and day nurseries – in the interests of child health). But others would include large-scale reallocation of priorities, for example a decision to reduce the rate of expansion in expenditure of one major social service, such as education, and greatly increase the rate of expansion of another, such as health. For this, however, support independent of central administration may be required, as we argue below. We appreciate that there are a wide range of possibilities, and that a joint approach could mean a great deal or very little. But considering that the government accepted, in the early 1960s, the need for plans for hospitals and for community care and that since then there have been a stream of plans of wider and lesser scope, developments in the actual co-ordination of social policies, as distinct from the reorganization of individual services, has been slow. (The progress since the JASP initiative has been traced by Plowden, 1977.) No doubt this is attributable to the precedence currently given not only by the government but by other bodies to economic over social objectives in policy, to a failure to appreciate the interrelatedness of policies, but above all to the stultifying effects of public expenditure control which has dominated all attempts of planning during the mid- and late-1970s. In the last fifteen years social planning has been, for the central government, predominantly one of control of public expenditure (Diamond, 1975; Glennerster, 1976; Heclo and Wildavsky, 1976). It would be wrong to suppose that this form of control could be changed overnight, because it has penetrated administrative practice at every level, or that there will not be financial and institutional constraints on more imaginative social planning. But the formulation of new social objectives by the government can only be sustained if certain changes are also made in the mechanisms of planning and administration.

A Health Development Council

Finally, and distinct from this machinery, although with the same objective in mind, we *propose the establishment of a Health Development Council*. This would be an independent body, with a small staff of seconded civil servants. Strictly its functions would be advisory, but the Council would, we recommend, play a key role in social planning. It would be invited to consider and spell out longer-term strategies to reduce inequalities of health and improve general family living standards, evaluate progress in relation to this aim, with particular reference to the roles of particular government and local authority departments and services, marshal a range of outside expertise, consult the public at every stage and play a major part in explaining the need for certain developments. Opportunities should be afforded to it of commenting on, and contributing to, plans, including expenditure programmes, which are to be published by the government on matters relevant to its concerns.

Although we are aware of the arguments against proliferation of such standing advisory bodies, we make this proposal for three particular reasons. First, the existence of the Council would provide some guarantee that, when initial enthusiasm had abated, the attempt at inter-departmental coordination through a Cabinet sub-committee did not 'run out of steam', as some would say happened with the original JASP initiative. Second, by virtue of its public existence such a body could serve both to keep the issue of health inequalities in the public eye, and enlist widespread support. This is essential, and the development of comparable machinery at the local level (perhaps based on existing Health and Local Authority Joint Consultative Committees) could be invaluable. Third, the Council would be in a position to assist Ministers in formulating longer-term strategies.

Conclusion and summary

In discussing actions outside the health care system which need to be taken to diminish inequalities of health we have been necessarily selective in this chapter. We have attempted to pay heed to those factors which are correlated with the *degree* of inequalities. Secondly, we have tried to confine ourselves to matters which are immediately practicable, in political, economic and administrative terms, which will none the less, properly maintained, exert a long-term structural effect. And thirdly, we have continued to feel it right to give priority to young children and mothers, disabled people and measures concerned with prevention. Above all we consider that the *abolition of child poverty should be adopted as a national goal for the 1980s*. We recognize that this requires a redistribution of financial resources far beyond anything achieved by past programmes and is likely to be very costly. Our recommendations here are presented as a modest first step which might be taken towards this objective.

i. As an immediate goal the level of child benefit should be increased to $5\frac{1}{2}$ per cent of average gross male industrial earnings, or £5.70 at November 1979 prices.

ii. Larger child benefits should be progressively introduced for older children, after further examination of the needs of children and consideration of the practice in some other countries.

iii. The maternity grant should be increased to £100.

iv. We recommend the introduction of an infant care allowance over a five-year period, beginning with all babies born in the year following a date to be chosen by the government.

Beyond these initial elements of an anti-poverty strategy, a number of other steps need to be taken.

v. Provision of meals at school should be regarded as a right. Representatives of local authorities and community dietitians should be invited to meet representatives of parents and teachers of particular schools at regular intervals during the year to seek agreement to the provision and quality of meals. Meals in schools should be provided without charge.

vi. The Health Education Council should be provided with sufficient funds to mount child accident-prevention programmes in conjunction with the Royal Society for the Prevention of Accidents. These programmes should be particularly directed at local authority planners, engineers and architects.

vii. A comprehensive disablement allowance for people of all ages should be introduced by stages at the earliest possible date, beginning with people with 100 per cent disablement.

viii. Representatives of the DHSS and DE, HSE, together with representatives of the trade unions and CBI, should draw up minimally acceptable and desirable conditions of work.

ix. Government departments, employers and unions should devote more attention to preventive health through work organization, conditions and amenities, and in other ways. There should be a similar shift of emphasis in the work and functions of the Health and Safety Commission and Executive, and the Employment Medical Advisory Service.

x. Local authority spending on housing improvements under the 1974 Housing Act should be substantially increased.

xi. Local authorities should increasingly be encouraged to widen their responsibilities to provide for all types of housing need which arise in their localities.

xii. Policies directed towards the public and private housing sectors need to be better co-ordinated.

xiii. Special funding, on the lines of joint funding, for health and local authorities should be developed by the government to encourage better planning and management of housing, including adaptations and provision of necessary facilities and services for disabled people of all ages by social service and housing departments.

Our recommendations reflect the fact that the reduction in health inequalities depends upon contributions from within many policy areas, and necessarily involving a number of government departments. Our objectives will be achieved *only* if each department makes its appropriate contribution. This in turn requires a greater degree of co-ordination than exists at present.

xiv. Greater co-ordination between government departments in the administration of health-related policies is required, by establishing interdepartmental machinery in the Cabinet Office under a Cabinet subcommittee along the lines of that established under the Joint Approach to Social Policy (JASP), with the Central Policy Review staff also involved. Local counterparts of national co-ordinating bodies also need to be established.

xv. A Health Development Council should be established with an independent membership to play a key advisory and planning role in relation to a collaborative national policy to reduce inequalities in health.

Summary and Recommendations

1. Most recent data show marked differences in mortality rates between the occupational classes, for both sexes and at all ages. At birth and in the first month of life, twice as many babies of 'unskilled manual' parents (class V) die as do babies of professional class parents (class I) and in the next eleven months nearly three times as many boys and more than three times as many girls. In later childhood the ratio of deaths in class V to deaths in class I falls to 1.5–2.0, but increases again in early adult life, before falling again in middle and old age. A class gradient can be observed for most causes of death, being particularly steep in the case of diseases of the respiratory system. Available data on chronic sickness tend to parallel those on mortality. Thus self-reported rates of long-standing illness (as defined in the General Household Survey) are twice as high among unskilled manual males and $2\frac{1}{2}$ times as high among their wives as among the professional classes. In the case of acute sickness (short-term ill-health, also as defined in the General Household Survey) the gradients are less clear.

2. The lack of improvement, and in some respects deterioration, of the health experience of the unskilled and semi-skilled manual classes (class V and IV), relative to class I, throughout the 1960s and early 1970s is striking. Despite the decline in the rate of infant mortality (death within the first year of life) in each class, the difference in rate between the lowest classes (IV and V combined) and the highest (I and II combined) actually increased between 1959–63 and 1970–72.

3. Inequalities exist also in the utilization of health services, particularly and most worryingly of the preventive services. Here, severe under-utilization by the working classes is a complex result of under-provision in working-class areas and of costs (financial and psychological) of attendance which are not, in this case, outweighed by disruption of normal activities by sickness. In the case of GP, and hospital in-patient and out-patient attendance, the situation is less clear. Moreover it becomes more difficult to interpret such data as exist, notably because of the (as yet unresolved) problem of relating utilization to need. Broadly speaking, the evidence suggests that working-class people make more use of GP services for themselves (though not for their children) than do middle-class people, but that they may receive less good care. Moreover, it is possible that this extra usage does not fully reflect the true differences in need for care, as shown by mortality and morbidity figures. Similar increases in the use of hospital services, both in-patient and out-patient, with declining occupational class are found, though data are scanty, and possible explanations complex.

4. Comparison of the British experience with that of other industrial countries, on the basis of overall mortality rates, shows that British perinatal and infant mortality

rates have been distinctly higher and are still somewhat higher than those of the four Nordic countries and of the Netherlands, and comparable with those of the Federal Republic of Germany. Adult mortality patterns, especially for men in the younger age groups, compare reasonably with other Western industrialized countries: the comparison for women is less satisfactory. The rate of improvement in perinatal mortality experienced by Britain over the period since 1960 has been comparable to that of most other countries. In the case of infant mortality (which is generally held to reflect social conditions more than does perinatal mortality) all comparable countries – especially France – have shown a greater improvement than has Britain. France, like Britain and most other countries considered (though apparently not Sweden), shows significant class and regional inequalities in health experience. It is noteworthy that through the 1960s the ratio of the post-neonatal death rate (between four weeks and one year) in the least favoured social group to that in the most favoured fell substantially in France. Also important probably has been a major French effort to improve both attendance rates for ante-natal care and the quality of such care. Very high rates of early attendance are also characteristic of the Nordic countries; so too are high rates of attendance at child welfare clinics, combined with extensive 'outreach' capacity. In Finland, for example, whenever an appointment at a health centre is missed, a health visitor makes a domiciliary call. We regard it as significant also that in Finland health authorities report not on the volume of services provided, but on the proportion of all pregnant women and of all children of appropriate ages who register with Health Centres.

5. We do not believe there to be any single and *simple explanation* of the complex data we have assembled. While there are a number of quite distinct theoretical approaches to explanation we wish to stress the importance of differences in material conditions of life. *In our view much of the evidence on social inequalities in health can be adequately understood in terms of specific features of the socio-economic environment:* features (such as work accidents, overcrowding, cigarette-smoking) which are strongly class-related in Britain and also have clear causal significance. Other aspects of the evidence indicate the importance of the health services and particularly preventive services. Ante-natal care is probably important in preventing perinatal death, and the international evidence suggests that much can be done to improve ante-natal care and its uptake. But beyond this there is undoubtedly much which cannot be understood in terms of the impact of so specific factors, but only in terms of the more diffuse consequences of the class structure: poverty, working conditions, and deprivation in its various forms. It is this acknowledgement of the *multicausal* nature of health inequalities, within which inequalities in the material conditions of living loom large, which informs and structures our policy recommendations. These draw also upon another aspect of our interpretation of the evidence. We have concluded that early childhood is the period of life at which intervention could most hopefully weaken the continuing association between health and class. There is, for example, abundant evidence that inadequately treated bouts of childhood illness 'cast long shadows forward', as the Court Committee put it.

6. We have been able to draw upon national statistics relating to health and mortality of exceptional quality and scope, as well as upon a broad range of research studies. We have, however, been conscious of certain inadequacies in the statistics and of major lacunae in the research. For example it is extremely difficult to examine health experience and health service utilization, in relation to income and wealth.

7. Moreover, we consider that the *form* of administrative statistics may both reflect and determine (as the Finnish example quoted above suggests) the way in which the adequacy and the performance of a service is understood: hence it acquires considerable importance. We also consider systematic knowledge of the use made of the various health services by different social groups to be inadequate: though this is less the case in Scotland than in England and Wales. While conscious of the difficulties in collecting and reporting of occupational characteristics within the context of administrative returns, we feel that further thought must be given to how such difficulties might be overcome. We argue that the monitoring of *ill-health* (itself so imperfect) should evolve into a system also of monitoring *health* in relation to social and environmental conditions. One area in which progress could be made is in relation to the development of children, and we propose certain modifications to community health statistics.

(1) *We recommend that school health statistics should routinely provide, in relation to occupational class, the results of tests of hearing, vision; and measures of height and weight. As a first step we recommend that local health authorities, in consultation with educational authorities, select a representative sample of schools in which assessments on a routine basis be initiated.* (Chapter 7, p. 127)

8. *Accidents* are not only responsible for fully one-third of child deaths, but show (with respiratory disease) the steepest of class gradients.

9. We should like to see progress towards routine collection and reporting of accidents to children indicating the circumstances, the age and the occupational class of the parents. In relation to traffic accidents there should be better liaison between the NHS and the police, both centrally and locally.

(2) *We therefore recommend that representatives of appropriate government departments (Health and Social Security, Education and Science, Home Office, Environment, Trade, Transport), as well as of the NHS and of the police, should consider how progress might rapidly be made in improving the information on accidents to children.* (Chapter 7, p. 128)

10. The Child Accident Prevention Committee, if suitably constituted and supported, might provide a suitable forum for such discussions, to be followed by appropriate action by government departments. Further,

(3) *We recommend that the Health Education Council should be provided with sufficient funds to mount child accident prevention programmes in conjunction with the Royal Society for the Prevention of Accidents. These programmes should be*

particularly directed at local authority planners, engineers and architects. (Chapter 9, p. 182)

11. While drawing attention to the importance of the National Food Survey as the major source of information on the food purchase (and hence diet) of the population, we are conscious of the scope for its improvement.

(4) *We recommend that consideration be given to the development of the National Food Survey into a more effective instrument of nutritional surveillance in relation to health, through which various 'at risk' groups could also be identified and studied.* (Chapter 7, p. 128)

12. We have already referred to the difficulties in examining health experience in relation to income and wealth. In principle this can be done through the General Household Survey in which the measure of income now (since 1979) corresponds to the more satisfactory measure employed in the Family Expenditure Survey. However,

(5) *We recommend that in the General Household Survey steps should be taken (not necessarily in every year) to develop a more comprehensive measure of income, or command over resources, through either (a) a means of modifying such a measure with estimates of total wealth or at least some of the more prevalent forms of wealth, such as housing and savings, or (b) the integration of income and wealth, employing a method of, for example, annuitization.* (Chapter 1, p. 41)

13. Beyond this, we feel that a comprehensive research strategy is needed. This is best regarded as implying the need for careful studies of a wide range of variables implicated in ill-health, in their *interaction over time*, and *conducted in a small number of places*. Such variables will necessarily include social conditions (and the interactions of a variety of social policies) as well as individual and behavioural factors. Any major advance in our understanding of the nature of health inequalities, and of the reason for their perpetuation, will require complex research of a multi-disciplinary kind.

(6) *The importance of the problem of social inequalities in health, and their causes, as an area for further research needs to be emphasized. We recommend that it be adopted as a research priority by the DHSS and that steps be taken to enlist the expertise of the Medical Research Council (MRC), as well as the Social Science Research Council (SSRC), in the initiation of a programme of research. Such research represents a particularly appropriate area for departmental commissioning of research from the MRC.* (Chapter 7, p. 129)

14. We turn now to our recommendations for policy, which we have divided into those relating to the health and personal social services, and those relating to a range of other social policies. Three objectives underpin our recommendations, and we recommend their adoption by the Secretary of State:

- To give children a better start in life.

– To encourage good health among a larger proportion of the population by preventive and educational action.

– For disabled people, to reduce the risks of early death, to improve the quality of life whether in the community or in institutions, and as far as possible to reduce the need for the latter.

Thirty years of the Welfare State and of the National Health Service have achieved little in reducing social inequalities in health. But we believe that if these three objectives are pursued vigorously inequalities in health can now be reduced.

15. We believe that *allocation of resources* should be based on need. We recognize that there are difficulties in assessing need, but we agree that standardized mortality ratios (SMRs) are a useful basis for broad allocation at regional level. At district level, further indicators of health care and social needs are called for. These should be developed as a matter of urgency, and used appropriately to reinforce, supplement or modify allocation according to SMRs. *However, a shift of resources is not enough: it must be combined with an imaginative (and in part necessarily experimental) approach to health care and its delivery.*

(7) *Resources within the National Health Service and the personal social services should be shifted more sharply than so far accomplished towards community care, particularly towards ante-natal, post-natal and child health services, and home-help and nursing services for disabled people. We see this as an important part of a strategy to break the links between social class or poverty and health.* (Chapter 8, p. 136)

(8) *The professional associations as well as the Secretary of State and the health authorities should accept responsibility for making improvements in the quality and geographical coverage of general practice, especially in areas of high prevalence of ill-health and poor social conditions. Where the number or scope of work of general practitioners is inadequate in such areas we recommend health authorities to deploy or redeploy an above-average number of community nurses attached where possible to family practice. The distribution of general practitioners should be related not only to population but to medical need, as indicated by SMRs, supplemented by other indicators, and the per capita basis of remuneration should be modified accordingly.* (Chapter 8, p. 145)

16. Moreover, we consider that greater integration between the planning process (and the establishment of priorities) and resources allocation is needed. In particular the establishment of revenue targets should be based not upon the current distribution of expenditure between services, but that distribution which it is sought to bring about through planning guidelines: including a greater share for community health.

(9) *We recommend that the resources to be allocated should be based upon the future planned share for different services, including a higher share for community health.* (Chapter 8, p. 142)

17. Our further health service-related recommendations, designed to implement the objectives set out above, fall into two groups.

18. We first outline the elements of what we have called a District Action Programme. By this we mean a general programme for the health and personal social services to be adopted nationwide, and involving necessary modifications to the structure of care.

19. Second, we recommend an experimental programme, involving provision of certain services on an experimental basis in ten areas of particularly high mortality and adverse social conditions, and for which special funds are sought.

District action programme

Health and Welfare of mothers and pre-school and school children

(10) *A non-means-tested scheme for free milk should now be introduced beginning with couples with their first infant child and infant children in large families.* (Chapter 8, p. 134)

(11) *Areas and districts should review the accessibility and facilities of all ante-natal and child-health clinics in their areas and take steps to increase utilization by mothers, particularly in the early months of pregnancy.* (Chapter 8, p. 143)

(12) *Savings from the current decline in the school population should be used to finance new services for children under 5. A statutory obligation should be placed on local authorities to ensure adequate day care in their area for children under 5, and that a minimum number of places (the number being raised after regular intervals) should be laid down centrally. Further steps should be taken to reorganize day nurseries and nursery schools so that both meet the needs of children for education and care.* (Chapter 8, p. 146 and Chapter 9, p. 174)

(13) *Every opportunity should be taken to link revitalized school health care with general practice, and intensify surveillance and follow-up both in areas of special need and for certain types of family.* (Chapter 8, p. 147)

20. Some necessary developments apply to other groups as well as children and mothers.

(14) *An assessment which determines severity of disablement should be adopted as a guide to health and personal social service priorities of the individual, and this should be related to the limitation of activities rather than loss of faculty or type of handicap.* (Chapter 8, p. 147)

21. Though we attach priority to the implementation of this recommendation in the care of disabled children, we believe that it must ultimately apply to all disabled people. We recognize that such assessments are now an acknowledged part of 'good practice' in providing for the disabled – we are anxious that they should become standard practice.

The care of elderly and disabled people in their own homes

22. The meaning of community care should be clarified and much greater emphasis given to tendencies favoured (but insufficiently specified) in recent government planning documents. (See Recommendation 7.)

(15) *A Working Group should be set up to consider:*

   i. *the present functions and structure of hospital, residential and domiciliary care for the disabled elderly in relation to their needs, in order to determine the best and most economical balance of future services;* (Chapter 8, p. 151)
   and

   ii. *whether sheltered housing should be a responsibility of social service or of housing departments, and to make recommendations.* (Chapter 8, p. 149)

(16) *Joint funding should be developed and further funding of a more specific kind should be introduced, if necessary within the existing NHS budget to encourage joint care programmes. A further sum should be reserved for payment to authorities putting forward joint programmes to give continuing care to disabled people – for example, post-hospital follow-up schemes, pre-hospital support programmes for families, and support programmes for the severely incapacitated and terminally ill.* (Chapter 8, p. 152)

(17) *Criteria for admission to, and for continuing residence in, residential care should be agreed between the DHSS and the local authority associations, and steps taken to encourage rehabilitation, and in particular to prevent homeless elderly people from being offered accommodation only in residential homes. Priority should be given to expansion of domiciliary care for those who are severely disabled in their own homes.* (Chapter 8, p. 149)

(18) *The functions of home helps should be extended to permit a lot more work on behalf of disabled people; short courses of training, specialization of functions and the availability of mini-bus transport, especially to day centres, should be encouraged.* (Chapter 8, p. 152)

Prevention: the role of government

23. Effective prevention requires not only individual initiative but a real commitment by the DHSS and other government departments. Our analysis has shown the many ways in which people's behaviour is constrained by structural and environmental factors over which they have no control. Physical recreation, for example, is hardly possible in inner city areas unless steps are taken to ensure that facilities are provided. Similarly, government initiatives are required in relation to diet and to the consumption of alcohol. Legislation and fiscal and other financial measures may be required and a wide range of social and economic policies involved. We see the time as now opportune for a major step forwards in the field of health and prevention.

(19) *National health goals should be established and stated by government after wide consultation and debate. Measures that might encourage the desirable changes in people's diet, exercise and smoking and drinking behaviour should be agreed among relevant agencies.* (Chapter 8, p. 154)

(20) *An enlarged programme of health education should be sponsored by the government, and necessary arrangements made for optimal use of the mass media, especially television. Health education in schools should become the joint responsibility of LEAs and health authorities.* (Chapter 8, p. 153)

24. The following recommendation should be seen not only as a priority in itself but as illustrative of the determined action by government necessary in relation to many elements of a strategy for prevention:

(21) *Stronger measures should be adopted to reduce cigarette-smoking. These would include:*

a. *Legislation should be rapidly implemented to phase out all advertising and sales promotion of tobacco products (except at place of purchase);*

b. *Sponsorship of sporting and artistic activities by tobacco companies should be banned over a period of a few years, and meanwhile there should be stricter control of advertisement through sponsorship;*

c. *Regular annual increases in duty on cigarettes in line with rises in income should be imposed, to ensure lower consumption;*

d. *Tobacco companies should be required, in consultation with trades unions, to submit plans for the diversification of their products over a period of ten years with a view to the eventual phasing out of sales of harmful tobacco products at home and abroad;*

e. *The provision of non-smoking areas in public places should steadily be extended;*

f. *A counselling service should be made available in all health districts, and experiment encouraged in methods to help people reduce cigarette-smoking;*

g. *A stronger well-presented health warning should appear on all cigarette packets and such advertisements as remain, together with information on the harmful constituents of cigarettes.* (Chapter 8, p. 154)

We have already recommended that steps be taken to increase utilization of antenatal clinics, particularly in the early months of pregnancy (Recommendation 11). Given early attendance there are practical programmes for screening for Down's Syndrome and for neural tube defects in the foetus. In relation to adult disease, screening for severe hypertension is practicable, and effective treatment is available.

(22) *In the light of the present stage of knowledge we recommend that screening for neural tube defects (especially in high risk areas) and Down's Syndrome on the one hand, and for severe hypertension in adults on the other, should be made generally available.* (Chapter 8, p. 156)

Additional funding for ten special areas

(23) *We recommend that the government should finance a special health and social development programme in a small number of selected areas, costing about £30 m. in 1981-2.* (Chapter 8, p. 157)

25. At least £2 m. of this sum should be reserved for evaluation research and statistical and information units. The object would be both to provide special help to redress the undeniable disadvantages of people living in those areas but also to permit special experiments to reduce ill-health and mortality, and provide better support for disabled people. Some elements of such a programme are illustrated, particularly in connection with the development of more effective ante-natal services. (Chapter 8, pp. 157-9)

Measures to be taken outside the health services

26. In discussing actions outside the Health Care system which need to be taken to diminish inequalities of health we have been necessarily selective. We have attempted to pay heed to those factors which are correlated with the *degree* of inequalities. Secondly, we have tried to confine ourselves to matters which are practicable now, in political, economic and administrative terms, and which will none the less, properly maintained, exert a long-term structural effect. Third, we have continued to feel it right to give priority to young children and mothers, disabled people, and measures concerned with prevention.

27. Above all, we consider that the *abolition of child-poverty* should be adopted as a national goal for the 1980s. We recognize that this requires a redistribution of financial resources far beyond anything achieved by past programmes, and is likely to be very costly. Recommendations 24-27 are presented as a modest first step which might be taken towards this objective.

(24) *As an immediate goal the level of child benefit should be increased to $5\frac{1}{2}$ per cent of average gross male industrial earnings, or £5.70 at November 1979 prices.* (Chapter 9, p. 171)

(25) *Larger child benefits should be progressively introduced for older children, after further examination of the needs of children and consideration of the practice in some other countries.* (Chapter 9, pp. 170-71)

(26) *The maternity grant should be increased to £100.* (Chapter 9, p. 171)

(27) *An infant care allowance should be introduced over a five-year period, beginning with all babies born in the year following a date to be chosen by the government.* (Chapter 9, p. 172)

28. Beyond these initial elements of an anti-poverty strategy, a number of other steps need to be taken. These include steps to reduce accidents to children, to which we have referred above (Recommendation 3). Further.

(28) *Provision of meals at school should be regarded as a right. Representatives of local authorities and community dietitians should be invited to meet representatives of parents and teachers of particular schools at regular intervals during the year to seek agreement to the provision and quality of meals. Meals in schools should be provided without charge.* (Chapter 9, p. 180)

(29) *A comprehensive disablement allowance for people of all ages should be introduced by stages at the earliest possible date, beginning with people with 100 per cent disablement.* (Chapter 9, p. 183)

(30) *Representatives of the DHSS and DE, HSE, together with representatives of trade unions and CBI, should draw up minimally acceptable and desirable conditions of work.* (Chapter 9, p. 187)

(31) *Government departments, employers and unions should devote more attention to preventive health through work organization, conditions and amenities, and in other ways. There should be a similar shift of emphasis in the work and function of the Health and Safety Commission and Executive, and the Employment Medical Advisory Service.* (Chapter 9, pp. 187–8)

(32) *Local authority spending on housing improvements under the 1974 Housing Act should be substantially increased.* (Chapter 9, p. 189)

(33) *Local authorities should increasingly be encouraged to widen their responsibilities to provide for all types of housing need which arise in their localities.* (Chapter 9, p. 190)

(34) *Policies directed towards the public and private housing sectors need to be better co-ordinated.* (Chapter 9, p. 189)

(35) *Special funding, on the lines of joint funding, for health and local authorities should be developed by the government to encourage better planning and management of housing, including adaptations and provision of necessary facilities and services for disabled people of all ages by social services and housing departments.* (Chapter 9, p. 191)

29. Our recommendations reflect the fact that reduction in health inequalities depends upon contributions from within many policy areas, and necessarily involves a number of government departments. Our objectives will be achieved *only* if each department makes its appropriate contribution. This in turn requires a greater degree of co-ordination than exists at present.

(36) *Greater co-ordination between government departments in the administration of health-related policies is required, by establishing inter-departmental machinery in the Cabinet Office under a Cabinet sub-committee along the lines of that established under the Joint Approach to Social Policy (JASP), with the Central Policy Review Staff also involved. Local counterparts of national co-ordinating bodies also need to be established.* (Chapter 9, p. 193)

(37) *A Health Development Council should be established with an independent membership to play a key advisory and planning role in relation to a collaborative national policy to reduce inequalities in health.* (Chapter 9, p. 194)

30. Within such co-ordinating machinery major initiatory responsibility will be vested in the Department of Health and Social Security, and we recommend that the Cabinet Committees we have proposed be chaired by a Minister, and by a senior DHSS official respectively, having major responsibility for health and prevention. Similarly it will be an important obligation upon the DHSS to ensure the effective operation of the Health Development Council.

Appendix of Tables

Table 1. *Percentage of economically active men in different occupational classes 1931, 1951, 1961, 1966, 1971 (England and Wales)*

Occupational class (Registrar General)	1931*		1951*		1961†	1966‡	1971
I	1.8	(2.2)	2.7	(3.2)	4.0	4.5	5.0
II	12.0	(12.8)	12.8	(14.3)	14.9	15.7	18.2
III	47.8	(48.9)	51.5	(53.4)	51.6	50.6	50.3
IV	25.5	(18.2)	23.3	(16.2)	20.5	20.6	18.0
V	12.9	(17.8)	9.7	(12.9)	8.9	8.8	8.4
Total	100.0	(100.0)	100.0	(100.0)	100.0	100.0	100.0
Number (thousands)	13,247		14,064		14,649	15,686	15,668

* Percentages have been weighted to allow for changes in classification between the 1931 and 1961 censuses: *The General Report, 1951* and *The General Report, 1961* allow the percentage change for each class between censuses to be calculated and the figures to be adjusted accordingly to bring both the 1931 and 1951 figures into line with the 1960 classification. Figures in brackets are based on the classification at that time. The estimates for 1931 and 1951 are necessarily crude – the latter partly for the reasons carefully listed in *The General Report 1961*, p. 193.

† Substantial numbers who were unclassified in 1961 (518,000) have been excluded. (Only 84,034 unclassified in 1971 have been excluded.)

‡ Percentages given are for economically active and retired males. Substantial numbers who were unclassified in 1966 have been excluded.

Sources: Census 1951, *General Report*, Table 66, p. 147; Census 1961, *General Report*, Table 55, p. 193; Census 1966, *Economic Activity Tables Part III*, Table 30, p. 416; Census 1971, *Economic Activity Tables Part IV*, Table 29, p. 96 (10 per cent sample).

Table 2. *Percentage of men aged 25 and over in five occupational classes in 1951, 1961 and 1971 (England and Wales), according to 1960 (and 1970) classification of occupations*

Age	Year	Professional I	Intermediate II	Skilled III	Partly skilled IV	Unskilled V
	1951	2.1	7 9	54.5	26.8	8.6
25–34	1961	5.3	12.9	55.9	18.4	7.5
	1971	7.5	18.1	53.2	15.2	6.1
	1951	2.1	12.6	49.0	26.7	9.8
35–44	1961	4.3	16.6	53.4	18.8	6.9
	1971	6.2	20.7	50.5	16.1	6.6
	1951	1.9	13.1	43.5	28.5	12.9
45–54	1961	3.3	18.8	48.5	21.1	8.2
	1971	4.8	21.3	48.8	17.9	7.3
	1951	1.8	14.0	39.9	29.5	14.7
55–9	1961	2.9	17.8	45.0	23.5	10.8
	1971	4.0	20.5	46.3	20.2	9.1
	1951	1.7	13.6	38.3	30.0	16.3
60–64	1961	2.6	17.5	42.7	24.5	12.7
	1971	3.7	18.7	45.3	21.4	10.9
	1951	1.9	13.3	42.6	29.1	15.0
65–9	1961	2.7	17.9	41.8	24.5	13.1
	1971	3.4	17.2	43.2	22.5	13 7
	1951	1.9	14.7	46.1	25.4	11.8
70+	1961	3.2	19.2	41.7	24.0	11.9
	1971	3.3	19.4	44.0	21.6	11.8
	1951	1.9	11.9	47.1	27.5	11.5
Total	1961	3.9	16.8	49.3	21.0	9.0
	1971	5.2	19.7	48.8	18.1	8.3

Note: An attempt has been made in this table to allow for changes of classification brought about after the introduction of the 1960 Classification of Occupations (there were only a few further changes in the 1970 classification and the figures from the 1961 and 1971 Censuses did not need to be adjusted before being compared). However, for 1951 we have changed the figures for each age-group by the proportion suggested for all age-groups in an exercise reported in *The General Report*, General Register Office, Census 1961, Great Britain, HMSO, 1968, p. 193. The 1961 data were re-classified for a sample using the 1951 classification and compared with the 1961 data classified according to the 1960 Classification of Occupations. We have worked back to the 1951 data for social classes and changed the figures for each class by the proportion suggested by the results of the exercise carried out by the GRO. The 1951 figures given above must be treated as approximate only. But they are more nearly comparable with the 1961 and 1971 Census results than the figures published in the 1951 Census reports.

The table gives estimates by age as well as class of the distribution in 1951, 1961 and 1971. For men aged 25 and over the percentage in class V declined from 11 to 8 and in class IV from 27 to 18 in the twenty years 1951 to 1971 (most of the corresponding increase taking place in class II, but also class I). However, the rate of change slowed down in 1961–71 and it can be seen that between a fifth and a quarter of those in the youngest age-groups continued to be found in classes IV and V. Overall, substantially more than a quarter of economically active men remained in class IV and V in 1971.

Sources: General Register Office, Census 1951, England and Wales, Occupation Tables, HMSO, 1956; General Register Office, Census 1961, England and Wales, Occupation Tables, HMSO, 1966, Table 20; Office of Population Censuses and Surveys, Census 1971, Great Britain, *Economic Activity Tables, Part IV*, HMSO, 1975, Table 29.

Table 3. *Two versions of trends in the distribution of wealth (Britain)*

Year	Inland Revenue data series B*				Atkinson and Harrison (assumption B3)†			
	Top 1%	Top 5%	Top 10%	Top 20%	Top 1%	Top 5%	Top 10%	Top 20%
1960	38.2	64.3	76.7	89.8	34.4	60.0	72.1	83.6
1964	34.4	59.3	73.5	88.4	34.7	59.2	72.0	85.2
1966	31.8	56.7	71.8	87.8	31.0	56.1	69.9	84.2
1968	32.7	59.0	73.8	89.4	33.6	58.6	72.0	85.4
1970	29.0	56.3	70.1	89.0	30.1	54.3	69.4	84.9
1972	29.9	56.3	71.9	89.2	32.0	57.2	71.7	85.3

* Assuming that persons not covered by the Inland Revenue estimates have no wealth.
† Assuming that the value of certain property not accounted for by estate data but estimated by means of the balance-sheet method is distributed between the population included in the estate data and the population excluded. This is their 'central estimate'.

Sources: Royal Commission on the Distribution of Income and Wealth, *Report No. 5 Third Report on the Standing Reference*, Cmnd 6999, HMSO, 1977, p. 76; A. B. Atkinson and A. J. Harrison, *Distribution of Personal Wealth in Britain*, Cambridge University Press, 1978, p. 159.

Table 4. *Distribution of personal income – study of the incidence of taxes and benefits (1961 to 1975, UK). Percentage shares of final income received by given quantile groups, and supplementary statistics (1961 to 1975). Income unit: households.*

Quantile group	Final income			
	1961	1965	1971	1975
Top 10 per cent	23.7	23.3	23.7	22.4
11–20 per cent	15.1	15.2	15.6	15.4
21–30 per cent	12.8	12.8	12.8	13.0
31–40 per cent	11.1	11.1	11.0	11.2
41–50 per cent	9.8	9.8	9.6	9.7
51–60 per cent	8.6	8.5	8.3	8.4
61–70 per cent	7.2	7.1	6.9	7.0
71–80 per cent	5.8	5.7	5.4	5.7
81–90 per cent	4.3	4.3	4.1	4.3
91–100 per cent	1.7	2.3	2.5	2.9
Difference as a percentage of the median between highest and lowest deciles	149	149	158	149
Upper and lower quartiles	75	77	83	81
Median £ pw	15	18	26	52
GINI coefficient %	32.9	32.2	33.0	31.1

Note: While this table shows no pronounced trend in the distribution of final income, it is also true that fringe benefits (employer welfare and public sector subsidies) have grown in importance, and probably this has been to the relative advantage of higher income groups. (See for example Royal Commission on Distribution of Income and Wealth Report, No. 13, Chapter 4 and Appendix H, 1975.)

Source: Royal Commission on the Distribution of Income and Wealth.

Table 5. *Recent trends in death rates by occupational class men aged 15–64 (England and Wales)*

Occupational class	Age-standardized death rate per 100,000 living at ages 15–64		
	1951	*1961*	*1971*
I	103	82	79
II	108	87	83
III	116	106	103
IV	119	108	113
V	137	134	123

Note: Adjustments have been made by the OPCS to improve comparability between censuses.

Source: OPCS, *Occupational Mortality, Decennial Supplement, 1970–72, England and Wales*, HMSO, 1978, p. 174 (supplemented by the OPCS).

The Health Divide

Preface

Reproduced below is the original preface to *The Health Divide*, which stirred strong reaction – favourable and otherwise.

This final report from the Health Education Council before its demise on 31 March 1987 is, in my opinion, an essential element in the public debate which must occur on health inequalities in the United Kingdom.

Such inequity is inexcusable in a democratic society which prides itself on being humane. To eliminate or even reduce it substantially would be a major contribution to the health of the people of this country.

DR DAVID A. PLAYER
Director General
Health Education Council, 1982–7

Foreword

In the seven years since the Black Report was submitted new evidence has been published, and a number of the propositions, both scientific and practical, in that report have been examined publicly. Some elements in the discussion – like the relationship between unemployment and health, the renewed concern with housing, the evidence of greater social polarization, the changes taking place in the diet and life-styles of millions of people – are of enormous public interest and are important too for any understanding of patterns of health and the choice of health policies.

The World Health Organization regional office for Europe has set targets for 'Health for All by the Year 2000' which were endorsed in 1984 by all member countries. The first of the thirty-eight targets in the programme is equity in health defined as to bring about a reduction of at least 25 per cent in the differences in health status between groups and countries, by improving the level of health of disadvantaged groups.

For Britain the implication would be to aim, among different operational possibilities, to cut the annual number of deaths among persons under the pensionable ages in the poorer manual groups by some 20,000 from the figure that might be projected from present trends for the last year of the century. If an effective programme were now to be introduced thousands of deaths each year would be saved, building up to the figure of 20,000 in the last year of the century. Another implication of the programme would be to cut the likely number of chronically sick and disabled people under the pensionable ages in the poorer manual groups at the end of the century by approximately 100,000. On the basis of the latest data from the social and medical sciences these kinds of objectives are, in our judgement, attainable.

As the WHO recognizes, the undertaking to reduce health inequalities will remain an empty gesture unless radical steps are taken by governments to seek better information, undertake large-scale experiments, introduce anti-poverty policies, give priority to healthier life-styles and monitor the effects of those on the health of the population as a whole and on the poorest groups in particular. The Health Education Council's aim to bring the latest data together in a new report is very welcome. It is a major contribution to public knowledge and to the fresh consideration of social inequalities in health in the much larger international, and not only national, context agreed among nations. We believe that this review of the up-to-date evidence and of current scientific discussion will provide a valuable stimulus to the public debate which necessarily must take place.

Sir Douglas Black
Professor J. N. Morris
Dr Cyril Smith
March 1987   Professor Peter Townsend

Chapter 1

Setting the Scene

The Health Divide came to be written because of the pressing need for an update on inequalities in health as the number of studies on the subject mounted at a quite extraordinary rate. This chapter explains the purpose behind the initiative. It describes some of the terms and measures used and outlines the main questions the body of the report sets out to answer.

The purpose of the project

In 1980 the research Working Group chaired by Sir Douglas Black produced an authoritative report documenting inequalities in health in Britain since the war. As soon as it was published it stimulated a widespread response from the research community both here and abroad and since then much more evidence has accumulated on several different fronts. By the end of 1985 it was obvious that the non-specialist would find it difficult to keep abreast of all the developments. Additionally, there was a growing desire to know what the picture on inequalities in health looked like in the 1980s, as the Black Report, because of the time-lag in analysing official statistics, drew much of its data from the early 1970s.

For these reasons the Health Education Council in early 1986 commissioned an update of the evidence. The brief was quite open-ended: to review the evidence on social inequalities in health published since 1980 and in addition to comment on the progress made on the thirty-seven recommendations of the Black Report. The initiative should be seen as one of three major updates which the HEC was sponsoring at the time. The Council had already joined with the National Children's Bureau and the Institute of Child Health to commission a review of child health services in Britain over the decade since the Court Report was published. That review came out in June 1987 and is drawn upon in Chapter 8 where it relates to children and deprivation. The third project was an update of the 1976 DHSS report, 'Prevention and Health: Everybody's Business'. Sponsored jointly by the HEC, the King's Fund and the London School of Hygiene and Tropical Medicine, this was an ambitious project to review the health of the nation and to assess the prospects for prevention, and the progress made towards the main thrusts of 'Prevention and Health' (Smith, Alwyn, 1988). It was hoped that these three projects would together provide a comprehensive commentary on some of the major themes running through the field of health promotion. One of the reasons why *The Health Divide* does not cover the overall health of the population in more detail is because of the existence of the companion project which set out to do just that.

The main aims of *The Health Divide* were to draw together and summarize the wide-ranging new evidence and to describe what had happened and could happen, in policy development. It was felt that the report needed to be sufficiently detailed and fully referenced to be useful both as an insight into the literature for those wishing to study the subject further, and a resource for those working in diverse fields who wanted more of an overview of the subject. The story of its development and reception is, of course, told in the introduction to this volume.

Social justice and health

Before going any further it is necessary to be clear about the meaning of some of the terms and about precisely what is being measured. It is widely accepted that there are natural differences in health in the population – human beings vary in health as they do in every other aspect of life. What is being addressed in this report is the extent of unfair or unacceptable inequalities: what some would call 'inequities'. Deciding what is fair and just comes down to a subjective judgement in the end, but the comments on social justice expressed at a recent World Health Organization meeting would probably command widespread support:

In health care, the principle of social justice 'leads to equal access to available care, equal treatment for equal cases and equal quality of care'.
In health terms, 'ideally everyone should have the *same opportunity* to attain the highest level of health and, more pragmatically, none should be unduly disadvantaged'. (WHO, 1985a)

One of the major issues is whether we have anything approaching social justice in health in the UK. Are there groups in the population who are disadvantaged to such an extent that it affects their opportunity to achieve good health? For instance, does a person's financial resources, social position, ethnic origin or gender affect their chances of good health? Are certain areas of the country or certain neighbourhoods unduly disadvantaged in health terms? Are the unemployed disadvantaged compared with those in work? Does the health care system treat some people more favourably than others? Are the resources available to the NHS fairly distributed around the country? These are the sorts of issues that arise when trying to answer the question of whether social justice in health has been achieved. There are two quite different orientations in the studies in this field: those concerned with inequalities in health and those concerned with deprivation and health. Those dealing with *inequality* consider the gradient in health over the whole population through the various grades from top to bottom of the social scale. Those focusing on *deprivation* single out the most disadvantaged subgroup whose welfare falls below the average or below a reasonable minimum standard of the society in which they live. Both types of study are included here in an attempt to give a broad overview, though it should be borne in mind that each may have quite different policy implications. Policies related to deprivation may be targeted exclusively to the worst-off. Policies to reduce inequalities may be wide-ranging and encompass changes at all levels of society.

Measuring health

Work on clarifying the meaning of health and health promotion has moved forward since 1980. The World Health Organization in particular has been active in helping to define these terms for practical policy-making purposes. A consensus is emerging from WHO discussions in which *health* is conceived as 'the extent to which an individual or group is able, on the one hand, to realize aspirations and satisfy needs and on the other hand, to change or cope with the environment. Health is therefore seen as a resource for everyday life, not the objective of living: it is a positive concept emphasizing social and personal resources as well as physical capacities' (WHO, 1984).

Expressed in this form, health is a complex rather than a simple concept, with several dimensions to it which may not all be capable of measurement. Two recent reviews have given clear accounts of the measurement of the various aspects which go to make up the concept of health (Macintyre, 1986a; Blaxter, 1987a).

Traditionally, the negative end of the health spectrum concerned with death and disease has been most extensively investigated. The expected length of life is calculated from death rates and the relative chances of death at a stated age are expressed as a ratio – the Standardized Mortality Ratio (SMR), used extensively in the chapters which follow. Short-term (acute) and long-term (chronic) disease rates are calculated from medical records or self-reports of complaints. It should be noted that statistics based on the use of health services or absence from work are not valid measures of the extent of disease in the population because they are influenced by different administrative arrangements and individual circumstances (Blaxter, 1987a).

However, the 1980s have seen a concerned effort to document other dimensions of health, including ones which consider the more positive end of the spectrum, incorporating various 'quality-of-life' measures. Whether people feel ill in themselves is considered an important dimension, affecting their quality of life and influencing subsequent behaviour. *Illness* is defined as the subjective experience of symptoms of ill-health, and has been measured in the Health and Life-style Survey, for example, by a symptom check-list to obtain an 'illness score' (Cox *et al.*, 1987). Paradoxically, people can be diseased without feeling ill and feel ill without having a medically recognizable disease. Studies using the Nottingham Health Profile have brought in the physical, social and emotional effects illness can have on an individual's everyday life (Hunt and McEwen, 1980). More use has also been made of measures like the General Health Questionnaire to assess minor psychiatric illness in the community and a modified form of this score has been used to assess psycho-social well-being/malaise. Growth and development, especially in babies and children, has been measured by height, weight, percentage of babies of low birth-weight and so on.

There is a certain amount of scepticism from the medical profession about the validity of health measures based on a layperson's own reported experience. However, when checked against doctors' records or other clinical measurements the self-reports are found to agree remarkably well. Studies using these additional measures are introduced wherever possible in the pages that follow and the techniques employed are described in greater detail in Chapter 7. These new measures are intended to supplement rather than replace traditional indicators.

Measuring social factors

In order to compare the health of people in different social circumstances in society, a variety of indicators has been employed in the studies quoted. The two most frequently used are based on the occupation of the head of the household. The first is the Registrar General's scale of five social or occupational classes, based on the skills and status of the job, ranging from professionals in class I to unskilled manual workers in Class V (the full scale is outlined on p. 227). The second is the scale of socio-economic groups which brings together people with similar skills and life-styles. A condensed scale of six categories is normally used:

Socio-economic groups
1. Professional
2. Employers and managers
3. Intermediate junior non-manual
4. Skilled manual
5. Semi-skilled manual and personal service
6. Unskilled manual.

Both are taken as a rough guide to the way of life and living standards experienced by the separate groups and their families. They correlate fairly well with other components of social position, like education and income. Measures based on occupation have their limitations though, which are discussed in more detail in Chapters 3 and 7. Increasingly, information from this source is being supplemented by data from other measures. For example, three categories of housing tenure – local authority tenant, private tenant and owner-occupier – are being used as a guide to resources available to individuals. Car ownership is also used as an indirect indicator of poverty or affluence. Employment status has been used in several studies examining the difference between those who are employed, unemployed, retired, permanently sick, housewives, etc. It is also now much easier to use the census data to study basic amenities and housing conditions in quite small areas to assess the degree of material and social deprivation in an area. These have been used in the regional studies quoted in Chapter 2, and the details and merits of some of the major deprivation indicators are discussed in Chapter 7.

Limited data on ethnic origin are obtained from the country of birth as recorded on death certificates and from the mother's country of birth which appears on birth certificates.

Summary

The purpose of *The Health Divide* is to bring together and review the array of studies published since 1980 on the issue of social inequalities in health in Great Britain, and to document any initiatives which have been taken to tackle this pressing problem.

In line with the social and ecological concepts of health, evidence quoted looks not only at mortality but also at the growing body of evidence on other dimensions of health which can have a profound influence on the quality of life of individuals and groups. The existence of long-standing disease and the experience of illness, restrictions on day-to-day living and measures of psycho-social health are included, as are measures of growth and development and of health-related behaviour.

The Registrar General's occupational class scale is still the most frequently used indicator of social inequalities in this report. But research on social inequalities has been greatly extended over the last few years into areas concerned with unemployment, income, housing, and material and social deprivation in small areas. There is also more discussion about gender and ethnic inequalities. For ease of reference *The Health Divide* follows a very similar format to that of the Black Report, with an updated chapter on each of the topics covered by Black.

Chapter 2

Health Inequalities Today

In Britain in the 1980s, does everyone have the same opportunity to attain the highest level of health? Are some unduly disadvantaged? This chapter makes a start at answering these questions by looking first of all at the present pattern of health across groups in the population with differing social circumstances. It considers for instance the latest evidence on how health varies with occupational class, employment status, housing tenure, gender and ethnic origin and asks if certain areas of the country or neighbourhoods are disadvantaged in health terms. Evidence on trends and possible causes of inequalities in health will help complete the picture in later chapters.

Occupational class and health

Much of the evidence on social differences in health is measured in terms of social or occupational class. Occupation is recorded in the census, on birth and death certificates and on some, but not all, health records. From that information the Registrar General classifies people into the five social classes listed below. Men and single women are classified by their own occupation, children by the occupation of the head of the household, and married women by their husband's occupation, though their own occupation is available for analysis now and is used in studies on p. 237.

It is important to realize that although this classification is based on occupation it is not just a measure of working conditions. The intention is to group together people with broadly similar living standards and way of life indicated by their occupation. When the scale was first devised it was intended to reflect both the wealth or poverty and the culture associated with each class. Although it is obviously not a very precise measure it is still, even today, useful as a general guide to social position (see pp. 311–13 for its limitations and alternatives).

The five classes consist of the following:

I. Professional (for example lawyer, doctor, accountant)

II. Intermediate (for example teacher, nurse, manager)

IIIN. Skilled non-manual (for example typist, shop assistant)

IIIM. Skilled manual (for example miner, bus driver, cook)

IV. Partly skilled manual (for example farm worker, bus conductor)

V. Unskilled manual (for example cleaner, labourer).

Using this scale, clear evidence emerges of occupational class differences in mortality in the 1980s. This applies at every stage of life from birth, through to adulthood and well into old age. Fig. 1, for instance, illustrates the typical pattern found in early life and in men and women of working age. It can be seen that in 1984 rates of stillbirth and death at various stages in the first year of life increased progressively from occupational class I to V. Thus babies whose fathers had unskilled jobs ran approximately twice the risk of stillbirth and death under one year than babies whose fathers worked in the professions.

Up-to-date statistics on older children will be published by the Office of Population Censuses and Surveys some time in 1988, and these are awaited with great interest as wide differences in health could be seen from the 1970–72 data on this age range. The evidence on adults in Fig. 1 is taken from the Registrar General's latest Decennial Supplement covering the years 1979–83 (OPCS, 1986b). Death rates are expressed as Standardized Mortality Ratio (SMR) to show the relative chances of death at a given age. The average for the population as a whole is 100, so SMRs below 100 indicate lower than average chances of death and SMRs above 100 indicate higher than average. The distinct gradient in mortality in adults can be seen to increase in a stepwise fashion from class I to class V, so that, for example, unskilled workers run at least twice the risk of death as professionals.

Note that the Decennial Supplement records a very high SMR for class V. For technical reasons related to the reclassification of occupations by the Registrar General in 1980, it is thought that class V figures may be artificially raised and data from the OPCS Longitudinal Study may provide more reliable figures for this class. The OPCS Longitudinal Study selected a 1 per cent sample of the population of England and Wales from the 1971 census and has continued to follow vital events in the sample and the associated families by use of flagged birth, death and cancer registrations. The study has been able to look at mortality in 1976–81 by occupational class in broad age-groups, and data for 1981–3 are just becoming available. Fig. 2 shows that from this second, independent study a clear social gradient in adult mortality is again evident, with a twofold difference between the top and bottom of the social class scale for people of working age. Even at ages after retirement there are clear mortality gradients for men which are

* England and Wales.

† Great Britain.

Figure 1. *Occupational class and mortality in babies and adults, early 1980s. (Source. OPCS, 1986a and 1986b.)*

Hatched areas represent approximate 95% confidence intervals for SMRs; each SMR is indicated by a horizontal line within the hatched area.

Figure 2. *Mortality of men by social class and broad age groups, 1976–81. (Source: Fox et al., 1986. OPCS Longitudinal Study. Crown Copyright.)*

almost as steep as those found in the latter stages of working life. Thus even in old age, men from occupational class V had more than 50 per cent higher death rates than those in occupational class I (Fox *et al.*, 1986). These are the first reliable estimates of the social class gradient in England and Wales at these older ages, as previous work could not assess the gradient past retirement age.

When the causes of death are investigated it becomes apparent that the social gradient in death is not limited to one or two specific causes but applies to a wide range of conditions. In order to make use of the mass of information in the latest Decennial Supplement and overcome the technical difficulties, it is necessary to group all the manual classes together and compare them with all the non-manual classes. Alternatively, data on classes I and II can be combined and then compared with data on combined classes IV and V, to compare the health of the richest and poorest classes. Analyses of this nature have already begun. For example, Marmot and McDowall (1986) carried out a careful study of some of the major causes of death for men and married women in the two distinct categories: manual and non-manual. Table 1 shows the results of this study and reveals that, for all the causes analysed, non-manual workers in 1979–83 had a lower risk of death than manual workers. This was particularly striking

Table 1: *SMRs* for select causes of death in Great Britain 1979–83 among men aged 20–54 and 55–64*

Cause of death	Age	*Non-manual*	*Manual*	*NM/M*
		1979/83		
All causes	20–54	76	115	0.66
	55–64	82	117	0.70
	20–64	80	116	0.69
Lung cancer	20–54	60	133	0.45
	55–64	67	128	0.52
	20–64	65	129	0.50
Coronary heart disease	20–54	80	113	0.71
	55–64	90	117	0.77
	20–64	87	114	0.76
Cerebro-vascular disease	20–54	73	121	0.60
	55–64	77	119	0.65
	20–64	76	120	0.63

* For each cause, and within each age-group, the SMR for all men in 1979/83 is 100.

Source: Marmot and McDowall (1986).

in the younger age range, and married women showed a similar pattern.

Another study of the 1979–83 data compared the two highest and the two lowest occupational classes. In 65 of the 78 disease categories for men, SMRs for classes IV and V were higher than for either class I or II. Only one cause, malignant melanoma, showed the reverse trend. This is a form of skin cancer associated with over-exposure to the sun. For women, 62 of the 82 categories of disease showed higher SMRs for classes IV and V and only 4 showed the reverse – cancer of the breast and the brain, malignant melanoma and chronic lymphoid leukaemia. The remainder showed no consistent pattern (Townsend *et al.*, 1988).

This work illustrates that most of the major and minor killer diseases now affect the poorest occupational classes more than the rich. This applies equally well to coronary heart disease, stroke and peptic ulcer, which are still sometimes misleadingly referred to as 'diseases of affluence' or 'executive diseases' when in fact they are more common in the manual classes. It is thought that the confusion has arisen partly because of misdiagnosis in the past and partly because these diseases are more common in developed or affluent societies than in developing ones. The fact that they predominantly affect the poor in affluent societies has been overlooked. Clearly in this country nowadays 'diseases of affluence' have all but disappeared and what is left is a general health disadvantage of the poor.

Evidence from a second major longitudinal study has become available since the publication of the Black Report and sheds light on another important point: whether the national data under-estimate or over-estimate the social class gradient. The Whitehall study of civil servants examined over 17,000 office-based civil servants in London from 1967 to 1969 and has been following the health of men in different grades of the service for more than a decade now. The study has found that the lower the grade, the higher the mortality for every cause of death except genito-urinary disease. There is a greater than threefold difference between the highest and the lowest grade: a much steeper gradient than the occupational class gradient found in the national data (Rose and Marmot, 1981; Marmot *et al.*, 1984b).

Other studies of single occupations have also found steeper gradients. For example, a study of mortality from coronary heart disease in different ranks in the British Army in 1973–7 found increasing mortality with decreasing rank, with a sixfold difference between the highest and lowest rank (Lynch and Oelman, 1981).

It seems that the national gradients may underestimate the real differences between social groups, because each class is made up of occupations with a range of mortality rates. Studies on single occupations are more homogeneous and can reveal a sharper distinction between top and bottom groups.

However, death rates measure only one dimension of health. Fortunately in the past eight years much more information has emerged about other dimensions, like the experience of illness, restrictions on everyday activity, and the levels of fitness and well-being in different groups. When these are investigated it appears that not only do lower occupational classes have higher death rates, but they also experience more sickness and ill-health throughout their lives. Indeed Blaxter (1988) argues that morbidity or general health status are more important indicators of inequality now that people are living longer and degenerative disease is becoming more prominent. One of the main sources of information on morbidity is the annual General Household Survey in which people are asked about both chronic and acute sickness. For such purposes six socio-economic groups are used, which correspond fairly well to the Registrar General's scale (see p. 225). Rates of sickness by socio-economic group have shown the same pattern each year throughout the 1980s, revealing great inequalities between the groups (OPCS, 1986d). The gradient is steepest for limiting long-standing illness, where the rates in the unskilled manual group are more than double those of the professional group for both men and women. It is not quite as steep, but still marked, for long-standing illness without limitation; while for acute sickness the differential is only evident at ages over 45. When days of restricted activity are counted, however, the gradient reappears.

When age as well as socio-economic group is taken into consideration it is in middle age that the differences between the socio-economic groups are greatest. Fig. 3, for example, shows very little difference in illness rates between the groups up to the age of 45, but after that a dramatic gradient develops which is steepest for the age-group 45–65. From similar data Blaxter (1988) concludes that health deteriorates more rapidly in those who are socially disadvantaged. As a Hungarian researcher put it, 'Sickness appears in the case of the majority sooner or later, but the worse off you are the sooner it hits' (Ferge *et al.*, 1985).

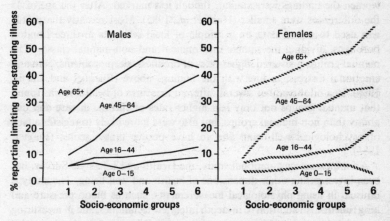

Figure 3. *Percentage of population reporting limiting long-standing illness by age and socio-economic group, 1984. (Source: OPCS, 1986d.)*

In order to check the findings of the Black Report, the data from the 1976 General Household Survey were re-examined to identify the main factors influencing the presence absence of long-standing illness in adults (Burchell, 1981). Age and sex were found to be the most important factors. Controlling for these, the Survey confirmed the conclusions drawn by the Black Working Group: that the rates of long-standing illness rose with falling socio-economic status. As a number of other variables like smoking behaviour, education, marital status and overcrowding factors were also relevant, it was suggested that occupational class may be acting as a proxy for a more complex combination of these variables.

Unfortunately, the GHS data give no insight into the nature of the reported illnesses. During the 1980s a number of surveys have used the Nottingham Health Profile to study differences in self-perceived health and its impact on daily lives. The nature of ill-health is considered under six main headings: lack of energy, pain, sleep disturbance, physical immobility, emotional distress and social isolation. The profile was used in a survey in 1981 that found clear differences in perceived health problems between occupational classes, but only in the 20–44 age-group: the lower the occupational class the greater the amount and severity of perceived distress. For example, men from classes IV and V had scores twice as high as men in classes I and II in the sections measuring lack of energy and emotional distress, over three times as high in the section measuring sleep disturbances, and over four times as high concerning feelings of social isolation. For women the findings were similar, though less marked. After the age of 45 the differences were smaller (Hunt *et al.*, 1985). Most recently the profile was used to collect data on a sample of local residents in three London boroughs, dividing the sample into manual and non-manual classes. The manual groups registered higher rates of tiredness, sleep problems, pain and emotional distress, in line with the findings above (Bucquet and Curtis, 1986). In a pilot study of several different measures of health, it was found that manual groups not only had higher rates of chronic disease and dis- ability than non-manual groups, but also were more likely to register a lack of psychological well-being and to have poorer fitness scores (Blaxter, 1985).

An important new national study, the Health and Life-style Survey, has been investigating other dimensions of health and well-being. The study is unusual in using physiological measurements, such as blood pressure and lung function, in addition to in-depth interview techniques, and in measuring income, education and housing as well as social class. A remarkably regular and in some cases steep social class gradient was found with a variety of measures of morbidity and fitness. For example, with self-perceived health the percentage of men believing their own health was only fair or poor increased from 12 per cent of class I to 36 per cent of class V. Analyses by income and education yielded similar results. Likewise when the experience of illness was assessed using a list of twenty-four common symptoms, the gradient appeared for a wide range of conditions from persistent cough and back trouble in men to headaches, palpitations, deafness and anxiety in women. When the prevalence of self-reported disease was assessed, lower social classes had higher rates of many common diseases like bronchitis, arthritis/rheumatism and varicose veins. With psychosocial health (ability to sleep well, to concentrate, etc.), high rates of 'malaise' were declared by lower social classes, with the steepest gradients found in middle age in women and older ages in men. Physiological measures of fitness, like weight, blood pressure and lung function, showed the same trend. The author of the study concluded that there was strong evidence of a high degree of inequality in health at the present time, not just in a particularly disadvantaged sub-group but throughout the social scale (Blaxter, 1987b; Cox *et al.*, 1987).

Most of the above studies were based on self-reported health, but there are numerous studies based on objective medical and dental observations which confirm the overall picture. For example, OPCS data for 1984 showed that low birth-weight was still much more common in babies born into lower occupational class families (OPCS, 1986a). (Low birth-weight is considered to be the single most powerful predictor of death in the first month of life.)

In contrast, in the 1980 national survey of heights and weights, childhood and adult obesity was a problem more common in men in class IIIM and women in classes IV and V (Knight, 1984). This was supported by a cohort study of children born in 1946. By 1982 (when the sample was thirty-six years old) higher rates of obesity were found in lower social groups in both men and women (Braddon *et al.*, 1986). Height, which can be taken as an indicator of general health, varies with occupational class. The 1980 survey found that in almost every age-group people from manual class households were shorter on average than people from non-manual class households (Knight, 1984). The Whitehall study found that height was significantly related to grade in the Civil Service. For example, the administrators in the highest grade were on average 4.7 cm taller than men in the lowest grade. In the same study, men in lower grades in the Civil Service had higher blood pressure and lower levels of glucose tolerance than those in the top grades (Marmot *et al.*, 1984b).

Looking at survival rates from cancer and coronary heart disease in men and women in the OPCS Longitudinal Study, it was found that lower occupational class people with cancer had poorer survival prospects, confirming earlier studies (Leon and Wilkinson, 1988).

The adult dental health survey of 1978 found that the proportion of people from class I with no natural teeth was much lower than in the other classes, though classes IV and V had shown a marked improvement over the previous decade (OPCS, 1982). The OPCS survey of children's dental health in 1983 found poorer health in lower occupational classes on several counts. For example, among 5-year-olds on average twice as many teeth were actively decayed among those from the manual classes compared with those from the non-manual classes. They also had more teeth missing as a result of decay (Todd and Dodd, 1985).

To sum up, the studies quoted above show that the risk of death for lower occupational classes in the 1980s was much higher than that of the highest occupational classes at every stage of life. Thus stillbirths, deaths under one year, deaths in adults of working age and deaths in old age show this gradient from lower mortality in the richer classes to higher mortality in the poorer classes. The evidence presented also shows that it is not just one or two specific causes of death which are to blame for the higher mortality, but that the full range of diseases, with very few exceptions, are affecting the poorer classes more than the rich. Only a wide-ranging general explanation could account for such a phenomenon. In addition, examples are given from the growing body of evidence showing that lower occupational classes experience much more illness and a poorer quality of self-perceived health during their lives. The evidence has been extended into other dimensions of health concerned with the experience of illness, fitness and well-being, and still wide differences are found.

Housing tenure and health

Conclusions about the extent of inequalities in health are not based solely on occupational class studies. Other measures based on assets, such as house and car ownership, are increasingly being used to investigate the association between poverty and ill-health. They are used as indirect indicators of wealth and command over resources.

Three tenure groups are identified from the census, depending on whether the house is owner-occupied, privately rented or local authority rented, and this reveals persistent differences in mortality and morbidity. For example, higher stillbirth and infant mortality rates have been found in babies born to private tenants compared with owner-occupiers (Macfarlane and Mugford, 1984). The National Child Development Study found marked and consistent differences between those in owner-occupied and local authority accommodation at ages 7 and 23 for five different health measures (height, 'malaise', self-reported health, hospital admissions and psychiatric morbidity), with the owner-occupiers having better health (Fogelman *et al.*, 1987).

In adults, the OPCS Longitudinal Study found that owner-occupiers had lower mortality than private tenants who in turn had lower mortality than local authority tenants (Fox and Goldblatt, 1982). This study is valuable in being able to look at mortality in relation to a range of socio-economic indicators. Table 2 shows mortality of men and women in the ten years from 1971 to 1981 by their housing tenure, education and access to cars. The same pattern is seen in both men and women, with lower than average mortality in the most favoured groups like the owner-occupiers, degree-holders and car-owners, rising to above-average mortality in the least-favoured groups such as the local authority tenants, those with no qualifications and no access to cars (Goldblatt, 1987).

Table 2: *Mortality of men and women in 1971–81 by housing tenure, education and access to cars (England and Wales)*

Socio-economic indicator	Standardized Mortality Ratios Men (aged 15–64 at death)	Women (aged 15–59 at death)
Housing tenure:[1]		
Owner-occupied	84	83
Privately rented	109	106
Local authority	115	117
Education:[2]		
Degree	59	66
Non-degree higher qualification	80	78
A-levels only	91	80
None or not stated	103	102
Access to cars:[1]		
One or more cars	85	83
No access to a car	121	135

1. Aged 15 years and over in 1971.   2. Aged 18–70 years in 1971

Source: Goldblatt (1987), OPCS Longitudinal Study, unpublished data. Crown Copyright reserved.

Even larger differences in mortality are found if two or more of these socio-economic indicators are combined. In this context current work in the Longitudinal Study is focusing on inequalities in women's health to see if some combination of social indicators would provide a better measure of the social circumstances of women than occupational class alone (which for married women is based on the husband's occupation). For instance, mortality differentials have been examined using a woman's occupation and that of her husband (if married), as well as housing tenure and house-hold access to a car. Three separate groups of women were considered:

single with an occupational class, married with an occupational class, and housewives (Moser *et al.*, 1987b). Distinct groups with high and low mortality could be differentiated by these methods. For example, among single women those with non-manual jobs and a car had SMR of 69, those with manual jobs and no car had SMR of 178. Among married housewives, those living in owner-occupied housing, with a car and a husband with a non-manual occupation, had SMR of 65; those in rented housing, with no car and a husband with a manual occupation, had SMR of 161. Among married women with an occupation the differentials were not quite as marked, but still evident. Those with non-manual jobs with non-manual husbands who were owner-occupiers and car-owners had SMR of 70, while those who had manual jobs and manual husbands in rented housing with no car had SMR of 113. This approach shows promise for the future, as it can pinpoint advantaged and disadvantaged groups of women with widely differing mortality rates.

Yet another approach has been used in the Longitudinal Study to look at the relationship between housing tenure and mortality in different types of local authority ward. Thirty-six distinct ward types have been identified in England and Wales from previous census studies (Webber and Craig, 1975), ranging from residential retirement areas to new towns and inner-city areas. In thirty-five of the thirty-six types of ward, owner-occupiers had lower SMRs than local authority tenants (Fox *et al.*, 1984). Table 3 gives the evidence on four different ward types illustrating the familiar tenure gradient.

Table 3: *Mortality in 1971–81 of males in selected clusters by housing tenure (1971)*

	Housing tenure		
	Owner-occupied	Privately rented	Local authority
Cluster	SMR	SMR	SMR
Residential retirement areas	83	97	104
New towns	78	78	112
Older industrial settlements with low stress	94	115	119
Inner areas with low-quality, older housing	112	137	134

Source: Fox *et al.* (1984); OPCS Longitudinal Study.

But it also highlights another point: that in each tenure category there was quite a large variation in death rates in different areas. For example, owner-occupiers in residential retirement areas had much lower mortality ratios than owner-occupiers in inner-city areas. Why this should be so is as yet unclear.

Such studies all point in the same direction and indicate that however poverty or social disadvantage is measured the link with ill-health is clear and consistent. Evidence on housing *conditions* and health can be found in Chapter 6.

Employed or unemployed: the health difference

Another factor which has been used as a general indicator of poverty or social disadvantage is unemployment, and it has become of increasing concern in the 1980s. Several reviews have been valuable in bringing together the evidence on particular aspects of the subject (Jahoda, 1979; Smith, 1985–6, 1987a; Platt, 1984; Warr, 1984; Macfarlane and Cole, 1985).

As in previous decades, the unemployed in the 1980s tend to have much poorer health than those in work, and areas of the country with high levels of unemployment have worse health records than areas with low levels of unemployment. For example, high death rates for unemployed men have been recorded in various recent studies, including the British Regional Heart Study of 1978–80 (Cook *et al.*, 1982), and the OPCS Longitudinal Study which found particularly high levels of lung cancer, suicide, accidents and heart disease (Moser *et al.*, 1984; Fox and Shewry, 1987).

Many studies have confirmed this association between suicide (or attempted suicide) and unemployment. For instance, one study found that in each year since 1977 the unemployment rate in Great Britain had been positively and significantly correlated with the total suicide rate (Kreitman and Platt, 1984). A study in Edinburgh during 1968–82 found that the unemployed had a much greater risk of attempted suicide than employed men of the order of 11:1 (Platt and Kreitman, 1984). The risk ratio increased sharply with the length of the spell of unemployment, as follows:

Duration of unemployment in 1982 (men)	*Ratio of risk of attempted suicide of unemployed to employed*
Less than 6 months	6:1
6–12 months	10:1
Over 12 months	19:1

Similarly, a study in Oxford in 1979–82 found that the attempted suicide rates for unemployed men were twelve to fifteen times higher than those for employed men, and again were particularly high for the long-term unemployed (Hawton and Rose, 1986). Studies of national economies and national health statistics have also shown consistent correlation between indicators of recession and mortality in several countries (Brenner, 1979, 1983).

The unemployed experience higher levels of illness, too. For example, age-standardized illness ratios have been calculated from the General Household Survey for 1981–2 to give an indication of the relative risk of illness in different groups. Employed men were nearly 20 per cent less likely to report limiting chronic illness than all men, while the unemployed were over 40 per cent more likely to report such illness. The retired and permanently sick had even higher ratios. Unemployed women had chronic illness ratios 16 per cent above the average for all women, while the ratios for housewives were even higher at 23 per cent above average. In contrast, those who worked full-time had ratios 19 per cent below the average and part-time workers had even better health with ratios 25 per cent below the average for all women (Arber, 1987). This study also looked at how social class influenced the unemployment and ill-health picture, bearing in mind that the unemployed were concentrated in the lower social classes. The results showed that the class gradient in health among the jobless was much greater than the class gradient in health for those in work, i.e. class seems to affect the jobless to an even greater extent than it does those in employment and should be taken into consideration more in future studies (Arber, 1987).

Poorer health and development have also been found in the children of the unemployed. Using data from the 1981 census it was found that children living in deprived districts of Glasgow were nine times more likely to be admitted to hospital than children in non-deprived districts. Overcrowding and parental unemployment were the aspects of deprivation most strongly correlated with hospital admission rates (Maclure and Stewart, 1984). A study of births in the Greater Dublin area found a higher incidence of low birth-weight in babies with unemployed fathers than in those whose fathers were employed (Dowding, 1981). In addition, children with unemployed fathers, especially the long-term unemployed, tended to be shorter than those whose fathers were in work (Macfarlane and Cole, 1985).

In the face of such abundant evidence of inequality the problems of interpretation need to be borne in mind. Are people who are in poor health more likely to become unemployed, or does the experience of unemployment itself have an adverse effect on health? Is it unemployment or an associated factor which causes areas of high unemployment to have high mortality and morbidity rates? Is the poor health experienced by a nation in times of recession a result solely of unemployment or is it also the result of deteriorating safety standards and increased stress on those in work? Separating the effect of unemployment from these other factors has been difficult. Some recent studies, however, show promise in disentangling cause and effect.

For example, the British Regional Heart Study of 1978–80 investigated, in particular, cardiovascular disease in middle-aged men selected at random from general practices in twenty-four towns. The unemployed sample was subdivided into those who said they were unemployed because of ill-health (the 'ill unemployed'), and those who considered that their unemployment was not due to illness (the 'not-ill unemployed'). It found that the frequencies of bronchitis, obstructive lung disease and ischaemic heart disease were indeed higher in the 'ill unemployed' than in the employed group. The rates of ischaemic heart disease were also significantly higher in the 'not-ill unemployed' compared with the employed population. Although smoking and heavy drinking were more common among the unemployed, once adjustments to the data had been made to allow for social class and town of residence, only smoking was slightly higher among the unemployed. Overall the authors concluded that the ischaemic heart disease rate was significantly higher in the 'not-ill unemployed' than the employed, when standardized for age, social class, town of residence and cigarette-smoking. However, this evidence was subject to the limitations of cross-sectional research, and a longitudinal follow-up is under way (Cook *et al.*, 1982).

The OPCS Longitudinal Study has been following a sample of men who were 'seeking work' at the time of the 1971 census and their mortality was recorded over the next ten years. As mentioned previously, the study found that these men had high mortality rates (SMR of 136) compared with that of all men in the study (SMR of 100). Some of the excess was 'explained' by occupational class factors, as unemployment was concentrated heavily in classes IV and V; but when adjustments were made to control for occupational class, it still left a 21 per cent excess in mortality unexplained. Two factors argue against any suggestion that these men became unemployed simply because they were already unhealthy. Firstly, those labelled as 'seeking work' in 1971 would be selected for *good* health, since there were two 'sickness' categories in the census to describe those not working because of poorer health. Secondly, women whose husbands were 'seeking work' were found to have raised mortality rates too (SMRs of 120 when compared with 100 for all married women in private households), suggesting a real effect of unemployment on families (Moser *et al.*, 1984). The latest preliminary results of the Longitudinal Study, relating to men who were seeking work in 1981, follow a similar pattern. The high death rates of men seeking work in 1981 could not be explained by the state of their health or social class before unemployment. Taken together the results lend support to the argument that unemployment had a genuine effect on the mortality rates (Moser *et al.*, 1987a). The latest evidence from this source shows that ill-health, marriage breakdown, movement into local authority housing and downward occupational mobility *followed* unemployment in the 1970s (Fox and Shewry, 1987). In contrast, the DHSS cohort study of unemployed men could find no evidence of a deterioration in self-reported health with unemployment, using the simple question: 'Has your health got better, got worse, or stayed about the same since registration?' (Moylan *et al.*, 1984).

The evidence that unemployment causes a deterioration in mental health is extremely strong. Several studies of people moving in and out of work have shown a decline in mental health on becoming unemployed and an improvement following re-employment. For example, numerous studies of minor psychiatric illness using the General Health Questionnaire found significant improvements in mental health when the unemployed were in work again (Warr, 1984, 1985).

In a most significant study in 1982 the General Health Questionnaire was used to assess young people moving from employment to unemployment or vice versa. It was able to test the young people before they left school and at intervals afterwards. Psychiatric symptoms increased significantly in those who left school and became unemployed and decreased in those who found work. As there had been no significant difference in mental health between the two groups while they were still at school, this is the clearest evidence yet of unemployment being the *cause* of poorer health (Banks and Jackson, 1982). Studies which have adopted an in-depth case-study approach have been able to document the effect of unemployment on family life and have shown that wives and children of unemployed men can also suffer psychologically (Fagin and Little, 1984).

In a study based on one general practice in England, researchers have been tracing the health of workers from a meat-product factory over the course of eight years. They found a significant increase in GP consultation rates and out-patient referrals when the workers were made redundant, while a control group in stable employment in neighbouring factories showed no such increase. Furthermore, the decline in health was evident two years prior to job loss, dating from the time when the threat of redundancy became apparent. The results suggested that the *threat* of redundancy may be a stress equal to the actual event (Beale and Nethercott, 1985, 1986a, 1986b).

To sum up, the unemployed population continues to have poorer health than those in work. Studies in Britain since 1980 have provided firm evidence that unemployment can cause a deterioration in mental health. The evidence that unemployment *causes* physical ill-health and suicide is less conclusive, though the OPCS Longitudinal Study provides evidence of excess mortality in the unemployed which cannot easily be explained away.

Sex differences in mortality and morbidity

The renewed interest in sex differences in health is not purely academic. The question is whether any of the recorded differences are environmentally determined and, if so, whether there is scope for improvement in health in either sex.

Life-expectancy estimates show that in 1983 new-born girls could expect to live six years longer than new-born boys, to 77 years and 71 years respectively, an improvement of over two years since 1971 (Central Statistical Office, 1986). In addition there are higher levels of male deaths in every age-group from birth right through to adulthood, when the adult ratio of male to female deaths is approximately 2:1 (Hart, 1988). Furthermore, the causes of death vary between men and women for different age-groups. One striking difference in young people is in accidental deaths. In 1985 in England and Wales, 40 per cent of deaths in boys aged 1–14 were due to accidents and violence compared with 26 per cent of deaths in girls. By middle age, circulatory disease had assumed prominence for men while cancer claimed a high proportion of lives in women (DHSS, 1986b).

In general the pattern of differences in morbidity is reversed. Overall, women consistently record higher levels of chronic and acute sickness, as shown in Fig. 4. This illustrates the trend from 1972 to 1984.

The picture is not quite as simple, though, when other factors like age, type of illness, social class and employment status are considered separately or in combination. Then certain groups of women can be seen to have less illness than their male counterparts, and among women themselves the rates of illness differ greatly with their differing social circumstances, as is the case for men.

When different ages are considered, for example, boys and young men are found to have higher rates of serious illness than girls. The National Survey of Health and Development found that serious illness in 21–25-year-olds was significantly more common in young men (15.8 per cent) than in young women (11.8 per cent) and the relationship held within each social class (Wadsworth, 1986). In 1983 boys between the ages of 5 and 15 were significantly more likely to suffer a long-standing illness than girls, while at 65 years and over women were more likely than men to report an illness. In

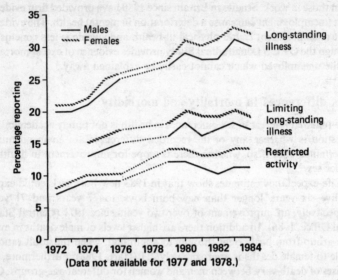

Figure 4. *Percentage of males and females reporting (a) long-standing illness; (b) limiting long-standing illness; (c) restricted activity in the 14 days before interview Great Britain, 1972 84. (Source: OPCS, 1986d. Crown Copyright.)*

the middle years there was no significant difference between the sexes (OPCS, 1985). Psychological well-being also showed different patterns with age in men and women. In a pilot study men showed a steady decline in well-being with age, though for women well-being was lower in young women under 30 and older women over 70, but was much improved in the years between 50 and 59 (Blaxter, 1985).

When social class and employment status are brought into the equation the picture becomes even more complex. For example, whether paid employment outside the home is beneficial to a woman seems to depend very much on her social circumstances and family responsibilities. Among women with children, paid employment seems to be associated with less illness for middle-class women but more illness for working-class women. This finding has been supported most recently by the results of the Health and Life-style Survey on differences in rates of mainly physical illness between working and non-working married women (Cox *et al.*, 1987). The evidence on this matter has been reviewed by Arber *et al.* (1985), who concluded that 'full-time work for young mothers may be detrimental for their health unless there are adequate financial resources to help with the burden of maintaining the multiple roles of housewife, mother and employee, or until sexual division of labour in the home changes'.

Working-class women living in urban areas have also been found to run a very high risk of depression, with a threefold difference between the rates for working-class and professional women (Brown and Harris, 1982).

An interesting Scandinavian study found great variation between men and women in the four countries, depending on the *type* of illness under study. For example, women were more often chronically ill than men in Denmark, Norway and Sweden, but not in Finland. When levels of anxiety were measured the rates were much higher for women than for men in Denmark and Norway, but there was much less of a difference in Finland and Sweden. When psychiatric admission rates were considered, they were higher for women than for men in Norway, whereas in Finland and Sweden men had higher rates. When social position and physical illness were considered, white-collar men and women had similar rates, and in fact in Finland and Norway white-collar women were physically healthier than men. Women in farming and manual occupations had high illness rates which influenced the overall figures (Haavio-Mannila, 1986).

A common finding in many countries is that illness among men and women varies with marital status. For instance, mental health tends to be best among married men, followed by single men and women, with most psychiatric problems found in married women (Haavio-Mannila, 1986).

All in all, these studies raise more questions than answers and the whole field is ripe for further research. However, one point is clear that social circumstances of both men and women are important factors which merit closer attention in future health studies.

Regional differences

The Black Report commented on differences in mortality between the major regions of the UK, with mortality rates increasing from the South and South-East to the North and North-West of the country. These regional differences have persisted into the 1980s, as illustrated in Table 4.

Table 4 gives the age-standardized death rates for men and women of working age in various regions of Britain. The general North/South gradient is evident for men and married women, though it is not as distinct for single women. Likewise, an analysis of deaths from smoking-related diseases by health authority, local authority, and parliamentary constituency areas showed great variation, for example from 155 deaths/100,000 population in Oxford to 242/100,000 in the Northern Region (Roberts and Graveling, 1985).

Table 4: *Mortality of men and women in different regions of Britain (1979–80 plus 1982 3)*

| | Direct age-standardized death rate*1,000 | | |
Region	Men (20–64)	Single women (20–59)	Married women (20–59)
Central Clydeside	7.86	1.78	3.23
Strathclyde	7.14	1.66	3.06
North	6.43	1.56	2.50
North-West	6.37	1.69	2.52
Remainder of Scotland	6.13	1.47	2.58
Wales	5.86	1.43	2.34
Yorkshire and Humberside	5.83	1.48	2.32
West Midlands	5.72	1.54	2.26
East Midlands	5.28	1.40	2.14
South-East	4.88	1.29	1.97
South-West	4.82	1.32	1.93
East Anglia	4.37	1.14	1.79
Scotland	6.92	1.62	2.89
England and Wales	5.43	1.41	2.17
Britain	5.57	1.43	2.23

Source: Townsend *et al.* (1986b), derived from OPCS (1986b).

The interaction between area of residence and occupational class is illustrated by Table 5, where distinct regional differences in the size of the health gap between the richest and the poorest occupational classes can be seen. As the table shows, it is in the North that the gap between the health of the rich and the poor is at its greatest – mortality in classes IV and V is 188 per cent of that for class I and II men, and for women the figure is 170 per cent (Townsend *et al.*, 1987b).

Information on differences in death rates has now been supplemented by data on disease and fitness and these, on the whole, reinforce the familiar picture. For instance, the North and Midlands had higher rates of chronic disease than the South when the age composition of each region was taken into account, though Wales and Scotland did not have as high rates as expected. The North/South gradient showed up for most disease conditions, for example arthritis/rheumatism, bronchitis, stomach disease, depression and heart disease, though asthma rates showed the reverse trend. Indicators of fitness showed people in Wales and Scotland in a poorer state of health (Cox *et al.*, 1987).

Table 5: *SMRs for all causes, 1979–80, 1982–3, by region and occupational class (men aged 20–64 and women aged 20–59)*

	Men			Women		
Standard region/country	I & II	IV & V	IV & V as % of I & II	I & II	IV & V	IV & V as % of I & II
North	81	152	188	80	136	170
Wales	79	144	182	79	125	158
Scotland	87	157	180	91	141	155
North-West	83	146	176	86	135	157
Yorkshire & Humberside	79	134	170	78	120	154
West Midlands	75	127	169	77	113	147
South-East	67	112	167	71	100	141
East Midlands	74	122	165	73	110	151
South-West	69	108	156	70	96	137
East Anglia	65	93	143	69	81	117
Great Britain	74	129	174	76	116	153

Note: SMR for all men, and for all women, in Great Britain in 1979–80, 1982–3, is 100. Regions ranked by SMR for classes IV and V combined as a proportion of SMR for classes I and II combined. Women classified on own, or husband's, occupation.

Source: Townsend (1987), derived from OPCS (1986b).

Coupled with this, further insight into the pattern of regional differences has been gained by the series of small area analyses which have flourished since 1980. Previous studies had examined differences at the level of large areas such as regions and counties. However, several authors have detailed the potential for studies based on smaller areas and a number of recent technical advances, explained in Chapter 7, have made such studies possible (Carstairs, 1981a).

Details of some of the major ones are listed in Table 6. A number of general points can be made about the findings:

1. Large differences exist between communities within one administrative area. In Sheffield, for instance, there was a difference in men's life expectancy of over eight years between the most affluent and the most deprived wards (Thunhurst, 1985a). And as the Greater Glasgow Health Board reported in 1984: 'In several communities [in the GGHB area] death rates are as low as or even lower than in the healthiest countries in the world –

whereas in many others death rates are among the highest anywhere.'

2. These large variations suggest that the concept of the North/South gradient in Britain is far too simplistic. In studies in the Northern Region and in Bristol, for instance, it was found that the healthiest areas in the Northern Region compared well with the healthiest areas in and around Bristol. Such evidence is masked when analysis is carried out at the County or Regional Health Authority level. This issue should be considered in the light of point 3 below.

3. Several of these studies have shown very clearly the association between poor health and various indicators of social and material deprivation. This may be the key to the North South gradient. Although there are very affluent areas in Scotland and the North, there is also the greatest concentration of material deprivation. It is this factor which may determine the overall regional health profile.

4. Some studies have been able to examine in more detail which particular factors in a deprived area are linked to the poor health record. Occupational class, unemployment rate and housing tenure differences 'explained' some but not all of the observed differences in health.

In addition to the studies in Table 6, several areas have produced local 'Black Reports' in which health profiles for specific areas have been drawn up and in some reports strategies have been put forward for local action on inequalities in health. Areas for which reports have been produced include: Merseyside (Ashton, 1984); Coventry (Binysh *et al.*, 1985); Manchester (Manchester City Council, 1985); Grimsby (Cubbon, 1986); Glyndon, Greenwich (Betts, 1985); Moyard, Belfast (Ginnety *et al.*, 1985) and Glasgow (Greater Glasgow Health Board, 1984).

Further 'small area' studies cover unemployment and hospital admissions in children (Stirland, 1985) and the mapping of childhood accidents in Haringey (Constantinides and Walker, 1985).

Health and ethnic origin

It is useful to define precisely what is meant by the terms in this section. Adopting Donovan's definition (1984),

'minority', 'ethnic', or 'ethnic minority' group is used to describe any group of people who share a cultural heritage, are not part of the majority, and may experience varying degrees of discrimination the term 'black people' in general tends to refer to people of Asian or Afro-Caribbean descent who share the common experience of differentiation or racial discrimination in Britain because of the colour of their skin.

Table 6: *Deprivation and ill-health. Small area analyses*

Study	Findings
Carstairs (1981b). 37 municipal wards in Glasgow, 23 in Edinburgh	Good evidence of greater mortality and morbidity in areas of greater deprivation (except for perinatal and infant deaths)
Thunhurst (1985a). 29 wards in Sheffield	Clear correlation between 'areas of poverty' and mortality for men and women. For men, life expectancy over eight years greater in most affluent wards compared with most deprived
Townsend *et al.* (1985). 28 wards in Bristol	Poor health significantly correlated with deprivation
Townsend *et al.* (1986a). 755 wards in London	Mortality rates in the most deprived wards nearly double that of the least deprived wards
Townsend *et al.* (1986b). 678 wards in Northern Region	Correspondence between ill-health and deprivation extremely close. The strongest association between health and deprivation variables was with lack of a car (proxy for low income)
Fox *et al.* (1984). 36 geographic clusters of wards in England and Wales. Longitudinal study individuals linked directly to data	Pattern of low mortality in high-status clusters and high mortality in low-status clusters

It is also important to point out that it can be misleading to lump all members of ethnic minorities into one disadvantaged category. There is great variation in health status among the ethnic minorities and it is more fruitful to examine in which areas specific disadvantages lie.

It is we believe mistaken to treat being black, or old and alone, or single parenthood as part of the definition of deprivation. Even if many among these minorities are deprived, some are not and the point is to find out how many *are* deprived rather than operate as if all were in that condition. It is the form their deprivation takes and not their status which has to be measured. (Townsend *et al.*, 1986b)

Unfortunately, studies in this area are hampered by the way in which health information on ethnic groups is collected. Researchers have to rely almost entirely on the country of birth recorded on documents such as birth and death certificates to infer ethnic origin. This means that, apart from infant mortality data, there is still very little information on the health of British-born children of ethnic minority groups. The Black Report made this point (p. 51) and it is still as true eight years later. However, a little more information has come to light since then.

There are a number of specific illnesses which are nowadays far more common in certain ethnic minorities than in the population as a whole – for example, rickets in children of Asian origin, sickle-cell anaemia in people of Afro-Caribbean descent, and tuberculosis in several immigrant groups. The evidence on these is reviewed by Donovan (1984), and a particular focus on health in childhood is given by the National Children's Bureau (1987). McNaught (1985) reviews the evidence on health and health care for ethnic minorities and discusses race relations policy in the NHS.

In 1984 the first major Immigrant Mortality Study in England and Wales was published (Marmot *et al.*, 1984a). It focused on people born outside those two countries who were over twenty years of age. It therefore *excluded* British-born members of minority groups and *included* British subjects born abroad. The mortality rates for most immigrant groups were lower than that of their countries of birth, indicating that healthier than average individuals 'selected' themselves for immigration. The exception was for immigrants from Ireland whose mortality was higher than that in Ireland or in England and Wales. Table 7 summarizes the main findings. For many diseases the pattern of mortality varied considerably from that commonly found in the country as a whole. All immigrant groups had higher mortality than the average for England and Wales for tuberculosis and accidents, but lower than average for diseases like bronchitis. Immigrants from the Indian sub-continent also had low mortality from several cancers which are common in this country, but they had high mortality from liver cancer, ischaemic heart disease and diabetes. Those born in the African Commonwealth or the Caribbean had higher than average mortality from liver cancer, strokes, maternal conditions and (for the Caribbean only) diabetes.

In addition, a detailed analysis was carried out of deaths in England and Wales of people born in India, Pakistan or Bangladesh, for the years 1975–7 (Balarajan *et al.*, 1984). This confirmed the findings of the Immigrant Mortality Study described above and provided further insight into mortality differences. Observed mortality for these groups was higher than expected for infective and parasitic disease, diabetes, ischaemic heart disease, cerebrovascular disease and cirrhosis of the liver. Fewer than expected deaths were due to cancer (notably lung cancer) and chronic bronchitis. Comparing different groups from the sub-continent with each other, proportional mortality ratios for cancer were lower for Hindu groups than for Moslems,

Table 7: *Summary of main findings of Immigrant Mortality Study (England and Wales, 1970–78)*

Mortality by cause	Comparison with death rates for England and Wales
Tuberculosis	*High* in immigrants from the Indian sub-continent, Ireland, the Caribbean, Africa and Scotland
Liver cancer	*High* in immigrants from the Indian sub-continent, the Caribbean and Africa
Cancer of stomach, large intestine, breast	*Low* mortality among Indians
Ischaemic heart disease	*High* mortality found in immigrants from the Indian sub-continent
Hypertension and stroke	*Strikingly high* mortality among immigrants from the Caribbean and Africa – four to six times higher for hypertension and twice as high for strokes as the level in England and Wales
Diabetes	*High* among immigrants born in the Caribbean and the Indian sub-continent
Obstructive lung disease (including chronic bronchitis)	*Low* in all immigrants in comparison with ratio for England and Wales
Maternal mortality	*High* in immigrants from Africa, the Caribbean, and to a lesser extent the Indian sub-continent
Violence and accidents	*High* in all immigrant groups

Source: adapted from Marmot *et al.* (1984a).

and lowest for Punjabis. The rate for ischaemic heart disease was highest in Moslems. Significantly more Punjabi men died from cerebrovascular disease and cirrhosis of the liver. Diabetes was commonest among Gujaratis.

Analysis of the 1978 and 1980 General Household Survey showed that smoking and drinking habits varied considerably by country of origin. Heavy drinking was significantly higher in Irish men, with the lowest levels in those born in the Indian sub-continent. Heavy smoking was significantly higher in both Irish and Scottish men, with the lowest levels again recorded in those born in the Indian sub-continent. Similar smoking patterns were found for women (Balarajan and Yuen, 1986).

Attention has been focused in the early 1980s on the health of babies born to mothers coming from the New Commonwealth countries and Pakistan. Figure 5 gives the OPCS statistics on outcome of pregnancy for 1984, showing stillbirth, perinatal, neonatal and post-neonatal mortality by country of birth of mother. Infant mortality rates are strikingly high for babies of mothers born in Pakistan and to a certain extent in babies of mothers from the Caribbean (OPCS, 1986a).

A number of studies centred around maternity hospitals have tried to unravel the causes of these high rates. Terry *et al.* (1980) studied all births occurring in one hospital in Birmingham in 1979. Most mothers fell into the social class IV and V categories. A high proportion of the mothers of Indian origin would be classified in a low-risk group based on age and parity, but had the highest stillbirth and perinatal mortality rates. Congenital malformation rates were highest in the Pakistani and Bangladeshi groups. The study concluded that the difference in the perinatal mortality rate was apparently not related to maternal age, parity or social class Lumb *et al.* (1981), studying babies born to mothers of Asian origin in Bradford over the five years from 1974 to 1978, found that the perinatal mortality rate was persistently higher than for babies of mothers born in the UK. Factors operating in favour of Asian-born women were fewer teenage pregnancies, lower rates of illegitimacy and fewer smokers. Increased risks for the Asian group included more women over thirty-five, lower social class, higher parity, shorter pregnancy intervals, previous perinatal deaths, shorter duration of antenatal care, anaemia and shorter gestation.

Gillies *et al.* (1984) followed up this study in Bradford in 1975–81, looking at all births and infant deaths occurring in one health district. They found large differences in mortality between babies of Asian-born mothers and those of mothers born in the UK, associated with congenital abnormality, largely independent of social class. Risk factors (which the authors suggest might explain the findings) included low maternal height, poor antenatal attendance, anaemia, high parity of Asian-born mothers, late childbearing, high number of low birth-weight babies and consanguinity (marriages between first cousins were apparently common in Pakistani marriages in Bradford in 1981).

Studies like these have raised questions about the causes of some of the high mortality rates observed. What, for instance, would explain the high rates of coronary heart disease in people of Asian origin in the light of the lower prevalence of smoking and heavy drinking? A comprehensive review of the evidence on this question has been made by the Coronary Prevention

Figure 5. *Outcome of pregnancy by mother's country of birth, England and Wales, 1984. (Source: OPCS, 1986a.)*

Group (1986). The high rates were not explained in Asian groups by classic risk factors like high levels of smoking. blood cholesterol and high blood pressure. However. diabetes was higher and may have been an important factor. though this required further study. Several avenues for further research were indicated from the evidence, including the added effect on health of poverty. poor working conditions and unemployment. which were all more prevalent in Asian and other ethnic minority groups. The extra stress of migration and discrimination have also been put forward as possible causes of the high death rates from heart disease. but all these suggestions are untested as yet; they are in fact difficult to test. given the lack of routinely available statistics on ethnicity and health. Yet again this emphasizes the urgent need for better information collection to help investigate the health of ethnic minority groups.

Conclusions

Data on health inequalities in the early 1980s confirm much of what the Black Working Group found on health inequalities in the early 1970s, with the addition of extended analyses on several issues. For example. data on occupational class mortality have now been extended to ages over sixty-five. and still a substantial class gradient persists. The OPCS Longitudinal Study has provided data free of numerator/denominator bias. and has confirmed a clear gradient under such conditions.

The experience of illness by occupational class has been extended into areas of self-perceived health and well-being. Lower occupational groups have been found to experience more illness which is both chronic and incapacitating. Although it is taken for granted that sickness will happen to almost everyone sooner or later. it seems that lower occupational groups experience it earlier and this must be seen as a major inequality in a welfare society.

Other direct measures of affluence and poverty. such as housing tenure and employment status. also highlight inequalities in health. Owner-occupiers continue to have lower rates of illness and death than private tenants. who in turn have lower rates than local authority housing tenants. It is well known. and confirmed in recent studies. that the unemployed have much poorer health than those with jobs. It is now also beyond question that unemployment *causes* a deterioration in mental health and there is increasing evidence that the same is true of physical health.

Women can expect to live longer than men and have lower mortality rates at every stage of life. However. women record higher levels of morbidity than men, particularly from middle age onwards. Research is only just beginning to unravel the complexities of inequality in health for women. Health experience has been found to differ for women and men in relation to marital status, employment, and presence of children in the home, as well as occupational class.

The overall North/South regional differences in health in Britain are still evident, but what is now becoming apparent is the great inequality in health which can exist between small areas in the same region. Areas suffering social and material deprivation have been found to have much poorer health profiles than neighbouring affluent areas. Furthermore, the gap between the health of the rich and the poor is greatest in the North.

Information on the health of ethnic minorities is mainly limited to studies of adult immigrants born outside England and Wales; there is hardly any information on the health of the second generation. A varied picture emerges. Mortality rates from lung cancer and chronic bronchitis, for example, are lower in most ethnic groups than in those born in the UK. On the other hand, deaths from accidents are disturbingly higher in all immigrant groups. There is strikingly high mortality from hypertension and strokes among people of Caribbean and African origin, and markedly higher mortality rates for babies of mothers born in Pakistan and, to a certain extent, for babies of mothers from the Caribbean. We need more information about the health of members of ethnic minority groups born in this country.

Chapter 3

Recent Trends

There is no doubt that the health of the population as a whole has continued to improve over recent years, measured, for example, by life expectancy. In 1983 a new-born boy could expect to live to 71 years and a girl to 77 – an improvement over the previous decade of over two years. Other measures of the population's health, like height and dental health, show steady improvement since 1971–2 (DHSS, 1986b). As mortality rates from infectious diseases continue to decline, deaths in childhood have become less common, and a greater proportion of the population can now expect to live to middle and old age.

Nevertheless, inequalities in health between different *social groups* within the population still exist on a substantial scale – as the evidence in Chapter 2 confirms. An important question now is whether these inequalities in health are increasing, decreasing or remaining the same. The Black Report, reviewing evidence from 1931 to 1971, concluded that the gap in health between different social groups had either stayed the same, or in some cases had widened. New evidence has been presented since then on trends over the past decade, and reassessments of the 1931–71 evidence have also been carried out; these will be discussed below, after an outline of some of the measurement problems.

Measurement problems

The seemingly simple task of following trends in health over time is fraught with difficulties, particularly in relation to occupational class comparisons. These problems have been reviewed recently by Wilkinson (1986a), Illsley (1986), and LeGrand and Illsley (1986). Wilkinson (1986a, 1986b) has also detailed ways of overcoming many of the problems. From these reviews five main obstacles have been identified, which need to be borne in mind when assessing research on occupational class time trends:

1. *Numerator/denominator bias.* In the calculation of mortality rates the occupation of the deceased is taken from death certificates, while the total

number of people in each class is calculated from occupations recorded in the ten-yearly national census. Misrecording of occupation in either source introduces bias into the calculation. OPCS points to a considerable increase in numerator/denominator bias in the latest Occupation Mortality Decennial Supplement based on the 1981 census. This census used the Registrar General's 1980 classification of occupations which changed the social class of some occupations. The recording of occupations on death certificates, however, is still much less precise and has not led to the same shift in occupations between classes. The social class mortality rates, in the form presented in the Decennial Supplement. may be misleading – especially for class V unless analysed with care. Many believe that the data can be used by comparing manual with non-manual categories, or combining data on classes I and II and comparing it with data on classes IV and V combined.

2. *Re-classification.* Repeated re-classification of occupations at each census since 1931 has made it difficult to compare occupational classes over such a time-span, unless adjustments are made to allow for the re-classification. Acknowledging this, previous Registrars General have carried out bridging exercises to enable the old and new classifications to be compared and the effect of the changes to be gauged. Another way of overcoming this effect is to trace occupations which have stayed in the same class throughout the period under study.

3. *Changing size of classes.* The proportion of the population in each social class has changed over time. In particular, there is a smaller proportion of the population in class V and a larger proportion in classes I and II. because of an upward shift in occupations. It should be noted that class V is also being eroded by unemployment as well as by upward mobility into higher classes. Comparisons of class I with class V over thirty to fifty years are therefore not comparisons of similar-sized segments of the population. However, comparison of combined classes I and II with combined classes IV and V would compare large and roughly equal-sized slices of the population.

4. *Changing status.* Linked to the change in size of each class may be a change in the relative status of each class. For example, the status and life-style of the much smaller class I in 1921 or 1931 may have been very different from the status of the expanded class I in 1981, so again the studies may not be comparing like with like. As this is an entirely subjective matter. it is difficult to think how this could be tested.

5. *Use of a small proportion of total deaths as a basis.* Some comparisons have been based on the mortality of men aged 15-64. In 1921 deaths in this

group accounted for 40 per cent of all male deaths, but by 1971 they only accounted for 31 per cent. Therefore only limited conclusions can be drawn from such data, though it is still true to say that they give a representation of premature adult male mortality. While it is true that conclusions are limited if based on deaths under the age of 65, these are a very important group, representing as they do premature or untimely deaths – and in some cases the most avoidable deaths. Many comparisons do include deaths in all working and unemployed men, their wives and babies.

Trends in babies

Table 8 illustrates trends in deaths of babies in the first year of life, comparing combined classes I and II with combined classes IV and V. Since 1975 birth and infant death registrations have been linked, so there are no numerator/denominator problems with these figures. Over the ten years, although there was a general decline in death rates, the occupational class differences persisted for stillbirths and deaths in the first week of life (perinatal deaths). For example, the perinatal death rate of classes IV and V fluctuated at around 150 per cent of the rate for classes I and II during the whole period. A similar differential was found in 1970–72, so the situation has remained static for nearly fifteen years (Macfarlane and Mugford, 1984).

However, the picture for post-neonatal deaths (age one month to one year) is somewhat different. There was a clear narrowing of the mortality gap between classes I and II and IV and V in the early 1970s, though there has been little, if any, improvement since then. Trends in post-neonatal mortality since the Second World War have been traced. From 1949–50 to 1970–72 there was a rapid decline in death rates for classes I, II, III and IV, but as they reduced at the same pace the relative differential between these four classes remained the same. The decline in class V rates was much smaller, and therefore the differential between it and the other classes *widened* during that time. After 1970–72 there was another sharp overall decline in death rate but this time the greatest improvement was in class V, so the gap in mortality between the classes *narrowed* (Pharaoh and Morris, 1979).

Since 1975 post-neonatal death rates have improved very little for non-manual classes, and since 1979 there has been little improvement for manual classes either (Macfarlane, 1986). The mortality gap has thus remained fairly constant for the past five years, as illustrated in Fig. 6. The still unanswered question is why the earlier improvement in class V rates occurred. The reasons seem to be complex and are still being investigated,

Recent Trends 259

Table 8: Infant mortality by occupational class (1975–84)

Deaths	1975	1976	1977	1978	1979	1980	1981	1982	1983	1984
Perinatal deaths/1,000 total births										
Rate for classes I and II	15.0	13.8	12.6	12.1	11.4	10.7	9.3	8.7	8.1	7.7
Rate for classes IV and V	22.7	20.5	19.5	17.5	17.1	15.5	13.8	13.5	12.5	12.3
Rate for classes IV and V as % of rate for classes I and II	151	148	154	144	150	144	148	153	154	159
Post-neonatal deaths/1,000 live births										
Rate for classes I and II	3.1	2.7	2.9	3.0	2.9	3.1	2.8	3.1	2.8	2.5
Rate for classes IV and V	6.4	5.8	5.7	4.9	6.0	5.2	5.4	5.1	5.3	4.5
Rate for classes IV and V as % of rate for classes I and II	202	214	196	160	204	167	192	164	186	178

Source: derived from OPCS data Series DH3, various years

Figure 6. *Post-neonatal mortality by father's social class, England and Wales. (Source: Macfarlane, 1987. From OPCS Mortality Statistics.)*

but certainly one of several relevant factors appears to be the reduction in average family size, particularly in class V (Pharaoh and Morris, 1979; Macfarlane, 1986).

Trends in adults

To give a general picture, the Decennial Supplement data has been analysed for 1949–53 to 1979–83 by combining class I with class II and class IV with V (Townsend *et al.*, 1988). Over the past thirty years mortality rates for each age range declined more rapidly in the two top occupational classes compared with the two lowest occupational classes. For example, in men aged 45–54 death rates declined by 37 per cent in the top two classes but by only 7 per cent in the lowest two classes over the thirty years. The equivalent figures for women were 35 per cent and 7 per cent. In addition, a larger number of causes of death showed a class gradient, with higher mortality in the lower occupational classes. Is this apparent widening of the health gap substantiated by other evidence?

One important study chose to analyse death rates in men and married women in terms of manual and non-manual class to overcome numerator-denominator difficulties and thus be able to make use of the Decennial Supplement for 1979–83. The authors argued that even if some occupations had been re-classified into different social classes in the 1981 census data, there was no evidence that there would be any serious mis-classification between these two very distinct groups. They also restricted their analysis to the recent past to avoid long-term complications (Marmot and McDowall, 1986).

The 1970–72 figures were standardized with the 1979–83 ratios to allow

Figure 7. *Standardized mortality ratios* for select causes of death in Great Britain 1970–72 and 1979–83 for manual and non-manual groups. (Source: Marmot and McDowall, 1986.)*

* For each cause the SMR in 1979–83 is 100 for each sex.

direct comparisons across time periods and classes. Fig. 7 summarizes the results and shows that all-cause mortality for 1979–83 fell in both groups in men and women, but because it had declined more rapidly in non-manual groups the social gap widened. When major causes of death were examined, the trends for cerebrovascular disease and lung cancer in men were similar to that for all-cause mortality. However, coronary heart disease (CHD) mortality in men in non-manual occupations fell by 15 per cent over the decade, whereas in manual occupations it increased by 1 per cent. For married women both lung cancer and CHD mortality increased in manual classes while decreasing in non-manual classes. The decline in CHD mortality was evident in non-manual men in every part of Great Britain, but only in Wales was there a noticeable decline in mortality for manual men.

The authors went on to consider what could account for this widening gap. Changes in disease classification over the ten years were examined and discounted, as was the changing size of the classes. Over the decade there was a 5 per cent decrease in manual classes and a 4 per cent increase in non-manual classes for men. They argued that a change of this order would not convert a 1 per cent rise in CHD mortality in manual men to a fall of 15 per cent to be in line with that of non-manual men. Their conclusion was that this reflected a genuine widening of the health gap, not influenced by statistical changes.

The OPCS Longitudinal Study is specifically designed to be free of numerator/denominator bias as the sample's death certifications and other records have been linked to the census records. It can also correct for reclassification, and because it only covers deaths from 1971 onwards it does not face some of the problems of longer-term comparisons. Preliminary results from the study comparing the years following the 1971 census with 1981 3 show a widening gap in all-cause death rates between manual and non-manual classes. When specific causes of death were examined, the Longitudinal Study found that differentials had widened since 1971 for lung cancer and circulatory diseases, particularly ischaemic heart disease, while for other causes of death the gap appeared to have remained the same or narrowed (Goldblatt, 1986).

So far the focus has been on trends in death rates, but illness rates also show some interesting changes. Trends in chronic and acute illness recorded in the General Household Survey have been analysed for the decade from 1974 to 1984 and are shown in Fig. 8 (OPCS, 1986d). These cover all ages from birth to old age. In contrast to the general fall in mortality, there is no sign of illness rates falling; rather they appear to be rising. From this analysis manual groups had higher rates of long-term illness than non-manual groups throughout the decade and the gap between the two groups widened over the ten-year period. For men, the widening occurred particularly from 1974 to 1979 and since then the gap has remained fairly stable. For women, the gap between manual and non-manual groups widened throughout the 1970s and continued to widen in the 1980s. In both men and women, rates of acute illness were consistently higher for manual than for non-manual groups. There was a slight widening of the gap between the two groups between 1974 and 1979, and then it remained stable up to 1984. When different age-groups were considered, divergent trends were seen in all ages, but it was only at ages over 45 that the manual groups showed a significantly greater increase in chronic illness than the non-manual groups. The difference was particularly noticeable in the over-65s, where the proportion with a limiting illness remained roughly the same for non-manual groups at 37 per cent in 1974 and 38 per cent in 1984, but the proportion in the manual groups increased from 40 per cent to 48 per cent.

Another way of tackling the question is to look at trends in health measured by other socio-economic indicators which would not be subject to

Figure 8. Top *Percentage of males and females reporting long-standing illness and limiting long-standing illness by whether non-manual or manual socio-economic group;* Bottom *Percentage of persons reporting restricted activity in the 14 days before the interview by sex and whether non-manual or manual socio-economic group: Great Britain, 1974, 1979 and 1984. (Source: OPCS, 1986. Crown Copyright.)*

the same measurement problems. In the international study mentioned on p. 281 the level of education was used as an alternative measure of social position – ranging from groups with no qualifications to holders of degrees, aged eighteen and over. From this study, inequalities in mortality between different groups increased in England and Wales between the early 1970s and the 1980s because of an improvement in the higher education categories and little or no improvement in the lowest. This adds weight to the view that the widening health gap between top and bottom of the social scale is real and not dependent on the particular classification used (Valkonen, 1988).

So much for the trends over the last decade. The objections to comparisons over much longer time-spans are far more serious and need more sophisticated techniques to try to overcome them. Three studies recently have reassessed the data on mortality trends from 1921 to 1971, making adjustments for expansion and contraction of numbers in different classes; for changes in classification of occupations over fifty years; and covering the bulk of the population rather than relatively small sections (thus taking into account problems 2, 3 and 5 listed at the beginning of this chapter).

The first study applied three measures of inequality to the experience of men, women and children in England and Wales from 1921 to 1972. The measures were the Gini Coefficient, the Slope Index of Inequality and the Index of Dissimilarity. All three indices indicated increasing inequalities from 1930–32 onwards, with the greatest inequality in health reached in 1970–72. As the authors point out, 'All classes have profited from mortality decline, but higher-status' groups have profited more than most' (Preston *et al.*, 1981).

The second study confirmed these findings by using the Slope Index of Inequality, based on the mortality level of all five social classes and their proportionate share of the population. To overcome re-classification difficulties, 143 occupations were used, which could be traced consistently between 1921 and 1971. From this analysis the author concluded that class inequality in mortality among men declined in the 1920s but increased again during the 1950s and 1960s, so that by the early 1970s it was greater than it had been in the earlier part of the century. For married women there was a similar increase in inequality between 1949–53 and 1970–72. The class differentials in infant mortality declined dramatically in absolute terms, but still increased in relative terms, as did the adult trends (Pamuk, 1985).

The third study analysed causes of death by occupational class from 1921 to 1972 in England and Wales, using a modified Index of Dissimilarity as an indicator of the relative differentials between the classes. This index is the number or proportion of deaths which would need to be reallocated between classes in order to give equal death rates in all classes. The possible role of medical care in influencing the class differentials was also assessed by comparing trends in mortality from causes thought to be amenable to medical intervention with other diseases. The analysis of 'all causes' of death suggested that the differences between occupational classes had become much wider than they used to be and that change in the class composition of the population was not responsible for the increase in inequality. The class differentials were much larger at the beginning of the 1970s than ever before. The widening differentials could not be explained by a few specific diseases, because in 31 out of the 32 causes of death analysed the higher classes did better than the lower classes.

Turning to 'diseases of poverty' (i.e. diseases with a consistent inverse class mortality gradient) regarded as amenable to medical intervention (such as tuberculosis and cancer of the cervix), Koskinen found no evidence of diminishing class differentials in any of them. Among married women the growth of inequalities had been *fastest* in those diseases where medical treatment is thought to be effective. For 'diseases of poverty' not amenable to treatment there was a marked steepening of the class gradient, especially since the early 1950s. He concluded that the health care system had not succeeded in diminishing class inequalities (Koskinen, 1985).

If the methods used in these three studies can be shown to be appropriate for the analysis, they will have helped to settle the debate on whether class differentials have widened in the second half of this century.

Trends in the sex differential

In contrast to considerations of occupational class, trends in sex differentials in mortality do not have the same measurement problems. Life expectancy at birth has been increasing in both men and women throughout this century, but during that time women's life expectancy has always been greater than men's (Hart, 1988).

In recent decades the gap in life expectancy has been increasing. For example, in 1950 women could expect to live 5 years longer than men; by 1981 they could expect to live 6.4 years longer.

There is evidence, however, that the difference between the mortality rates for some major causes of death may be declining. For instance, Lopez (1984) has traced the sex ratio trends for lung cancer from 1950 to 1979. The sex ratio for lung cancer mortality showed a peak around 1960, when male death rates were nine times greater than female death rates in England and Wales. Since then the ratio has been steadily declining, mainly because the female death rate from lung cancer was rising faster than that for men.

By the late 1970s the male death rate had fallen from nine times to four times the female rate. For other causes of death showing a large excess of male deaths, such as accidents, the ratio of male to female death rates has been falling. Unfortunately, some of this reduction in inequality seems to have been brought about by rising female rates for these particular causes of death.

Have inequalities in health widened?

There are a number of fundamental problems in measuring health trends over time, but several recent studies show promise in overcoming them satisfactorily. The results of these studies, taken together, give convincing evidence of a widening of health inequalities between social groups in recent decades, especially in adults. In general, death rates in adults of working age have declined more rapidly in the higher than in the lower occupational classes, contributing to the widening gap. Indeed in some respects the health of the lower occupational classes has actually deteriorated against the background of a general improvement in the population as a whole. While death rates have been declining, rates of chronic illness seem to have been increasing, and the gap in the illness rates between manual and non-manual groups has been widening too, particularly in the over-65 age-group.

The exception to the widening trend was in relation to deaths in babies under one year. While there has been little change in the differential for deaths around birth and in the first month of life, great improvements have occurred in the post-neonatal period (age range from one month to one year). There was a dramatic decline in post-neonatal death rates during the 1970s in all classes, but especially for class V, and thus the gap in mortality narrowed considerably. Although there has been very little further improvement from 1980 to 1984 for manual or non-manual classes, the evidence does illustrate that the class differential is not inevitable and can be reduced. The regional differences in post-neonatal mortality are also not as wide as they were.

Chapter 4

Health Services: Equal Access for Equal Need?

There has been much debate about whether the national health services are equally accessible to all social groups. Some of the studies reviewed by the Black Working Group suggested that access to those who needed care was in some cases biased in favour of the non-manual socio-economic groups. Equality in this context can have a variety of meanings. On p. 222 aspects of equality were mentioned: equal access to available care, equal treatment for equal cases and equal quality of care. A fourth aspect is equal access to the service for equal need. The fourth aim may lead to an element of positive discrimination in services in favour of those with the greatest need. Measuring true 'need', however, is an exceedingly difficult, if not impossible, task. That is perhaps why the argument continues about whether or not equal access for equal need has been achieved.

Physical access

Studies which have looked at availability of services in different areas and physical access problems give a mixed picture of progress. For example, a study of the location and accessibility of GP surgeries in Aberdeen found that the location of the surgeries clearly favoured the longer-established middle-class districts of the city, and that the deprived areas were poorly served. When car ownership was considered as an additional factor, it was found that the high levels of car ownership in the owner-occupied outlying areas of the city extended accessibility to services quite markedly, while there continued to be very low levels of accessibility in the outlying local authority estates (Knox, 1979). Another study confirmed that transport difficulties to GP surgeries appeared to have a deterrent effect on the use of the service (Whitehouse, 1985).

In 1985 the availability of dental services in Newcastle upon Tyne was clearly greater in more affluent areas and poorer in officially designated 'priority areas' (Carmichael, 1985). In contrast, improvements were reported in the distribution of hospice care for terminally ill patients. A 1980 survey had shown considerable regional inequalities in provision, with the

South-East generally much better off than the rest of the country. Since then the imbalance has been reduced by differential funding for hospices (Lunt, 1985).

An OPCS national survey in 1977 investigated access to primary health care in terms of ease of journey, use of appointment systems, doctors' approachability, ease of getting home-visits and so on. Most people found the services easily accessible. The proportion of people reporting difficulties was relatively small, between 5 per cent and 10 per cent of all informants, though the report did point out that this would represent over two million people nationally. As expected, those in rural areas were more likely to experience difficulties than urban dwellers, but age, sex and social class proved to be more important factors. Problems were most common among the elderly, especially manual-group women. People in social classes IV and V were less likely than others to use ophthalmic, dental and chiropody services, a finding in line with previous studies on preventive services (Richie *et al.*, 1981).

Quality of care

The quality of services is also important. Further studies on GP consultations have shown differences in GP responses to different social groups. For example, one study found that higher social class patients received more explanations voluntarily than did lower social class patients (Pendleton and Bochner, 1980).

A study of home-visiting in a large inner-London general practice found that there was a steady increase in the proportion of home-visits from class II to class V, but the proportion of home-visits was highest of all in occupational class I. When distance was also taken into consideration, class I patients living close to the health centre had by far the highest proportion of home-visits – more than double that of any other occupational class. Of the patients living farthest away from the health centre, occupational class I again had the highest proportion of visits and class V the lowest (Bucquet *et al.*, 1985).

There is also evidence that classes I and II patients are more likely to be referred to specialist services by their GP than classes IV and V patients, particularly in the case of older women (Blaxter, 1984).

On a larger scale, an attempt was made in 1983 to examine the quality of health care delivery in the ninety-eight Area Health Authorities in England and Wales (Charlton *et al.*, 1983). This study chose the eleven diseases regarded as most amenable to medical intervention (excluding conditions controlled mainly by prevention). Mortality for these diseases in the different Area Health Authorities was found to vary considerably, even after adjusting for socio-economic differences between areas. Could differences in quality of health services in these areas account for the variation in death rates? The study raised this question and suggested that the findings warranted further investigation.

Treatment received by ethnic minorities, particularly for mental illnesses, has been called into question. For example, one study of psychiatric hospital patients found that black patients tended to receive harsher forms of treatment (such as electroconvulsive therapy) than their white counterparts with similar ailments (Littlewood and Cross, 1980). Although there are few studies in this area and the extent of differential treatment in the NHS is not known, it is a topic which has been heightening the concern of ethnic minority groups.

Use of primary care services

There is plenty of evidence that members of lower occupational classes make less use of preventive services for themselves and their children. Analysis of the second national morbidity survey of general practice confirmed the occupational class gradient in uptake of preventive services (Blaxter, 1984; Crombie, 1984). Differential use of services has also been recorded for screening and preventive services in Wales (Nutbeam and Catford, 1987); attendance at local authority developmental assessment clinics for preschool children (Fisher *et al.*, 1983); frequency of attendance for dental services (Todd and Dodd, 1985; Eddie and Davies, 1985); attendance at well-woman, well-man and cervical cytology clinics (Marsh and Channing, 1986); and use of orthodontic services (Jenkins *et al.*, 1984). This raises the question of *why* these services are used less frequently by the lower socio-economic groups. Is it because of difficulties encountered in using the services or different perceptions of the need for preventive care? Possible explanations are discussed further in Chapter 6.

When the full range of primary care services (preventive and curative) is considered, the problem of assessing 'need' arises. Fig. 8 on p.263 indicated the *potential demand* for health care and suggested that manual groups would have greater need for health services than non-manual groups. Fig. 9 shows use of GP services by the two groups and indicates that manual groups do indeed use GP services more than non-manual groups. But does their use of services completely match their increased need? This is a key question and one which has proved difficult to answer, particularly when sex and age differences in use are also taken into consideration.

In 1980 newly available data from the 1974 General Household Survey were examined (Collins and Klein, 1980). In 1974 (but not in other years)

Figure 9. *Percentage of males and females consulting a NHS GP in the 14 days before interview by whether non-manual or manual socio-economic group, Great Britain, 1974, 1979 and 1984. (Source: OPCS, 1986d. Crown Copyright.)*

people who reported both illness and GP consultation were asked whether their consultations had been about the reported illness, thus allowing a more direct comparison of the link between use and need. They found that among men who reported no illness the professional group had higher consultation rates than the rest of the population. Among men who reported acute sickness or chronic sickness without limitation manual groups had higher consultation rates than non-manual groups. For men with chronic limiting illness and for women in all categories consultation rates were not systematically related to socio-economic group. From these results it was concluded that 'the NHS had achieved equity in terms of access to primary health care'. This study has been widely criticized for drawing such sweeping conclusions from the limited data and from the restricted aspect of the system studied (Scott-Samuel, 1981). For example, critics have pointed to the fact that the study was based on figures for only one year, that it was based on numbers of users of primary care and not on frequency of use, and that it took no account of the higher numbers of partly skilled and unskilled workers in the chronic sick category. As it did not cover children's access, severity of need, or nature of conditions, it was premature to suggest that equity of access throughout the NHS had been achieved (Townsend and Davidson, 1982).

The GHS has also recently re-analysed the 1974 data, with some refinements on the technique used by Collins and Klein and with the inclusion of data on children. The study found that for given rates of sickness those in the manual socio-economic groups were more likely to consult a GP than those in the non-manual groups. The result was clearer for acute than for chronic sickness and more marked for men than for women. The conclusion was that, from 1974 data, 'for the aspect studied there was no evidence of bias' (OPCS, 1986d). As similar information was collected in the 1986 GHS, an updated analysis is planned when the data become available.

Looking at the issue from a different perspective, 1980 GHS data were examined to see if the health and social services discriminated in favour of the poor and disabled. Of the elderly, 56 per cent were found to be living in poverty (defined as having income up to 40 per cent above the supplementary pension scale rate). There was no significant difference in service use between the 'poor' and the 'not poor'. When their degree of disability was taken into consideration, no substantial difference in contact rates were observed between the 'poor' and 'not poor' for *health* services (except the district nursing service for the severely disabled). But for the *social* services, especially home-helps, the highest usage rates were found in the 'not poor'. The authors concluded that neither health nor social service departments, for a given level of disability, discriminate in favour of the poor (Victor and Vetter, 1986).

In 1984 two studies using the same data source came to very different conclusions about use of services. One inferred from the results that doctors were discriminating in favour of occupational class V patients. The other study put a completely different interpretation on the findings. Using the national morbidity survey of general practice, Crombie (1984) investigated consultation rates by dividing them into two groups: first-time consultations .nitiated by the patient, and repeat appointments initiated by the doctor. In the ones initiated by patients, lower occupational classes had fewer consultations for preventive services than higher classes but more consultations for acute episodes like accidents and violence, so that overall there was little difference in consultation rates between the classes. However, for repeat consultations initiated by the doctor, Crombie noted that occupational class V patients had more consultations for a given episode of illness. He reasoned that doctors were compensating for lack of coping skills in class V patients by giving them more return appointments. Blaxter (1984) looked at the conditions for which patients were consulting their doctors. She also found higher consultation rates for occupational classes IV and V, but concluded that these higher rates were justified by the more severe nature of the illness they experienced. The lower occupational classes had more illness which was life-threatening and more painful in nature than higher classes. These two studies illustrate clearly the difficulty of interpreting research in the health service field.

In a community survey of three London Boroughs the Nottingham Health Profile was used to compare self-reported morbidity with service use by manual and non-manual classes. The study also aimed to identify which types of morbidity were likely to trigger a consultation and which were not. There were substantial differences in the prevalence of ill-health between social groups. The manual groups were particularly susceptible to tiredness, sleep disturbance, pain and emotional distress. However, their higher levels of morbidity were not matched by higher consultation rates for these conditions (Bucquet and Curtis, 1986).

A detailed local study in general practice has recently tackled the issue of deprivation and health in one practice serving 15,500 patients (Marsh and Channing, 1986). They selected a sample of 587 'deprived' patients from their register and these were paired with matched controls from a 'more endowed' area. Data on patients for the previous three to five years were abstracted for analysis. Deprived patients were found to have 60 per cent more hospital admissions, 75 per cent more casualty attendances, and almost three times as much mental illness as the control group. Comparisons of serious physical illness, consultant referrals and GP consultations all showed the same trend. There was significantly more non-attendance for appointments and much poorer immunization rates and other preventive care in the deprived group. In total, the deprived patients had provided a 50 per cent higher morbidity load to the health services than their matched controls. The authors go on to describe what a practice can do, in practical terms, to try to improve the health of its deprived patients.

Allocating resources fairly

Before the NHS was set up, resources available for health care varied greatly from one region to another. The NHS inherited this unequal distribution, but since 1976, when the Resource Allocation Working Party (RAWP) reported, the service has been committed to the principle of allocating resources more fairly across the country. At that time the expenditure/head of population in the wealthiest regions was approximately 30 per cent higher than that of the poorest regions. The RAWP formula for calculating budget allocation was applied to try to solve the problem.

A decade later, are resources distributed more fairly? At the regional level there certainly has been a reduction in inequality, with the gap in expenditure/head between the richest and poorest reduced to less than 10 per cent (Holland, 1986). In this particular respect the formula has worked well, though it has not been achieved without penalty. In a period of growth, the NHS might have achieved the redistribution relatively painlessly by keeping current expenditure levels fairly steady in some sectors while giving more to others. As it has turned out, there have been severe financial restrictions on the service, and under such circumstances almost the only way of giving more to one region is to cut resources and services in another. This has produced its own brand of unfairness, which the RAWP formula is incapable of solving – it is more a national question of deciding the size of the cake to be shared out (Holland, 1986).

It is also important to understand that RAWP only deals with geographical inequalities of resources in the health service. It was not designed to tackle inequalities between different social groups in their access to health care, or inequality in resources provided for different services, in particular the lesser priority given to preventive and community health care services compared with the high technology hospital sector. These have yet to be addressed.

Has equality been achieved?

It is difficult to get a comprehensive overview of how the position has changed in the health services over the past decade. Although some recent studies could find no evidence of bias in favour of any social group in relation to GP consultation rates, there is no room for complacency. Other studies have highlighted examples of poorer provision of services in more deprived areas; physical access difficulties for a small proportion of the population – notably among the elderly and manual groups; differences in the quality of care which appeared to favour higher occupational classes; and much lower uptake of preventive services by lower social groups. What is not known is the extent of such inequalities. On the other hand, there are certainly examples of health and social service workers making strenuous efforts to reduce the inequalities they have identified, and these important initiatives are outlined in Chapter 8.

Chapter 5

International Comparisons

How does Britain's health record compare with those of other developed countries? Do they all experience inequalities in health between their various population groups, and if so, is the size and scale of the inequality the same in each country? Can we learn anything from other countries' attempts to reduce their inequalities? Answering such questions would be of value in developing health policy for the future, but it is no easy task.

The problem is that each country has different methods of collecting information, different definitions of each social group, and covers different time-spans and topics. Only rarely can direct comparisons be made on the type of social factors which are of particular interest here. The difficulties in making international comparisons on inequalities have been reviewed in detail for perinatal and infant mortality (Macfarlane and Mugford, 1984); for chronic illness (Blaxter, 1988); for health services (Macintyre, 1988); and for mortality differentials in general (Lynge, 1984). In what can only be a brief overview, this chapter outlines the extent of present-day inequalities in a number of European countries. It gives some of the findings of the few comparative studies available, as well as looking at notable policy developments.

The international league table

One way of forming a general picture of how Britain's health record compares with that of other countries is to look at life expectancy and death rates at various ages, before going on to consider the health of different social groups. Table 9 shows mortality rates for 1983 and illustrates several points:

1. In all developed countries female life expectancy is greater than that of males by several years. Nepal and Bangladesh have been included to illustrate a common characteristic of developing countries, where the sex differential is reversed and males can expect to live longer than females.

2. Death rates are lower for women than for men at each stage in life in developed countries. In countries like Bangladesh, high maternal mortality

in child-bearing years contributes to higher mortality rates in women at these ages.

3. England and Wales still compare unfavourably with the Nordic countries on infant mortality, but have a better record than most on deaths in early adulthood, due mainly to a low accident rate. The countries' record deteriorates again for deaths in late middle age. Scotland and Northern Ireland compare even more unfavourably with most European countries.

4. The pattern differs for each country. For example, Finland has had an excellent record on infant health for several years, but a poor record with respect to the middle-aged and older men in the population. Japan comes out favourably at all stages of life. Hungary consistently comes out badly in comparison with other developed countries.

Macfarlane and Mugford (1984) conclude from their analysis of international comparisons that, at least as far as perinatal mortality is concerned,

Table 9: *Mortality from all causes in selected countries* (*latest available year around 1983*)

| | Expectation of life at birth | | Death rate/1,000 population in selected age-groups | | | | | |
| | | | Age under 1 year | | Age 20–24 | | Age 55–59 | |
	Male	Female	Male	Female	Male	Female	Male	Female
England and Wales	71.3	77.3	11.4	9.0	0.8	0.3	13.2	7.4
Scotland	69.3	75.4	12.8	9.7	1.0	0.3	17.5	9.4
Northern Ireland	69.2	75.6	15.0	12.4	1.2	0.6	14.0	8.9
Denmark	71.5	77.5	8.7	6.4	1.1	0.4	13.2	7.9
Finland	70.1	77.9	6.6	5.9	1.1	0.4	15.6	5.8
Iceland	73.9	79.4	7.0	5.4	1.1	0.5	12.4	5.2
Norway	72.6	79.5	8.7	6.9	1.2	0.3	11.2	5.4
Sweden	73.6	79.6	7.0	7.0	1.0	0.3	10.0	4.8
France	70.4	78.4	12.3	9.0	1.8	0.6	13.8	5.4
Netherlands	72.7	79.4	9.3	7.5	0.8	0.4	11.2	5.4
Hungary	65.5	79.4	21.3	16.4	1.6	0.5	22.7	10.1
USA	71.0	78.3	12.7	10.2	1.5	0.5	13.8	7.3
Japan	74.2	79.7	6.8	5.6	0.9	0.4	9.1	4.4
Bangladesh	55.3	54.4	128.4	119.5	1.6	2.9	21.2	21.8
Nepal	46.6	45.1	Not available		Not available		Not available	

Source: United Nations, *Demographic Yearbook for 1984* (1986).

the performance of England and Wales in the 1980s is not quite as bad as some observers have suggested. Nor would the UK countries be 'near the bottom of the league' if there was a uniform international classification.

Another study, however, draws attention to our much poorer record on premature mortality in men and women aged 45–64. From a comparison of twelve European countries in 1980 it was concluded that mortality was considerably higher in the UK than elsewhere. This applied to circulatory and respiratory diseases, cancer, and 'all causes'. Our relatively low mortality from accidents reduces the overall mortality difference, but it is still striking. Comparing mortality from all causes in 1950 and 1980, the authors concluded that France and Finland made notably better advances in health than the UK countries for this age-group (Catford and Ford, 1984).

The extent of inequalities

The above statistics, of course, do not say anything about the extent of the inequalities in health *within* each country. Different countries use different social variables to measure inequalities: occupation; income; education; social circumstances; rural/urban residence, and so on. But however inequality is measured, every country is found to have disadvantaged and advantaged groups which differ in their experience of health (Blaxter, 1983).

Inequalities between social groups show up in most countries when chronic disease and limiting long-standing illness are measured, with middle-aged men commonly showing rates of chronic disease 40 per cent to 50 per cent higher in the lowest compared with the highest social group (Blaxter, 1988). Examples of inequalities in chronic illness in five European countries are shown in Fig. 10.

Low income is also commonly associated with poorer health, particularly for chronic illness and disability in middle age. In one survey in Finland, for example, the proportion of middle-aged people with chronic illness ranged from 18 per cent in the highest income group to 42 per cent in the lowest group. In France the chronic illness rate ranged from 30 per cent in the high income bracket to 57 per cent in the lowest. These surveys are not comparable, but they do illustrate the common link between low income and high illness rates (Blaxter, 1988). The experiences of the following European countries give further insight into the issue.

Figure 10. *Some examples of social trends in chronic illness.* (*Source: Blaxter, 1988. Copyright Gower Press.*)

Denmark

From Table 9 it can be seen that infant mortality (death under one year) in 1983 was very low in Denmark compared with many countries, including England and Wales. Comparisons between occupational groups in the country show that throughout the 1970s initial differences in neonatal mortality declined so that by 1977 the differences had been almost eliminated. The figures given on p. 89 of the Black Report can now be updated in Table 10 to illustrate the point. This shows negligible differences between the five occupational groups by 1977.

Table 10: *Denmark: neonatal mortality/1,000 live births*

Parent's occupation	1974	1977
Self-employed	5.7	6.6
White-collar	7.5	5.3
Skilled worker	8.1	5.6
Unskilled worker	9.0	5.6
Other/unknown	8.8	6.1
Average	8.0	5.7

Source: Holstein (1985).

Furthermore, the infant mortality rate does not differ between married and unmarried women as it did in the 1960s. Of these reductions in inequality, Holstein comments: 'This result is, in my view, a very important one. It demonstrates that inequalities in health should not be interpreted as an unavoidable "natural law" but as open to change by public health intervention' (Holstein, 1985).

For adults of working age, however, there are still obvious inequalities in health. For example, a longitudinal study, examining deaths from 1975 to 1980 in men, found that mortality in the lowest, unskilled group was 37 per cent higher than that of the highest professional group. For women, mortality was 20 per cent higher in the equivalent groups (Andersen, 1985). From studies quoted later it seems that occupational differences in Denmark are smaller than in several other European countries. Morbidity studies have found the familiar pattern of increasing disease rates with decreasing social class, except in the 20–29 age range, where professional classes have poorer health.

Although regional differences in infant mortality have been noted, these change from year to year without showing a stable pattern of regions with high and low rates, so the differences appear to be the result of random fluctuations (Holstein, 1985).

On the other hand, the regional differences in dental health in Denmark seem to be more systematic. Comparing the Copenhagen area with Western Jutland in the 1980s the ratio of children with decayed teeth was 1:2 – a difference which reflects the variations in preventive programmes and regular dental examinations in these areas. The Danish municipalities with public dental care for children have 10 per cent less caries than those without public dental care.

In relation to health services, no major differences in use of services are apparent, and use of free primary health care varies only slightly with income. However, use of dental care, which is not always free for adults, varies considerably with social class and income (Holstein, 1985).

Finland

Detailed reports on inequalities in health and health care have recently been prepared for Finland (Koskinen *et al.*, 1985).

The country has an excellent record in reducing the proportion of low birth-weight babies and consequently reducing perinatal and infant mortality. Between the early 1950s and the 1970s the proportion of low birth-weight babies fluctuated around 5.5 per cent of all births. Between 1975 and 1979 the incidence went down to 4.2 per cent, and in the region with previously relatively high rates the incidence fell to just below 4 per cent. As a comparison, the rates for England and Wales were approximately 7 per cent. Now the rates of low birth-weight and infant mortality are among the lowest in the world, but Finland aims to improve on that record still further. By the year 2000 Finland has set itself the target of reducing the number of low birth-weight infants to less than 3 per cent (Koskinen *et al.*, 1985).

In contrast, mortality for older adults in Finland is relatively high, particularly for men, with evidence of social inequality. In the years 1976 to 1980 mortality in unskilled male workers was 89 per cent higher than in the top professional group, and for women was 20 per cent higher (Marin, 1986). There was also a regional pattern with north-eastern Finland considered less healthy than the south-western parts. Over the decade from 1970 to 1980 mortality declined in all four provinces but the differential in mortality between them remained the same. However, over the same period the differences between cities and rural areas in mortality rates for men aged 35–75 disappeared. Among women there were no obvious urban/rural differences.

Interesting changes have occurred in relation to the health services.

In 1964 there were noticeable regional differences in consultation rates with doctors in the state-subsidized health care system. Residents in the 'healthier' south of the country made more use of doctors' services than those in the 'less healthy' east and north. However, between then and 1976 these regional differences had diminished, especially among those who were chronically sick, and the relative differences are now said to be negligible in the rural areas and much reduced in the urban areas. Later in this chapter some of the policies thought to be responsible for reductions in inequalities will be discussed.

What has still to be tackled in Finland, though, is the inequality in the use of health services by different income groups. Consultation rates with doctors increased with increasing income, when adjustments were made for the variation in the number of days sick. Hospital use also varied with income, and large regional differences still persist in the use of the private dental services (Koskinen *et al.*, 1985).

France

According to Valkonen there are no recent data on socio-economic differences in infant mortality in France to update those quoted in the Black Report. Then, the differences were roughly the same as in England and Wales (Valkonen, 1987). For adult mortality the results of a longitudinal study linked to the 1975 census have become available. For the years 1975 to 1980 the usual occupational class gradient was observed in this study, with a wide differential between top and bottom grades of the order of 2.8:1 for men and 2:1 for women. The health gap between non-manual and manual classes of working age widened between the late 1950s and the late 1970s as mortality declined more rapidly in the non-manual sector (Desplanques, 1984).

Norway

The rate of infant mortality in Norway declined over the thirty years from 1951 to 1981, from 26 deaths/1,000 live births to less than 8/1,000, comparing favourably with that for England and Wales. By 1983 the Social Survey found that there had been a general decline all over the country, with a decrease in inequality between the different regions (Måseide, 1985). For adults, though, regional mortality differences have remained unchanged for over thirty years, with high rates in northern Norway and low rates in the west. For example, in 1976–80 the mortality for men was 26 per cent above average in the most northerly county and 18 per cent below average in the south-west, though very little difference in chronic illness was found between the various counties (Måseide, 1985).

In socio-economic groups mortality of unskilled men in 1975-80 was 35 per cent higher than the top professionals and for unskilled women the difference was of the order of 9 per cent (Borgan and Kristofersen, 1986). The working class had nearly 60 per cent more chronic illness than the highest social class (Måseide, 1985).

Sweden

For many years the infant mortality rate in Sweden has been one of the lowest in any developed country, though Finland now appears to be challenging that position. In 1980 just over 4.6 per cent of babies had a low birth-weight, which is also an excellent record.

A 1984 study examined perinatal mortality in 1976-7 linked to the census records so that several socio-economic factors could be studied. Mortality in the lowest socio-economic groups was only 17 per cent higher than in the most privileged group – a difference which was not statistically significant (Ericson *et al.*, 1984). This supports the conclusion, expressed by many, that social inequalities in health in early life are negligible in Sweden, at least in those areas where information is available.

Adult mortality rates are also low compared with those of other countries, but information on inequalities within the country is sparse. The results of one of the comparative studies quoted in the next section suggest that socio-economic differences in adult mortality are small.

Comparative studies

A number of recent studies have tried to compare several countries in relation to social inequalities in health.

Valkonen (1988), for example, compared mortality by level of education in Denmark, England and Wales, Finland, Hungary and Norway in the 1970s and 1980s for the age range 35–54. Among men, mortality rates were highest in Hungary and Finland, and among women, in Hungary and Denmark. Death rates were found to decline with increasing years of education with a remarkably similar pattern in all six countries. Changes in inequalities over the decade were also analysed. The gap in mortality between groups with different levels of education had increased in England and Wales in the 1970s. In men there was no change in mortality in the lowest educational category, whereas there was a decline of between 10 per cent and 20 per cent in the other categories. In women there had been a large increase in the health gap due to a decline of more than 40 per cent in the death rates for the higher educational category. No significant increases in inequality were noted for the Nordic countries over the same period (Valkonen, 1988).

Occupational mortality in the four Nordic countries has been compared for 1971–80, making use of compatible census-linked longitudinal studies. Standardized Mortality Ratios were based on the *whole* Nordic population who were economically active (Andersen *et al.*, 1987). Clear differentials in mortality in men could be seen between occupational groups. Finnish men had the highest mortality in almost every occupational group, followed by Denmark, then Norway and Sweden. It was noticeable that the same groups were advantaged and disadvantaged in each of the four countries. Thus non-manual groups (especially teachers, nurses and doctors) had relatively low mortality, while manual groups had high mortality (particularly those in heavy industrial jobs, and in hotel and domestic work). When causes of death were investigated in the study it was found that groups with high mortality overall had high mortality for almost all causes of death, not just for a few specific occupational hazards (Andersen *et al.*, 1987). Valkonen (1987) has used the results from the above study to compare the gap in mortality between white-collar and blue-collar occupations in the four Nordic countries. Mortality was between 9 per cent and 14 per cent higher for blue-collar occupations than for white-collar occupations in Denmark, Norway and Sweden, while in Finland the difference was 25 per cent. This suggested that inequalities in mortality were greater in Finland than in the other three countries, which had roughly equivalent levels of inequality (Valkonen, 1987).

In a detailed review of these and other comparative studies in 1987, Valkonen came to the following conclusions:

For working age adults,
* inequality in mortality is greatest in France, somewhat less marked in England and Wales, Hungary and Finland, and smallest in Denmark, Norway and Sweden;

* inequality in mortality among men in different occupational classes had increased during the last two decades in France, Hungary, and England and Wales, but has remained constant in Norway, Denmark and Finland;

* there are smaller gradients in mortality among married women than among men but changes in inequality reflect those seen in men, with increased inequality in England and Wales and Hungary but not in the Nordic countries.

For babies,

* in Denmark and Sweden socio-economic differences in infant mortality throughout the first year of life have all but disappeared. In most of the other countries discussed above the differences are still marked, though they have decreased somewhat in England and Wales (Valkonen, 1987).

Policies for reducing inequalities in health

Reduction in inequalities has been most noticeable in the Nordic countries in relation to the health of babies. To what do they attribute this success? In Denmark the reduction has been attributed in part to an intensive preventive public health effort, coupled with social changes concerned, for example, with freer access to abortion services (Holstein, 1985).

In relation to the Finnish record on low birth-weight and infant mortality the Black Report has already outlined the rapid development of primary health care services in Finland which aim to cover a large proportion of the population with outreach programmes (p. 98). Since then, further improvements have been made. To advance the target set on low birth-weight, new social maternity benefits for all pregnant and nursing mothers were introduced in the 1970s. By 1982 all women were entitled to 258 days of paid maternity leave (compared with 72 days in 1971), and men were entitled to 6 to 12 days of leave around the time of birth, and between 25 and 100 days' paternity leave in exchange for some of the maternity leave (compared with nil in 1971). Twenty per cent of men take advantage of this benefit.

The reduction in regional differences in health care in Finland has been attributed to the very active policy-making which was adopted to combat inequalities. It was recognized that there was an unfair geographical distribution of medical personnel, and an Act of 1972 enforced a two-pronged strategy:

1. Health resources were preferentially allocated to northern and eastern parts of the country. Cities which had hospitals and health centres were deliberately left lagging behind. Subsidies were offered to set up new medical posts in priority areas. Higher salaries were offered in community health centres than in the hospital sector.

2. Building expenditure was switched from hospital to health centre buildings. By 1981 the community and hospital sectors were taking equal shares of the building budget (formerly the hospital sector took the major share).

The policy seems to have been successful because the health centres in rural areas in Lapland and eastern Finland 'are today better manned than those in the big cities There has been a corresponding improvement in the number of nurses and dentists in the priority areas, too. In effect, primary health care has become the centrepiece of the national health service rather than playing a subordinate role. For the future, Finland is following through its commitment to the World Health Organization's 'Health for All' goal, with a national health strategy containing detailed targets for the country and with the full backing of central government (Koskinen *et al.*, 1985). (The Swedish government is also mobilizing action in support of the WHO strategy.)

In Norway interest in inequalities in health has increased progressively over the decade, but it became apparent that the available information on this issue in the country was inadequate. Therefore in 1987 the Ministry of Health commissioned what could be seen as a 'Norwegian Black Report': a three-year research project to analyse and document the extent of the problem and to identify priority areas for action (Vandeskog, 1987).

One major health policy development in Norway has already won international acclaim and is relevant to discussions on reducing inequalities. In 1976 the Norwegian parliament passed a national nutrition and food policy the first of its kind in the world. It had four main goals:

1. To encourage healthy dietary habits, by pricing policies and improvement in the food distribution networks;

2. To help stabilize the world food supply by contributing to emergency food reserves and decreasing reliance on imported food;

3. To promote consumption of domestically produced food;

4. To strengthen and stabilize the rural economy, stopping the decline in the number of small farms by making farming more profitable and attractive.

National dietary goals were set and, uniquely, the policy focused on structural changes to encourage the desired dietary changes, rather than emphasize the individual's responsibility alone. Differential food pricing and incentives for production of healthy food were proposed, with the whole policy co-ordinated across the nine government departments which could have an influence on the issue. The aim was to provide reasonably priced, nutritious food accessible to all.

After ten years of the policy, evaluations show mixed progress. On the positive side, it has been noted that the policy has survived three different governments; all the goals and objectives are still valid and indeed have been strengthened by subsequent research findings; all the major political parties still support it, and there have been great efforts at cooperation at national and local level. In addition, the proportion of the gross national product given in aid to developing countries has also increased over the decade, reaching 1.15 per cent in 1984. The level of farming incomes and the area of cultivated land has also increased (Klepp and Forster, 1985).

On the negative side, it has proved very difficult to change existing farming and pricing policies in the face of a strong lobby from the agricultural sector, in effect protecting the producers rather than the consumers. Even the inter-departmental government committee is reported to be dominated by the Ministry of Agriculture. Against this background the policy has made most progress in a wide variety of health education programmes, and much less on the pricing and food-production fronts (Winkler, 1987). The strategy, however, has not been abandoned but is entering a second phase, supplemented by more intensive research on how to change pricing policy and build on the successes so far.

Conclusions

So what conclusions can be drawn from these international comparisons? Certainly the UK is not alone in experiencing inequalities in health. Every country to a greater or lesser extent experiences differences in health between regional, social or income groups. The question of whether some countries have less inequality in health than others is very difficult to answer. The comparative studies quoted lend support to the suggestion that the Nordic countries, particularly Denmark, Sweden and Norway, experience less social inequality in health than other European countries, including England and Wales.

What is instructive in these comparisons is the examples of concrete strategies which have been adopted to reduce specific inequalities. The Finnish example of reduction in regional (particularly rural/urban) variations in health care is illuminating. It is also obvious that the Nordic countries have for many years put national health policy high on their agendas.

Chapter 6

Explaining Health Inequalities

Of crucial importance is the question of how health inequalities are generated and maintained. The Black Working Group examined the evidence on causes of occupational class differences in health under four main headings: artefact, health selection, cultural/behavioural and materialist/structuralist explanations. Material and structural factors were judged to be the main contributors to inequalities, though the other explanations were not mutually exclusive and could be seen to play some part at varying stages of life.

This chapter looks at fresh evidence published since 1980 which has taken the discussion further forward. A number of useful reviews are available (Macintyre, 1986b; Wilkinson, 1986a; Blane, 1985).

The artefact explanation

This approach, described in depth by Illsley (1986) and Jones and Cameron (1984), suggests that the method of measuring occupational class – by the Registrar General's social class classification – artificially inflates the size and importance of health differences. The authors maintain that the Registrar General's classification and the nature of occupations open to the labour force have changed so much in recent decades that any comparisons with earlier decades this century are meaningless, using this classification as a tool. The arguments and evidence concerning this explanation have already been outlined in greater detail on pp. 256–65. Briefly, the recent evidence continues to point to very real differences in health between social groups which cannot convincingly be explained away as artefact.

Firstly, important new evidence has come from the OPCS Longitudinal Study showing the existence of a clear occupational class gradient in mortality, free from one of the statistical problems – numerator/denominator bias, as outlined on p. 228. Secondly, Chapter 3 has already given examples of recent studies which have made serious attempts to control for some of the other measurement problems concerned with occupational class, and none of the results alter the picture to any great extent. Thirdly, the 1980s have seen an upsurge in studies (quoted in Chapter 2) which have used other indicators of social circumstances to examine their relationship with health. Whether social position is measured by income, housing tenure, household possessions or education, a similar pattern emerges on inequalities in health between the top and the bottom of the social scale, consistent with that found by using occupational class. Finally, results from another major longitudinal study, the Whitehall Study, have provided fresh evidence of a social class gradient in mortality between different grades of the Civil Service, with a differential *greater* than that found when occupational class is used as a measure. This and other studies suggest that the Registrar General's classification might be under-estimating the size of the class gradient rather than over-estimating it (see p. 232). There can be no doubt that these inequalities exist, however imperfect the measuring tool.

The argument that we could do with a better measure of social class than one based on occupation is widely accepted. Occupation is just one of the many interrelated factors which contribute to the concept of social class. It has been pointed out that there is a tendency for some social groups to be relatively privileged in almost every respect – power, status, income, education, etc. – and for other groups to be relatively disadvantaged in almost every respect. That the disadvantaged groups have poorer health than the privileged groups is at the heart of the studies on inequality.

Theories of natural and social selection

Explanations in terms of selection accept that social inequalities in health exist, but suggest that the differences are caused by a health selection process. According to this explanation, people in poor health would tend to move down the occupational scale and concentrate in the lower social classes, while people in good health would tend to move up into higher classes. The gap between the health of the higher and lower classes would therefore be kept open indefinitely and would be inevitable whatever overall improvements in health occur over the entire population. The same sort of explanation has been discussed on p. 240 in relation to unemployment – the possibility that ill-health may lead to subsequent unemployment rather than unemployment leading to ill-health.

Has any new evidence shed more light on this explanation? Further data have been presented for the three decades from 1951 to 1980 which confirm early studies on first-time mothers in Aberdeen and the outcome of their pregnancies. There was a gradient in perinatal mortality, birth-weight of babies and height of mothers between the occupational classes. It was noted that taller women tended to move up the occupational classes at marriage, while shorter women tended to move down at marriage. As height can be taken as an indicator of health before marriage, this evidence shows that some sort of health selection was taking place at marriage and contributing to the class differential (Illsley, 1986).

The 1980 OPCS survey of heights and weights in Great Britain confirmed that the 'shortest women were least likely to raise their social class through marriage and that, to a lesser extent, the tallest were most likely to raise their social class in this way'. However, OPCS were less certain about what interpretation to put on these findings (Knight, 1984).

Data from the National Survey of Health and Development cohort study have shown that *serious* illness in childhood can affect social mobility. Whatever their class of origin, seriously ill boys were more likely than others to experience a fall in occupational class by the time they were twenty-six (Wadsworth, 1986). This kind of evidence suggests that unhealthy people are more likely to move down the social scale, but estimates suggest that this effect would not make more than a small difference in the overall figures. For example, one estimate based on the data on first-time mothers in Aberdeen suggests that movement between classes accounted for little more than 10 per cent of the social class gap in the perinatal mortality rates (Wilkinson, 1986b). An estimate of the effect of serious childhood illness suggests that only about 1.5 per cent of those seriously ill in their early twenties had suffered a drop in occupational class as a result of previous childhood illness (Wilkinson, 1986a).

Additionally, the 'National Child Development Study, which has been following a cohort of children born in 1958, has been used to check this explanation. Preliminary results confirm that some social mobility in childhood was related to health, but again this mobility did not account for the social class gradient in health observed (Power *et al.*, 1986). A second study from this project has used housing tenure as well as occupational class to check the results. It compared not only the health of young adults who were upwardly or downwardly mobile, but also the health of those who had stayed in stable socio-economic circumstances from birth to the age of twenty-three. Significantly, the health of those young people whose circumstances were stable differed between socio-economic groups as much, if not more, than that of those who were mobile; this difference in health could not be explained by social mobility because there had been none (Fogelman *et al.*, 1987).

Similarly, the Longitudinal Study examined health-related selection in older adults and concluded that for men over fifty years of age health-related mobility between classes did not contribute to the mortality differentials (Fox *et al.*, 1986).

In the Whitehall study the men were given a rigorous medical examination on entry to the study. Among those with no detectable disease at the beginning of the study, there were still much greater death rates in lower than higher grades. Recruitment of sicker men into lower grades in the Civil Service would not explain the gradient in this case (Marmot *et al.*, 1984b).

To sum up, there is some evidence that health selection operates at younger ages, and new evidence for men over fifty that no such selection effect is evident after this age. Estimates of the size of the selection effect suggest that it accounts for only a small proportion of the overall differential between the social classes.

Cultural/behavioural and materialist/structuralist explanations

The health selection explanation suggests that health can determine subsequent social position. The third and fourth explanations both take the view that social circumstances can affect subsequent health, but differ in where they put the emphasis.

The cultural/behavioural explanation stresses differences in the way individuals in different social groups choose to lead their lives: the behaviour and voluntary life-styles they adopt. In this explanation inequalities in health evolve because lower social groups have adopted more dangerous and health-damaging behaviour than the higher social groups, and may have less interest in protecting their health for the future.

The structuralist/materialist explanation emphasizes the role of the external environment: the *conditions* under which people live and work and the pressures on them to consume unhealthy products. Inequalities in health in this context would come about because lower social groups are exposed to a more unhealthy environment. They do more dangerous work, have poorer housing, and have fewer resources available to secure the necessities for health and to use the available health services. At a more general level, the whole structure of society is implicated.

But several commentators are beginning to question whether the distinction between the two approaches is artificial, as behaviour cannot be separated from its social context (Blane, 1985; Blaxter, 1983). The classic example of childhood accidents has been quoted to illustrate the point. The observation that children from lower social groups have more accidents than children from higher groups may be explained by the behavioural view as due to more reckless, risk-taking behaviour in this group and inadequate care by parents. The materialist view would highlight the unsafe play areas, the lack of fenced-off gardens and the greater difficulty of supervising children's play from high-rise housing. In the latter view, the environment is dictating the behaviour of both mother and child.

The following new evidence supports the behavioural and the structural/materialist explanations but shows that the two are interrelated rather than mutually exclusive.

Evidence on cultural/behavioural differences

Latest evidence confirms previous observations that there are life-style differences between the social classes which are related to health. Cigarette-smoking would be a prominent example.

Smoking habits

Table 11 gives the percentages of cigarette-smokers in each socio-economic group over the period 1972–84. It is clear that in every year the percentage

Table 11: *Prevalence of cigarette-smoking in Great Britain, 1972–84, by sex and socio-economic group* [1] (*persons aged 16 and over* [2]): *percentage smoking cigarettes*

	Professional	Employers and managers	Intermediate and junior non-manual	Skilled manual and own account non-professional	Semi-skilled manual and personal service	Unskilled manual	All aged 16 and over
Men							
1972	33	44	45	57	57	64	52
1974	29	46	45	56	56	61	51
1976	25	38	40	51	53	58	46
1978	25	37	38	49	53	60	45
1980	21	35	35	48	49	57	42
1982	20	29	30	42	47	49	38
1984	17	29	30	40	45	49	36
Women							
1972	33	38	38	47	42	42	42
1974	25	38	38	46	43	43	41
1976	28	35	36	42	41	38	38
1978	23	33	33	42	41	41	37
1980	21	33	34	43	39	41	37
1982	21	29	30	39	36	41	33
1984	15	29	28	37	37	36	32

[1] Members of the Armed Forces, persons in inadequately described occupations, and all persons who have never worked have not been shown as separate categories. They are, however, included in the figures for all persons.

[2] Aged 15 and over in 1972.

Source: OPCS (1986d). Crown Copyright.

Table 12: *Prevalence of cigarette-smoking in Great Britain, 1984, by region*[1] (*persons aged 16 and over*)

Region	Percentage smoking cigarettes	Base = 100%
England		
North	36	1,020
Yorkshire and Humberside	39	1,662
North-West	35	2,133
East Midlands	31	1,334
West Midlands	33	1,791
East Anglia	24	651
Greater London	37	2,090
South-East	31	3,415
South-West	30	1,383
Wales	37	925
Scotland	39	1,801

[1] It should be noted that the data in this table have not been standardized to take account of differences in age-structure between regions.

Source: OPCS (1986d). Crown Copyright.

of smokers increased steadily from the professional group through to the unskilled manual group. For example, in 1984 17 per cent of professional group men and 15 per cent of professional group women were smokers compared with 49 per cent of men in the unskilled manual category and 36 per cent of women in that category.

The table also shows that there has been a decline in the prevalence of smoking in most socio-economic groups, but the decline has been more rapid in some groups than in others. For example, prevalence in women in the manual groups has shown very little reduction over the decade, whereas that in the professional group has shown a pronounced decline.

Smoking habits varied with economic status, too. For example, in 1984 36 per cent of men in work were smokers, compared with 61 per cent of unemployed men. The corresponding figures for women were 34 per cent and 48 per cent. Table 12 gives an indication of the regional variations in smoking in 1984 (although the data have not been standardized for age).

Class trends in mortality from lung cancer and coronary heart disease show some similarity to the smoking trends. Thus there is a social class gradient in mortality for both diseases, with lower rates in the professional classes to highest in the unskilled manual class. In addition, mortality over the decade has been declining faster in non-manual groups than in manual groups, as Fig. 7 on p. 261 has illustrated (Marmot and McDowall, 1986).

Mortality from lung cancer and coronary heart disease is higher in the unemployed than in the employed population, and regional variations in mortality from the diseases mirror the smoking variations to a certain extent.

In the case of coronary heart disease, there are further similarities. Before 1950 mortality from the disease in men was marginally higher in classes I and II than in IV and V, but during the 1950s the gradient reversed and mortality became higher in classes IV and V than in I and II (Marmot *et al.*, 1981; Morris, 1979).

Alcohol

Drinking habits also vary between the social groups, but in a much more complex way. Heavy drinking is more common among manual groups than among non-manual groups. For example, 26 per cent of unskilled manual group men were classed as heavy drinkers in 1984, compared with 8 per cent of professional men. At a regional level the highest proportion of heavy drinkers was found in the North (including the North-East) and Wales, and the lowest in East Anglia and the outer South-East of England. However, the pattern varied considerably in relation to other categories of drinker. For example, the unskilled manual group had the highest percentage of abstainers as well as the highest percentage of heavy drinkers. This group also had a lower proportion of 'frequent light drinkers', whereas the professional and managerial groups, both men and women, had the highest proportion of this type of drinker (OPCS, 1986d). Which pattern of drinking would ultimately be more detrimental to the health of each group is debatable. There is some evidence that mortality from chronic liver disease and cirrhosis was lower in class I men and high in class V men in 1979–83, but apart from that the situation is unclear.

Food and nutrition

There are differences between social groups in the quantity and nutritional quality of the food they eat. In this context comparisons are made between income groups. Groups A to D represent households with at least one earner. Group A contains the richest 10 per cent, group D the poorest 10 per cent, and groups B and C are intermediate, each representing 40 per cent of households with one earner. Table 13 shows consumption of some of the main food categories by income group in 1976 and 1984. It is interesting to note how the pattern has changed over that period, bearing in mind that recent nutritional advice has stressed the need to eat more fibre (for instance in bread, particularly brown and wholemeal), more fresh fruit and vegetables including potatoes, and to cut down on sugar, salt and fat, particularly animal fat. In both years the richest group consumed more brown and wholemeal bread, more fresh fruit and vegetables, and less white bread, potatoes, sugar and fat than the poorest group. By the mid 1980s all income groups had increased their consumption of brown and wholemeal bread and potatoes, and had cut down on sugar. (By 1986 brown and wholemeal bread accounted for 25 per cent of all bread consumed, compared with 10 per cent in 1976.) However, consumption of fresh fruit and vegetables had increased only marginally in groups A, B and C, and in the poorest group had actually declined. There was a small reduction in the consumption of total fats across all income groups, but a substantial change in the *type* of fats consumed. Butter, lard and compound cooking fat consumption declined markedly, and there was a corresponding increase in margarine and 'all other fats' consumption in all income groups (MAFF, 1977, 1986). Thus in terms of the foodstuffs listed the richest income group continues to have a healthier diet than the poorest group. However, there are signs that, within the limits of their income, the poorest group may have responded to nutritional advice to the same extent as other groups, for example in wholemeal bread consumption. How much the poorest group's choice of food is restricted by low income is discussed in greater detail on pp. 299–302.

Table 13: *Food consumption by income group (Great Britain, 1976 and 1984)* (*oz./person/week*)

Income Group	White bread		Brown bread, incl. wholemeal		Sugar		Total fats		Fruit (fresh)		Vegetables (fresh)		Potatoes	
	1976	1984	1976	1984	1976	1984	1976	1984	1976	1984	1976	1984	1976	1984
A	19.8	12.3	4.1	8	12.3	8	9.8	9.1	22.5	25.3	27.3	30.7	29.8	33.4
B	26.2	18.3	3	6	13.4	9.4	10.5	9.5	18.3	19	24	24.4	35	36.5
C	30.4	23.0	3	5.9	14.5	10.9	11	10.4	15.2	16	24.8	25.5	38.2	42.4
D	29.9	26.0	2.7	5.2	15.7	11.5	11	10	15.2	13	24.9	21.5	42.3	48.3

Source: MAFF (1977, 1986).

There is also evidence of higher consumption of sweets by children in lower social groups (Charles and Kerr, 1985).

The links between nutrition and health are many and varied, ranging from effects on growth, to links with specific diseases like coronary heart disease and obesity, to general resistance to infections, and all of these show higher rates in lower social groups.

Exercise in leisure-time

Data on leisure-time activities by socio-economic group were available in the 1973, 1977 and 1983 General Household Surveys. Table 14 shows two of the most popular activities: walking and swimming. In both, the professional group had the highest participation rates and the unskilled manual group the lowest. There was an increase in participation from 1977 to 1983 for all groups, but the social gradient remained.

Exercise may be linked to health in several ways, including a possible protective effect against coronary heart disease mortality, which is, of course, class-related (Morris, 1981).

Poorer take-up of preventive services by lower social classes has already been noted; it is clearly a possibility that this is due to cultural norms and voluntary behaviour choices rather than to material barriers to take-up, such as limited access.

Table 14: *Exercise in leisure-time in Great Britain by socio-economic group. Persons aged 16 and over (1977 and 1983): % participating.*

Socio-economic group	Walking (over 2 miles)		Indoor swimming	
	1977	1983	1977	1983
Professional	29	30	9	12
Employers and managers	23	24	6	9
Intermediate – non-manual	27	27	7	11
Junior – non-manual	20	22	5	10
Skilled manual	15	16	4	5
Semi-skilled manual	12	15	1	4
Unskilled manual	10	13	2	3

Source: OPCS *General Household Survey* for 1977 and 1983.

How much of the differential does life-style explain?

The evidence outlined above suggests that differences in life-style can indeed account for some of the class differential in health, but how much of it do the life-style factors account for? A more systematic investigation of coronary heart disease risk factors was carried out in the Whitehall study (Marmot *et al.*, 1984b). The two major smoking-related diseases, coronary heart disease and lung cancer, were related both to smoking and employment grade. Of the top grade, 29 per cent were smokers, compared with 61 per cent of the lowest grade. However, it was found that even for non-smokers coronary heart disease was strongly associated with grade, with higher rates in lower grades. Table 15 shows what happened to the class gradient for coronary heart disease when controlled for age, smoking, systolic blood pressure, plasma cholesterol, height and blood sugar. The risk associated with employment grade reduced by less than 25 per cent. Likewise, controlling for exercise in leisure-time had little effect on the differential. In addition, steep gradients were found for diseases thought not to be related to smoking.

Table 15: *Relative risk * of CHD death in ten years controlling for (a) age, and (b) age, smoking, systolic blood pressure, plasma cholesterol concentration, height and blood sugar.*

	Administrators	Professional executive	Clerical	Other
(a) Controlling for age	1.0	1.6	2.2	2.7
(b) Controlling for other risk factors	1.0	1.5	1.7	2.1

* Calculated by multiple logistic regression.

Source: Marmot *et al.* (1984b).

In the United States similar results have been found from an important cohort study, the Alameda County Study in California (Berkman and Breslow, 1983; Kaplan, 1985). The study has been assessing levels of health in the sample and trying to determine factors associated with health since 1965. When family income was studied, those with 'inadequate' income had much poorer survival chances over eighteen years of follow-up. For example, compared with the richest group, the poorest group had more than double the risk of death over that period. The study went on to analyse whether harmful behaviour patterns accounted for the increased risk. Even when the data were adjusted to take account of thirteen known risk factors including smoking, drinking, exercise and race, there was still a substantial gradient of risk associated with income. For example, the poorest group still had one and a half times the risk of death as the richest group. They concluded that behaviour patterns were not the major factors related to the increased risk of death, and suggested that factors related to the general living conditions and environment of the poor were more likely to be implicated. This line of enquiry is continuing.

Likewise, in the study of unemployed and employed groups reported on p. 241, excess mortality in the unemployed group was still evident when the study controlled for smoking and drinking (Cook *et al.*, 1982).

All these studies suggest that the differences in life-style between social groups account for some, but not all, of the observed health gap. Indeed in some cases *most* of the difference in health is not explained by these factors.

Several new studies have touched on the cultural aspect of this explanation – the suggestion that beliefs about health and health care may differ among social groups. The 'culture of poverty' idea – that poorer groups have more negative concepts of health and a lack of orientation towards the future which inhibits preventive health action – has been re-examined. For example, Calnan and Johnson (1985) compared the health beliefs of women from social classes I and II with those of social classes IV and V on two issues: concepts of health and perception of vulnerability to disease. Both of these issues are claimed to be related to decisions to take action on health. Findings showed that there was no social class difference ir theories about vulnerability, or in concepts of health when defined in relation to personal health. Only when health was defined in the *abstract* were there marked social class differences and this may have been because middle-class women found it easier to express abstract ideas.

Similarly, Blaxter and Paterson (1982), in a study of disadvantaged mothers and daughters in Scotland, found no evidence that would fit a simple 'culture of poverty' model in either generation. Problems in health service use in the younger generation seemed to stem more from a lack of skill in dealing with the system rather than from adverse cultural beliefs. These and other studies (Pill and Stott, 1985a, 1985b) suggest that the importance of the 'culture of poverty' model as an explanation of poor service use and health-damaging behaviour may have been over-estimated in the past, and new appraisals of health behaviour are needed.

Evidence that material factors affect health or health-related behaviour

Several studies published recently have investigated how material and structural factors affect health. Others have looked at how such factors influence behaviour or limit choice about health. The evidence for a clear causal link between unemployment and mental ill-health has already been presented on pp. 241–3, together with evidence of higher mortality in the unemployed which cannot easily be explained away other than by some direct or indirect effect of unemployment. The strong association with aspects of material deprivation and ill-health in small area studies has also been discussed on pp. 247–9. This section therefore concentrates on a number of additional factors, such as housing and income, to add to the evidence in previous chapters.

Housing conditions and health

This subject has been badly neglected until recently and is only beginning to be studied again, mainly in the public sector. Some of the studies look at aspects of poor housing, like damp and mould, in relation to physical health. Others are concerned more with the stress and safety aspects imposed on people by poor design.

A study in Gateshead was carried out in 1983 on eight council housing areas, from the very best to the very worst in the district. Controlling for age, there were marked and consistent differences in self-reported health between individuals from different areas. People from 'bad' housing areas reported poorer health, more long-standing illness, more recent illness and more symptoms of depression than those living in 'good' housing areas. The position was reversed for the over-65s because of a local authority letting policy which gave priority to the less-fit elderly. Nearly a third of households reported defects in houses which they thought affected health, and these came disproportionately from the three 'bad' areas, especially in connection with respiratory conditions. 'Bad' council housing areas did not necessarily conform to the stereotype of non-traditional construction and high-rise flats. Location, poor environment and low quality of construction were the important factors (Keithley *et al.*, 1984).

A further paper by the same team looked in greater detail at respiratory conditions in council house tenants. It was found that smoking, an unhealthy working environment and age were the most important determinants of respiratory problems. When these were held constant, people in areas of 'bad' housing reported more respiratory conditions than those in 'good' housing areas. The problems were associated with flats rather than houses, and with older accommodation (McCarthy *et al.*, 1985).

A large-scale study investigated whether the design of buildings could lead to social malaise among the inhabitants. It covered over 4,000 blocks of flats and 4,000 houses in London, with additional information from around the country and abroad. Fifteen design variables in blocks of flats were identified which affected the behaviour of at least some of the residents, especially children. The degree of social malaise was indicated by the extent of litter, graffiti, vandalism, children taken into care, and urine and faecal pollution. Circumstances worsened with larger buildings and grounds, as the number of interconnecting walkways increased, and also where residents could not see or control the approach to their dwellings. The study concluded that such badly-designed blocks 'made it difficult for normal people to cope', and thus contributed to social malaise (Coleman, 1985).

Also of relevance is the growing problem of infestation of housing estates, with the associated health risks. It has been pointed out that the design of high-rise buildings, with their interconnecting ducts and heating systems, allows rapid spread of vermin over which the individual tenants have very little – if any – control (Young, 1980).

An analysis of 'difficult to let' council housing in Liverpool concluded that the unsatisfactory housing conditions on one estate were contributing to high rates of infectious diseases, respiratory disease and mental illness. One source of infection was traced to unhygienic mobile food vans which residents used because no shops had been provided on the estate. Respiratory illnesses were aggravated by ducted warm-air heating and the practice of drying clothes indoors because of inadequate facilities (Department of the Environment, 1981a). Another study of families living in flats found that serious accidents among children were linked to the design of the building (Department of the Environment, 1981b).

The Housing and Environmental Health Departments of the Wirral, Merseyside, identified serious design and construction faults in their high-density housing. Water penetration, ventilation, heating and insulation problems, inadequate under-floor electric heating, deck access and high child-densities 'combined to produce disaster'. These faults resulted in dangerous and severely limiting conditions for the tenants, including lack of privacy and play facilities, noise, lack of clothes drying facilities, dependence on lifts, inadequate refuse disposal, and the obvious safety aspects of the height of buildings (Darley, 1981).

On the subject of damp, a study in South Wales suggested that respiratory symptoms may be aggravated by damp housing and by open coal fires which were thought to cause some pollution of the air inside the house (Burr *et al.*, 1981). Another found clear effects of damp housing on the health of children in a deprived area of Edinburgh in 1986. In particular, respiratory/bronchial symptoms, headaches and diarrhoea were much more common among children living in damp housing. The effect of damp was independent of the effect of low income or smoking in the household (Hunt *et al.*, 1986). A previous study in Edinburgh in 1984 had also found an association between respiratory problems in children, reported by their parents, and damp or mouldy housing. However, such environmental factors were not linked to GP consultation rates for these illnesses. This highlights the dilemma of which measure of morbidity to use in community studies (Strachan, 1986).

Income

There have been few studies in this country of the direct effect of income on health, partly because of the enormous difficulties encountered and partly because of political sensitivity. To be meaningful, all sources of income would have to be assessed, including the value of fringe benefits, property, etc., and such statistics are not readily available in this country. A preliminary analysis has been carried out on occupational incomes and mortality in twenty-two occupations, comparing 1951 and 1971. Over twenty years those occupations which had increased their income relative to average earnings tended to experience a relative decrease in mortality rates. In occupations where income had gone down relative to the mean, mortality rates tended to go up relative to the mean. The death rates of old people also seemed to vary in a similar way with changes in the real value of state pensions over the years from 1965 to 1982. As Wilkinson notes, this work will have to be repeated and extended before firm conclusions can be drawn (Wilkinson, 1986c).

Another study has looked at the effect of income, but this time on children's height. A study of families in poor areas in London in 1973–6 found that a low amount of money spent on food/person/week in a household was highly correlated with poor growth in children. Among these children protein intake was 92 per cent of the recommended daily intake, iron 80 per cent and vitamin D 40 per cent of that recommended. Of the children in the survey 11 per cent were mildly or moderately malnourished (Nelson and Naismith, 1979).

The *indirect* effect of income on health, for example on choice of diet and eating habits, has been more widely investigated. As outlined on p. 293, people from low-income households tend to eat less fruit, vegetables and high-fibre foods, and more fat and sugar, than people from high-income households.

Studies of why this should be so have found lack of money to be a major factor, restricting food choice as well as limiting the quantity of food consumed. For example, a study of sixty-five families living on supple-mentary benefit in 1980 found that some parents went without food to provide enough for their children, and lack of money was frequently cited as the reason for lack of fruit and vegetables in the diet (Burghes, 1980). In a study of 1,000 low-income people in the North of England in 1984, approximately a quarter of respondents reported that they did not have a main meal every day. One third of these said this was because of cost. Four out of ten unemployed people went without a main meal because of lack of money (Lang *et al.*, 1984). An in-depth study of 107 women living with pre-school children in Milton Keynes in 1984 found that 51 per cent of single parents and 30 per cent of low-income mothers in two-parent families were cutting down on food consumption for financial reasons. Of low-income women, 67 per cent found it difficult to afford what they considered to be a healthy diet for their children (Graham, 1986).

It is commonly found in such studies that food is treated as a flexible item in the household budget (unlike rent and rates); when money is short, spending on food tends to be cut back. Unfortunately the cheaper foods are often higher in fat and sugar.

A number of 'desk-top calculations' have been carried out to estimate the cost of following advice on a 'healthy diet', to see whether recommendations are realistic for people on low incomes. One, looking at the cost of an 'adequate' diet in pregnancy, concluded that the cost may be beyond the means of families dependent on low wages or benefits. For example, an average couple living on supplementary benefit in 1984 spent 9 per cent to 10 per cent of their income (excluding housing) on one person's food. However, it was estimated an 'adequate' diet for a pregnant woman would have taken up 28 per cent of the couple's income (Durward, 1984). The British Dietetic Association has considered the dietary problems of special groups at risk of malnutrition – children, pregnant women, ethnic minor-ities, the handicapped and elderly – and concluded that existing benefits for some members of these groups were insufficient for their dietary needs (Haines and de Looy, 1986). One recent study, basing the 'healthy diet' on the advice of the National Advisory Committee on Nutrition Education, calculated that the recommended diet could cost up to 35 per cent more than the typical diet of a low-income family (Cole-Hamilton and Lang, 1986). Some would dispute the figure of 35 per cent and suggest that community studies are now needed to check how valid these calculations are in real-life settings.

In recent years an increasing number of studies have gone out into the community to do just that: to document how people in different circumstances live and how they cope with aspects of health. In the field of family health care, Graham (1984) has collected and reviewed over 250 studies relevant to the question: 'How do parents meet their responsibility to family health?' This provides a valuable insight into the literature. It becomes obvious from such studies that all household resources have the potential to influence health – income, housing, fuel, food and transport. The pattern of spending on these basics varies between rich and poor families. For example, in 1985 poor households spent 56 per cent of income on necessities (food, fuel, housing), whereas rich households spent 36 per cent of their income on these products (Department of Employment, 1986). While 95 per cent of professional households have at least one car available, only 38 per cent of unskilled manual households have one (OPCS, 1986d). It is found that the poorest families may have little choice of fuel, and often have to rely on the most expensive kind (Boardman, 1986). Families who are economizing on fuel risk making their homes cold, damp and prone to condensation. Even within families, there is evidence of resources not being shared out equally. For example, parents may go without food to provide for the children, and the adult breadwinner may be given more food than those who stay at home. If a family has a car it cannot be assumed that women and children have access to it for food shopping and health appointments during the day. Frequently it is found that the male breadwinner in a household has priority over use of the car for work. The issue of transport has been growing in importance as food outlets and medical services become centralized. The time and money spent on travelling becomes a factor to be considered in health service use. One study of pregnant women found that women going to the hospital ante-natal clinic spent twice as long travelling and waiting than mothers going to local GP clinics. They also experienced great problems in travelling with young children (Graham, 1979).

Several studies examine how mothers cope with the stress of caring for the family on a low income, which often involves a juggling act of keeping within a very limited budget while at the same time seeing that the children are well and relatively contented. There is evidence that mothers find a variety of ways of relieving stress in the short term without leaving the child alone. Graham (1984) points out that this often leads to parents going against medical advice. Sweets tend to be used as a quick and easy way of keeping children quiet on shopping trips and on other stressful occasions (Charles and Kerr, 1985), breast-feeding may be abandoned to allow more time for other members of the family (Graham, 1980), and babies' milk may be mixed with cereal to help cope with crying and sleep problems (Graham and McKee, 1980). Cigarette-smoking was used by some mothers as a way of easing tension without leaving the room (Graham, 1976). Another review has also recently highlighted the use of smoking by women to help them survive their stressful workload (Jacobson, 1986).

Graham (1984) points out that such actions, which would be labelled irresponsible by some professionals, may be the only way in which mothers can stay sane and act responsibly towards their family. Poor attendance for preventive health services is also examined in terms of costs and benefits. Graham concludes: 'For poor families in particular a *rational* decision may be one which rejects professional care. The mother may choose instead to invest her limited resources of time, money, and energy in other areas of family health' – in food for the family for example, or in keeping her children warm (Graham, 1984).

These studies on family health, in particular, indicate a complex relationship between individual behaviour and structural and material factors. When researchers start to ask why behaviour differs between classes, it becomes clear that socio-economic circumstances do play an important part. It is far too simple an explanation to put it all down to ignorance or laziness.

Explaining sex differences in health

Parallels can be drawn between the explanations of social class inequalities and those of sex inequalities in health. The artefact, natural selection, behavioural/cultural and materialist/structuralist explanations have all been applied to sex differentials.

For instance, some of the sex differences in morbidity (with high rates for women) have been attributed to artefact, though the exact extent of this is unknown. Morbidity may be under-estimated for men relative to women due to more proxy reporting for men in surveys; or women may have a greater predisposition to report illness. Additionally, women may be more inclined to take care of their health, resulting in increased consultation rates or days of restricted activity for the same amount of illness (Waldron, 1983). All these points need further investigation and, of course, none of them can explain away the sex differential in mortality.

The natural selection or genetic explanation suggests that women's greater longevity and low mortality rate is an intrinsic feature of the human species. This view is supported by the fact that even before birth female foetuses have better survival rates than male foetuses (Hart, 1988). Whatever the merits of the genetic explanation, evidence that the sex differential in mortality is reversed in less developed countries (like Nepal and Bangladesh), and that even the morbidity differential is not a fixed phenomenon in the same country, suggests that the social and cultural environment and health services can play a powerful part in modifying the differential. If that is so, then there should be scope for improvement in health for both sexes.

Very little work has been published on the causes of the sex differential in Britain, though studies in the United States and Europe attempt to answer the question: 'Why do women live longer than men?' Male mortality exceeds female mortality by 100 per cent for seven of the major causes of death in the United States: coronary heart disease, lung cancer, emphysema, motor-vehicle and other accidents, cirrhosis of the liver and suicide. These causes account for 75 per cent of the sex differential in mortality in the United States. Reasons for the differential have been analysed at the behavioural/cultural level. It was estimated, for example, that well over half the difference between male and female death rates could be accounted for by differences in behaviour, for example cigarette-smoking, alcohol consumption and occupational hazard. The study concluded that sex differences in behaviour are more important causes of higher male mortality than genetic factors (Waldron, 1976).

A comparison of sex differentials in health and illness in Sweden, Denmark, Finland and Norway found great variation in the morbidity differential. For example, the sex differential in symptoms of anxiety was much smaller in Finland and Sweden than in Denmark and Norway. Type of employment also had an effect on the differential. There was excess female morbidity in agricultural and manual workers. In white-collar groups, students and pensioners, however, men and women had similar standards of health. In some countries, like Finland and Norway, white-collar women were healthier than their male counterparts. Overall, the excess female morbidity rate was mainly due to higher rates for female manual workers and full-time housewives (Haavio-Mannila, 1986). In general it was concluded that in countries where many women work outside the home, rates of illness and hospitalization for women are lower than those for men. In countries, and at certain periods of time in the same country, when women mostly stay at home, women's illness rates are higher than for men (Haavio-Mannila, 1986). In Britain employment outside the home was found to be a benefit to some groups of women and a burden to others, depending on their social circumstances, as explained on p. 244 (Arber *et al.*, 1985).

Another study in 1985 was interested in the causes of the difference in life expectancy between men and women. The authors argued that if much of the difference between males and females was due to environmental factors, then there may be situations where the difference could be reduced. They hypothesized that kibbutz life might be capable of narrowing the gender gap in life expectancy by providing a closely matched environment for men and women with less difference in gender roles than in other developed countries. Calculating the expected gap in life expectancy from international data, they found that in the kibbutz the observed gap was much smaller – at birth the gap was 4.5 years instead of the expected 7.1 years, and at age fifty the gap was 2.7 years instead of the expected 5.1 years. The gap had been reduced by improvements in male life expectancy rather than by a reduction in female life expectancy (Leviatan and Cohen, 1985).

These recent studies open up intriguing possibilities for improvements in the sex differentials in health, though investigations are only at a preliminary stage. They certainly illustrate the potential importance of social and environmental factors on the health of both men and women.

Conclusions

The four possible explanations of inequalities in health put forward by the Black Working Group have been reviewed in the light of new evidence. From the evidence, the inequalities between social groups are genuine and cannot be explained away as artefact. Further evidence has confirmed the existence of a health selection effect – in particular, showing that serious illness in childhood can cause a fall in occupational class later on. There is also renewed evidence of selection for height at marriage. Estimates suggest that the selection effect is small and does not account for the much larger differentials in health observed.

The weight of evidence continues to point to explanations which suggest that socio-economic circumstances play the major part in subsequent health differences. For example, the evidence that health-damaging behaviour is more common in lower social groups continues to accumulate, especially concerning smoking and diet. But can such life-style factors account for all the observed differential in health between different social groups? The short answer is: no. When studies are able to control for factors like smoking and drinking, a sizeable proportion of the health gap remains and factors related to the general living conditions and environment of the poor are indicated. In this context there is also a growing body of evidence that material and structural factors, such as housing and income, can affect health. Most importantly, several studies have shown how adverse social conditions can limit the choice of life-style and it is this set of studies which illustrates most clearly that behaviour cannot be separated from its social context. Certain living and working conditions appear to impose severe restrictions on an individual's ability to choose a healthy life-style.

The evidence suggests that policies to reduce inequalities which focused entirely on the individual would be misguided. The importance of social and material factors highlighted by the research suggests that broader policies incorporating structural improvements in living and working conditions would be required in addition.

Chapter 7

The Research Response

As soon as it was published, the Black Report attracted great interest within the research community. Although individual criticisms of details of the report were put forward, as documented on p. 5, it was appreciated as an authoritative collection of evidence, rekindling debate on inequalities in health. Even its critics acknowledged that its main findings were sound and paid tribute to the contribution it had made to the literature in the field:

> No one reading the report could easily contradict the conclusion from the weight of evidence it assembles that systematic class-related differences in health experience do exist; that these are associated with the structure and operation of the socio-economic system within which people are born, live and die; and that a way out of these inequalities will involve very much more than individual responses: the government is inextricably involved. (Gray, 1981)

Several bodies responded by setting up meetings to discuss its implications. The Faculty of Community Medicine, for instance, commented that 'it is a mine of information and will merit study for many years to come' (Brotherston, 1980).

The Faculty suggested that a working party could have been set up by the Secretary of State to study the report in more detail and identify immediately practical recommendations. The Social Science Research Council (now the Economic and Social Research Council) set up a survey of researchers in 1981 to identify further research stemming from the report's findings. In 1983 it also organized a workshop to clarify research priorities – some papers from which appear in Wilkinson (1986a). There was general agreement on the major problems hampering further research and a desire to remedy the situation.

Little progress

In 1980, the Black Working Group found that statistics on many important issues were not collected routinely or were missing altogether. For all concerned this greatly hampered the task of planning and evaluating policies to reduce inequalities in health. Consequently the Working Group considered that it would be easier to trace and assess continuing inequalities

○ if school health statistics routinely recorded the height, weight, hearing and other health indicators of school children in relation to occupational class;

○ if statistics on accidents to children routinely recorded the circumstances of the accident, and the age and occupational class of the parents;

○ if the National Food Survey were adapted to be a more effective measure of nutritional status, and be able to identify 'at risk' groups in the population;

○ if the General Household Survey developed a more comprehensive measure of income and command over resources, so that the influence of poverty/affluence could be related to self-reported illness in the Survey.

It also recommended that the problems of social inequalities in health and their causes should be officially adopted as an area of further research by the DHSS, in association with the Medical Research Council and the Social Science Research Council, and co-ordinated centrally.

None of the four recommendations on data collection has been adopted in the intervening eight years, so policy-makers still have to rely on special surveys carried out from time to time at national or local level. Nor have the major research-funding bodies adopted the subject of social inequalities in health as a priority issue for co-ordinated action. Furthermore it has become even more difficult to obtain information on social class and health even from the traditionally available sources. The Black Working Group drew heavily on detailed analyses from the occupational mortality supplements of the Registrar General's Office produced for the years around each census. However, the latest supplement, published in 1986, did not carry out such analysis of the data, and several researchers have expressed their frustration at this latest obstacle to research (Townsend *et al.*, 1988; Morris, 1986).

There was an even stronger reaction from the *British Medical Journal* in a leader entitled 'Lies, damned lies and suppressed statistics'. It commented:

The latest [supplement] has just been published, and something strange has happened – reference to the social class differences in mortality have almost slipped out. Why is this? Could it be because somebody in the government or in the Registrar General's office is anxious to play down the widening gap in mortality between rich and poor . . . it would seem that yet again the government is exerting its influence and suppressing potentially adverse information. (*British Medical Journal*, 1986)

This implication was flatly denied by the chief medical statistician responsible for producing the supplement. He argued that the information on occupational class in the supplement was less reliable than in previous decades and was also no longer suitable for studying the very deprived groups in society, and that was why the customary analysis had not been carried out. Because in the months that followed there was still much disquiet about the affair, the Medical Research Council called a meeting in May 1987 to consider the collection of information on inequalities in health. Several researchers pointed out that the information on occupational class collected by the Registrar General was still valuable if used properly. Indeed it was considered one of the best sources for investigating deaths by different causes or in a variety of sub-groups because of the large number of deaths it covered. There were plenty of suggestions for improving the reliability of data, including more field surveys, more longitudinal studies following people over a period of time, and the use of 'marker' occupations representing each occupational class. Many ideas for further research were put forward, including greater understanding of the ways in which unemployment, psycho-social differences and nutrition could bring about inequalities in health. However, the *British Medical Journal* commented that the government's chief medical statistician 'did almost too good a job at demolishing the value of the data that he is responsible for collating, and other researchers at the meeting had to reassure him that they were still valuable' (Smith, 1987b).

Despite this rather negative picture at national level and the difficulties encountered, there have been notable developments in this field, including the following examples.

Post-coding

Social indicators from the census small-area statistics are now readily available on tape from OPCS, down to the level of wards. From this, over 250 variables are available for analysis, including housing and overcrowding factors, consumer-durable ownership, employment status, family composition and so on. Since 1981 (1974 in Scotland) OPCS has provided post-coded death records, and also post-coded birth records. Since 1982 birth-weight has been recorded almost universally on birth and perinatal death certificates. In Scotland all in-patient statistics and cancer registrations have been post-coded since 1975.

This opens up much wider opportunities for analysing small areas below the level of local authority or health district. For instance, it makes it much easier to pinpoint areas of poor health and to explore which social and other factors in those areas are implicated. In this context, the Black Report called for further research 'on the development of area social conditions and health indicators for use in resource allocation' and 'the study of the interaction of the social factors implicated in ill-health over time, and within small areas'. Numerous studies of this kind have been undertaken by health and local authorities in direct response to the Black Report, making use of these newly available data. These studies have already been outlined in Chapter 2, but in the following section some of the technical considerations will be discussed.

Developing measures of social inequality

Small-area analysis does have some unique problems which have been reviewed by Carstairs (1981a). In particular, small areas produce small numbers of events, for example only a handful of deaths in a year. To compensate for small numbers, results have sometimes been aggregated over several years. Alternatively, results for areas with similar social profiles have been combined. OPCS sponsored a series of studies in the 1970s to find ways of identifying and grouping together wards with similar socio-economic composition irrespective of where they were in the country (Webber and Craig, 1975). For example, in the Craig–Webber classification forty variables from the census data have been employed to group census wards together to form thirty-six socially distinct 'clusters'. Clusters range from 'high-status suburban areas' to 'poor-quality housing in areas of economic decline', and this classification has been used in other studies – for example in the OPCS Longitudinal Study described on p. 238. A Classification of Residential Neighbourhoods (ACORN) is a similar approach which has been developed commercially, based on the age structure of an area together with its employment level, family composition, type of housing, car ownership and social status. Only the post-code is required to identify the social profile of a neighbourhood. The value of using the ACORN system in health studies is being investigated (Morgan, 1983; Morgan and Chinn, 1983).

Other studies have combined several indicators of social and material deprivation into a composite deprivation index. Areas can then be ranked by their degree of disadvantage or affluence according to their score on the index. The question of which social indicators to include in the index is crucial and has been thoroughly discussed in two recent papers (Thunhurst, 1985b; Townsend *et al.*, 1986b). The points made there warrant closer inspection. Table 16 shows the social indicators used to define deprivation in five area-based studies.

Table 16: *A comparison of the social indicators used in five area-based studies*

	Proportion of:
Department of the Environment (1983) Indicators of urban deprivation	unemployed persons; overcrowded households; single-parent households; households lacking exclusive use of basic amenities; pensioners living alone; population change; residents living in households where head of household was born in the New Commonwealth or Pakistan. Standardized Mortality Ratio.
Jarman (1983, 1984) Underprivileged Area Score	children aged under 5; ethnic minorities; single-parent households; elderly living alone; lower social classes; highly mobile people; non-married-couple families (indicating less stable family groups). Overcrowding factor. Poor housing factor. Unemployment.
Scott-Samuel Score (1984)	persons aged over 15 with temporary sickness; households overcrowded; households severely overcrowded; households owner-occupied; households rented from local authority; households lacking a car; men aged 16–64 out of employment; women aged 16–59 out of employment; private households with 3 or more dependent children; one-parent families; working-age people permanently sick.
Townsend et al. (1985) Bristol Study	households with fewer rooms than persons; households lacking a car; economically active persons seeking work (or temporarily sick); children aged 5 15 who receive school meals free; households experiencing disconnection of electricity.

Table 16 – *cont.*

Townsend et al. (*1986b*) *Northern Region Study*	economically active residents aged 16–59/64 who are unemployed; private households lacking a car; private households which are not owner-occupied; private households with more than one person per room.

Note that some indices combine direct indicators of deprivation, like overcrowding and unemployment, with indirect measures of the number of people *at risk of deprivation*, for instance the proportion of one-parent families, elderly people or ethnic minorities in an area. The problem is that not all people in such groups are deprived. Mixing material conditions and 'at risk' groups like this can result in certain pitfalls. For example, Townsend points out that the Department of the Environment's score finds that the ten most deprived local authority areas in England are all in London, with none in the North. Similarly the Jarman index finds seven of the ten most deprived health districts are in London and none in the Northern Region: figures which fly in the face of other observations. Thunhurst (1985b) points out that such results are obtained when an index is dominated by certain highly skewed variables such as ethnic minority and one-parent family households which are more highly concentrated in the inner London boroughs than elsewhere. If no correction is made for this skewed distribution, then high-scoring areas on the index may simply be high-scoring areas for ethnic minority or single-parent households.

Ways of overcoming this problem have been put forward, for example by the use of more sophisticated statistical techniques and by using 'grass-roots' surveys to check and extend the statistical results (Thunhurst, 1985b). Townsend and his colleagues solve the problem by choosing only indicators of material deprivation, such as the proportion of households with no car, or with electricity disconnected, or with an unemployed head. Likewise social class is not included in the composite index, but is analysed separately so that the interrelationship between health, deprivation and social class can be investigated.

Beyond occupational class

Although occupational class has traditionally been used to measure social class it is not without its problems, particularly in relation to women (McDowall, 1983). In mortality statistics and studies on morbidity (in the

General Household Survey, for instance) married women have often been classified by their husband's occupational class and single women by their own occupation. At least three major problems arise:

1. 52 per cent of married women now work outside the home either full-time or part-time. Classifying them by their husband's occupation may conceal health hazards linked to their own employment.

2. Such classification may also conceal differences in health between married women who are housewives, those who are unemployed and those who are in paid employment.

3. The earnings of working women may well influence the standard of living and material resources of the household, but this is not taken into account if the husband's occupation alone is used.

Difficulties also arise with the unemployed, the elderly and children. For these groups, occupational class may not fully encapsulate the circumstances in which they live.

Several alternative approaches have been put forward and are being investigated. For instance, Arber (1988) suggests that the most appropriate measure would be *household class*, rather than individual class, based on the occupation of the spouse who is economically dominant. Groups can also be differentiated by their assets, for example by house and car ownership, and the OPCS Longitudinal Study has done extensive work on this as detailed on p. 237. Promising measures are emerging from this study in relation to the social circumstances of women.

In relation to children, one alternative measure is the Social Index developed for use in the Child Health and Education Cohort Study and intended to be more in tune with the home environment of the child than occupational class alone. This incorporates seven socio-economic variables associated with the child's environment:

occupational status of head of household;
parents' education;
social rating of neighbourhood;
tenure;
crowding index (persons/room);
bathroom availability;
type of accommodation.

If any one variable, such as occupational class, is not available, a score can still be obtained for the family by adjusting the index accordingly. The Social Index provides a continuous scale running from the most disadvantaged to the most advantaged social groups, and appears to be more sensitive to social inequalities in childhood than the Registrar General's social class scale. For example, it has identified disadvantaged groups experiencing difficulties in health service use which were not detected by the use of occupational class (Osborn and Morris, 1979).

Developing measures of health

The Black Report also contained the recommendation that policy decisions on, for example, resource allocation should not be based on area mortality data alone.

There were calls for the use in area studies of morbidity data and measures of positive health, like height and weight, in addition to mortality rates. With the advent of post-coded birth records containing birth-weights, the incidence of low birth-weight in small areas can now be used as a health indicator in such studies. For example, it has been used in the study of health inequalities in the Northern Region (Townsend *et al.*, 1986b), and the Greater Glasgow Health Board used it in their review of deprivation and ill-health in the City of Glasgow (Greater Glasgow Health Board, 1984).

Another promising tool for surveying health problems is the Nottingham Health Profile (Hunt and McEwen, 1980). It defines, much more specifically than, say, the General Household Survey, the *nature* of health problems in the population and the impact of those problems on everyday activities. The profile is in two parts. Part I assesses health in six problem areas considered to be important by the lay population, i.e. pain, energy, physical mobility, sleep, social isolation and emotional reaction. Part II measures the effect of these health problems on paid employment, ability to perform jobs around the house, and the effect on relationships, sexuality and so on. Each section carries a score of 100 – the higher the score, the greater the number of problems experienced. The profile has been shown to relate well to more traditional measures such as the presence of chronic illness and the seeking of medical care, but it provides an added insight for policy-making. Studies using this profile were described in Chapter 2.

Blaxter has reviewed the many different measures commonly used as health indicators in inequality studies and has been experimenting with five measures of health to assess their usefulness for future large-scale surveys. The five dimensions are disease, functional disability, 'illness' or frequent symptoms, 'malaise' (lack of psychological well-being) and fitness. The problems of measuring health are considered in depth in this study (Blaxter, 1985).

The Health and Life-style Survey, a national sample study of 9,000 people, is beginning to provide data on a whole range of health factors which have not been available on a national scale before. As well as collecting data on illness symptoms and conditions in the sample, the Survey has taken physiological measurements and collected information on life-style factors, self-assessment of health and orientation towards healthy behaviour, and can relate these to a variety of socio-economic parameters including income (Cox *et al.*, 1987).

The Welsh Heart Health Survey of 1985 (to be repeated in 1990) is also providing valuable data in the realm of positive health. In the nine health authorities in Wales 20,000 people were interviewed to provide a baseline of health indicator and life-style factors against which to assess health promotion activities (Nutbeam and Catford, 1987).

One of the issues highlighted for further research by the Black Working Group was in the field of disability and handicap. The Working Group called for prevalence studies of disability in the community which made assessments of the severity of disablement, for example by self-care criteria. They also wanted studies on the *interaction* of processes leading to physical and mental handicap and disadvantage, and on how some children escape the effects of disadvantaged conditions (p. 137). The Child Health and Education Study, based on a cohort of children born in 1970, has been engaged in studies of this nature. One of its aims has been to investigate the extent of disability and learning difficulties in the national sample of ten-year-old children. To do this, it has been developing a measure of disability based on an inventory of skills and behaviour. With the inventory the parents of each child in the sample can make an assessment of the child's ability, and norms for the population can be derived. Results from groups of disabled children can then be compared with the norms. In addition it is making assessments of educational achievement, undertaking medical examinations to assess physical health, and collecting information on a range of social and environmental factors associated with each child. From the data it may be possible to map the development of disability and learning difficulties and to assess the importance of the factors involved (Butler *et al.*, 1982).

Conclusions

The Black Working Group highlighted major deficiencies in data collection, and eight years later these deficiencies have still not been remedied. Improvements have been made in some fields, for example in the production of statistics for use on a small-area basis, but the inherent problem spreads far beyond research on inequalities in health to encompass public health research in general. The Australian Better Health Commission has recently confirmed a similar situation existing in Australia and has outlined a number of prerequisites for public health research, including the need to develop a comprehensive and accessible data base of national health statistics; the need to find methods of widely disseminating statistical information and ensuring that it is understood by the public; and the need to establish administrative structures and appropriate funding strategies which will guarantee funds over a long period (Better Health Commission, 1986).

Many argue that a first and most important step towards improved health statistics would be a regular National Health Survey similar to that conducted in Canada, to provide the necessary data base. This would benefit not only research in social inequalities but the whole field of public health. Also of considerable potential help would be the inclusion of health questions in the census.

Despite the shortcomings in data collection there has been an upsurge in research on social inequalities in health, as the numerous studies reported in earlier chapters testify. It is significant that many of these studies were directly stimulated by the publication of the Black Report in 1980.

Chapter 8

What Are the Health and Social Services Doing?

At least seventeen of the thirty-seven recommendations of the Black Report relate directly to policy-making within the caring professions. Although the evidence presented in that report – and confirmed by the latest research – suggests that health and social services cannot be expected to solve the problem of inequalities in health single-handed, the Working Group was convinced that there was a vital role for these services to play. The improvement in the quality of life which health care can bring about, particularly for the most disadvantaged groups, was considered to be of substantial importance.

The policy outlined on pp. 133–64 has three main thrusts: priority for children, for disabled or elderly people, and for preventive and educational action. Has this policy been adopted in part or in whole? What are the most promising initiatives? Are there any pointers for the future?

A voice for children

Recommendations concerning child health included a shift in the resources of the NHS and social services towards community care, particularly ante-natal, post-natal and child health services; improvement in the facilities and accessibility of ante-natal and child health clinics; greatly expanded nursery school and day-care provision for the under fives, and a revitalized school health service linked in an effective way to general practice to intensify surveillance and follow-up. Such a strategy, it suggested, would give some support to parents while mitigating some of the effects of a poor environment for many young children, as well as improving the identification and treatment of children most at risk.

In general, the response to these recommendations has been disappointing. Although there is a consensus that a shift towards community care is desirable, it has not been translated into a comprehensive commitment. Events in the child health services over the past ten years have been thoroughly reviewed by the National Children's Bureau (1987) and the findings are very relevant here. Overall the Bureau found that, since the Court

Committee reported in 1976. 'Progress in the organization and delivery of treatment and more especially preventive services to children has been, at best, patchy. In some respects there has been a decline in those areas in which the Court Committee had hoped to see improvement' (National Children's Bureau, 1987). Much of the concern was related to changes in the organization and overseeing of services. At a national level a 'watchdog' body had been recommended in 1976, drawn from national politicians and professional and voluntary workers, to keep the quality and development of services for children constantly under review. The DHSS set up this 'Children's Committee' in 1978, but it was disbanded in 1981 by the government, so one more voice of concern for children has disappeared.

The NHS also experienced major reorganizations in 1974 and 1982, as well as substantial changes in management structure in 1984, and at each stage child health services have been affected. Since 1974 specialists in community medicine and in nursing with special responsibility for child health were appointed at the *Area* Health Authority level to help develop an integrated service coterminous with social and educational services. However, with reorganization in 1982 the Area tier of management in the NHS disappeared, and with it these special child health posts and often the multidisciplinary bodies which co-ordinated specialist services for children (for example on child abuse). It was no longer obligatory to have such posts. With responsibility falling on *District* Health Authorities it was not always efficient or effective for them to provide some of the expert services for the smaller population.

With the 1984 management changes there has been a trend away from organizing services for particular client groups, like children or the elderly, and towards different types of service or topics, for instance acute or community services, or mental health. This trend has further discouraged the development of integrated services for children, as well as creating difficulties in monitoring the resources going into child health services. The danger with this situation is that administrators may lose sight of children as a priority. Indeed a survey of District Health Authorities in 1986, inquiring about budgets for child health services, found that these services were treated differently in each district. There was no underlying strategy linking the development of the services throughout the country. In fact, some districts could not separate resources given to child health services from the rest of the budget, which made it difficult to evaluate progress (Kurtz, 1986). The work of health visitors and social workers has also moved away from specialization on children or other client groups and towards a more general approach. Again, the special skills for work with children may no longer be acquired or practised as a result of this trend.

The review found that the delivery of the preventive child health services also seemed to vary greatly around the country. A survey in 1983 found that some districts ran five times more child health clinics than others. Service provision was not related to any obvious criterion of *need* in the community (Macfarlane and Pillay, 1984).

Although some general practitioners were becoming involved in screening and monitoring services, overall the level of involvement was thought to be most disappointing. In addition, a major problem has been highlighted in inner cities, where a fair proportion of primary care appears to be carried out in local accident and emergency departments of hospitals, with little opportunity for follow-up of preventive work or continuity of care.

As for the school health service, the National Children's Bureau was concerned that it was failing to meet the needs of children, parents and teachers. Once again a survey found that each district had its own way of managing and integrating the services with others related to children. There had been virtually no move to improve services for adolescents who were ill or had stressful life-problems.

Why has there been such a decline in the quality of the services? The National Children's Bureau put it down to two main factors. Firstly, economic constraints, or in some areas decline, had led to a lack of commitment to the care of children at the level of government, health and local authority. Secondly, inter-professional disagreements about who should have responsibility for the services coupled with a lack of government leadership to deal with them 'have resulted in uncertainty about using even the limited resources that have been available'.

The picture on local authority day-care for children under five is very variable across the country, but in most areas it is overstretched and largely concentrated on the most deprived groups. The rapid expansion in provision in the 1970s has slowed down considerably in the 1980s, so the aim of extending it to a wide section of the community as envisaged in the Black Report (recommendation 12) has not been achieved.

A better start in life

Although the overall picture on services for children is patchy there have been outstanding efforts in certain areas, especially in relation to the Black recommendation that 'districts should review the accessibility and facilities of all ante-natal and child health clinics in their areas, and develop plans to increase utilization by mothers'.

This recommendation has been taken seriously by many groups around the country, and services in the ante-natal care field in particular have improved enormously. Dowling (1983) has made a comprehensive review of new developments in preventive health care in pregnancy and early childhood and has documented over sixty schemes operating in England and Wales which have tried to ensure that services reach those who need them. The review concludes that, 'when attention is given to the life-styles and needs of the parents, most families can be contacted, often with surprising ease'. How is this done?

For a start, attention has been given to the difficulties of parents with young children trying to reach the clinics. Transport, for example, is a particular problem for people on low incomes relying on public transport – which can be expensive, time-consuming and fraught with stress if small children have to be taken along too. Both rural areas like the Isle of Wight and urban areas like Hounslow and Edinburgh have been running de-centralized ante-natal clinics staffed by a consultant and community midwives. Mobile clinics have been used by Southwark to improve im-munization in areas with low take-up rates, and by Ormskirk District to take child health services to outlying areas. Other health authorities have organized mini-buses and other forms of transport to bring parents and children into central ante-natal and child health clinics. Another successful approach has been the timing of clinics to suit parents who work during the day, or mothers with children who need to be collected from school in mid afternoon, or Asian women reluctant to visit the clinic at times when their husbands cannot accompany them. Some hold evening clinics, for example, while others make sure that mothers with school-age children to collect are given early-afternoon appointments. Many now provide play areas for children in clinics and general practitioners' surgeries to relieve the stress of long waits. The point is that quite large improvements can be made in access and convenience of the services for the patient without necessarily costing large amounts of money.

Then there are projects which have gone out to provide opportunistic health care for those who would not usually use preventive services. Shopping centres are obvious choices. Bolton Community Health Council and Health Authority, for example, set up a pregnancy walk-in clinic in the centre of the town, staffed by a midwife. The TUC and the Spastics Society have pioneered workplace ante-natal care projects in Scotland and Oldham for pregnant women mainly working on the factory floor (Dowling, 1983).

New initiatives are continually being evolved to try to help deprived communities. In Nottingham, for example, an experimental programme has been investigating the organization of a child health clinic serving a deprived population. A community paediatric team approach has been used and has resulted in attracting older, more deprived pre-school children, and the detection of more treatable medical disorders (Nicoll, 1986). In the same city extra health-visiting has been provided for deprived groups. In this case areas of the city suffering from deprivation were first identified by a City Council project. From this, babies at high risk of post-neonatal death could be identified and their families supported with extra health-visiting. As the ratio of health visitors to population was already well below the DHSS recommended level, any transfer of staff from one area to another was considered unfair on the community in general. The solution was to obtain joint funding for extra health visitors from City Council and Department of the Environment sources (Madeley, 1982).

In the primary care setting, a group of GPs in the North-East of England has been exploring ways of improving preventive care for deprived patients, with various outreach programmes and schemes for tracing and responding to missed care through patients' records. Action is based on comprehensive, computerized medical records. The front of each record card shows the missing care for each member of the patient's household. An offer of preventive care can therefore be made whenever the doctor sees the patient for a sickness appointment – and the care is given immediately, to avoid return appointments. In addition, letters go out to each household listing and offering the missing care, with follow-up letters sent to non-responders from time to time. To make use of every opportunity, health visitors are provided with household lists with the missing care for each household member so that the topic can be brought up when visiting. The GPs involved believe that there are many advantages for their patients in this system and evaluation continues (Marsh and Channing, 1986).

Caring for the disabled and elderly

The recommendations in this field were aimed mainly at improving the care of elderly and disabled people in their own homes. The strategy involved reviewing hospital, residential and domiciliary care for the disabled elderly, reviewing sheltered housing provision, encouraging joint care programmes and increasing community support especially in the form of nursing services for disabled people and home-help services with greatly extended functions (recommendations 15–18).

There is no evidence of a substantial shift in resources to community care for the disabled and elderly in the 1980s. In 1986 the government-appointed Audit Commission reported on its study of community care policies. Were policies such as those in the DHSS 'Care in Action' document being adopted in practice? Were funding and organizational policies helping or hindering the desired developments? The Commission concluded:

There are serious grounds for concern about the lack of progress in shifting the balance of services towards community care. Progress has been slow and uneven across the country; and the near-term prospects are not promising. In short the community care policy is in danger of failing to achieve its potential . . . community care is far from a reality for many of the very people it is intended to help. (Audit Commission, 1986)

For the elderly, the Commission found that although there had been a decrease in the numbers accommodated in hospitals, this had been more than offset by an increase in accommodating old people in private residential homes. Apart from an increase in local authority day-care in the late 1970s, home-based services like home-helps, meals-on-wheels and community nursing had not increased in real terms but had been struggling to keep pace with the growing number of elderly in the population.

Furthermore there were great regional differences in the provision of care. For example, home-help provision by local authorities ranged from 7/1,000 people aged over 75 in some authorities, to 44/1,000 in others. The level of private and voluntary residential accommodation for the elderly varied from 7.6/1,000 people aged over 75 in Cleveland to over 70/1,000 in Devon. Indeed, all along the south coast of England there was much greater provision of this kind of service in relation to the relevant population than in the rest of the country. This could have far-reaching effects, as will become apparent shortly. The rapid expansion of private residential and nursing homes began in 1983 when the DHSS for the first time allowed local authority social service departments to make payments to private residential homes to place frail elderly people. Homes have been springing up all over the country and DHSS payments to them in 1983 totalled £102 million, rising to £200 million in 1984 and over £500 million in 1986 (Audit Commission, 1986). The BMA points out that this large expenditure on private residential homes conflicts with the government's stated policy of redirecting resources to community care. There is also the fear that elderly people may be pressured into accepting places in nursing homes when they could continue in their own homes *if they had adequate support* (BMA, 1986).

Support for this concern came from a 1985 study of elderly people admitted to residential homes in three authorities. About half the residents did not need to be there. They could have been supported in the community if the necessary resources had been available (Audit Commission, 1986).

Because of the perverse way in which the social security system works, it appeared to be easier to obtain supplementary benefit payments for board and lodging in private residential homes than to obtain either Attendance Allowance or Invalid Care Allowance for care in a person's own home. And the amount of the benefit was greater. 'In short the more residential the care, the easier it is for people to obtain benefits and the greater the size of the payment.' Under this system there was, and still is, a further temptation for local authorities to turn some of their council-owned homes over to private management so that eligible residents could claim supplementary benefit to cover their fees. Substantial 'savings' have been made by local authorities by doing just that. The overall effect, however, is a serious undermining of community care initiatives because:

○ it is encouraging high-cost residential care while starving some of the low-cost, home-based options;

○ it is undermining the efforts of RAWP and the Rate Support Grant by channelling public funds to people in the better-off, least deprived areas of the country.

What is more, local authorities which have increased expenditure to fund community care have often been penalized by having their Rate Support Grant cut. As a result of this, the Audit Commission made recommendations for immediate action on funding and managerial policies. The Commission warned that if action was not taken, 'the result will be continued waste of scarce resources and, worse still, care and support that is either lacking entirely, or inappropriate to the needs of some of the most disadvantaged members of society and the relatives who seek to care for them' (Audit Commission, 1986).

Improvements in the quality of life

It would be wrong to give the impression that nothing was being done in this field. Currently there are a number of experiments attempting to improve the quality of life of elderly and disabled people, particularly those who do need residential care. The aim of several of these projects is to give residents as much independence as possible, with their own furniture and possessions around them and more privacy, but with nursing facilities on site if and when required (Graham, 1983). In a new approach to community care, boroughs like Camden have introduced foster care schemes for the elderly and disabled. Volunteers are paid to take disabled people into their own homes and care for them on a long-term basis. The 'Age Well' programme of the Health Education Council and Age Concern has since 1984 been encouraging and disseminating information on initiatives which promote independence in old age, especially those organized by the elderly themselves. In Scotland, the Scottish Health Education Group has an ongoing in-service training programme for a variety of professionals and para-professionals with the aim of de-medicalizing the care of the elderly and encouraging independence. The aim is to make helpers aware of when they are creating dependence in the people they care for and help them reverse the process (Thompson, 1986).

There has been a promising development in relation to the role of home-helps. Several social service departments have recognized that home-helps can do much more valuable work on behalf of disabled people, as recommended by Black, and have extended their functions accordingly. For example, in Cheshire the home-help service is being replaced totally by a 'home-care' service. Home-care assistants are being trained in the care of elderly and disabled people and employed on a similar basis to care assistants in residential homes. Provision of this service is still not at an optimum level (Constable, 1986).

In Hillingdon a complete re-think of services for elderly people is taking place, built upon knowledge of the *needs* of the elderly in the area. The Borough Council and the health authority have jointly reviewed social services and housing. The needs of elderly people already receiving care were re-assessed and a theoretical pattern of services drawn up which would meet those needs. This was then compared with the existing pattern and many inconsistencies became obvious. For example, some old people were in hospital beds when they no longer required treatment, while others were unable to obtain a place. Residential homes were sometimes occupied by people who could have been independent in the community, given the appropriate support. In many cases there was a mismatch between domiciliary services and needs. As a result of the review the challenge has been to devise services more closely matched to the needs of the elderly. A major shift in services is under way, involving the combining and expanding of home-care and auxiliary nursing services, the promotion of neighbourhood and voluntary care, and the accommodation in residential homes of those elderly people who really are in need of this kind of care.

These are just a few examples of the very many initiatives taking place, but they do illustrate what can be done. There is no doubt, however, that the need for community support services is undiminished. The British Medical Association report on the elderly recommends the urgent development of respite care to help the carers of disabled and elderly people, as well as greater provision of home-help services, telephone alarms, laundry services, meals-on-wheels and so on – all services which allow disabled people to remain in their own homes (BMA, 1986).

Priority for preventive and educational action

The recommendations under this heading were mainly concerned with action the government could take in the field of prevention and education to encourage good health. These included

* the setting of national health goals;
* an enlarged programme of health education with particular focus on schools;
* stronger measures to reduce cigarette-smoking;
* specific screening programmes;
* the funding of a series of intensive health and social development programmes in ten disadvantaged areas on an experimental basis.

There have been attempts to draw up detailed national health goals for the UK (Catford, 1983) but this particular recommendation has now been superseded by this country's adoption of the World Health Organization's thirty-eight 'Targets for Health for All by the Year 2000' (WHO, 1985b). What is now needed is wider publicity for and discussion on these targets with all the agencies involved in their implementation. As a discussion opener the Faculty of Community Medicine has published its proposals on action to be taken in this country on the WHO targets, which will be covered on p. 347 below when the wider community strategy is considered.

The question of whether an 'enlarged programme of health education' (recommendation 20) has been funded is a difficult one to answer. More money has certainly been provided for specific emergency purposes such as drugs and AIDS education, but the amount provided for more comprehensive health education programmes, which might start to tackle the issues of inequality, has not noticeably been increased. For example, the budget of the Health Education Council for the past ten years has remained at roughly 0.1 per cent of the NHS hospital expenditure. In April 1987 the Council was incorporated into a special Health Education Authority with additional responsibility for AIDS education, so resources for general health education may change completely.

Despite past limitations on funding health education has developed considerably, particularly in the school sector. For example, even in the early 1970s health education in schools was still very limited – restricted mainly to hygiene and sex education – with little or no co-ordination. School inspectors noted that it was rare to find a school with a broad concept of health and active learning methods were not widely used. In contrast, by the early 1980s approximately 68 per cent of secondary schools and 30 per cent of primary schools had a planned programme of health education, and between a third and a half of secondary schools had a co-ordinator to plan health education across the curriculum. The concept of health and health education in a fair proportion of schools had become broader and more positive, associated with self-esteem, mental health and relationships – very much in line with the WHO concept of health as a resource for life. In Scotland every secondary school now has a well-developed 'guidance system', and in an increasing number of English and Welsh schools equivalent structures are developing. In 1981, the Department of Education and Science recognized for the first time that health education should be an essential part of the curriculum for every pupil. Although the recommendation has yet to be fulfilled in many areas, it was an important milestone (Whitehead, 1988). The question now is whether these advances will be maintained or reversed by the changes to the curriculum proposed in the current Education Bill.

Measures taken to reduce cigarette-smoking have been piecemeal and progress, though evident, has been linked mainly to higher social classes. For example, while tobacco advertising and sales promotions are still very much with us, the 1986 voluntary agreement has banned such advertising from cinemas and certain women's magazines. Current negotiations on sports and arts sponsorship between the tobacco companies and the government may at last lead to restrictions, but in the meantime both the BBC and ITV have imposed their own house rules to reduce exposure of tobacco companies' logos, etc., in sponsored sporting events. Although it has not become official government policy, taxes on cigarettes have gone up by about 30 per cent in the last five years, and in the last budget the Chancellor acknowledged that the latest price rise was in response to the health lobby. The health warning is still on the side of the cigarette pack rather than on the front, but the size has been enlarged and the wording varied to try to create more impact (White, 1986).

It is in local authorities that noticeable initiatives on smoking in public places have taken place. A 1985 survey by Action on Smoking and Health (ASH) found that 83 per cent of local authorities had smoking bans or restrictions in council meetings (compared with 78 per cent in 1983). Almost 20 per cent of councils also had smoking restrictions in their offices and staff canteens; 16 per cent had banned tobacco promotion on council-owned poster sites (ASH, 1986).

Screening for neural tube defects and Down's syndrome, as recommended in the Black Report, is now generally available. Screening for hypertension in adults is not so widespread, though there are major community projects incorporating blood pressure screening in Wales, Oxford and Glasgow.

The intensive health and social development programmes in selected deprived areas, envisaged in the Black Report, have not been funded, but there have been several smaller-scale initiatives. The HEC has been funding a series of community development experiments over the past five years. For example the Mansfield Community Health Project has, since 1982, been developing ways of reaching in particular young mothers and isolated elderly people in the community (HEC, 1984). The Catford project was located in an inner-city deprived area and explored the feasibility of a Community Health Council employing a health worker to help local people identify and act on their own health needs (Reason, 1985). The Paddington and North Kensington Health Authority has funded a research project to examine the use of community development methods for health visitors, and is currently developing a model for health authority action in a deprived inner-city area, with emphasis on the community development approach (Farrant, 1986). In the Greater Glasgow area the Health Board has been involved in such projects for a number of years. In one initiative a community development health education officer was employed to work in a severely deprived area. The local community identified high food prices (leading to poor nutrition) as a major priority, and the officer helped them to set up and run their own food cooperative providing reasonably priced fresh fruit and vegetables (Black, 1984). This last example perhaps illustrates the approach better than any, with its emphasis on what the local community feels is important rather than what an outsider has decided is good for them.

A few District Health Authorities, like Cambridge, have built action on inequalities in health into their strategic plans for the next ten years. Cambridge has selected for priority the low-paid, one-parent families, the unemployed, the overcrowded, the disabled, ethnic minorities and lone pensioners. Several others have drawn up health profiles of their locality to reveal the extent of local inequalities in health, as detailed on pp. 247–9. These include the Northern Regional Health Authority, and District Health Authorities/Health Boards in Grimsby, Sheffield, Coventry, Glasgow and Northern Ireland. Still others, like Bloomsbury and Sheffield, have become involved in drawing up targets in response to the WHO strategy for 'Health for All', with its emphasis on reducing inequalities, described in greater detail in Chapter 9. Bury Community Health Council has shown how Community Health Councils can document inequality in access to health services in a deprived part of a town and put practical suggestions to the health authority for making services more accessible (Walsh *et al.*, 1985). Slowly but surely a focus on inequality in health is taking shape in the health care sector.

Action on unemployment and health

Since the Black Report was written there has been a dramatic rise in unemployment in this country, and with it has come growing concern for the possible health consequences and a questioning of the action the caring services could take on the matter.

In 1985 a research project funded by the HEC explored the issue with three professional groups. Health visitors, health education officers and social workers in London, the Midlands and Scotland were interviewed to discover how unemployment was affecting their work and their response to it. The study found that 80 per cent of the sample of health visitors and social workers and 50 per cent of health education officers, considered that unemployment was affecting their day-to-day practice. The study found that the increase in poverty was the most striking feature, though health visitors and social workers also found added individual and family problems created or exacerbated by unemployment. Most were ignorant of local initiatives and were responding in an *ad hoc* way to the situation. Though well-meaning, very few had stopped to think whether their actions were really suitable for dealing with the problem. The poor response was put down to lack of time and resources, but for some their attitudes were holding them back. For example, some felt that it was not really a task for them, but was for other professions. There was also confusion about what could be done, or a lack of conviction of the effectiveness of their actions – a realization that they would only be ameliorating rather than removing the difficulties. Some were apprehensive that their superiors would not see unemployment and its effects on health as a legitimate issue for health workers to tackle. The next phase of this project is currently developing and testing training materials for these professionals (Popay *et al.*, 1986).

But what response can realistically be given? The Unemployment and Health Study Group (1986) and a series of articles by Smith (1985–6) have examined the question in depth and put forward suggestions for action:

Responding to unemployment

District Health Authorities could

1. monitor unemployment and its health effects in the locality;
2. have a clear strategy to deal with the issue;
3. relay the information to staff;
4. take unemployment into account when targeting responses and resources to those most in need;

5. train staff in benefits and facilities available to the unemployed;
6. liaise with local authorities over local community initiatives;
7. create jobs and work.

Source: adapted from Harris and Smith (1987).

Recommendations from these reviews include the drawing-up by health authorities of clear strategies to deal with unemployment and health; the monitoring of local unemployment and its effects on health using the special expertise of the district medical officer and community medicine specialist, for instance; the training of all health workers on the health effects, the state benefits and local help available to the unemployed; and the setting-up of appropriate counselling services for them. Recognizing that the NHS is a major local employer, it was further suggested that health authorities could create jobs and work opportunities for the unemployed and handicapped people through the Manpower Services Commission, for instance, and ensure that orders for supplies went wherever possible to local firms. An important role for Community Health Councils was also advocated in raising the awareness of both the public and the health authorities of what could and is being done about the problem.

At the end of 1986 a survey of District Health Authorities was carried out to find out what they were doing about unemployment and health. Encouragingly, about half the health authorities in Britain were found to be responding to the problem in some way. For instance, those in areas of high unemployment were more active than those in low unemployment areas. There was great variability in the extent of the action, though, with health education and community medicine departments leading the way. The monitoring of health and social factors, including unemployment, had been undertaken by many districts, though only a few had passed the information to staff (Harris and Smith, 1987).

Some authorities, like Somerset, had been training staff in the benefits available to the unemployed, and the Greater Glasgow Health Board had produced a comprehensive study pack – originally intended for the unemployed, but which had become popular for professional training purposes (Black and Laughlin, 1985). Resource allocation to areas of high unemployment had proved difficult, though, because of the large proportion of expenditure taken up by hospital services. South Sefton Health Authority had been at the forefront of action in creating work opportunities. It now employs 250 long-term unemployed through the Manpower Services Commission Community Programme, covering such topics as dental health education, community surveys and hospital security. Other districts have been following this example.

Wider strategies are, of course, needed to tackle unemployment. But the point made by these commentators is that local action to ease the situation is possible at a very practical level.

Planning services for ethnic minorities

The issue of ethnic minorities and the health and social services has been attracting more attention in recent years, although there have been suggestions that the health professions have been slow to recognize that this client group may have special needs (Johnson, 1984). For example, the NHS has been criticized for a lack of effective action on two conditions which especially affect ethnic minority groups – sickle-cell anaemia and rickets. People of Afro-Caribbean origin are particularly at risk from sickle-cell anaemia, but although a test for it can be carried out at birth, as yet there is no comprehensive screening programme. With rickets, caused by a deficiency of vitamin D, the Asian population appears to be most at risk. Pressure to have Asian food fortified with vitamin D has, however, failed so far (Radical Statistics Health Group, 1987).

Donaldson and Odell (1984) list seven areas of concern where cultural differences may have implications for services: uptake of and encounters with services; perceptions of health and presentation of illness; lifestyle and cultural practices; differing patterns of disease and the use of alternative medicine. It is clear that in order to plan and provide health services with the needs of ethnic minorities in mind, routinely available information is required at the District Health Authority level. But does this information exist?

A survey in 1984 set out to discover what information bases were used at local level, what special services were provided (in this case for the Asian population), and whether health workers were undertaking training and research on transcultural health issues. Only health authorities with Asian populations over 500 were included. The vast majority of these authorities (81 per cent) derived estimates of the size of the Asian population from the census, which indicates country of birth only. Others had incorporated local data into the census data (16 per cent) and still others used data from local surveys only (8 per cent). Only 19 per cent had details of the religious composition of their Asian population. A total of 21 per cent of authorities had further details, such as the language spoken by various groups, but the two latter measures were mostly based on guesswork or general impressions. Authorities did not have morbidity data available by ethnic origin, though a number did have the country of birth recorded on some of their information systems. Despite these deficiencies many District Health Authorities were providing special services – mostly health education and special diets in hospital. Thirty per cent were also providing staff in-service training, and a high proportion were making use of informal interpreters, mainly relatives and volunteers (Donaldson and Odell, 1984). This study highlights the urgent need for sample surveys at a local level and suitable health information collection to provide the necessary data on ethnic minority populations. A plea was made in this study for renewed efforts to devise an acceptable question on ethnic origin for the 1991 census.

Many of the initiatives developed so far have centred on services for mothers and babies. Tower Hamlets, for example, has employed interpreters in ante-natal and child health clinics. Some employ health aides who, in addition to interpreting, give information about nutrition, child development, family planning and so on. Others have established new ante-natal clinics in Asian communities, staffed by people who can speak the relevant languages (Dowling, 1983).

Such ideas could be developed further if health workers became more aware of the issues. In this context the National Extension College, with the DHSS and HEC, has been developing training materials for the health professions, and the College has also carried out a survey of training needs on health and race, to identify priority topics in this area (National Extension College, 1984, 1986; Pearson, 1985; Larbie and Mares, 1986).

One possible way forward in the promotion of health services more sensitive to the needs of ethnic minority groups is that taken by Liverpool Health Authority, which in May 1987 agreed a ten-year race relations strategy. The strategy's four goals are broken down into objectives and action programmes, together with time-scales for achieving them. A staff training programme supports the strategy, and targets will feature in the performance review of senior managers. The goals are notable in covering health care issues as well as employment matters.

Summary

The seventeen recommendations of the Black Report relating to health and social services were aimed mainly at improving the opportunities for good health and the quality of life of the most vulnerable groups in society – children, the disabled and the elderly. This was seen as a vital role for the caring professions, even if wider measures outside the control of the services were needed to tackle fully the roots of the problem of inequality.

Progress on most of these recommendations has been painfully slow, at least at a national level. Independent concern about the state of the child health services was expressed by the National Children's Bureau following a survey of developments since 1976. Hoped-for improvements in the delivery and co-ordination of services for children had not materialized and there was little evidence that children were being given the desired priority. Other services, such as local authority day-care for children under five appeared overstretched and incapable of expanding further without additional funding. Nevertheless, tremendous efforts were being made in some health authorities to improve facilities and accessibility of ante-natal and child health clinics to ensure that they reached those who needed them most. Examples of imaginative schemes could be found throughout the country.

Recommendations on improving the care of the elderly and the disabled in their own homes had made little headway. A government Audit Commission found a lack of progress in shifting resources to community care, and indeed many health and local authorities were struggling against conflicting DHSS policies. For example, some policies were inadvertently encouraging high-cost residential care for the elderly, while starving some of the preferred home-based services. Yet in some parts of the country services were still making valiant efforts against all odds.

Priority for preventive and educational action was also recommended and here again the picture was of little action at the national level, for example in the setting of national health goals, or the shift of resources towards prevention and education; but there were plenty of 'grass-roots' initiatives. For instance, there had been noticeable progress in health education in schools and in some health authorities which had given health promotion and community development a high profile.

Two additional questions have come to the fore since the Black Report was published: what action should caring services be taking on unemployment and health, and how should services be planned with ethnic minorities in mind? Concerned bodies have put forward relevant suggestions and some agencies have started to develop appropriate policies.

Chapter 9

The Wider Strategy and Beyond

As material living standards and social circumstances were seen to play a major role in maintaining inequalities in health, a broad social policy was proposed by the Black Working Group through the three main strategies outlined on pp. 165–97. First and foremost the abolition of child poverty was proposed as a national goal for the 1980s, achieved through various means involving

○ increases in child benefit and maternity grants;

○ the introduction of an infant care allowance;

○ attention to nutrition of children, particularly in school meals, which should be free for all;

○ increased pre-school education and action on child accidents mentioned previously.

Secondly, the Working Group recommended improvements in housing and working conditions, together with a fairer deal for disabled people through a comprehensive disability allowance and special funding for housing adaptations and services (recommendations 29–35).

Thirdly, a co-ordinated government policy was envisaged, involving national and local government and an overseeing Health Development Council responsible for planning and monitoring progress of the policy (recommendations 36, 37).

So what has happened? What has been the response to this strategy? The following sections bring together some of the evidence on the present situation and on the initiatives which have been taken, before going on to consider a possible way forward.

No more child poverty?

The goal of abolishing child poverty is nowhere in sight. That was the conclusion of two reports which reviewed the changing scene over the past ten and twenty years (Piachaud, 1986; Walker and Walker, 1987). In fact the situation has become much worse in recent years as more families with young children have fallen into the low-income category. There are several ways of demonstrating this. For instance, we can look at which groups occupy the bottom 20 per cent of the income range, i.e. the poorest fifth of the population. In 1971, 52 per cent of families in this category were pensioners and 22 per cent were families with children. By 1982, pensioner families only accounted for 27 per cent of this poorest section while the proportion of families with children accounted for 30 per cent (Central Statistical Office, 1986).

This approach tells us who the poor are but will not, of course, say anything about how widespread poverty is in the population. To answer this question we have to choose a minimum standard of decency and assess the number or proportion of the population falling below that level. Problems arise here because there is no universally agreed poverty line. Some define it in *absolute* terms, assessing a minimum level of income required for basic subsistence and defining anyone with less than that minimum as in poverty. Others believe that poverty is *relative* to the standard of living common in the rest of society. Those who cannot afford to participate in the normal activities of the community and have only enough income to 'exist' are defined as poor in relative terms.

There is no agreement about what the basic necessities are, either. Sir Keith Joseph has been quoted as arguing that 'a family is poor if it cannot afford to eat' (Joseph and Sumption, 1979). On the other hand, a MORI poll of the general public in 1983 found a broader concept of a minimum standard of living which included damp-free housing with basic amenities; clothing and shoes; money for public transport; adequate heating and carpeting; and toys for the children (Mack and Lansley, 1985). By Joseph's definition there may be very few poor people in Britain today (though we have no way of knowing), while defined by public opinion the numbers run into millions (Pond and Burghes, 1986).

For want of a better measure, most studies work around the supplementary benefit standard (SB), which represents the amount of money the state provides for those with little or no income. Many studies describe those living on or below the level of SB as living in poverty, and those living on incomes above SB but within 140 per cent of that level as living on the margins of poverty or on low incomes. An increasing number of social researchers choose 140 per cent of SB as a more realistic cut-off point for poverty, partly because of studies which show that the SB level is inadequate for decent living.

Table 17 shows the number of children living below, on, or just above the

Table 17: *Children in or on the margin of poverty (Great Britain)*

	1979		1983	
	No. of children	% of children	No. of children	% of children
Below SB	290,000	2	400,000	3
On or below SB	1,170,000	9	2,030,000	16
140% of SB and below	2,360,000	18	3,880,000	31

Source: DHSS (1986a).

SB level in 1979 and 1983 (latest figures available). Wherever the poverty line is drawn, the impression gained remains the same – that there is a serious problem of child poverty, which is getting worse.

It can be seen from the table that 2 per cent of children lived in families below the SB level in 1979, and 3 per cent in 1983. A total of 18 per cent of children lived below 140 per cent of the SB level in 1979, compared with 31 per cent in 1983. Put another way, by 1983 approximately one third of all children in Britain were living in families in or on the margin of poverty. Roughly half these children came from working families on low wages and half from families where the head was unemployed. Table 18 updates that on p. 108, and shows the total number of adults and children living in or on the margins of poverty in 1979–83.

It shows, for instance, that the numbers dependent on supplementary benefit rose from 3.9 million in 1979 to 6.1 million in 1983, and there were corresponding increases in other categories too.

Table 18: *Changes in the extent of poverty, Great Britain, 1979–83*

	1979		1981		1983	
	No. of people (millions)	%	No. of people (millions)	%	No. of people (millions)	%
Below SB	2.09	4	2.6	4.9	2.7	5
Receiving SB	3.90	7.6	4.8	9.1	6.1	11.4
At or up to 40% above SB level	5.50	10.4	7.2	13.5	7.5	14.1
Total	11.5	22	14.6	27.5	16.3	30.5

Source: DHSS (1986a).

Why has there been this increase in poverty? If the supplementary benefit standard had become more generous then more people would automatically be classified into the low-income category without any real social decline. Measured against the retail price index there has been a small increase (of about 5 per cent since 1978) in the purchasing power of SB, and the DHSS has argued that up to 40 per cent of the increase in the number of people in or close to poverty since 1979 could be attributed to this rise in value of the SB. However, most of the increase, equivalent to 3 million people, cannot be explained in this way (Piachaud, 1987). On the contrary, bodies like the Child Poverty Action Group argue that SB levels should be measured against *average incomes* rather than *prices*. In such a comparison, CPAG calculates that SB levels have declined relative to general income levels in Britain and that the poor therefore have not shared in the general rise in living standards over the past two decades (Piachaud, 1986).

Piachaud examined a number of other explanations; for example, has the increased child poverty been concentrated in large families? Could the growth of one-parent families be to blame? He found that most of the additional children in poverty were in one- or two-child families, not larger families, and that less than one quarter of the increase in poor children occurred in one-parent families. It was the dramatic rise in unemployment that accounted for three-quarters of the increase (Piachaud, 1986).

What about welfare benefits?

Against this growth in poverty, what has happened about the recommendations for increased support for families with children as part of a wide-ranging, anti-poverty strategy? There have been many complex changes in the benefit system since 1980, and the biggest-ever reorganization of social security is still under way but will not be fully functional until 1988. It is therefore very difficult to get a clear overview of what the changes have meant to the people for whom the benefits were actually intended. Analyses by advice agencies and pressure groups for the poor and homeless suggest that gains in some benefits have been offset by losses in others, so that in the end the poor are no better off than at the beginning of the decade and may very well be worse off with the forthcoming reorganization. For example, through the CPAG and Maternity Alliance there has been a successful fight to retain a universal child benefit, but its real value has dropped since 1979, rather than increased as recommended. The rates for family income supplement, maternity allowance, maternity grant and one-parent benefit have also fallen behind inflation (Walker and Walker, 1987).

In April 1987 the £25 maternity grant for all mothers was abolished, but women on family income supplement and SB could apply to the newly formed Social Fund for a grant of £80. At first sight this might seem like an improvement for the poorest women, but under the old system some of them would have applied for and received a payment for maternity needs of up to twice that amount.

Also in 1987, administration of the maternity allowance was transferred from the DHSS to employers, and women who were not employed during the year prior to their pregnancy lost entitlement to this allowance (Esam, 1987).

As more families with children face long-term unemployment, one particular defect in the benefit system has become more apparent. People who have been on supplementary benefit for over a year normally receive an increased rate of benefit in recognition of the wear-and-tear replacements that they would have to make. This does not apply to the unemployed, who are not entitled to the long-term rate however long their unemployment lasts. Many agencies, from the British Medical Association to the churches, have been calling for this anomaly to be put right to prevent added hardship in these families. In general, the fact that applications to the new Social Fund will be means-tested and payments will often be in the form of loans rather than grants has increased concern that yet more obstacles will be put in the way of the poor needing help, and that there will be low take-up of the benefits as a result

Children and nutrition

On other fronts the situation has also worsened, for example in relation to the nutrition of children. The school meals service, for instance, envisaged by Black as a source of free, nutritionally sound meals for all children, is in jeopardy in many local authorities. In 1980 price maintenance and nutritional standards for school meals were abolished, and since then great differences have developed between regions in what is provided for children and its cost. As the price of a school meal goes up the numbers taking meals tend to go down, and many authorities have had to resort to self-service, fast-food arrangements to keep the service going at all. While there were doubts about the nutritional standards of some school meals before 1980, these new arrangements suggest that standards may have fallen even further since then.

From 1979 to 1986 the proportion of children taking free school meals rose from 12 per cent of all pupils to 18 per cent, but there are fears that the quality and quantity of food offered to these most needy children may, in some cases, be most unsatisfactory. For example, there have been reports of children entitled to free school meals not being given a full meal because their allowance was below the cost of it (Roll, 1985).

Concern over the nutrition of British children was heightened in 1986 by the publication of a DHSS survey of the diets of 10- to 15-year-old schoolchildren (DHSS, 1986c). Consumption of crisps, chips and sweets was high and consequently more than three-quarters of the children were obtaining high levels of their energy from fats. Although the average intake of most minerals and vitamins was above the daily recommended allowances (DRA), a quite substantial proportion of children failed to reach the recommended intakes. For girls especially, iron intake was low: the average intake was less than 75 per cent of the DRA. From the kinds of foodstuffs eaten it would appear that the average child in the 1980s had a diet high in fat, sugar and salt, and low in fibre – the opposite of that recommended in current nutritional advice. Data from the same survey suggested that free school meals were an important factor in the nutrition of older children, helping to keep energy intakes up to the levels of those children who had packed lunches or ate at home (Cole-Hamilton and Lang, 1986).

Agencies like the London Food Commission have been advocating a return to national nutritional guidelines for school meals, but ones which reflect the modern consensus among nutritionists, together with a coherent food and nutrition policy for local authorities and the nation, with special regard for the young. Some local authorities, like the London Borough of Haringey, have taken on board many of these recommendations by developing a comprehensive food policy for the community services under the council's control. Haringey, in fact, has a 'Charter for Health' which aims at action on many aspects of health inequality in the borough.

While applauding such action, it has been stressed that local authorities can only do so much to alleviate food-related ill-health:

Low income is the key link between food, poverty and health. Tackling low income goes entirely beyond the capacity of the local authority and into the realms of welfare benefit policy. Above all it needs national, not just local action. (Lang, 1987)

And the rich get richer

Conversely, as more people have fallen into poverty in the 1980s the rich appear to be getting richer, after decades of a gradual closing of the wealth gap. According to Inland Revenue statistics (1986), the share of marketable *wealth* (including houses, stocks and shares, etc.) owned by the richest 1 per cent of the population dropped steadily after the war until 1980. In that year the richest 1 per cent owned 20 per cent of the total wealth. In 1981 their share increased slightly to 21 per cent, where it stayed until 1984. Likewise, the richest 5 per cent's share of wealth, which had been dropping steadily, has stabilized at 39 per cent of total wealth since 1980. Trends in the distribution of *income* between 1976 and 1984 also reflect growing inequality (Central Statistical Office, 1987). This has been attributed to several factors, including a boom in the stock market, the easing of certain capital taxes, and cuts in income taxes linked with substantially bigger increases in gross pay for those on high incomes (Huhne, 1986). All these factors have particularly benefited those who were already wealthy, while doing little to help those who were poor.

Consequently a review of social trends in the United Kingdom pointed to a growing social division since the mid 1970s between the prosperous majority and the poor minority (Halsey, 1987).

Improvements in housing and working conditions?

Many people consider decent housing to be one of the prime prerequisites for health, and certainly the Black Working Group saw it as such. But there are still sections of the population in this country who have yet to attain that goal. The housing charity Shelter reviewed the issue in 1986 and showed that many of the hoped-for improvements in housing conditions have still not materialized (McKechnie and Wilson, 1986). The following statistics are taken from this and other Shelter publications.

On the issue of *homelessness*, comparable figures go back only to 1978. In that year 53,000 households in England were accepted by councils as homeless. By 1985 the figure had risen to 94,000, which was expected to top 100,000 with the addition of Scotland and Wales. This represented an increase of nearly 80 per cent in seven years, and as three-quarters of these households consisted of families with children the number of homeless *people* probably exceeded 250,000. These figures did not include the majority of childless couples or homeless single people for whom local councils did not have a statutory responsibility. In 1985, 14,000 families were placed in temporary bed-and-breakfast accommodation – an unsafe and disadvantaged environment for children.

The latest major survey on housing conditions was carried out in 1981 and showed that 1.2 million homes in England and Wales were 'unfit for human habitation', while an additional 1 million lacked one or more basic amenities. Added to this were homes needing major repairs, to give a total of 4 million properties classed as substandard (one in four of the housing stock).

Over the past twenty years there have been considerable improvements in the provision of basic amenities – in 1967, 4 million homes lacked one or more basic amenities while in 1981 the figure had dropped to 1 million. The number of houses classed as 'unfit for human habitation' also dropped rapidly from 1.8 million in 1967 to 1.3 million in 1971 under the slum clearance schemes, but with very little improvement since then. In contrast, the number of houses needing major repairs increased by nearly 50 per cent from 1967 to 1981.

There have been real improvements in the matter of overcrowding. 'Extreme overcrowding' (more than 1.5 persons/room) was experienced by over 1.6 million people in Britain in 1966, but by 900,000 in 1981. 3.4 million people were classed as living in 'overcrowded' conditions in 1981 (more than 1 person/room) – a fall of 40 per cent since the 1960s. Within these categories the ethnic minorities were at particular risk of overcrowding. For instance, households with a head from the New Commonwealth or Pakistan were seven times more likely to be overcrowded, and fourteen times more likely to be extremely overcrowded, than households whose head was born in the UK.

Much of the improvement in housing conditions took place in the 1960s and the beginning of the 1970s, with very little progress made since then. Two additional factors are now giving concern for the future – the shortage of houses and the poor state of repair of existing houses. In 1977 it was estimated that 200,000 new dwellings/year were needed throughout the 1980s. In reality there has been a severe drop in building to the level of 40,000 dwellings/year in the public sector, with the private sector unable to make up the difference. Shelter has estimated that the public sector has experienced a 60 per cent cut in investment since 1979, so efforts have had to be concentrated on the repair of existing stock rather than on new building programmes. However, the housing stock is in a poor condition. In addition, home improvement grants have dropped to a very low level since 1982. In 1981 the Parker Morris standard for council housing was suspended, and a substantial proportion of houses built since then – at least in the Greater London area – have fallen below that standard. These developments go directly against the Black recommendation that local authority spending on housing improvements should be substantially increased.

Working conditions are also causing concern. One report found that there had been a 23.6 per cent increase in serious industrial accidents in the UK in the 1980s, suggesting that safety standards for those in employment may be deteriorating (Nichols, 1986). While there is no evidence of a concerted effort by government, employers and unions to develop acceptable and desirable conditions at work, or even to monitor conditions more effectively, some industries have been leading the way. A review of health promotion activities in the workplace in 1986 (Webb *et al.*, 1987) found that over half of Britain's workers (and 80 per cent of workplaces) had no access even to basic occupational health services other than first aid. However, the survey did find that some of the major public and private sector employers and leading trades unions had begun to develop programmes for prevention and health promotion in the workforce. The survey noted a change in emphasis between 1976 and 1986, with occupational disease reduction now seen as just as important as accident prevention, and in the last year or two much more attention given to health promotion. As well as giving examples of good practice from the survey, this study is valuable in recommending targets for health at work for the year 2000, and in outlining the action needed to develop a comprehensive workplace health service.

There are notable examples of unions raising the level of awareness of health issues among their members as a legitimate area of concern. The National Union of Public Employees (NUPE), for instance, formally adopted a policy on health in 1987, to be used both as a framework for organizing and negotiating, and a target for campaigning. With the aim of 'equality in health' it sets out the union's policy on specific issues and makes proposals for improving the health-promoting services. Its penetrating proposals for health at work encompass the collection of more complete figures on accidents and illness at work; a greater preventive role for the Employment Medical Advisory Service; a higher priority for occupational health in medical and nursing training; 'no fault' compensation; and changes within the NHS itself to improve its record on health and safety at work. In addition, various trades unions have played a part in developing the local authority initiatives described in the next few pages.

As far as the fairer deal for disabled people is concerned, the complex benefit changes have been reviewed recently and reveal a picture of gains and losses similar to that for child and family benefits (Walker and Walker, 1987). There are still inequalities and anomalies in the system, which mean that some disabled people are worse off than others. In June 1987 the Disability Alliance launched a campaign to publicize the wide differences in benefit which depended on how a person's disability was acquired. For example, someone born with a disabled leg would be entitled to much less than someone with a similar condition acquired as a result of a work accident, or war. The need for an adequate disablement allowance which takes account of the degree of disability rather than its cause is still just as pressing now as it was in 1979.

The government response

The initial response of the government to the recommendations of the Black Working Group has been well documented in the introductory chapter to this volume. All the recommendations were rejected as too expensive, costed by government economists at £2 billion. Those which would have cost very little appear to have been overlooked in the overall rejection. Doubt was also cast on the existence of some inequalities in health. This was in contrast to the assessment made by the research community, which accepted the Black Report as a sound and authoritative document (see p. 306).

Consequently, a co-ordinated policy tô reduce inequalities in health in the U K has not been adopted. 'Greater co-ordination between government departments in the administration of health-related policies – by establishing inter-departmental machinery in the Cabinet Office' (recommendation 36) is still very much required. Local counterparts of this national structure have not been encouraged, nor has an overseeing Health Development Council been set up. On the other hand, the government has committed the U K to the W H O targets for 'Health for All', one of which is the reduction of inequalities in health between groups in this country (see p. 347). This could signal a renewed commitment to solving the problems of health inequality. However, there is little indication as yet that the D H S S sees any wider commitment beyond the regional reallocation of N H S funds through R A W P (Scott-Samuel and Szalai, 1988). Precisely what would be involved in a firm commitment to the W H O targets is examined in the final sections of this chapter.

Putting inequalities in health on the agenda

Just because there has been a lack of national action does not mean that the subject has been abandoned. Some exceptional initiatives have been taking place, together with a growing movement towards a new kind of health policy.

First, there have been what might be called 'agenda-setting' exercises around the country. For example, the Health Education Council, with bodies like the B M A and T U C, have been organizing conferences on deprivation and ill-health, and on the community development approach to deprivation, in an attempt to inform and motivate professional action on the subject (T U C, 1986). Similarly, the Scottish Health Education Coordinating Committee convened a working party on multiple deprivation which has reviewed projects and action on the issue throughout Scotland,

and has made recommendations for wide-ranging action (Scottish Health Education Co-ordinating Committee, 1984). Following on from this, bodies like the Royal College of Physicians and Surgeons of Glasgow held symposia on the subject in 1986 and June 1987 (Davies, 1987). Various professional bodies, like the Health Visitors Association, the BMA and the Faculty of Community Medicine have all addressed the issue from their own particular perspectives.

Adding a further dimension to the debate, the Archbishop of Canterbury set up a Commission in 1983 to examine social and economic conditions in the urban priority areas. When it was published in 1985 the Commission's report, entitled 'Faith in the City', was influential in forcefully focusing public attention on the plight of the inner cities. In graphic detail it set out the structure of inequality within the cities; the economic and physical decline and social disintegration experienced in the outer housing estates as well as in the central urban areas. It concluded:

Chapter after chapter of our Report tells the same story: that a growing number of people are excluded by poverty or powerlessness from sharing in the common life of our nation. A substantial minority are forced to live on the margins of poverty or below the threshold of an acceptable standard of living. The critical issue to be faced is whether there is any serious political will to set in motion a process which will enable those who are at present in poverty and powerlessness to rejoin the life of the nation. (Archbishop of Canterbury's Commission, 1985)

The recommendations for the nation stemming from the study were very much in tune with those of the Black Report, with radical proposals for concerted action on poverty, unemployment, housing conditions, homelessness, community care, public safety and national policies on health.

In July 1987 a new organization, the Public Health Alliance, was formed to bring together individuals from the health, local government, voluntary and consumer sectors, with the aim of making sure that the public health aspect was given priority on a wide range of national matters. These range from poverty and food policy to housing and transport. It was thought that if such an organization could raise the awareness of policy-makers to such issues, then there would be a greater chance that recommendations on reducing inequalities in health would at last be taken seriously (Smith, 1986).

The World Health Organization's ambitious project, 'Healthy Cities', which began in 1986, is focusing on how cities can promote health. The aim is to develop in ten to twelve European cities a broadly based approach to health promotion in partnership with the people in those cities, firmly rooted in the principle of 'equity in health' (Ashton, 1986). Although only two cities in Britain are officially part of the project (Liverpool and Bloomsbury), several more have been stimulated by the project to formulate targets of their own concerning health promotion, as will become apparent in the next few pages.

All these developments were part of a re-awakening of interest in the social influences on health, which perhaps are most clearly illustrated by the activities of the local authorities.

Action by local authorities

Although there is no unifying national lead on the issue, nevertheless what has been done by individuals and organizations in the context of policy-making should not go unrecorded.

As noted in Chapter 2, p. 248, many local councils and health authorities have instituted their own 'local Black Reports' to help with resource allocation and service planning. These were directly inspired by the findings of the original Black Report. The Association of Metropolitan Authorities is currently attempting to co-ordinate the data-base needed to describe indicators of poverty and health in cities for further small-area analyses. A 1985 survey by the A M A found that at least a third of its members possessed a health committee or an equivalent group serving the same function. Since then the number of such committees has continued to expand, encouraged by the A M A Working Group. At least six have also appointed health liaison officers to make communication easier with the various departments and organizations influencing health across the full range of services to the community. It has been pointed out that such figures do not give a complete picture of the work going on in local authorities. Many long-established environmental health departments, for example, have been taking the lead in this field over many years. A more comprehensive picture of local authority activities concerned with health should shortly be available, following a 1987 survey by the charity Health Rights. The experiences of Manchester, Sheffield and Oxford illustrate the kind of developments which have taken place so far.

In Manchester, shortly after the Black Report was published, the City Council sponsored two seminars for health authority, City Council and Community Health Council members, with the aim of publicizing the findings of the report and considering what to do locally. Out of those seminars came a ten-point plan identifying those areas of action which could be implemented fairly swiftly. These included action to improve the take-up of welfare benefits, to improve the statistical information on health available at ward level (for example on accidents to children) and to continue improvements in housing to tackle the problem of damp, as well as the promotion of strategies on cigarette-smoking and nutrition. A 'Black Report Working Group' was set up in 1981 composed of officers from the City Council planning department and the three District Health Authorities. Among other projects, this Working Group was concerned to improve local information on health and in 1985 it published a report on 'Health Inequalities in Manchester', with an update in 1986. During the same period the City Council had also agreed a wide-ranging policy on smoking with the North-Western Regional Health Authority, including the designation of no-smoking areas and the setting up of smoking cessation groups. A healthy eating policy was also pursued in the Education and Social Services Departments, and also in the catering section of the Council. This led to a review of nutrition in Manchester schools. A joint working party with the health authorities was also set up to look at the question of accidents to children.

In parallel with these developments, an Anti-poverty Sub-committee of the City Council was set up to promote measures to tackle poverty across the city as well as in the most deprived areas. Included in the anti-poverty programme were initiatives to stimulate employment, to tackle low pay and to promote uptake of welfare benefits. In this context twenty welfare rights officers are working around the city encouraging uptake of benefits and training other Council staff in the help available to low-income groups (Manchester City Council. 1986).

As the health component of the Council's work increased, a health campaign worker was appointed in April 1986 to liaise on health matters with community groups and to co-ordinate the work of the Council representatives on all the various community committees and health bodies. A specialist in community medicine was also appointed (jointly with the North Manchester Health Authority) to focus specifically on housing and health inequalities. Springing from this appointment a report is currently being prepared on 'Health and the Physical Environment', to complement the information on social inequalities documented in the local 'Black Report'. This will cover aspects of housing, access to services, pollution and community safety, with a view to devising remedial action. A desire by Manchester City Council to put health higher on the agenda led in July 1986 to the formation of a Health Sub-committee of the Council, which is considering, among other projects, the city's responses to the WHO targets for 'Health for All'. All such initiatives are being pulled together into a City of Manchester health strategy which is currently being developed, but will almost certainly feature the reduction of inequality in health as one of its main themes (Morris, 1987).

The experience of Sheffield City Council is of particular interest because it was the first to establish a focus for health policy across all the Council departments. In 1981 it set up a Health Care Strategy Group, initially to co-ordinate the Council's responses to the four District Health Authorities within its boundaries, but it soon took on a wider role. In 1983 and 1984 the group sponsored two conferences with Greenwich on 'Progressive Strategies for Health', which were influential in raising the profile and interest in public health in local government across the country. During this time the Strategy Group considered the recommendations of the Black Report and decided that a local study in Sheffield was needed. This was commissioned jointly by the Environmental Health Department and the Central Policy Unit, and was published in 1985 under the title 'Poverty and Health in the City of Sheffield' (Thunhurst, 1985a). This analysis came to similar con-clusions to those in the Black Report and made a number of recom-mendations, including the adoption of a comprehensive health policy for the city. Towards this end a new Health and Consumer Services Committee was created in May 1986 and a health unit was formed within the En-vironmental Health Department. Meanwhile the Sheffield Health Authority had been compiling a health profile of the city's electoral wards in terms of disease and health care, which revealed striking inequalities in provision of local health services in relation to need (Sheffield Health Authority, 1986).

Both the City Council and Health Authority reports made recom-mendations which have yet to be implemented, but promising initiatives have been taken on some fronts. For example, the local authority is pushing forward with a food policy and is looking at the ways in which more nutritious food can be supplied and promoted in all the authority's outlets. Schools and residential homes for the elderly are particular priorities. Simi-larly, a city smoking policy is being developed to control tobacco advertising and promote non-smoking in Council-controlled sites. A mobile clinic for cervical cytology targeted on certain areas is being developed by the health authority as a result of the deficiencies in health care which showed up in the city's health profile. Most recently, the two agencies have come together with the Family Practitioners Committee and voluntary agencies to examine the issues raised by the WHO 'Healthy Cities' project and to plan a joint public health programme with specific targets set for the year 2000. The aim of reducing inequalities in health by 25 per cent is the prime target under consideration (Sheffield City Council, 1987).

Oxford has seen a dramatic expansion of its health promotion role over the past four years, dating from 1984 when a Health Liaison Committee was formed within the Council after intense lobbying from the health trades unions. In May 1985 this was merged with the Environmental Health

Committee and by July 1986 the Council had adopted a 'City Health Strategy'. Included in the strategy were two important aims: 'to offset health inequalities related to social class, gender, ethnic origin, age and disability', and 'to secure and sustain a safe and healthy environment within the city'. Many practical initiatives stemming from the strategy are now well under way. The Environmental Health Department, for example, now has a health liaison and promotion section consisting of officers concerned with health liaison, AIDS liaison, home safety and smoking prevention. But health promotion is being introduced into other areas too, to extend the traditional work of the department. In the food hygiene section, for instance, a community dietician has been appointed to develop a healthy eating programme for the city. In the housing section an energy and heating officer is developing a programme to tackle ill-health and deaths associated with inadequate heating. Each of the Council's departments has been asked to produce health targets to focus their work on the overall goals of the health strategy, and to date 100 targets have been identified and are being refined with the help of community physicians. The Planning Department has been investigating ways of producing a health data-base for the city and has already ranked the neighbourhoods against a deprivation index in readiness for health profiles of the areas to be drawn up. A community development project is under way in one of the more deprived neighbourhoods, sponsored jointly with the health authority. This combines action on fitness testing, welfare benefits, health screening and home safety.

The city engineers and Recreation Department have developed safe cycle routes for schoolchildren, and a community fitness programme. As a major employer itself, the City Council is also attempting to develop a model occupational health policy with smoke-free atmospheres in offices and workplaces, smoke cessation courses, a health screening programme and so on, with the aim of extending the policy to workplaces across the city.

Oxford too has been inspired by the WHO 'Healthy Cities' project and initiated a 'Healthy Oxford 2000 Campaign' in November 1986, with twenty-five target areas for development within the city which complement the existing City Health Strategy (Fryer, 1987).

All these examples are indicative of the growing awareness in local authorities of their important role in health promotion. In 1974 the local authorities, who had a proud tradition of public health action for over a century, lost responsibility for community health services to the health authorities; with that change they also lost the key post of Medical Officer of Health, whose function it was to promote health in the community. As a consequence for several years there was no health focus in local government outside the Environmental Health Departments, and interest in the field waned. But then the Black Report came along in 1980, followed by the WHO developments, and both underlined the importance of housing, primary health care, social services and other local authority functions in promoting health and reducing inequalities. In several cases the national and international influences seemed to act as catalysts for a complete re-think of council policies and the formation of committees with the power, theoretically, to carry these policies through, though there are still many practical obstacles to action (Moran, 1986). Fryer (1987) expresses the growing mood of optimism:

> Though it is recognized that the solutions to major public health problems do not reside, for the most part, in the hands of local government, there is a growing conviction that local authorities can play an effective role in advancing public health in their localities.

Towards 2000: the WHO targets

Previous sections have noted the influence of the WHO 'Health for All by the Year 2000' programme on local and health authorities and also this country's commitment to the programme for the next twelve years or so. But what would this commitment entail if it were to be taken on wholeheartedly? And how does it fit in with the discussions on inequalities in health?

In 1984 the European Region of the WHO drew up a strategy for attaining 'Health for All by the Year 2000' and in 1985 issued detailed targets to which the UK has agreed. Firstly, it acknowledged that there are certain fundamental conditions which have to be met before any real improvements can be made – the prerequisites for health:
* freedom from the fear of war;
* equal opportunities for all;
* satisfaction of the basic needs for food, basic education, clean water and sanitation, decent housing, secure work and a useful role in society;
* political will and public support to launch the necessary action.

'Without peace and social justice, without enough food and water, without education and decent housing, and without providing each and all with a useful role in society and adequate income, there can be no health for the people, no real growth and no social development' (WHO, 1985b).

Secondly, it recognized that the region would have to come to grips with two major issues if the European goal is to be reached by the year 2000: the reduction of health inequalities among countries and among groups within countries, and the placing of just as much emphasis on strengthening health as on reducing disease and its consequences.

Not surprisingly, therefore, the first of the thirty-eight detailed targets which followed this statement was concerned with 'equity in health', which has already been quoted in full on p. 219. The WHO considered that this target could be achieved 'if the basic prerequisites for health were provided for all; if the risks related to life-styles were reduced; if the health aspects of living and working conditions were improved; and if good primary health care were made accessible to all'. It emphasized that the main determinants of present health differences were living and working conditions; that the struggle against poverty and social deprivation was an integral part of any policy for better health; and that approaches to changing life-styles should be supportive rather than victim-blaming and should recognize the limits placed on the choice of a healthy life by social and economic conditions. It also stressed the need for responsive, outreach health services. What the WHO strategy goes on to do is to carry the theme of 'equity in health' right through the rest of the targets to form a broad, long-term policy touching on many aspects of health.

These points and the finer details of the strategy were in complete agreement with the policies advocated by the Black Working Group. The two analyses agree on the main problem, the underlying causes and the most likely solutions. The documents can be read and considered together as outlining a way forward for the future. It is obvious that this is precisely what is happening already in some local government and health authorities, and also in the discussions taking place in the professional bodies. For example, the Faculty of Community Medicine issued a Charter for Action in 1986 to identify the specific actions that would be required in the UK to pursue the WHO targets successfully (Faculty of Community Medicine, 1986). This spelt out in detail what the targets would mean for central and local government, for health authorities and health professions, for training institutions, for all organizations and for individuals.

The British Medical Association, in direct response to its members' concern about the Black Report, set up a working group to consider the evidence on deprivation and ill-health and came up with recommendations from a medical perspective (BMA, 1987). There are two strands to the action proposed in the BMA discussion document: short-term health initiatives which could lessen the incidence of specific illness in deprived groups, and long-term structural changes in social policy.

The suggested health service initiatives included:
* strengthening of the role of community physicians to collect data on the health of populations and to translate that data into recommendations for action;
* better co-ordination between different local services;

* a wider view of health education by health professionals to consider social, not just individual, factors;
* a role for health professionals in raising public awareness of health issues;
* the adoption of a community development approach;
* the encouragement of the convenient availability of preventive services;
* the training of health professionals to help them encourage take-up of welfare benefits;
* the development of a standard format for recording ethnicity in official statistics;
* quotas for community nursing and health-visiting provision to take account of socio-economic factors, and such factors to be taken into consideration in all health service planning;
* a role for Community Health Councils in representing and actively advocating the needs of the most disadvantaged users of the services.

The long-term suggestions on structural changes included:

* action on unemployment;
* financial support for vulnerable groups;
* school meals;
.* an enlightened approach to inner-city building and the safety of children;
* a review of legal control of workplace health and safety;
* a new generation of public health laws to combat present-day problems of housing design, damp and disrepair.

The report does emphasize, however, that the problem cannot be solved by juggling existing resources between different health and social services. There would need to be a national commitment to take action and to provide the necessary resources to do so.

As such examples indicate, there is a distinct movement in this country which believes not only that something *should* be done about inequalities in health, but that something *can* be done. There are clear pointers emanating from the United Kingdom and abroad which indicate the best way forward.

Public attitudes

Before leaving the subject, it is worth looking at what has been happening to public attitudes to social inequalities over the same period. From survey evidence there appears to be a softening of attitudes to poverty by the general public, with the poor now attracting greater sympathy. For instance, a Gallup poll in 1977 found that 33 per cent of people blamed the poor for their own plight. In 1986 the same question was asked and this time only 17 per cent blamed the poor, while 53 per cent blamed 'circumstances beyond their control' (Lipsey, 1986). In 1984 a MORI poll found that 74 per cent of people thought that the gap between the rich and the poor was too great and there was widespread support for increasing benefits even at the cost of higher taxation (Golding, 1986). Perhaps the community at large would now more than ever appreciate concerted action on inequalities in health.

Conclusions

One of the most important features of the recommendations of the Black Working Group was the recognition that good health and the reduction of inequalities could only be achieved by mobilizing the efforts of a wide spectrum of agencies outside the health care sector as well as within it. The Working Group maintained that there had to be a united attack on poverty, poor nutrition, and poor housing and working conditions. To achieve this would require co-ordinated action by national and local government, health authorities and all the other agencies with an influence on health.

Disappointingly, in the intervening eight years there seems to have been little progress on the basic problems underlying inequality in health, or on the specific recommendations of the report. There is evidence, for example, that the number of children living in poverty has increased rather than decreased, that welfare benefit policy has failed to improve the living standards of the poor to any appreciable extent and that poor nutrition, housing and working conditions abound. There just has not been a recognizable national effort to tackle inequalities in health.

Against this extremely negative picture can be set the many positive initiatives which have been taken around the country. There has been a dramatic re-awakening of interest in public health in the local authorities, a growing concern and pressure for action from the various professional associations, and numerous examples of individual health workers and health authorities doing their best to counteract the inequality in health and health care which they face in their day-to-day work.

All this activity has been given added impetus by the international initiatives springing from the World Health Organization's strategy for 'Health for All by the Year 2000' and associated 'Healthy Cities' projects. Added to this, the international research community has been brought together by the efforts of the WHO to focus on aspects of inequality in health. The WHO targets, with the theme of 'equity in health' running right through them, reaffirm the policy recommendations of the Black Report and show clear pointers for the way forward. But they, like the Black Report itself, stress that any real progress can only be made with a strong political will to make things happen.

Summary

Background and format

The pattern of health inequalities in Britain was thoroughly documented by the Black Working Group, drawing on evidence from the early 1970s. But what does the picture on inequalities in health look like in the 1980s? How has it changed, and what progress, if any, has been made towards implementing the recommendations of the Working Group?

These questions formed the starting-point for the present review, which summarizes the evidence on social inequalities in health published since 1980 and draws attention to some of the recent initiatives which have been undertaken in this field. Closely following the format of the original Black Report, the review first considers how the experience of health of people living in Britain in the 1980s varies with their occupational class, employment status, gender, area of residence, ethnic origin and housing tenure. It goes on to look at whether the health gap between the occupational classes has widened or narrowed in recent years; whether there are differences in the use and availability of health services for different social groups; and whether international comparisons can offer further insight. New studies investigating the causes of inequalities in health are outlined and discussed. The final chapters cover some responses to the Black Report's recommendations, including improvements in data collection, initiatives taken by the health and social services, and the wider response of national and local government. Finally some pointers for the future are considered.

Health inequalities today

The evidence presented in Chapter 2 confirms that serious social inequalities in health have persisted into the 1980s. Whether social position is measured by occupational class, or by assets such as house and car ownership, or by employment status, a similar picture emerges. Those at the bottom of the social scale have much higher death rates than those at the top. This applies at every stage of life from birth through to adulthood and well into old age.

Neither is it just a few specific conditions which account for these higher death rates. All the major killer diseases now affect the poor more than the rich (and so do most of the less common ones). The less favoured occupational classes also experience higher rates of chronic sickness and their children tend to have lower birth-weights, shorter stature and other indicators suggesting poorer health status.

The unemployed and their families have considerably worse physical and mental health than those in work. Until recently, however, direct evidence that unemployment *caused* this poorer health was not available. Now there is substantial evidence of unemployment causing a deterioration in mental health, with improvements observed on re-employment.

The well-established pattern of women having lower death rates than men but experiencing higher sickness rates still holds good in the 1980s. Recent studies have shown that the situation is far more complex, though. Women's health varies with social class, employment and marital status in ways which are only just beginning to be understood. The health of working-class women is particularly poor.

Striking regional disparities in health can still be observed. Death rates were highest in Scotland, followed by the North and North-West regions of England, and were lowest in the South-East of England and East Anglia, confirming the long-established North/South gradient. What is becoming increasingly clear from fresh evidence, though, is the great inequalities which exist between communities living side by side in the same region. Numerous studies at the level of local authority wards have pinpointed pockets of very poor health corresponding to areas of social and material deprivation. Alongside them, areas with much better health profiles can be detected and these exhibit more affluent characteristics. Although such deprived areas can be found throughout the country, the North has a higher concentration of them than the South and South-East.

The health of ethnic minorities presents a varied picture. Strikingly high mortality from hypertension and strokes is found among people of Afro-Caribbean origin, and high mortality rates for babies of mothers born in Pakistan. High death rates from accidents for all immigrant groups also cause concern. However, most ethnic minority groups have lower death rates from other major diseases like lung cancer and chronic bronchitis than people born in the UK. These findings are based on country of birth as an indicator of ethnic origin, which is not a very precise measure and which of course says nothing about the health of members of ethnic minority groups who were born in this country. As many suffer poor housing and working conditions and a high risk of unemployment, there are fears that the health of some ethnic minority groups may be poor, but we need better information collection to help investigate this possibility.

Recent trends

Chapter 3 considers whether the health inequalities have increased or decreased in recent years. In the decade from 1971 to 1981 there was a fall in 'all cause' death rates in Britain, but these improvements in health were not experienced equally across the population. Non-manual groups experienced a much greater decline in death rates than manual groups; as a result the gap between the two groups widened. Furthermore, death rates among women from coronary heart disease and lung cancer actually rose in manual groups over the ten-year period, while showing a substantial decline for non-manual women. There was also a widening gap between manual and non-manual groups in their rates of chronic sickness from 1974 to 1984.

The more controversial issue of long-term trends is discussed and new assessments of the data reviewed in the Black Report are summarized. The studies confirm the original conclusions of the report: that inequalities in health have widened since the 1950s for adults of working age. The exception to this trend is in relation to babies aged one month to one year. There was a dramatic decline in their death rates during the 1970s in all classes, but especially in class V, bringing about a reduction in the health gap. Although there has been very little further improvement since 1980 for manual or non-manual classes, the evidence does illustrate that the class differential is not inevitable. It can be reduced.

Use of health services

Chapter 4 considers access to and use of health services by different groups in the community. On the issue of the availability of services, there are still examples of poorer provision in more deprived areas, and poorer quality, though no overall picture of the extent of inequality around the country is available.

There is general agreement that semi-skilled and unskilled manual groups still make less use of preventive services than professional and managerial groups, but have higher rates of general practice consultations. Whether the rates of use of the primary care services fully match the different levels of perceived illness within each group is a vital question. Although there have been a few studies in this field since 1980, the evidence on this issue is still inconclusive. Claims that all socio-economic groups have equal access to and opportunity to make use of NHS services are certainly premature.

International comparisons

In Chapter 5 comparisons are made with other developed countries. The UK is certainly not alone in experiencing social inequalities in health. Every country to a greater or lesser extent experiences differences in health between regional, occupational or income groups. One of the most important questions for such a comparison is whether any countries have managed to reduce inequalities in the population and if so, how.

In this context, examples from the Nordic countries are illuminating. Policies to reduce regional differences in health care in Finland and to set up a national nutrition and food policy in Norway deserve special attention.

Explaining health inequalities

Explanations of continuing inequalities are considered in Chapter 6. From the evidence, it is concluded that health inequalities between social groups are genuine and cannot be explained away as artefact. There is evidence of some selection, in which those in poor health move down the social scale. However, this is not sufficient to account for the large differentials in health found between social groups. On the other hand, the evidence that socio-economic circumstances have a major impact on health is now extremely strong. Fresh evidence shows that life-style and material living conditions influence health and vary with occupational class. Furthermore, recent in-depth studies have increased understanding of how living and working conditions can impose severe restrictions on an individual's ability to choose a healthy life-style. They provide fresh insight into the way behaviour is influenced by social conditions and argue for a policy which recognizes the link between the two, in preference to policies which focus solely on the individual.

The research response

Chapters 7, 8 and 9 deal with progress made on the recommendations of the Black Report. None of the recommendations concerned with improving the collection of information or the monitoring of social inequalities in health has been adopted. In many cases the information required to carry out vital research is still not available. What is even more frustrating is the fact that in recent years the traditional sources of information on social class and health, and deprivation and health, have also virtually dried up. For example, in the past many have relied on the Registrar General's occupational mortality Decennial Supplements for authoritative information, but the latest supplement (1986) scarcely addresses the issue.

Despite these difficulties, notable advances have been made in the way data are collected. Post-coding of birth and death records, for instance, has made it much easier to carry out small-area studies and this field has developed considerably as a result. The development of measures of area social inequality was called for by the Black Report and much progress has been made towards this end. More sensitive ways of measuring social class continue to be explored to supplement the use of occupations. Measures of health are being developed which take more account of the impact of certain factors on a person's daily life, to supplement traditional measures like mortality and morbidity rates.

The response to policy recommendations

Many recommendations in the report focused on what the health and social services could do to reduce inequalities in health, together with proposals for action in the wider community.

The response to the recommendations has been characterized by a lack of action, particularly at national and central level. No unifying lead has been taken to guide and motivate a response which would have translated recommendations into action. Some of the services the Working Group wanted to see built up and revitalized have remained at the same level, or in some cases may have deteriorated. For example, the child health services, provision of day care for under-fives, and the school health services, which were seen as ways of giving children a better start in life, are all giving cause for concern. Similarly with services for disabled people; the shift in resources towards support for people in their own homes has been minimal. Prevention and health education are still not being given the priority recommended.

In the wider community, the Working Group saw the abolition of child poverty as number one priority for the 1980s. Improvements in housing and working conditions were also recommended, as was a proper mechanism for co-ordinating health-related policy at a national and local level.

In reality what has happened over the past eight years is a disturbing increase in the number of children growing up in poverty, and an increase in families becoming homeless. Policies deliberately designed to reduce child poverty have not been adopted, and the situation has been exacerbated by a sharp rise in the level of unemployment which has affected families with young children in particular.

A concerted effort to improve housing conditions has not been made and there is now growing concern over the shortage of houses and the poor state of repair of existing dwellings. There is no evidence, except in isolated cases, that government, employers and trades unions have come together to formulate plans for creating healthier working conditions or to monitor the working environment more effectively. Mechanisms for co-ordinating policies on health in local and national government have not been set up on a significant scale, even though it is widely acknowledged that health promotion policies need to involve many agencies outside the health sector, such as housing, environmental control, transport, food and agriculture and – above all – the Treasury.

So far, much of this summary may have sounded very negative. It would be wrong to give the impression that no one cares about inequalities in health and that no attempts have been made to remedy them. Although a co-ordinated policy has not been set in motion, a great deal has been done by individuals and by organizations in direct response to the Black Report. A selection of the many initiatives is described, including health and social service projects to improve the access of deprived communities to primary health care; to explore the community development approach; and to encourage independence in old age – to name a few.

Chapters 8 and 9 also note the tremendous efforts being made by some health and local government authorities to compile local 'Black Reports' and to build up health data-bases as well as to work out health strategies. The renewed interest in public health policy in local authorities is particularly noticeable. In addition, the report highlights the work of many professional bodies and organizations concerned about inequalities. Some have formulated policy and plans for tackling the problem of health inequalities from their own particular perspectives.

Now the World Health Organization's strategy for 'Health for All' is taking shape with the theme of 'equity in health' as one of its major principles. This is acting as a catalyst for co-ordinated action to tackle the health divide. Together these initiatives will continue to keep the issue of health inequality firmly on the agenda.

References

Introduction to *Inequalities in Health*

Black, D. (1981a), 'Inequalities in Health', *British Medical Journal*, 282, p. 1468.

Black, D. (1981b), 'Inequalities in Health', lecture in memory of Dr Christie Gordon, mimeo.

Bosanquet, N. (1985), *Public Expenditure on the NHS: Recent Trends and the Outlook*, Institute of Health Service Management, 75 Portland Place, London W1N 4AN, p. 8.

British Medical Association (1987), 'Deprivation and Ill-health', British Medical Association.

British Medical Journal (1986), 'Whatever Happened to the Black Report?', 293, pp. 91–2.

COHSE (1980), Research Bulletin, occasional series, Confederation of Health Service Employees, December.

Deitch, R. (1981), 'The Debate on the Black Report', *Lancet*, ii, pp. 158–9.

Gray, A. (1981), *On the Black Report: Inequalities in Health, a Summary and Comment*, Aberdeen, Health Economics Research Unit, University of Aberdeen.

Griffiths (1983), The National Health Service Management Inquiry (Griffiths) Report, Department of Health and Social Security.

Hart, N. (1987), 'The Health Divide: Class Still Reigns', *Poverty*, 67, pp. 17–19.

Illsley, R. (1986), 'Occupational Class, Selection and the Production of Inequalities in Health', *Quarterly Journal of Social Affairs*, 2 (2), pp. 151–65.

Illsley, R. (1987a), 'Occupational Class, Selection and Inequalities in Health – Rejoinder to Richard Wilkinson's Reply', *Quarterly Journal of Social Affairs*, 3 (3), pp. 213–23.

Illsley, R. (1987b), 'The Health Divide: Bad Welfare or Bad Statistics?', *Poverty* 67, pp. 16–17.

Illsley, R., and LeGrand, J. (1986), *Measurement of Inequality in Health*, No. 12 in the Welfare State Programme of STICERD, London School of Economics.

Kilmarnock (1987), House of Lords Hansard, 1 April, col. 645.

Lancet (1987a), 'Suspicion about the New Health Education Authority', i, p. 517.

Lancet (1987b), 'The Health Education Council Goes Out with a Flourish', i, p. 816.

Lancet (1987c), 'The Health Divide: Swan-song of the Health Education Council', i, pp. 724–5.

LeGrand, J. (1985), *Inequalities in Health: the Human Capital Approach*, No. 1 in the Welfare State Programme of STICERD, London School of Economics.

LeGrand, J. (1987), *An International Comparison of Inequalities of Health*, No. 16 in the Welfare State Programme of STICERD, London School of Economics.

LeGrand, J., and Rabin, M. (1986), 'Trends in British Health Inequality, 1931–83' in A. J. Culyer and B. Jonsson (eds.), *Public and Private Health Services*, Oxford, Basil Blackwell.

Marmot, M., and McDowall, M. (1986), 'Mortality Decline and Widening Social Inequalities', *Lancet*, ii, pp. 274–6.

Morris, J. N. (1980a), 'Social Inequalities Undiminished', *Lancet*, i, pp. 87–90; *Health Visitor*, 53, pp. 361–5.

Morris, J. N. (1980b), 'Equalities and Inequalities in Health', *British Medical Journal*, 281, p. 1003.

Morris, J. N. (1980c), 'Medicine's Order of Priorities', *The Times*, 19 September.

National Association of Health Authorities (1986), *NHS Economic Review*, available from NAHA, Garth House, 47 Edgbaston Park Road, Birmingham B15 2RS.

OECD (1985), *Measuring Health Care 1960–1983*, Paris, OECD.

Radical Community Medicine (1980), 4.

Seear (1987), House of Lords *Hansard*, 30 March, col. 358.

Townsend, P. (1982), 'The Policy Implications of a Positive Approach to Health', *Health Visitor*, 55, pp. 97–101.

Townsend, P., Phillimore, P., and Beattie, A. (1986), 'Inequalities in Health in the Northern Region: an Interim Report', Northern Regional Health Authority/Bristol University.

TUC (1981), *The Unequal Health of the Nation*, a TUC summary of the Black Report, TUC.

Watkins, S., and Elton, P. (1981), 'Inequalities in Health: a Response', paper prepared for a working party of the North-West Regional Health Authority (unpublished).

Whitney, R. (1987a), House of Commons *Hansard*, 6 April, col. 53.

Whitney, R. (1987b), House of Commons *Hansard*, 6 April, col. 54.

Wilkinson, R. G. (1986), 'Occupational Class Selection and Inequalities in Health: a Reply to Raymond Illsley', *Quarterly Journal of Social Affairs*, 2 (4), pp. 415–22.

Wilkinson, R. G. (1987), 'A Rejoinder', *Quarterly Journal of Social Affairs*, 3 (3), pp. 225–8.

World Bank, *World Development Report 1981*, Oxford, Oxford University Press.

The Black Report

1: Concepts of Health and Inequality

Abel-Smith, B., *The Hospitals 1800–1948*, Heinemann, 1964.

Birch, H. G., and Gussow, J. D., *Disadvantaged Children: Health, Nutrition and School Failure*, New York, Harcourt, Brace and World, 1970.

Black, D., 'The Paradox of Medical Care', *Journal of the Royal College of Physicians*, 13, 57, 1979.

Brown, G. W., and Harris, T., *Social Origins of Depression: A Study of Psychiatric Disorder in Women*, Tavistock, 1978.

Culyer, A. J., Lavers, R. J., and Williams, A., in Shonfield, A., and Shaw, S. (eds.), *Social Indicators and Social Policy*, Heinemann, 1972.

Disability Rights Handbook for 1980, Disability Alliance, 1979.

Dollery, C., *The End of an Age of Optimism*, Nuffield Provincial Hospitals Trust, 1978.

Dubos, R., *Mirage and Health*, Allen & Unwin, 1960.

Help for the Disabled, Louis Harris International, 1974.

McKeown, T., *The Role of Medicine: Dream, Mirage or Nemesis?*, Nuffield Provincial Hospitals Trust, 1976.

Marshall, W. A., *Human Growth and Its Disorders*, Academic Press, 1977.

Mechanic, D., *Medical Sociology: A Selective View*, New York, Free Press, 1968.

Morris, J. N., *Uses of Epidemiology*, 3rd edn, Churchill Livingstone, 1975.

Royal Commission on the Distribution of Income and Wealth, Reports Nos. 1, 4, 5 and 7, Cmnds 6171, 6626, 6999 and 7595, London, HMSO, 1975–9.

Sackett, D. L., Chambers, L. W., MacPherson, A. S., Goldsmith, C. H., and Macauley, R. G., 'The Development and Application of Indices of Health: General Methods and a Summary of Results', *American Journal of Public Health*, Vol. 67, No. 5, 1977.

Sigerist, H. E., *Civilisation and Disease*, University of Chicago Press, Phoenix Edition, 1962 (first published Cornell University Press, 1943).

Stevenson, T. H. C., 'The Vital Statistics of Wealth and Poverty', *Journal of the Royal Statistical Society*, Vol. 91, 1928.

Susser, M. W., and Watson, W., *Sociology in Medicine*, Oxford University Press, 1971.

Tuckett, D. A. (ed.), *An Introduction to Medical Sociology*, Tavistock, 1976.

2: The Pattern of Present Health Inequalities

Gans, B., 'Health Problems and the Immigrant Child', in CIBA Foundation, *Immigration: Medical and Social Aspects*, 1966.

Hood, C., Oppé, T. E., Pless, I. B., and Apte, E., *West Indian Immigrants: A Study of One-Year-Olds in Paddington*, Institute of Race Relations, 1970.

Logan, W. P. D., and Cushion, A. A., *Morbidity Statistics from General Practice*, HMSO, 1960.

Ministry of Pensions and National Insurance, *Report of an Inquiry into the Incidence of Incapacity for Work*, HMSO, 1964.

OPCS, *Occupational Mortality 1970–72, Decennial Supplement*, HMSO, 1978.

Oppé, T. E., 'The Health of West Indian Children', *Proceedings of the Royal Society of Medicine*, 57, 1967, pp. 321–3.

Smith, D., *The Facts of Racial Disadvantage: A National Survey*, PEP, 1976.

Thomas, H. E., 'Tuberculosis in Immigrants', *Proceedings of the Royal Society of Medicine*, 61, 1968.

3: Trends in Inequality of Health

Fit for the Future: The Report of the Committee on Child Health Services (Court Report), Cmnd 6684, HMSO, 1977.

McKeown, T., *The Role of Medicine*, Nuffield Provincial Hospitals Trust, 1976.

Morris, J. N., 'Health and Social Class', *Lancet*, 7 February 1959.

OPCS, *Occupational Mortality, Decennial Supplement, 1970–72, England and Wales*, HMSO, 1978.

Registrar General's Decennial Supplement England and Wales, 1961: Occupational Mortality Tables, HMSO, 1971.

4: Inequality in the Availability and Use of the Health Service

Bone, M., *Family Planning Services in England and Wales*, HMSO, 1973.

Brotherston, J., 'Inequality: Is It Inevitable?', in Carter and Peel (eds.), *Equalities and Inequalities in Health*, Academic Press, 1976.

Bulman, J. S., Richards, N. D., Slack, G. L., and Willcocks, A. J., *Demand and Need for Dental Care*, OUP, 1968.

Buxton, M. J., and Klein, R. E., 'Distribution of Hospital Provision: Policy Themes and Resource Variations', *British Medical Journal*, 1, 1976, p. 299.

Cartwright, A., *Human Relations and Hospital Care*, Routledge, 1964. *Parents and Family Planning Services*, Routledge, 1970.

Cartwright, A., and O'Brien, M., 'Social Class Variations in Health Care', in Stacey, M. (ed.), *The Sociology of the NHS*, Sociological Review Monograph 22, 1976.

Clarke, M., *Trouble with Feet*, Occasional Papers on Social Administration, Bell, 1969.

Coombe, V., 'Health and Social Services and Minority Ethnic Groups', *Journal of the Royal Society of Health*, 96, 1976.

Douglas, J. W. B., and Rowntree, G., 'Supplementary Maternal and Child Health Services', *Population Studies*, 2, 1949.

Forster, D. P., 'Social Class Differences in Sickness and General Pracitioner Consultations', Health Trends, 8, 1976, p. 29.

General Household Survey Reports, 1971–7.

Gordon, I., 'Social Status and Active Prevention of Disease', *Monthly Bulletin of the Ministry of Health*, 10, 1951.

Gray, P. G., et al., *Adult Dental Health in England and Wales in 1968*, HMSO, 1970.

Jones, D. R., and Masterman, S., 'NHS Resources: Scales of Variation' *British Journal of Preventive and Social Medicine*, 30, 1976, p. 244.

Martin, D., *Social Aspects of Prescribing*, Heinemann, 1957.

Martin, J., and Morgan, M., *Prolonged Sickness and the Return to Work*, HMSO, 1975.

Martini, C. J. M., et al., 'Health Indexes Sensitive to Medical Care Variation', *International Journal of Health Services*, 7, 1977, p. 293.

Morris, J. N., *The Uses of Epidemiology*, 3rd edn, Churchill Livingstone, 1975.

Noyce, J., Snaith, A. H., and Trickey, A. J., 'Regional Variations in the Allocation of Financial Resources to the Community Health Services', *Lancet*, 1974.

Rickard, J. H., 'Per Capita Expenditure of the English Area Health Authorities', *British Medical Journal*, 1, 1976, p. 299.

Sheiham, A., and Hobdell, M. H., 'Decayed, Missing and Filled Teeth in British Adult Populations', *British Dental Journal*, 126, 1969, p. 401.

Skrimshire, A., *Area Disadvantage, Social Class and the Health Service*, Department of Social and Administrative Studies, University of Oxford, 1978.

Titmuss, R. M., *Commitment to Welfare*, Allen & Unwin, 1968.

Townsend, P., *The Last Refuge*, Routledge, 1962.

Townsend, P., and Wedderburn, D., *The Aged in the Welfare State*, Bell Occasional Papers on Social Administration, 1965.

Tudor Hart, J., 'The Inverse Care Law', *Lancet*, 1, 1971.

West, R. R., and Lowe, C. R., 'Regional Variations in Need for and Provision and Use of Child Health Services in England and Wales', *British Medical Journal*, October 1976, p. 843.

5: International Comparisons

Anderson, O. W., *Health Care – Can There Be Equity?*, New York, Wiley, 1972.

Chase, H. C., 'Infant Mortality and Its Concomitants 1960–1972', *Medical Care*, 15, 8, August 1977, p. 662.

Denmark, *Medicinsk Fødselsstatistik*, Copenhagen, 1974.

Derrienic, F., Ducimetière, P., and Kritsikis, S., 'La mortalité cardiaque des Français actif d'âge moyen selon leur catégorie socio-professionelle et leur région de domicile', *Revue d'Épidémiologie, Médecine Sociale, et Santé Publique*, 25, 1977, p. 131.

Dinh Quang Chi, and Hemery, S., 'Disparités régionales de la mortalité infantile', *Économie et Statistiques*, 1977, 85, pp. 3–12.

Doguet, M. L., 'Les prestations familiales en France: Bilan et perspectives', *Revue Française des Affaires Sociales*, 32, 1, January–March 1978, pp. 3–48.

Geijerstam, G., 'Low Birth Weight and Perinatal Mortality', *Public Health Report*, 84, November 1969, pp. 939–48.

Germany, *Bevölkerung und Kultur*, Reiche 7: *Gesundheitswesen 1974*, Wiesbaden, Statistisches Bundesamt, 1974.

Kaminsky, M., Blondel, B., Bréart, G., Franc, M., Du Mazaubrun, C., 'Issue de la grossesse et surveillance prénatale chez les femmes migrantes. Enquête sur un échantillon représentatif des naissances en France en 1972', *Revue d'Épidémiologie, Médecine Sociale, et Santé Publique*, 26, 1, 1978, pp. 29–46.

Lerner, M., and Stutz, R. N., 'Have We Narrowed the Gap between the Poor and the Non-Poor? Narrowing the Gaps 1959–61 and 1969–71 – Mortality', *Medical Care*, 15, 8, August 1977, p. 620.

Lindgren, Gunilla, 'Height, Weight and Menarche in Swedish Urban School Children in Relation to Socio-Economic and Regional Factors', *Annals of Human Biology*, 3, 1976, 6, pp. 501–28.

Maynard, A., 'The Medical Profession and the Efficiency and Equity of Health Services', *Social and Economic Administration*, 12, 1, 1978, p. 3.

Morris, J. N., 'Scottish Hearts', *Lancet*, 3 November 1979.

Naytia, S., 'Social Group and Mortality in Finland', *British Journal of Preventive and Social Medicine*, 31, 4, 1977, p. 231.

Netherlands. *Compendium Gezondheidsstatistiek Nederland*. Centraal Bureau voor de Statistiek. 1974.

Norway. *Sosialt Utsyn 1977*. Oslo. Statistisk Sentralbyra. 1977.

Pharaoh. P. O., and Morris, J. N.. 'Postneonatal Mortality'. in Sartwell. P. E. (ed.), *Epidemiological Reviews* I. 1979. pp. 170–83.

Purola. T.. Kalimo. E.. Nyman. K.. and Sievers. K.. *The Utilization of the Medical Services and its Relationship to Morbidity. Health Resources and Social Factors*. Helsinki. Research Institute for Social Security. 1968.

Rona. R. J.. Swan. A. V.. and Altman. D. G.. 'Social Factors and Height of Primary School Children in England and Scotland'. *Journal of Epidemiology and Community Health*. 32. 1978. pp. 147 54.

Rumeau-Rouquette. C.. *et al*.. 'Evaluation épidémiologique du programme de santé en périnatologie. I Région Rhône-Alpes 1972 1975'. *Revue d'Épidémiologie. Médecine Sociale. et Santé Publique*. 25. 1977. p. 107

Salkever. D. S.. 'Economic Class and Differential Access to Care: Comparisons among Health Care Systems'. *International Journal of Health Services*. 5. 1975. 3. p. 373.

Sjolin. S.. 'Infant Mortality in Sweden'. in Wallace. Helen M. (ed.). *Health Care of Mothers and Children in National Health Services*. Cambridge. Mass. Ballinger. 1975.

Wilson. R. W.. and White. E. L.. 'Changes in Morbidity. Disability and Utilization Differentials between the Poor and the Non-Poor. Data from the Health Interview Survey 1964 and 1973'. *Medical Care*. 15. 8. 1977. p. 636.

Wynn. M.. and A.. *The Protection of Maternity and Infancy* (A Study of the Services for Pregnant Women and Young Children in Finland with Some Comparisons with Britain). Council for Children's Welfare. 1974. *Prevention of Handicap of Perinatal Origin* (An Introduction to French Policy and Legislation). Foundation for Education and Research in Childbearing. 1976.

6: *Towards an Explanation of Health Inequalities*

Abel-Smith. B.. and Townsend. P.. *The Poor and the Poorest*. Bell. 1965.

Baird. D.. 'Epidemiology of Congenital Malformations of the Central Nervous System in (a) Aberdeen and (b) Scotland'. *Journal of Biosocial Science*. 6. 1974. p. 113. 'The Epidemiology of Low Birth Weight: Changes in Incidence in Aberdeen. 1948 1972'. *Journal of Biosocial Science*. 6. 1974. p. 323.

Banks. J. and O.. *Feminism and Family Planning*. Routledge. 1964.

Bernstein. B.. *Class, Codes and Control*. Routledge. 1971.

Birch. H. G.. and Gussow. J. D.. *Disadvantaged Children: Health. Nutrition and School Failure*. New York. Harcourt. Brace and World. 1970.

Brennan. M. E.. 'Medical Characteristics of Children Supervised by the Local Authority Social Services Department'. *Policy and Politics*. 1. 1973. 3. p. 255.

Brenner. M. H.. 'Fetal. Infant. and Maternal Mortality during Periods of Economic Instability'. *International Journal of Health Services*. 3. 1973. 2. p. 145. 'Estimating the Social Costs of National Economic Policy: Implications for Mental and Physical Health and Criminal Aggression', Joint Economic Committee, US Congress, US Government Printing Office, Washington DC, 1976. 'Health Costs and Benefits of Economic Policy', *International Journal of Health Services*, 7, 1977, 4.

Brown, G., and Harris, T., *Social Origins of Depression*, Tavistock, 1978.

Colley, J. R. T., and Reid, D D., 'Urban and Social Class Origins of Childhood Bronchitis in England and Wales', *British Medical Journal*, 2, 1970, p. 213.

DHSS, *Eating for Health*, 1978.

DHSS, *Nutrition among the Elderly*, 1980.

Doll, R., Hill, A. B., and Sakula, J., *British Journal of Preventive and Social Medicine*, 1960.

Douglas, J. W. B., and Waller, R. E., 'Air Pollution and Respiratory Infection in Children', *British Journal of Preventive and Social Medicine*, 20, 1966, 1.

Eichenwald, H. F., and Fry, P. C., 'Nutrition and Learning', *Science* 163, 1969, p. 644.

Eyer, J., 'Hypertension as a Disease of Modern Society', *International Journal of Health Services*, 5, 1975, 4, p. 539. 'Prosperity as a Cause of Death', *International Journal of Health Services*, 7, 1977(a), 1, p. 125. 'Does Employment Cause the Death Rate Peak in Each Business Cycle?', *International Journal of Health Services*, 7, 1977(b), 4, p. 625.

Fuchs, V., *Who Shall Live? Health, Economics, and Social Choice*, New York, Basic Books, 1974.

Goldberg, E. M., and Morrison, S. L., 'Schizophrenia and Social Class', *British Journal of Psychiatry*, 109, 1963, p. 785.

Hellier, J., 'Perinatal Mortality 1950 and 1973', *Population Trends*, 10, Winter 1977.

Holman, R. T., *Poverty: Explanations of Social Deprivation*, Robertson, 1978.

Illsley, R., 'Social Class Selection and Class Differences in Relation to Stillbirths', *British Medical Journal*, 2, 1955, p. 1520.

Janerich, D. T., 'Maternal Age and Spina Bifida: Longitudinal Versus Cross-Sectional Analysis', *American Journal of Epidemiology*, 96, 1972, p. 389.

Lawrence, K. M., Carter, C. O., and David, P. A., 'Major CNS Malformations in South Wales II', *British Journal of Preventive and Social Medicine*, 22, 1968, p. 212.

Leeder, S. R., Corkhill, R., Irwig, L. M., Holland, W. W., and Colley, J. R. T., 'Influence of Family Factors on the Incidence of Lower Respiratory Tract Illness during the First Year of Life', *British Journal of Preventive and Social Medicine*, 30, 1976, p. 203.

Lewis, O., *The Children of Sanchez*, New York, Random House, 1967.

McKeown, T., *The Modern Use of Population*, Arnold, 1976.

Miller, F. J. W., Court, S. D. M., Knox, E. G., and Brandon, S., *The School Years in Newcastle-upon-Tyne, 1952 1962*, Oxford University Press, 1974.

Morris, J. N., *Uses of Epidemiology*, 3rd edn, Churchill Livingstone, 1975. 'Social Inequalities Undiminished', *Lancet*, 13 January 1979, 87.

Morris, J. N., and Heady, J. A., 'Social and Biological Factors in Infant Mortality: I. Objects and Methods', *Lancet*, 1955, i, p. 343.

Morris, J. N., and Titmuss, R. M., (a) 'Health and Social Change: I The Recent History of Rheumatic Heart Disease', *Medical Officer*, 26 August, 9 September

1944. (b) 'Epidemiology of Peptic Ulcer', *Lancet*, 30 December 1944, p. 841.

OPCS, *Occupational Mortality 1970–72*, HMSO, 1978. *Trends In Mortality*, HMSO, 1978.

Powles, J., 'Health and Industrialization in Britain', Proceedings First World Congress on Environmental Medicine and Biology, Paris, 1974.

Rutter, M., and Madge, N., *Cycles of Disadvantage*, Heinemann, 1976.

Stedman-Jones, G., *Outcast London*, Oxford, Clarendon Press, 1971.

Thompson, P., *The Edwardians*, Paladin, 1976.

Townsend, P., *Poverty in the United Kingdom*, Penguin Books, 1979.

Wilson, H., and Herbert, G. W., *Parents and Children in the Inner City*, Routledge, 1978.

8: Planning the Health and Personal Social Services

Acheson Report, *Primary Health Care in Inner London: A Report of a Study Group Commissioned by the London Health Planning Consortium*, 1981.

Action on Smoking and Health, *European Survey of Smoking in Public Places*, 1976.

Alberman, E. D., Morris, J. N., and Pharaoh, P. O., 'After Court', *Lancet*, 20 August 1977.

Brennan, M. E., and Lancashire, R., 'Association of Childhood Mortality with Housing Status and Unemployment', *Journal of Epidemiology and Community Health*, 32, 1978, 1.

Butler, J. R., Bevan, J. M., and Taylor, R. C., *Family Doctors and Public Policy*, Routledge, 1973.

Carstairs, V., and Morrison, M., *The Elderly in Residential Care*, Scottish Health Studies No. 19, Edinburgh, SHHD, 1972.

Department of Health and Social Security (and the Welsh Office), *The Census of Residential Accommodation 1970*, HMSO, 1975. *Priorities for Health and Personal Social Services in England: A Consultative Document*, HMSO, 1976. *Prevention and Health*, Cmnd 7047, HMSO, 1977. *The Way Forward*, HMSO, 1977. 'The DHSS Perspective', in Barnes, J., and Connelly, N., *Social Care Research*, Bedford Square Press, 1978. *A Happy Old Age*, 1978. Circular HC(78)5, *Health Services Development: Court Report on Child Health Services*, January 1978. *Local Authority Social Service Summary of Planning Returns 1976–77 to 1979–80*, HMSO, 1978. *Report of the Committee of Inquiry into Mental Handicap Nursing and Care* (Jay Report), Cmnd 7468, HMSO, 1979.

Expenditure Committee, First Report, Session 1976–7, *Preventive Medicine*, HC 169-i, HMSO, 1977. Ninth Report, Session 1976–7, Chapter V, 'Spending on the Health and Personal Social Services', HC, HMSO, 1977.

Fitzherbert, K., *Child Care Services and the Teacher*, Temple Smith, 1977.

Forster, H. D. P., Frost, B., Francis, B., and Heath, P., 'Need and Demand for Health Care', University of Sheffield.

Gardner, M. J., Crawford, M. D., and Morris, J. N., 'Patterns of Mortality in Middle and Early Old Age in the County Boroughs of England and Wales', *British Journal of Preventive and Social Medicine*, 23, 1969, 3.

Graham, H., 'Problems in Antenatal Care', unpublished paper, DHSS/CPAG conference, 'Reaching the Consumer in the Antenatal and Child Health Services', April 1978.

Kimbell, A., and Townsend, J., *Residents in Elderly Persons' Homes*, Cheshire CC Social Services Department, April 1974.

Lind, G., and Wiseman, C., 'Setting Health Priorities: A review of Concepts and Approaches', *Journal of Social Policy*, 7, 4, 1978.

Morris, J. N., 'Social Inequality Undiminished', *Health Visitor*, September 1980.

Plank, D., *Caring for the Elderly, Report of a Study of Various Means of Caring for Elderly People in Eight London Boroughs*, GLC, 1977.

Report of the Royal Commission on the National Health Service (Merrison Report), Cmnd 7615, HMSO, 1979.

Rutter, M., Tizard, J., and Whitmore, K., *Educational Health and Behaviour*, Longman, 1970.

Rutter, M., *et al.*, 'Attainment and Adjustment in Two Geographical Areas: Some Factors Accounting for Area Differences', *British Journal of Psychology*, 126, 1975.

Scottish Home and Health Department, *Towards an Integrated Child Health Service*, Edinburgh, HMSO, 1973.

Smith, D., *The Facts of Racial Disadvantage*, PEP, 1976.

Townsend, P., *The Last Refuge*, Routledge, 1962. 'The Needs of the Elderly and the Planning of Hospitals', in Canvin, R. W., and Pearson, N. G. (eds.), *Needs of the Elderly for Health and Welfare Services*, University of Exeter, 1973.

Tuckett, D., 'Choices for Health Education: A Framework for Decision Making', Health Education Studies Unit, 1979.

9: The Wider Strategy

Baker, J. A., *et al.*, 'School Milk and Growth in Primary School Children', *Lancet*, ii, 1978, p. 575.

Benjamin, B., *Social and Economic Factors Affecting Mortality*, Mouton, The Hague and Paris, 1965.

Bone, M., *Pre-School Children and the Need for Day Care*, OPCS Social Survey Division, HMSO, 1977.

Bradshaw, J., Edwards, H., Staden, F., and Weale, J., 'Area Variations in Infant Mortality 1975/77', *Journal of Epidemiology and Community Medicine*, November 1978.

Brown, G. W., and Harris, T., *The Social Origins of Depression*, Tavistock, 1978.

Cook, J., Altman, D. G., Moore, D. M. C., Topp, S. G., Holland, W. W., and Elliott, A., 'A Study of the Nutritional Status of School Children', *British Journal of Preventive and Social Medicine*, 27, 2, 1973.

Cook, J., Altman, D. G., Jacoby, A., Holland, W. W., and Elliott, A., 'School Meals and Nutrition of School Children', *British Journal of Preventive and Social Medicine*, 29, 3 September 1975.

Cook, J., Altman, D. G., Jacoby, A., and Holland, W. W., 'The Contribution Made by School Milk to the Nutrition of Primary School Children', *British Journal of Nutrition*, 1975, 34, 91.

Cook, J., Irwig, L. M., Chinn, S., Altman, D. G., Florey, C. du V., 'The Influence of Availability of Free School Milk on the Height of Children in England and Scotland', *Journal of Epidemiology and Community Health* (in press).

Department of Education and Science, *Nutrition in Schools*, Report of the Working Party on the Nutritional Aspects of School Meals, HMSO, 1975.

DHSS, *A Nutrition Survey of Pre-School Children 1967–68*, Reports on Health and Social Subjects, No. 10, HMSO, 1975.

DHSS, *Eating for Health*, HMSO, 1978.

DHSS and DES, *Joint Circular on Co-ordination of Provision for Under-5s*, January 1978.

DHSS and Supplementary Benefits Commission, *Response of the Supplementary Benefits Commission to 'Social Assistance: A Review of the Supplementary Benefits Scheme in Great Britain'*, HMSO, 1979.

Diamond, J., *Public Expenditure in Practice*, Allen & Unwin, 1975.

Disability Alliance, *Disability Rights Handbook for 1979*, November 1978.

Field, F., and Townsend, P., *A Social Contract for Families*, Poverty Pamphlet, 19. Child Poverty Action Group, 1975.

Field, F., *Children Worse Off under Labour?*, Poverty Pamphlet 32, London, Child Poverty Action Group, February 1978.

Fox, A. J., and Adelstein, A. M., *Journal of Epidemiology and Community Health*, 23, 1978, p. 73.

Glennerster, H. (ed.), *Labour's Social Priorities*, London's Fabian Research Series 327, 1976.

The Great Child Benefit Robbery, Child Benefit Now Campaign, London Child Poverty Action Group, April 1977.

Harris, I. A., *et al.*, *Income and Entitlement to Benefit of Impaired People in Great Britain*, Vol. 3 of *Handicap and Impairment in Great Britain*, HMSO, 1972.

Heclo, H., and Wildavsky, A., *The Private Government of Public Money*, Macmillan, 1976.

Howe, J. R., *Two-parent Families: A Study of their Resources and Needs in 1968, 1969 and 1970*, Statistical Report Series No. 14, HMSO, 1971.

Institute for Fiscal Studies, *The Structure and Reform of Direct Taxation*, Report of a Committee chaired by Professor J. E. Meade, Allen & Unwin, 1978.

Jacoby, A., Altman, D. G., Cook, J., Holland, W. W., and Elliott, A., 'Influence of Some Social and Environmental Factors on the Nutrient Intake and Nutritional Status of School Children', *British Journal of Preventive and Social Medicine*, 29, 2, June 1975.

Land, H., 'The Introduction of Family Allowances: An Act of Historic Justice?', in Hall, P., Land, H., Parker, R., and Webb, A., *Change, Choice and Conflict in Social Policy*, Heinemann, 1975.

Land, H., 'The Child Benefit Fiasco', in Brown, M., and Jones, K. (eds.), *The Yearbook of Social Policy in Britain 1977*, Routledge, 1978.

Ministry of Pensions and National Insurance, *Financial Circumstances of Retirement Pensioners*, HMSO, 1966.

Ministry of Social Security, *Circumstances of Families*, Report of an Inquiry by the Ministry of Pensions and National Insurance with the co-operation of the National Assistance Board, HMSO, 1967.

National Food Survey, *Household Food Consumption and Expenditure*, Ministry of Agriculture, Food and Fisheries Annual Report, 1977.

Plowden, W. J. L., 'Developing a Joint Approach to Social Policy', *The Yearbook of Social Policy in Britain 1976*, Routledge, 1976.

Reed, F. B., *Lancet*, 2, 1978, pp. 675–6.

Report of the Snowdon Working Party, *Integrating the Disabled*, National Fund for Research into Crippling Diseases, 1976.

Rona, R. J., Chinn, S., and Smith, A. M., 'Height of Children Receiving Free School Meals', *Lancet*, 8 September 1979, p. 534.

Royal Commission on the Distribution of Income and Wealth, *Report No. 6, Lower Incomes*, Cmnd 7175, HMSO, May 1978.

Safety and Health at Work (Robens Report), Cmnd 5034, HMSO, July 1972.

Select Committee on Tax Credit, Session 1972–3, Vol. I, *Report and Proceedings of the Committee*, Vol. II, Evidence, HMSO, 1973.

Social Trends, Cmnd 7439, HMSO, 1979.

Supplementary Benefit Report 1973, Annual Report of the SBC 1973, Cmnd 6615, HMSO, 1974.

Townsend, P., *Poverty in the United Kingdom*, Penguin Books, 1979.

Trades Union Congress, *Handbook of Safety and Health at Work*, TUC, 1978.

Wicks, M., *Old and Cold*, Heinemann, 1978.

Wilson, H., and Herbert, G. W., with Wilson, J. V., *Parents and Children in the Inner City*, Routledge, 1978.

Working Party on Housing of the Central Council for the Disabled, *Towards a Housing Policy for Disabled People*, 1976.

The Health Divide

Andersen, O. (1985), 'Dodelighed og erhverv 1970–80', Danmarks Statistik, *Statistiske Undersogelser* No. 41, quoted in Valkonen (1987).

Andersen, O., *et al.* (1987), 'A Comparative Study of Occupational Mortality in the Nordic Countries 1971–80', in *Proceedings of the 4th Meeting of the UN/WHO/CICRED Network*, Zamardi, Hungary, 13–16 September 1986, Hungarian Statistical Bureau.

Arber, S. (1987), 'Social Class, Non-employment, and Chronic Illness: Continuing the Inequalities in Health Debate', *British Medical Journal*, 294, pp. 1069–73.

Arber, S. (1988), 'Gender and Class Inequalities in Health: Understanding the Differentials', in A. J. Fox (ed.), *Inequalities in Health within Europe*, Gower Press, Aldershot.

Arber, S., Gilbert, G. N., and Dale, A. (1985), 'Paid Employment and Women's Health: a Benefit or a Source of Role Strain?', *Sociology of Health and Illness*, 7 (3), pp. 375–400.

Archbishop of Canterbury's Commission on Urban Priority Areas (1985), *Faith in the City: a Call for Action by Church and Nation*, Church House Publishing.

ASH (1986), 'Local Authority Policy on Smoking: a Report on a Survey of Councils in England and Wales', ASH.

Ashton, J. (1984), 'Health in Mersey: a Review', Department of Community Health, University of Liverpool.

Ashton, J. (1986), 'Healthy Cities – a WHO Project', Department of Community Health, University of Liverpool.

Audit Commission (1986), 'Making a Reality of Community Care', HMSO.

Balarajan, R., *et al.* (1984), 'Patterns of Mortality among Immigrants in England and Wales', *British Medical Journal*, 289, pp. 1185–7.

Balarajan, R., and Yuen, P. (1986), 'British Smoking and Drinking Habits: Variations by Country of Birth', *Community Medicine*, 8 (3), pp. 237–9.

Banks, M. H., and Jackson, P. R. (1982), 'Unemployment and Risk of Minor Psychiatric Disorder in Young People: Cross-sectional and Longitudinal Evidence', *Psychological Medicine*, 12, pp. 789–98.

Beale, N., and Nethercott, S. (1985), 'Job-loss and Family Morbidity: a Study of a Factory Closure', *Journal of the Royal College of General Practitioners*, 35, pp. 510–14.

Beale, N., and Nethercott, S. (1986a), 'Job-loss and Morbidity in Married Men with and without Children', *Journal of the Royal College of General Practitioners*, 36, pp. 557–9.

Beale, N., and Nethercott, S. (1986b), 'Job-loss and Morbidity: the Influence of Job Tenure and Previous Work History', *Journal of the Royal College of General Practitioners*, 36, pp. 560–63.

Berkman, L. F., and Breslow, L. (1983), *Health and Ways of Living: the Alameda County Study*, Oxford University Press.

Better Health Commission (1986), 'Interim Report, February 1986', Australian Government Publishing Service, Canberra.

Betts, G. (1985), 'Report of a Survey on Health in Glyndon Ward, Greenwich', Greenwich Health Rights Project.

Binysh, K., *et al.* (1985), 'The Health of Coventry', Department of Community Medicine, Coventry Health Authority.

Black, D. (1984), Evidence to the Scottish Health Education Co-ordinating Committee, 1984.

Black, D., and Laughlin, S. (eds.) (1985), 'Unemployment and Health: Resources, Action, Discussion, Information', Health Education Department, Greater Glasgow Health Board.

Blane, D. (1985), 'An Assessment of the Black Report's Explanations of Health Inequalities', *Sociology of Health and Illness*, 7, pp. 423–45.

Blaxter, M. (1983), 'Health Services as a Defence against the Consequences of Poverty in Industrialised Societies', *Social Science and Medicine*, 17, pp. 1139–1148.

Blaxter, M. (1984), 'Equity and Consultation Rates in General Practice', *British Medical Journal*, 288, pp. 1963–7.

Blaxter, M. (1985), 'Self-definition of Health Status and Consulting Rates in Primary Care', *Quarterly Journal of Social Affairs*, 1, pp. 131–71.

Blaxter, M. (1987a), 'Fifty Years On – Inequalities in Health', in J. Hobcraft and M. Murphy (eds.), *Proceedings of the British Society for Population Studies*, Oxford University Press (in press).

Blaxter, M. (1987b), 'Evidence on Inequality in Health from a National Survey', *Lancet*, ii, pp. 30–33.

Blaxter, M. (1988), 'A Comparison of Measures of Inequality in Morbidity', in A. J. Fox (ed.), *Inequalities in Health within Europe*, Gower Press, Aldershot.

Blaxter, M., and Paterson, L. (1982), *Mothers and Daughters: a Three Generational Study of Health Attitudes and Health Behaviour*, Heinemann.

BMA (1986), 'All Our Tomorrows: Growing Old in Britain', report of the Board of Science and Education, British Medical Association.

BMA (1987), 'Deprivation and Ill-health', Board of Science and Education, British Medical Association.

Boardman, B. (1986), 'Seasonal Mortality and Cold Homes', paper presented to the Institute of Environmental Health Officers/Legal Research Institute conference on 'Unhealthy Housing: a Diagnosis', Warwick University, 14–16 December 1986.

Borgan, J., and Kristofersen, L. (1986), 'Mortality by Occupation and Socio-economic Group in Norway 1978–80', Central Bureau of Statistics of Norway, *Statistiske Analyser*, 56, quoted in Valkonen (1987).

Braddon, F. E. M., *et al.* (1986), 'Onset of Obesity in a 36-year Birth Cohort Study', *British Medical Journal*, 293, pp. 299–303.

Brenner, M. H. (1979), 'Mortality and the National Economy: a Review and the Experience of England and Wales 1936–1976', *Lancet*, ii, pp. 568–73.

Brenner, M. H. (1983), 'Mortality and Economic Instability: Detailed Analysis for Britain and Comparative Analysis for Selected Industrial Countries', *International Journal of Health Services*, 13 (4), pp. 563–619.

British Medical Journal (1986), editorial, 'Lies, Damned Lies and Suppressed Statistics', *British Medical Journal*, 293, pp. 349–50.

Brotherston, J. (1980), Comments on the Black Report from the Faculty of Community Medicine to Patrick Jenkin, MP, 12 December 1980.

Brown, G. W., and Harris, T. (1982), 'Social Class and Affective Disorder', in Ihsam Al-Issa (ed.), *Culture and Psychopathology*, University Park Press, Baltimore.

Bucquet, D., and Curtis, S. (1986), 'Socio-demographic Variation in Perceived Illness and the Use of Primary Care: the Value of Community Survey Data for Primary Care Service Planning', *Social Science and Medicine*, 23 (7), pp. 737–44.

Bucquet, D., Jarman, B., and White, P. (1985), 'Factors Associated with Home Visiting in an Inner London General Practice', *British Medical Journal*, 290, pp. 1480–83.

Burchell, A. (1981), 'Inequalities in Health: Analysis of the 1976 *General Household Survey*', Government Economic Service Working Paper No. 48, DHSS.

Burghes, L. (1980), 'Living from Hand to Mouth: a Study of 65 Families Living on Supplementary Benefit', Child Poverty Action Group/Family Services Unit.

Burr, M. L., St Leger, A. S., and Yarnell, J. (1981), 'Wheezing, Dampness and Coal Fires', *Community Medicine*, 3, pp. 205–9.

Butler, N. R., *et al.* (1982), 'Research Findings from the 1970 Child Health and Education Study', *Journal of the Royal Society of Medicine*, 75, pp. 781–4.

Calnan, M., and Johnson, B. (1985), 'Health, Health Risks and Inequalities: an Exploratory Study of Women's Perceptions', *Sociology of Health and Illness*, 7, pp. 55–75.

Carmichael, C. L. (1985), 'Inner-city Britain: a Challenge for the Dental Profession. A Review of Dental and Related Deprivation in Inner-City Newcastle upon Tyne', *British Dental Journal*, 159 (1), pp. 24–7.

Carstairs, V. (1981a), 'Small Area Analysis and Health Service Research', *Community Medicine*, 3, pp. 131–9.

Carstairs, V. (1981b), 'Multiple Deprivation and Health State', *Community Medicine*, 3, pp. 4–13.

Catford, J. (1983), 'Healthy Living: Towards a National Strategy for Health Education and Health Promotion', report to the Health Education Council, June 1983.

Catford, J. (1985), 'Take Heart: a Consultative Document on the Development of Community-based Heart Health Initiatives in Wales', Heartbeat Report No. 1, Heartbeat Wales, Cardiff.

Catford, J., and Ford, S. (1984), 'On the State of the Public Health: Premature Mortality in the UK and Europe', *British Medical Journal*, 289, pp. 1668–70.

Central Statistical Office (1986), *Social Trends*, 16, 1986 edition, HMSO.

Central Statistical Office (1987), *Social Trends*, 17, 1987 edition, HMSO.

Charles, N., and Kerr, M. (1985), 'Attitudes towards the Feeding and Nutrition of Young Children', Research Report No. 4, Health Education Council.

Charlton, J. R. H., *et al.* (1983), 'Geographical Variation in Mortality from Conditions Amenable to Medical Intervention in England and Wales', *Lancet*, i, pp. 691–6.

Clarke, J. (1983), 'Sexism, Feminism and Medicalisation – a Decade Review of Literature on Gender and Illness', *Sociology of Health and Illness*, 5, p. 62.

Cole-Hamilton, I., and Lang, T. (1986), 'Tightening Belts: a Report on the Impact of Poverty on Food', London Food Commission.

Coleman, A. (1985), *Utopia on Trial: Vision and Reality in Planned Housing*, Hilary Shipman.

Collins, E., and Klein, R. (1980), 'Equity and the NHS: Self-reported Morbidity, Access and Primary Care', *British Medical Journal*, 282, pp. 1111–15.

Constable, D. (1986), Home Care Service Organiser, personal communication.

Constantinides, P., and Walker, G. (1985), 'Child Accidents and Health Inequalities in a London Borough', paper presented at 'Symposium on Accidents in Childhood', King's Fund Centre, 3 October 1985.

Cook, D. G., Bartley, M. J., Cummins, R. O., and Shaper, A. G. (1982), 'Health of Unemployed Middle-aged Men in Great Britain', *Lancet*, i, pp. 1290–94.

Coronary Prevention Group (1986), 'Coronary Heart Disease and Asians in Britain', Confederation of Indian Organizations and Coronary Prevention Group.

Cox, B., *et al.* (1987), 'Health and Life-style Survey: Preliminary Report', Health Promotion Research Trust.

Crombie, D. L. (1984), 'Social Class and Health Status. Inequality or Difference', *Journal of the Royal College of General Practitioners*, Occasional Paper 25.

Cubbon, J. (1986), 'The Health of Grimsby: a Review of Statistical Information on Mortality and Morbidity', Grimsby Health Authority.

Darley, C. D. (1981), 'High Density Housing: the Wirral's Experience', *Royal Society of Health Journal*, 101 (6), pp. 229 33.

Davies, J. K. (ed.) (1987), 'Health Promotion in Areas of Multiple Deprivation', report of a symposium held by the Royal College of Physicians and Surgeons of Glasgow, Scottish Health Education Group, Edinburgh.

Department of Employment (1986), 'Family Expenditure Survey: Report for 1985', HMSO.

Department of the Environment (1981a), 'An Investigation of "Difficult to Let" Housing', HMSO.

Department of the Environment (1981b), *Families in Flats*, HMSO.

Department of the Environment (1983), 'Urban Deprivation: Information Note No. 2 from the Inner Cities Directorate', Department of the Environment.

Desplanques, G. (1984), 'L'Inégalité devant la mort', *Économie et Statistiques* No. 162, quoted in Valkonen (1987).

DHSS (1976a), 'Prevention and Health: Everybody's Business', HMSO.

DHSS (1976b), 'Priorities for the Health and Personal Social Services in England', HMSO.

DHSS (1980), 'Inequalities in Health: Report of a Research Working Group Chaired by Sir Douglas Black', DHSS.

DHSS (1986a), 'Low Income Families 1983', DHSS.

DHSS (1986b), 'On the State of the Public Health: 1985', HMSO.

DHSS (1986c), 'The Diets of British Schoolchildren', DHSS.

Donaldson, L. J., and Odell, A. (1984), 'Planning and Providing Services for the Asian Population: a Survey of DHAs', *Journal of the Royal Society of Health*, 104 (6), pp. 199–202.

Donovan, J. (1984), 'Ethnicity and Health: a Research Review', *Social Science and Medicine*, 19 (7), pp. 663–70.

Dowding, V. M. (1981), 'New Assessment of the Effects of Birth Order and Socio-economic Status on Birth Weight', *British Medical Journal*, 282, pp. 683–6.

Dowling, S. (1983), *Health for a Change: the Provision of Preventive Health Care in Pregnancy and Early Childhood*, Child Poverty Action Group/National Extension College.

Durward, L. (1984), 'Poverty in Pregnancy', Maternity Alliance.

Eddie, S., and Davies, J. A. (1985), 'The Effect of Social Class on Attendance Frequency and Dental Treatment Received in the General Dental Service in Scotland', *British Dental Journal*, 159, pp. 370–72.

Ericson, A., *et al.* (1984), 'Pregnancy Outcome and Social Indicators in Sweden', *Acta Paediatrica Scandinavica*, 73, pp. 69–74, quoted in Valkonen (1987).

Esam, P. (1987), 'The Bottom Line: Has Conservative Social Security Protected the Poor?', in A. Walker and C. Walker (eds.), *The Growing Divide*, Child Poverty Action Group.

Faculty of Community Medicine (1986), 'Health for All by the Year 2000. Charter for Action', Faculty of Community Medicine.

Fagin, L., and Little, M. (1984), *The Forsaken Families*, Penguin Books.

Farrant, W. (1986), 'Health for All in the Inner City: a Proposed Framework for Health Promotion Policy Development within Paddington and North Kensington Health Authority', Paddington and North Kensington Health Authority.

Ferge, Z., Kremer, B., Losonczi, A., and Szalai, J. (1985), 'Health and Poverty: the Hungarian Case' (mimeo), quoted in M. Blaxter, paper prepared for the second meeting in a European Science Foundation series of workshops on 'Inequalities in Health', London, September 1985.

Fisher, M. J., *et al.* (1983), 'Patterns of Attendance at Developmental Assessment Clinics', *Journal of the Royal College of General Practitioners* (Scotland), 33 (249), pp. 213–18.

Fogelman, K., Fox, J., and Power, C. (1987), 'Class and Tenure Mobility. Do They Explain the Social Inequalities in Health among Young Adults in Britain?', National Child Development Study Working Paper No. 21, Social Statistics Research Unit, City University, London.

Fox, A. J., and Goldblatt, P. O. (1982), 'Socio-demographic Mortality Differentials: Longitudinal Study 1971–75', Series L.S. No. 1, HMSO.

Fox, A. J., Goldblatt, P. O., and Jones, D. R. (1986), 'Social Class Mortality Differentials: Artefact, Selection, or Life Circumstances?', in R. G. Wilkinson (ed.), *Class and Health*, Tavistock.

Fox, A. J., Jones, D. R., and Goldblatt, P. O. (1984), 'Approaches to Studying the Effect of Socio-economic Circumstances on Geographic Differences in Mortality in England and Wales', *British Medical Bulletin*, 40 (4), pp. 309–14.

Fox, A. J., and Shewry, M. C. (1987), 'New Longitudinal Insights into Relationships between Unemployment and Mortality', Working Paper No. 50, Social Statistics Research Unit, City University, London.

Fryer, P. (1987), 'Oxford's Aim of Health for All', *Health Service Journal*, 5 March 1987, pp. 274–5.

Gillies, D. R. N., *et al.* (1984), 'Analysis of Ethnic Influences on Stillbirths', *Journal of Epidemiology and Community Health*, 38 (3), pp. 214–17.

Ginnety, P., Kelly, K., and Black, M. (1985), 'Moyard: a Health Profile', Parts 1 and 2, Eastern Health and Social Services Board, Belfast.

Goldblatt, P. O. (1986), 'Social Class Mortality Differentials of Men Aged 16–64 in 1981: a Note on First Results from the OPCS Longitudinal Study for the Period 1981–83', Working Paper No. 42, Social Statistics Research Unit, City University, London.

Goldblatt, P. O. (1987), personal communication, unpublished update (provided by the Social Statistics Research Unit) of Table 13.2 of Fox and Goldblatt (1982).

Golding, P. (1986), 'Rich Man, Poor Man', *New Society*, 18 April 1986, pp. 16–17.

Graham, H. (1976), 'Smoking in Pregnancy: the Attitudes of Expectant Mothers', *Social Science and Medicine*, 10, pp. 399–405.

Graham, H. (1979), 'Problems in Antenatal Care', Department of Sociology, University of York.

Graham, H. (1980), 'Family Influences in Early Years on the Eating Habits of Children', in M. Turner (ed.), *Nutrition and Lifestyles*, Applied Science Publishers.

Graham, H. (1984), *Women, Health and Family*, Wheatsheaf Books, Brighton.

Graham, H. (1986), 'Caring for the Family', Research Report No. 1, Health Education Council.

Graham, H., and McKee, L. (1980), 'The First Months of Motherhood', Research Monograph No. 3, Health Education Council.

Graham, J. M. (1983), 'Experimental Nursing Homes for Elderly People in the NHS', *Age and Ageing*, 12, p. 273.

Gray, A., (1981), 'On the Black Report: Inequalities in Health, a Summary and Comment', Aberdeen University, Northern Health Economics Publication, Aberdeen.

Greater Glasgow Health Board (1984), 'Ten Year Report, 1974–1983', Greater Glasgow Health Board.

Haavio-Mannila, E. (1986), 'Inequalities in Health and Gender', *Social Science and Medicine*, 22 (2), pp. 141–9.

Haines, F. A., and de Looy, A. E. (1986), 'Can I Afford the Diet? The Effect of Low Income on People's Eating Habits with Particular Reference to Groups at Risk', British Dietetic Association, Birmingham.

Halsey, A. H. (1987), 'Social Trends Since World War II', in Central Statistical Office *Social Trends*, 17, pp. 11–19, 1987 edition, HMSO.

Harris, C., and Smith, R. (1987), 'What Are Health Authorities Doing about the Health Problems Caused by Unemployment?', *British Medical Journal*, 294, pp. 1076–9.

Hart, N. (1988), 'Sex Differentials in Mortality in Europe', in A. J. Fox (ed.), *Inequality in Health within Europe*, Gower Press, Aldershot.

Hawton, K., and Rose, N. (1986), 'Unemployment and Attempted Suicide among Men in Oxford', *Health Trends*, 8, pp. 29–32.

HEC/Age Concern (1985), 'Age Well Ideas Pack', Health Education Council, and 'New Initiatives in Self-health Care for Older People', Beth Johnson Foundation/University of Keele/Health Education Council.

HEC/Nottingham City Council (1984), 'Mansfield Community Health Project: Report to the Health Education Council', Health Education Council.

Holland, W. W. (1986), 'The RAWP Review: Pious Hopes', *Lancet*, ii, pp. 1087–90.

Holstein, B. (1985), 'Denmark Country Paper', in *Inequalities in Health and Health Care*, Nordic School of Public Health, NHV Report 1985:5, Göteborg, Sweden.

Huhne, C. (1986), 'Share Boom Halts Equality Trend', *Guardian*, 23 September 1986.

Hunt, S., and McEwen, J. (1980), 'The Development of a Subjective Health Indicator', *Sociology of Health and Illness*, 2, pp. 231–46.

Hunt, S., McEwen, J., and McKenna, S. P. (1985), 'Social Inequalities in Perceived Health', *Effective Health Care*, 2 (4), pp. 151–60.

Hunt, S., *et al.* (1986), 'Housing and Health in a Deprived Area of Edinburgh', paper presented to the Institute of Environmental Health Officers/Legal Research

Institute conference on 'Unhealthy Housing: a Diagnosis' at Warwick University, 14–16 December 1986.

Illsley, R. (1986), 'Occupational Class, Selection and the Production of Inequalities in Health', *Quarterly Journal of Social Affairs*, 2 (2), pp. 151–65.

Inland Revenue Board (1986), 'Inland Revenue Statistics', HMSO.

Jacobson, B. (1986), *Beating the Ladykillers: Women and Smoking*, Pluto Press, pp. 86–107.

Jahoda, M. (1979), 'The Impact of Unemployment in the 1930s and 1970s', *Bulletin of the British Psychological Society*, 32, pp. 309–14.

Jarman, B. (1983), 'Identification of Underprivileged Areas', *British Medical Journal*, 286, pp. 1705–9.

Jarman, B. (1984), 'Under-privileged Areas: Validation and Distribution of Scores', *British Medical Journal*, 289, pp. 1587–92. For critical response to the Jarman Score, *see* A. Scott-Samuel, 'Identification of Underprivileged Areas', *British Medical Journal*, 287 (1983), p. 130; J. R. H. Charlton and A. Lakhani, 'Is the Jarman Underprivileged Area Score Valid?', *British Medical Journal*, 290 (1985), pp. 1714–16; R. Leavey and J. Wood, 'Does the Underprivileged Area Index Work?', *British Medical Journal*, 291 (1985), pp. 709–11.

Jenkins, P. M., *et al.* (1984), 'The Effect of Social Factors on Referrals for Orthodontic Advice and Treatment', *British Journal of Orthodontics*, 11 (1), pp. 24–6.

Johnson, M. R. D. (1984), 'Ethnic Minorities and Health', *Journal of the Royal College of Physicians of London*, 18 (4), pp. 228–30.

Jones, I. G., and Cameron, D. (1984), 'Social Class: an Embarrassment to Epidemiology?', *Community Medicine*, 6, pp. 37–46.

Joseph, K., and Sumption, J. (1979), *Equality*, John Murray.

Kaplan, G. A. (1985), 'Twenty Years of Health in Alameda County: the Human Population Laboratory Analyses', paper presented to the Society for Prospective Medicine, Annual Meeting, San Francisco, 24 November 1985.

Keithley, J., Byrne, D., Harrison, S., and McCarthy, P. (1984), 'Health and Housing Conditions in Public Sector Housing Estates', *Public Health*, 98, pp. 344–53.

Klepp, K., and Forster, J. L. (1985), 'The Norwegian Nutrition and Food Policy: an Integrated Policy Approach to a Public Health Problem', *Journal of Public Health Policy*, 6, pp. 447–63.

Knight, I. (1984), 'The Height and Weight of Adults in Great Britain', OPCS/HMSO.

Knox, P. L. (1979), 'The Accessibility of Primary Care to Urban Patients: a Geographical Analysis', *Journal of the Royal College of General Practitioners*, 29 (220), pp. 160–68.

Koskinen, S. (1985), 'Time-trends in Cause-specific Mortality by Occupational Class in England and Wales', International Union for the Scientific Study of Population Conference, Florence, June 1985.

Koskinen, S., Melkas, T., and Vienonen, M. (1985), 'Finland Country Paper', in *Inequalities in Health and Health Care*, Nordic School of Public Health, NHV Report, 1985:5, Göteborg, Sweden.

Kreitman, N., and Platt, S. (1984), 'Suicide, Unemployment and Domestic Gas Detoxification in Great Britain', *Journal of Epidemiology and Community Health*, 38, pp. 1–6.

Kurtz, Z. (1986), personal communication.

Lang, T. (1987), paper presented to a conference on 'Rethinking Public Health', Birmingham, 14–15 July 1987.

Lang, T., *et al.* (1984), 'Jam Tomorrow?', Food Policy Unit, Manchester Polytechnic.

Larbie, J., and Mares, P. (1986), *A Training Handbook for Multiracial Health Care*, National Extension College, Cambridge.

LeGrand, J., and Illsley, R. (1986), 'The Measurement of Inequality in Health', paper presented to a meeting of the British Association for the Advancement of Science, Bristol, 1–5 September 1986.

Leon, D., and Wilkinson, R. G. (1988), 'Inequalities in Prognosis: Socio-economic Differences in Cancer and Heart Disease Survival', in A. J. Fox (ed.), *Inequalities in Health within Europe*, Gower Press, Aldershot.

Leviatan, U., and Cohen, J. (1985), 'Gender Differences in Life Expectancy among Kibbutz Members', *Social Science and Medicine*, 21, pp. 545–51.

Lipsey, D. (1986), 'Poverty – the Public *Does* Care', *New Society*, 18 April 1986.

Littlewood, R., and Cross, S. (1980), 'Ethnic Minorities and Psychiatric Services', *Sociology of Health and Illness*, 2, pp. 194–201.

Lopez, A. D. (1984), 'Sex Differentials in Mortality', *WHO Chronicle*, 38 (5), pp. 217–24.

Lumb, K. M., *et al.* (1981), 'Perinatal Mortality in British Asians', *Journal of Epidemiology and Community Health*, 35, pp. 106–9.

Lunt, B. (1985), 'Terminal Cancer Care Services: Recent Changes in Regional Inequalities in Great Britain', *Social Science and Medicine*, 20 (7), pp. 753–8.

Lynch, P., and Oelman, B. J. (1981), 'Mortality from CHD in the British Army Compared with the Civil Population', *British Medical Journal*, 283, pp. 405–7.

Lynge, E. (1984), 'Experiences in Estimating Differentials in Mortality in Developed Countries – Achievements and Shortcomings of the Various Approaches', in UN Department of International Economic and Social Affairs (ed.), *Data Bases for Mortality Measurement*, *Population Studies* No. 84, New York.

Macfarlane, A. (1986), letter to the *British Medical Journal*, 293, p. 504.

Macfarlane, A. (1987), personal communication.

Macfarlane, A., and Cole, T. (1985), 'From Depression to Recession – Evidence about the Effects of Unemployment on Mothers' and Babies' Health', in L. Durward (ed.), 'Born Unequal: Perspectives on Pregnancy and Childrearing in Unemployed Families', Maternity Alliance.

Macfarlane, A., and Mugford, M. (1984), 'Birth Counts: Statistics of Pregnancy and Childbirth', National Perinatal Epidemiology Unit in collaboration wih OPCS, HMSO.

Macfarlane, J. A., and Pillay, U. (1984), 'Who Does What, and How Much, in the Pre-school Child Health Services in England?', *British Medical Journal*, 289, pp. 851–2.

Macintyre, S. (1986a), 'Health and Illness', in R. Burgess (ed.), *Key Variables in Social Investigation*, Routledge & Kegan Paul.

Macintyre, S. (1986b), 'The Patterning of Health by Social Position in Contemporary Britain: Directions for Sociological Research', *Social Science and Medicine*, 23 (4), pp. 393–415.

Macintyre, S. (1988), 'The Role of Health Services in Relation to Inequalities in Health in Europe', in A. J. Fox (ed.), *Inequalities in Health within Europe*, Gower Press, Aldershot.

Maclure, A., and Stewart, G. T. (1984), 'Admission of Children to Hospital in Glasgow: Relation to Unemployment and Other Deprivation Variables', *Lancet*, ii, pp. 682–8.

McCarthy, P., *et al.* (1985), 'Respiratory Conditions: Effects of Housing and Other Factors', *Journal of Epidemiology and Community Health*, 39, pp. 15–19.

McDowall, M. (1983), 'Measuring Women's Occupational Mortality', *Population Trends*, 34, pp. 25–9.

McKechnie, S., and Wilson, D. (1986), 'Homes Above All: Housing in Britain, the Facts, the Failures, the Future', Shelter.

McNaught, A. (1985), 'Race and Health Care in the UK', Occasional Paper No. 2, Health Education Council.

Mack, J., and Lansley, S. (1985), *Poor Britain*, Allen & Unwin.

Madeley, R. J. (1982), 'Positive Discrimination in Child Health', *Public Health*, 96 (6), pp. 358–64.

MAFF (1977), 'Household Food Consumption and Expenditure 1976', Annual Report of the National Food Survey Committee, HMSO.

MAFF (1986), 'Household Food Consumption and Expenditure 1984', Annual Report of the National Food Survey Committee, HMSO.

Manchester (1985) Joint Consultative Committee (Health), 'Health Inequalities and Manchester', Manchester City Council/Health Authority.

Manchester City Council (1986), 'Poverty in Manchester', Manchester City Council.

Marin, R. (1986), 'Occupational Mortality 1971–80', *Central Statistical Office of Finland Studies No. 129*, quoted in Valkonen (1987).

Marmot, M. G., Adelstein, A. M., and Bulusu, L. (1984a), 'Immigrant Mortality in England and Wales 1970–78', *OPCS Studies on Medical and Population Subjects No. 47*, HMSO.

Marmot, M. G., *et al.* (1981), 'Changes in Heart Disease Mortality in England and Wales and Other Countries, *Health Trends*, 13, pp. 33–8.

Marmot, M. G., and McDowall, M. E. (1986), 'Mortality Decline and Widening Social Inequalities', *Lancet*, ii, pp. 274–6.

Marmot, M. G., Shipley, M. J., and Rose, G. (1984b), 'Inequalities in Death – Specific Explanations of a General Pattern?', *Lancet*, i, pp. 1003–6.

Marsh, G. N., and Channing, D. M. (1986), 'Deprivation and Health in One General Practice', *British Medical Journal*, 292, pp. 1173–6.

Måseide, P. (1985), 'Norway Country Paper', in *Inequalities in Health and Health Care*, Nordic School of Public Health, NHV Report 1985:5, Göteborg, Sweden.

Moran, G (1986), 'Health Promotion in Local Government: a British Experience', *Health Promotion*, 1, pp. 191–200.

Morgan, M. (1983), 'Measuring Social Inequalities: Occupational Classifications and their Alternatives', *Community Medicine*, 5, pp. 116–24.

Morgan, M., and Chinn, S. (1983), 'ACORN, Social Class and Child Health', *Journal of Epidemiology and Community Health*, 37, pp. 196–203.

Morris, J. (1987), personal communication.

Morris, J. N. (1979), 'Social Inequalities Undiminished', *Lancet*, i, pp. 87–90.

Morris, J. N. (1981), 'Coronary Heart Disease: a Tract for the Times', *Update*, 1 August 1981, pp. 323–31.

Morris, J. N. (1986), 'Inequality, Poverty and Health', *Lancet*, ii, p. 662.

Moser, K. A., *et al.* (1987a), 'Unemployment and Mortality: a Comparison of the 1971 and 1981 Longitudinal Study Census Samples', *British Medical Journal*, 294, pp. 86–90.

Moser, K. A., Fox, A. J., and Jones, D. R. (1984), 'Unemployment and Mortality in the OPCS Longitudinal Study', *Lancet*, ii, pp. 1324–8.

Moser, K., Pugh, H., and Goldblatt, P. O. (1987b), 'Inequalities in Women's Health: Developing an Alternative Approach', 31st Annual Scientific Meeting of the Society of Social Medicine, Dublin, 16–18 September 1987.

Moylan, S., Millar, J., and Davis, R. (1984), *For Richer, for Poorer? DHSS Study of Unemployed Men*, HMSO.

NACNE (1983), 'Proposals for Nutritional Guidelines for Health Education in Britain', Health Education Council.

National Children's Bureau (1987), 'Investing in the Future: Child Health Ten Years after the Court Report', National Children's Bureau.

National Extension College (1984), 'Providing Effective Health Care in a Multiracial Society', National Extension College, Cambridge.

National Extension College (1986), 'NHS Training Needs Survey', National Extension College, Cambridge.

Nelson, M., and Naismith, D. (1979), 'The Nutritional Status of Poor Children in London', *Journal of Human Nutrition*, 33 (1), pp. 33–46.

Nichols, T. (1986), 'Industrial Injuries in British Manufacturing in the 1980s – a Commentary on Wright's Article', *Sociological Review*, 34, pp. 290–306.

Nicoll, A. (1986), 'The Child Health Clinic: Results of a New Strategy of Community Care in a Deprived Area', *Lancet*, i, pp. 606–8.

NUPE (1987), 'Equality in Health: a Strategy for Change', National Union of Public Employees.

Nutbeam, D., and Catford, J. (1987), 'Pulse of Wales Social Survey Supplement', Heartbeat Report No. 7, Heartbeat Wales, Cardiff.

OPCS (1982), 'Adult Dental Health in England and Wales in 1978', OPCS/HMSO.

OPCS (1985), 'General Household Survey for 1983', HMSO.

OPCS (1986a), 'Mortality Statistics, Perinatal and Infant: Social and Biological Factors for 1984', Series DH3, No. 17, HMSO.

OPCS (1986b), 'Registrar General's Decennial Supplement on Occupational Mortality 1979–83', HMSO.

OPCS (1986c), 'Longitudinal Study 1981–83, SMRs for Men of Working Ages, England and Wales'. Data provided by Baroness Trumpington, Parliamentary Under-Secretary of State, DHSS, in a parliamentary written reply, quoted in *Population Trends*, 45, Autumn, pp. 2–4.

OPCS (1986d), 'General Household Survey for 1984', HMSO.

Osborn, A. F., and Morris, A. C. (1979), 'The Rationale for a Composite Index of Social Class and its Evaluation', *British Journal of Sociology*, 30 (1), pp. 39–60.

Pamuk, E. R. (1985), 'Social Class Inequality in Mortality from 1921–1972 in England and Wales', *Population Studies*, 39, pp. 17–31.

Pearson, M. (1985), 'Racial Equality and Good Practice – Maternity Care', National Extension College, Cambridge.

Pendleton, D. A., and Bochner, S. (1980), 'The Communication of Medical Information in General Practice Consultations as a Function of Patients' Social Class', *Social Science and Medicine*, 14, pp. 669–73.

Pharaoh, P., and Morris, J. N. (1979), 'Postneonatal Mortality', *Epidemiologic Reviews*, 1, pp. 170–83.

Piachaud, D. (1986), 'Poor Children: a Tale of Two Decades', Child Poverty Action Group.

Piachaud, D. (1987), 'The Growth of Poverty', in A. Walker and C. Walker (eds.), *The Growing Divide*, Child Poverty Action Group.

Pill, R., and Stott, N. C. (1985a), 'Choice or Chance: Further Evidence on Ideas of Illness and Responsibility for Health', *Social Science and Medicine*, 20 (10), pp. 981–91.

Pill, R., and Stott, N. C. (1985b), 'Preventive Procedures and Practices among Working Class Women: New Data and Fresh Insights', *Social Science and Medicine*, 21 (9), pp. 975–83.

Platt, S. (1984), 'Unemployment and Suicidal Behaviour: a Review of the Literature', *Social Science and Medicine*, 19, pp. 93–115.

Platt, S., and Kreitman, N. (1984), 'Unemployment and Parasuicide in Edinburgh 1968–1982', *British Medical Journal*, 289, pp. 1029–32.

Pond, C., and Burghes, L. (1986), 'The Rising Tide of Deprivation', *New Society*, 18 April 1986.

Popay, J., Dhooge, Y., and Shipman, C. (1986), 'Unemployment and Health: What Role for Health and Social Services?', Research Report No. 3, Health Education Council.

Power, C., Fogelman, K., and Fox, A. J. (1986), 'Health and Social Mobility During the Early Years of Life', National Child Development Study Working Paper No. 8, May 1986, Social Statistics Research Unit, City University, London.

Preston, S., Haines, M., and Pamuk, E. (1981), 'Effects of Industrialisation on Mortality in Developed Countries', in *Solicited Papers*, Vol. 2, IUSSP 19th International Population Conference, Manila, Part 2, Liegei Imprimerce Derouaux, pp. 233–54.

Radical Statistics Health Group (1987), 'Facing the Facts: What Really Is Happening to the NHS?', Radical Statistics Health Group.

Reason, L. (1985), 'Catford Community Health Project: Evaluation Report', Health Education Council.

Richie, J., Jacoby, A., and Bone, M. (1981), 'Access to Primary Health Care', OPCS/HMSO.

Roberts, J. L., and Graveling, P. A. (eds.) (1985), 'The Big Kill: Smoking Epidemic in England and Wales', published for the Health Education Council and the British Medical Association by the North West Regional Health Authority.

Roll, J. (1985), 'Poverty and Food', *Poverty* No. 6, Spring 1985.

Rose, G., and Marmot, M. G. (1981), 'Social Class and Coronary Heart Disease', *British Medical Journal*, 45, pp. 13–19.

Scottish Health Education Co-ordinating Committee (1984), 'Health Education in Areas of Multiple Deprivation', a report by the Scottish Health Education Co-ordinating Committee, Edinburgh.

Scott-Samuel, A. (1981), 'Social Class Inequality in Access to Primary Care: a Critique of Recent Research', *British Medical Journal*, 283, pp. 510–11.

Scott-Samuel, A. (1984), 'Need for Primary Health Care: an Objective Indicator', *British Medical Journal*, 288, pp. 457–8.

Scott-Samuel, A., and Szalai, J. (1988), 'Policy Issues in Health Inequality', in A. J. Fox (ed.), *Inequalities in Health within Europe*, Gower Press, Aldershot.

Sheffield City Council (1987), 'Good Health for All', Central Policy Unit, Sheffield.

Sheffield Health Authority (1986), 'Health Care and Disease – a Profile of Sheffield', Sheffield Health Authority.

Smith, Alwyn (chair) (1988), 'The Nation's Health: Strategy for the 1990s', report of an independent multidisciplinary committee, King's Fund on behalf of Health Education Authority/London School of Hygiene/Scottish Health Education Group (in press).

Smith, R. (1985–6), 'Occupationless Health', a series of articles in the *British Medical Journal*. *British Medical Journal*, 291, pp. 1024–7; 291, pp. 1107–11; 291, pp. 1191–5; 291, pp. 1263–6; 291, pp. 1338–41; 291, pp. 1409–12; 291, pp. 1492–5; 291, pp. 1563–6; 291, pp. 1626–9; 291, pp. 1707–10; 292, pp. 263–5; 292, pp. 320–23; 292, pp. 470–72.

Smith, R. (1986), 'The Need for a Public Health Alliance', *British Medical Journal*, 293, pp. 346–7.

Smith, R. (1987a), *Unemployment and Health* (based on the series of articles for the *British Medical Journal* listed above), Oxford University Press.

Smith, R. (1987b), 'Medical News', *British Medical Journal*, 294, p. 1358.

Stirland, H. (1985), 'Risk Factors in Childhood Accidents', paper presented to a symposium on 'Accidents in Childhood', King's Fund Centre, London, 3 October 1985.

Strachan, D. P. (1986), 'The Home Environment and Respiratory Morbidity in Children', paper presented to the Institute of Environmental Health Officers/Legal Research Institute conference on 'Unhealthy Housing: a Diagnosis', Warwick University, 14–16 December 1986.

Terry, P. B., *et al.* (1980), 'Analysis of Ethnic Differences in Perinatal Statistics', *British Medical Journal*, 281, pp. 1307–8.

Thompson, I. (1986), Scottish Health Education Group, personal communication.

Thunhurst, C. (1985a), 'Poverty and Health in the City of Sheffield', Environmental Health Department, Sheffield City Council.

Thunhurst, C. (1985b), 'The Analysis of Small Area Statistics and Planning for Health', *Statistician*, 34, pp. 93 106.

Todd, J. E., and Dodd, T. (1985), 'Children's Dental Health in the UK, 1983', OPCS/HMSO.

Townsend, P. (1987), personal communication, from secondary analysis of Registrar General's Decennial Supplement on Occupational Mortality, 1979 83.

Townsend, P., Corrigan, P., and Kowarzik, O. (1986a), 'Poverty and the London Labour Market: an Interim Report', Low Pay Unit.

Townsend, P., and Davidson, N. (1982), *Inequalities in Health: the Black Report*, 1982 edition, Penguin Books, Harmondsworth, p. 24.

Townsend, P., Phillimore, P., and Beattie, A. (1986b), 'Inequalities in Health in the Northern Region: an Interim Report', Northern Regional Health Authority/Bristol University.

Townsend, P., Phillimore, P., and Beattie, A. (1987), *Health and Deprivation: Inequality and the North*, Croom Helm.

Townsend, P., Simpson, D., and Tibbs, N. (1985), 'Inequalities in Health in the City of Bristol: a Preliminary Review of Statistical Evidence', *International Journal of Health Services*, 15 (4), pp. 637–63.

TUC (1986), 'Deprivation and Ill-health', report of HEC/British Medical Association/TUC Conference, 4 July 1986, TUC.

Unemployment and Health Study Group (1986), 'Unemployment: a Challenge to Public Health', Occasional Paper No. 10, Centre for Professional Development, Department of Community Medicine, University of Manchester.

United Nations (1986), *Demographic Year Book 1984*, United Nations, New York.

Valkonen, T. (1987), 'Social Inequality in the Face of Death', paper presented to the European Population Conference, Central Statistical Office of Finland.

Valkonen, T. (1988), 'Adult Mortality and Level of Education: a Comparison of Six Countries', in A. J. Fox (ed.), *Inequalities in Health within Europe*, Gower Press, Aldershot.

Vandeskog, G. (1987), personal communication.

Victor, C. R., and Vetter, N. (1986), 'Poverty, Disability and Use of Services by the Elderly: Analysis of the 1980 *General Household Survey*', *Social Science and Medicine*, 22 (10), pp. 1087–91.

Wadsworth, M. E. J. (1986), 'Serious Illness in Childhood and its Association with Later-life Achievement', in R. G. Wilkinson (ed.), *Class and Health: Research and Longitudinal Data*, Tavistock.

Waldron, I. (1976), 'Why Do Women Live Longer than Men?', *Social Science and Medicine*, 10, pp. 349–62.

Waldron, I. (1983), 'Sex Differences in Illness Incidence, Prognosis and Mortality: Issues and Evidence', *Social Science and Medicine*, 17, pp. 1107–23.

Walker, A., and Walker, C. (eds.) (1987), *The Growing Divide: a Social Audit 1979– 1987*, Child Poverty Action Group.

Walsh, J., *et al.* (1985), 'Access to Primary Health Care: a Study of East Ward, Bury', Bury Community Health Council.

Warr, P. (1984), 'Work and Unemployment', in P. J. D. Drenth *et al.* (eds.), *Handbook of Work and Organisational Psychology*, Wiley.

Warr, P. (1985), 'Twelve Questions about Unemployment and Health', in B. Roberts, R. Finnegan and D. Gallie (eds.), *New Approaches to Economic Life*, Manchester University Press.

Webb, T., Schilling, R., Babb, P., and Jacobson, B. (1987), 'Health at Work?', a report on Health Promotion in the Workplace, Health Education Council.

Webber, R., and Craig, J. (1975), 'Which Local Authorities are Alike?', *Population Trends*, 5, HMSO.

White, P. (1986), ASH, personal communication.

Whitehead, M. (1988), 'Education for Health: Achievements of a Decade', Scottish Health Education Group, Edinburgh.

Whitehouse, C. R. (1985), 'Effect of Distance from Surgery on Consultation Rates in an Urban Practice', *British Medical Journal*, 290, pp. 359–62.

WHO (1984), 'Report of the Working Group on Concepts and Principles of Health Promotion', Copenhagen, 9–13 July 1984, World Health Organization.

WHO (1985a), 'Social Justice and Equity in Health', a report from the Programme on Social Equity and Health meeting, Leeds, 22–26 July 1985.

WHO (1985b), 'Targets for Health for All: Targets in Support of the European Regional Strategy for Health for All by the Year 2000', World Health Organization Regional Office for Europe, Copenhagen.

Wilkinson, R. G. (1986a), 'Socio-economic Differences in Mortality: Interpreting the Data on their Size and Trends', in R. G. Wilkinson (ed.), *Class and Health: Research and Longitudinal Data*, Tavistock.

Wilkinson, R. G. (1986b), 'Occupational Class, Selection and Inequalities in Health: a Reply to Raymond Illsley', *Quarterly Journal of Social Affairs*, 2 (4), pp. 415–22.

Wilkinson, R. G. (1986c), 'Income and Mortality', in R. G. Wilkinson (ed.), *Class and Health: Research and Longitudinal Data*, Tavistock.

Winkler, J. T. (1987), 'Nurturing Nutrition the Norwegian Way', *Guardian*, 2 May 1987.

Young, B. (1980), 'Health and Housing: Infestation', *Roof*, July/August 1980, pp. 111–12.

Index

Abel-Amith, B., 33, 108
accidents
  causes of child death, 117–18, 243
  class differential, 118, 119, 181–2
  explanations for, 289
  importance of child-accident reporting, 128, 129, 130
  sex differences in, 243. 303
  strategy for child accident prevention, 181 2
  at work, 122, 124, 125, 185, 339
ACORN (A Classification of Residential Neighbourhoods), 309
Action on Smoking and Health (ASH), 325
Age Concern, 322
AIDS, 7, 324, 346
Alameda County Study, 11, 295
Alberman, E. D., 144
alcohol, 292
Alliance Party. 7
Andersen, O., 278, 282
Anderson, O. W., 87
ante-natal care, 73, 74, 79, 98 9, 100, 110, 126, 143, 155 6, 163, 164, 316–20
Arber, S., 240, 244, 303, 312
Archbishop of Canterbury's Commission on Urban Priority Areas, 10, 342
artefact explanation, 105, 286 7
Asclepius, 33
Ashton, J., 248, 342
Association of Metropolitan Authorities, 343

attempted suicide, 239–40
Audit Commission, The, 320–21, 322, 331
Australian 'Better Health' Commission, 315

Bailey, B., 8
Baird, D., 116
Balarajan, R., 250 52
Banks, J. and O., 114
Banks, M. H., 242
Beale, N., 242
Beattie, A., 12
behavioural/cultural explanation of health inequality, 110–15, 289–96
Berkman, L. F., 295
Bernstein, B., 113
Better Health Commission, The. 315
Betts, G., 248
Bevan, J. M., 146
Binysh, K., 248
Birch, H. G., 34, 121
birth
  class incidence of mortality and low birth-weight, 115, 235
  groups at risk, 115
  mortality rates, 115, 228–9
  see also ante-natal care; infant mortality; perinatal mortality
Black, David, 326, 328
Black, Douglas, 2, 4, 5, 7, 12, 34, 219, 221
Black Report
  action on recommendations of, 16, 306 15, 316 30, 332–49

Black Report – *contd*
  appointment of working group, 2
  and availability and distribution of
    resources, 17, 18, 19
  broad findings, 2
  and causes of inequalities in health, 2,
    5
  government reaction to, 3, 4, 5, 9, 10,
    11
  The Health Divide and, 6, 7, 9, 10, 16–
    17, 219, 221, 226
  purpose, 1
  recommendations of, 2
  WHO strategy and, 348
Black Working Group, 2, 17
Blane, D., 286, 289
Blaxter, M., 223, 224, 232, 233, 234, 235,
    244, 268, 269, 271, 274, 276, 277,
    289, 296, 313
Blume, S., xi
Boardman, B., 301
Bochner, S., 268
Bone, M., 169, 172, 173, 174, 188
Borgan, J., 281
Bosanquet, N., 22
Boxall, M., 147
Braddon, F. E. M., 235
Bradshaw, J., 135, 179
Brandon, S., 121
Brennan, M., 120, 140
Brenner, M. H., 109, 110, 240
Breslow, L., 295
British Dietetic Association, 300
British Medical Association, 10, 15, 321,
    323, 341, 342, 348
British Medical Journal, 3, 5, 16, 307
British Regional Heart Study, 239, 241
Brotherston, J., 1, 74, 306
Brown, G. W., 36, 38, 120, 189, 245
Bucquet, D., 234, 268, 272
Bulman, J. S., 74
Burchell, A., 233
Burghes, L., 300, 333
Burr, M. L., 299
Butler, J. R., 146

Butler, N. R., 314
Buxton, M. J., 79

Calnan, M., 296
Cambridge Health Authority, 326
Cameron, D., 286
Canada, 103, 315
car ownership
  and mortality, 237, 238
  as a social indicator, 225, 236
Carmichael, C. L., 267
Carstairs, V., 247, 249, 309
Carter, C. O., 115
Cartwright, A., 68, 71, 73
Catford, J., 269, 276, 314, 324
Catford Project, 326
census
  need for ethnicity question in, 254
  small area statistics, 308
Central Council for the Disabled, 190–
    91
Central Statistical Office, 243, 333, 338
cervical screening, 73–4, 268, 345
Channing, D. M., 269, 272, 320
Charles, N., 294, 301
Charlton, J.R. H., 268
Chase, H. C., 96
Child Benefit Act 1975, 170
Child Health and Education Study, 312,
    314
child health services, 143–7, 316–20
child poverty, 169–80, 332–5
Child Poverty Action Group, 172, 335
children
  causes of death and illness class
    related, 118–22, 235
  child benefit, 170–71, 195, 332, 335
  child guidance system, 147
  death from accidents, 117, 118, 119–
    20, 127–8, 243, 289
  diet of, 337
  handicapped children, 146, 147, 314
  importance of child-accident re-
    porting, 128, 129, 130
  infant care allowance, 171–2, 196, 332

need for health education in schools, 153, 159, 163, 324–5

need for more research into child health, 129, 130, 312, 314

need for provision of school health statistics in relation to class, 127–8, 307

nutrition, 299–302, 336–7

review of health services for, 221, 316–18

physical development affected by material deprivation, 121, 314

policy for elimination of child poverty, 169–72, 332–3

pre-school education and day care, 172–5, 318

priority for children at start of life, 133, 318–20

respiratory disease, 117, 118–19, 120, 121

school health work, 146–7, 318

school milk and meals, 175–80, 336–7

strategy for accident prevention, 181–2

unemployment and, 240, 334, 335

Children's Committee, 317

Chinn, S., 309

chiropody, 74, 75

cigarette-smoking, 110, 111, 124, 125, 131, 251–2, 290–92

need for anti-smoking policy, 154–5, 159, 163, 325

City Health Strategy, 346

class gradient in health standards

care of infirm and disabled, 76–7

and concepts of 'social class', 39, 311–12

and female mortality, 61–2, 243

and GP consultations, 53–4, 69–70, 269–72

illness and, 53–6, 232–6

and infant mortality, 62–3, 228–9

international comparisons, 82–101, 276–83

mortality of elderly and, 63, 230

mortality rates, 228–32

occupation as basis of, 40–41, 227–8, 311–12

trends in morbidity, 64–5, 262–3

use of hospital services, 72–3

use of preventive and promotive services, 73–4, 267–72

see also living standards, inequalities in; middle class; occupational class; working class

classes, changing size of, 257, 286

Cohen, J., 304

Cole, T., 239, 240

Cole-Hamilton, I., 300, 337

Coleman, A., 298

Colley, J. R. T., 118

Collins, E., 269, 270

Committee on Medical Aspects of Food Policy (COMA), 127, 175, 177

community care

conflicting DHSS policy on, 317, 320–22

crisis in, 23, 321–2

and elderly, 149–52, 320–23

and mentally handicapped, 148–9

shift of resources towards, 136–8, 142, 320–22

vagueness of DHSS definition, 135

Community Health Councils, 4, 16, 156, 319, 326, 328, 343, 349

Confederation of British Industry (CBI), 187

Confederation of Health Service Employees (COHSE), 4

Conservative Party, 3, 24, 27

Constable, D., 323

Constantinides, P., 248

Cook, D. G., 239, 241, 296

Cook, J., 177, 178

Coombe, V., 79

Corkhill, R., 118

Coronary Prevention Group, 253–4

country of birth, *see* ethnic minorities

Court Report, 221, 317

Court, S. D. M., 121

Cox, B., 224, 235, 244, 246, 314

Craig, J., 238, 309

Crawford, M. D., 140

Crombie, D. L., 269, 271

Cross, S., 269

Cubbon, J., 248

cultural/behavioural explanations of health inequalities, 110–15, 289–96

culture of poverty, 113, 296

Culyer, A. J., 37

Currie, E., 12

Curtis, S., 234, 272

Cushion, A. A., 53

Darley, C. D., 298

David, P. A., 115

Davidson, N., 270

Davies, J. K., 342

Davies, R., 269

day care, 172–5, 318

death, *see* accidents; infant mortality; mortality rates; neonatal mortality; perinatal mortality; post-neonatal mortality; Standardized Mortality Ratio.

Decennial Supplement, Registrar General's, 28, 228, 257, 307–8

Deitch, R., 4–5

de Looy, A. E., 300

Denmark, 82, 83, 84, 87–9, 245, 278–9

dental care, 74, 75, 235–6, 267, 269

Department of Education and Science, 325

Department of Employment, 301

Department of the Environment, 298, 310, 311

Department of Health and Social Security (DHSS), 3, 8, 21, 121, 125, 129, 131, 135, 139, 142, 143, 149, 153, 162, 164–5, 175, 176, 184, 187, 192, 193, 196, 221, 242, 243, 256, 307, 317, 320, 321, 331, 334, 335, 336, 337, 341

deprivation, 126, 223, 248–9. *See also* indicators; living standards, inequalities in; poverty

Derrienec, F., 91

Desplanques, G., 280

Diamond, J., 194

diet
  as health factor, 111, 112, 292–4
  in the North of England, 12–13
  nutrition: school milk and meals, 175–80, 336–7

Dinh Quang Chi, 90

Disability Rights Handbook for 1980, 38

Disability Alliance, 8, 183, 185, 340

disabled
  home help service for, 152, 162, 320–23
  housing for, 190–91
  inequalities in care of, 76–7, 320–22
  inequalities in different types of hospital, 148
  interpretation of concept, 38
  more co-ordination between health and social services needed, 151–2
  need for categorization of severity, 128, 151–2, 161–2, 340
  need for comprehensive disability allowance, 183–5, 340
  need for increased research and information, 130, 131, 314
  need for local authorities to report on, 128
  priority called for, 134, 320
  proposals for improved care at home, 147–52, 322–3

diseases
  of affluence, 231
  of poverty, 232, 265

Dodd, T., 236, 269

Doguet, M. L., 99

Doll, R., 115

Dollery, C., 34

Donaldson, L. J., 329, 330

Donovan, J., 248, 250

Douglas, J. W. B., 74, 118

Dowding, V. M., 240

Dowling, S., 319, 330

drinking habits, 251, 292

Dubos, R., 33, 34
Durward, L., 300

economic factors and health inequalities, 17–27, 106, 299–302. *See also* living standards, inequalities in; poverty
Eddie, S., 269
education, as social indicator, 234, 237, 263–4, 281–2
Eichenwald, H. F., 121
elderly
  access to health services and, 268, 320–23
  deprivation indicators and, 310–11
  explanation of health inequalities, 124–5
  improving quality of life of, 134–8, 322–3
  occupational class and mortality, 48, 63, 228, 230
  positive discrimination in services for, 23, 271
  poverty and, 333
  proposals for improved care at home, 149–52
  regional differences in provision of care for, 321
  trends in illness rates in, 263
Elton, P., 4
Employment Medical Advisory Service, 188, 196, 340
Ennals, David, 1
environmental health, committees and departments, 343, 345, 346
Ericson, A., 281
Esam, P., 336
ethnic minorities
  adult mortality and, 250–51
  definitions, 248
  explanations of health differences, 252–4
  health and social services initiatives relating to, 329–30
  housing conditions and, 339
  infant mortality and, 252–3

need for reliable statistics on, 51, 249–50, 254, 255, 349
  planning services for, 329–30
  rickets and, 250
  sickle-cell anaemia and, 250
  smoking and drinking habits of, 251–2
  specific illnesses in, 250
  use of health services and, 269
  see also ethnicity; race; immigrant mortality study
ethnicity
  and mortality, 50–52, 250–51
  and provision of health care, 79, 269, 329–30
exercise, 112, 294
Eyer, J., 110

Faculty of Community Medicine, 10, 306, 324, 342, 348
Fagin, L., 242
Family Allowances Act 1945, 170
Family Expenditure Survey (FES), 41, 184
family planning services, 73, 74, 114
Family Practitioner Service, 21, 345
Farrant, W., 326
Ferge, Z., 233
Field, F., 170, 179
Finland, 82, 83, 84, 85, 87, 91, 97–100, 102–3, 144, 245, 279–80, 283–4
Fisher, M. J., 269
Fitzherbert, K., 147
Fogelman, K., 236, 288
food, *see* nutrition
Ford, S., 276
Forsdick, A. J., xi
Forster, D. P., 146
Forster, J. L., 285
Fowler, N., 6
Fox, A. J., 7, 230, 236, 238, 239, 242, 249, 288
France, 82, 83, 84, 85, 87, 90, 91–2, 97, 99, 100, 102, 144, 280
Francis, B., 146

Frost, B., 146
Fry, P. C., 121
Fryer, 346, 347
Fuchs, V., 110

Gallup Poll, 349
Gans, B., 52
Gardner, M. J., 140
Geijerstam, G., 98
gender, health inequalities associated
  with, *see* sex differences
General Health Questionnaire, 224, 242
General Household Survey (GHS), 28,
  38, 41, 54, 64, 69, 72, 111, 127, 232,
  233, 240, 251, 269, 270, 294, 307,
  312
general practitioners
  class differences in diagnosis and
    consultation, 53–5, 69–72, 80, 267,
    268, 269–72
  initiatives on deprivation by, 320
  liaison with health visitors, 159
  low standard of service in some poor
    areas, 144–5
  need for involvement at early stage of
    child's life, 144, 318
  recommendations for improvement in
    coverage, 145–6
  recommended basis of distribution,
    161
  unequal access to, 267–8
Germany, West, 82, 83, 84, 85, 86, 87,
  92 3, 102
Gillies, D. R. N., 252
Gini coefficient, 264
Ginnety, P., 248
Glennerster, H., 194
Goldberg, E. M., 195
Goldblatt, P. O., 236, 237, 262
Golding, P., 350
Gordon, I., 74
Graham, H., 300, 301, 302
Graham, J. M., 322
Graveling, P. A., 245
Gray, A., 4, 74, 306

Greater Glasgow Health Board, 247,
  248, 313, 326, 328
Greece, ancient, 33
Griffiths, R., 24
Guillebaud Committee, 23
Gussow, J. D., 34, 121

Haavio-Mannila, E., 245, 303
Haines, F. A., 300
Halsey, A. H., 338
Hamilton, W., 5
handicapped children, 146, 147, 314
Haringey, 337
Harris, C., 328
Harris, T., 36, 38, 120, 183, 189, 245
Hart, N., xi, 15, 243, 265, 302
Hawton, K., 240
health
  ancient Greek concept of, 33, 34
  choice of indicators of, 37, 38, 223–4,
    225, 313–14
  choice of indicators of inequality, 39–
    41
  conceptions of inequality, 38–9, 222–
    3, 232
  construction and priorities of health
    care services, 17–27, 35–6
  development of medical education, 33
  different meanings given to idea of,
    33–7, 223–4, 324–5
  'social' and 'medical' approach, 34–7,
    225
  see also health education; health in-
    equalities, explanation of; health
    and social services, strategy for
    improving
Health and Life-style Survey, 15, 224,
  234, 244, 314
Health and Safety Executive, 187, 188
health and social services, strategy for
  improving
  anti-smoking measures, 154–5, 159,
    325
  care of disabled and elderly at home,
    147–52, 320–23

district action programme, 143-56, 325-6
equal access for equal need, 267-72
facilities for recreation, 153-4
health education, 153, 324-6
health and welfare of mothers and children, 143-7, 316-20
planning, 134-8, 316-31
prevention, 152-5, 162-4, 324-6
priority for children at start of life, 133-4, 316-17
priority for disabled, 134, 320-22
proposed programme for ten special areas, 156-9. 163-4
resource allocation, 17-22, 138-42
screening programmes, 155-6, 159, 163, 325
shift of resources towards community care, 136-8, 320-22
Health Divide, The
commissioning of, 6, 221
media response. 7-8
political reaction to, 9-11
professional reaction to, 13, 16
purpose of, 6, 221-2
support from health education officers for, 16, 327
health education, 7, 153, 324-6, 341-2
community development projects and, 326, 341-2, 349
priority given in funding for, 324
in schools, 153, 159, 163, 324-5
victim-blaming approach in, 10, 348
Health Education Authority, 6, 16, 324
Health Education Council, 6, 8, 181, 182, 196, 217, 221, 322, 325, 326, 327, 341
termination of, 6
health education officers, 16, 326, 327, 328
health inequalities
availability and use of NHS, 68-81, 267-73
care of infirm and disabled, 76-7, 320-23

consultation of GPs, 53-5, 69-72, 269-72
housing tenure and mortality, 52, 236-9
illness and class, 53-6, 232-6
and interaction of social and geographical disparities, 78-9, 81, 247
need for more information and research, 127-32, 306-15
occupational class and mortality, 43-4, 227-32
race, ethnicity and, 50-52, 248-54
regitional differences in mortality, 69-70, 245-8
sex differences in mortality, 48-9, 58-62, 243-5
trends in, 53-63, 256-66
unemployment and, 242, 327-9
use of hospital services, 72-3
use of preventive and promotive services, 73-5, 80, 269, 271, 272
see also health inequalities, explanation of; living standards, inequalities in
health inequalities: explantion of, 104-26, 286-305
in adult life, 122-6
artefact explanation, 104, 105, 122, 286-7
at birth and during infancy, 115-17
in childhood. 117-22
cultural/behavioural explanation, 11, 110-15, 125, 289-96
'culture of poverty' thesis, 113-14, 296
material life, 122, 123, 297
materialist or structuralist explanations, 106-10, 125, 289-90, 297-302
natural and social selection, 105-6, 287-9
in old age, 124-5
result of social division of labour, 125, 126
sex differential and, 302-4
unemployment and, 240-43

health policy
  economic arguments on, 17–27
  in other countries, 96–100, 283–5
  and NHS, 17–27, 316–331
  positive discrimination and, 23
  WHO targets for, 17, 284, 324–5, 347–8
health promotion, 222, 223
  in the workplace, 339–40
Health Rights, 343
health services
  action on Black Report's recommendations for, 316–31
  availability and distribution of resources, 17–26, 272–3
  growth of private medicine, 26–7
  % of GDP spent on, 22
  role of in reducing inequalities, 316–17, 320, 324
  what nation can afford to spend on, 17–20
  see also health and social services, strategy for improving; National Health Service
Health Services Act 1976, 27
Health Services Board, 27
Health Units in local authorities, 343
health visitors, initiatives by, 318–20, 326, 327
Health Visitors Association, 342
Heath, P., 146
Heclo, H., 196
Hellier, J., 115
Help for the Disabled, 38
Hemery, S., 90
Herbert, G. W., 120, 169
Hill, A. B., 115
Hobdell, M. H., 74
Holland, W. W., 118, 272, 273
Holman, R. T., 114
Holstein, B., 278, 279, 283
home care service, 323
home helps, 152, 320–21, 323
home visiting, 268
homelessness, 338

Hong Kong, 2
Hood, C., 52
hospital admissions: children, 240
hospital in-patient enquiry (HIPE), 28, 127, 128
hospital services
  class gradient in use of, 72–3
  inequalities in different types of care for the disabled, 148
housing
  of disabled, 190–91
  and mortality, 52, 140, 236–9
  need to improve conditions, 188–91, 338–9
  need for increased provision by local authorities, 190, 339
  see also housing conditions
Housing Act 1974, 189, 196
Housing Act 1977, 190
housing conditions
  bad design, 297–8
  and causes of health inequalities, 297–9
  homelessness, 338
  inadequate facilities, 298, 338–9
  as indicators of deprivation, 225, 309–11
  infestation, 298
  initiatives by local authorities on, 344, 346
  overcrowding and ethnic minorities, 339
  Parker Morris standard, 339
  shortage of houses, 339
  state of repair of housing stock, 339
  see also housing
housing tenure and health, 52, 225, 236–9
Huhne, C., 338
Hunt, S. M., 224, 234, 299, 313
Hygeia, 34

illness, definition of, 224
Illsley, R., 13, 14, 15, 116, 256, 286, 288
immigrant mortality, *see* ethnic minorities

Immigrant Mortality Study, 250–51
immunization and vaccination, 73, 74, 75, 110, 144, 154, 163, 272
income
  food choices and, 299–302
  and mortality, 107–10, 295–6, 299–300
  sickness and, 234, 276
Index of Dissimilarity, 264
indicators
  choice of indicators of health, 37–8, 223 4, 313 14
  choice of indicators of inequality, 39–41, 224 5, 309–13
  concept of need could be enhanced by additional, 140
  for international comparisons, 274
  more research necessary into development of, 131–2, 309–14
  of social and material disadvantage, 225
inequalities, *see* health inequalities; health inequalities, explanation of; living standards, inequalities in; regional differences; sex differences; ethnic minorities
infant mortality
  by mother's country of birth, 252–4
  class differences, 43 5, 228 9
  international comparisons, 82 3, 85–6, 90, 91–2, 94–5, 95–6, 101, 274 6, 278, 283
  and late attendance for ante-natal care, 74
  policies designed to reduce, 97 101, 283, 318–20
  regional, 140–42
  in the UK, 82, 228 9
infirm, inequalities in care of, 76–7
Inland Revenue Board, 337
Inner City Partnership Scheme, 141
Institute of Child Health, 221
international comparisons
  adult mortality rates, 84, 85, 274–6
  inequalities in health, 87–96, 276–83

perinatal mortality rates, 82–3, 85–6
provision of health care, 86–7, 283–4
reduction of inequalities, 96–101, 283–5
see also individual countries
Irwig, L. M., 118

Jackson, P. R., 242
Jacobson, B., 302
Jahoda, M., 239
Janerich, D. T., 115
Jarman, B., 310, 311
Jarman Underprivileged Area Score, 310
Jay Committee, 148
Jenkin, P., 3, 31
Jenkins, P. M., 269
Johnson, B., 296
Johnson, M. R. D., 329
Joint Approach to Social Policy (JASP), 193, 194, 195, 197
Jones, D. R., 79
Jones, I. G., 286
Joseph, K., 333

Kaminski, M., 99
Kaplan, G. A., 295
Keithley, J., 297
Kerr, M., 294, 301
Kilmarnock (Lord), 9, 10
King's Fund, 221
Klein, R., 79, 269, 270
Klepp, K., 285
Knight, I., 235, 288
Knox, E. G., 121
Knox, P. L., 267
Koskinen, S., 265, 279, 280
Kreitman, N., 239
Kristofersen, L., 281
Kurtz, Z., 317

Labour Party, 2, 4, 7
Labour Weekly, 4
Lancashire, R., 140
Lancet, 3, 7, 8, 10, 63

Land, H., 170
Lang, T., 11, 300, 337
Larbie, J., 330
Lansley, 333
Laughlin, S., 328
Lawrence, K. M., 115
Leeder, S. R., 118
LeGrand, J., 13, 14, 15, 256
leisure-time activity, 112, 294
Leon, D., 235
Lerner, M., 96
Leviatan, U., 304
Lewis, O., 113
life expectancy of sexes, 48–9, 57–8, 265,
    274 6, 302 4
life-style
    control over, 10, 11, 12, 289, 300–302
    regional differences in, 291, 292
    risk factors in, 290–94, 295–6
Lind, G., 135
Lipsey, D., 349
Lipworth, L., 63
Little, M., 242
Littlewood, R., 269
Liverpool Health Authority, 330
living standards, inequalities in
    accidents to children, 181–2, 289
    anti-poverty strategy, 165–9, 332 7
    child benefit, 170–71, 195, 332, 335
    comprehensive disability allowance,
        183 5, 340
    distribution of personal income, 212,
        332 4, 337 8
    evidence of multiple deprivation, 166
    housing, 188 91, 196, 297 9, 338 9
    improving working conditions, 185 8,
        196, 339 40
    individual or state accountability, 12
    infant care allowance, 171 2, 196
    need for co-ordinated government
        policy, 191 5, 196 7, 341
    need for encouragement of self-de-
        pendence, 168, 323
    need for fairer distribution of re-
        sources, 167 8

nutrition: school milk and meals, 175–
    80, 336–7
    policy for family and children, 169–
        82, 316–20
    pre-school education and day care,
        172–5, 318
    proposal for Health Development
        Council, 194–5, 197, 341
    trends in distribution of wealth, 209,
        337–8
    what is poverty?, 166–7, 333–4
local 'Black Reports', 248
local government authorities
    community care policy and, 320–22
    initiatives taken by, 322 3, 343 7
    local 'Black Reports' in, 248, 343
    rate-capping in, 23, 322
    services provided by, 23, 320–22
Logan, W P. D., 53
London Food Commission, 11, 337
London Health Planning Consortium,
    145
London School of Hygiene and Tropical
    Medicine, 221
Longitudinal Study, OPCS, 228, 230,
    236–8, 239, 262, 286, 288, 312
Lopez, A. D., 265
Lowe, C. R., 78
Lumb, K. M., 252
Lunt, B., 268
Lynch, P., 232
Lynge, E., 274

Macfarlane, A., 236, 239, 240, 258, 260,
    274, 275, 318
Macintyre, S., 223, 274, 286
Maclure, A., 240
McCarthy, P., 298
McDowall, M. E., 14, 230, 231, 261, 292,
    311
McEwen, J., 224, 313
McKechnie, S., 338
McKee, L., 302
McKeown, T., 33, 36, 57, 106
McNaught, A., 250

Mack, J., 333
Madeley, R. J., 320
Madge, N., 114
Manchester City Council
    initiatives taken by, 343–4
    local 'Black Report', 248, 344
Mansfield Community Health Project,
    326
manual workers
    cigarette-smoking, 111, 290
    GP consultations, 70–71, 269–70
    leisure pursuits, 112, 294
    morbidity trends, 64–5, 262–3
    mortality rates, 43–8, 230–31, 282
    occupational risks, 122, 124
    sex differences in mortality, 245
    sickness and medical consultation, 54–
        5, 232–4
    see also unskilled workers; working
        class
Mares, P., 330
Marmot, M. G., 7, 14, 230, 231, 232,
    235, 250, 251, 261, 289, 292, 295
Marsh, G. N., 269, 272, 320
Marshall, W. A., 34
Martin, J., 77, 78
Martini, C. J. M., 68
Måseide, P., 280, 281
Masterman, S., 79
material and structural factors (on in-
    equalities), 289–90, 297–302
material deprivation, 12, 289
Maternity Alliance, 335
maternity services, class gradient in use
    of, 73, 74. *See also* ante-natal care;
    post-natal care
Maynard, A., 88
meals, school, 178–80, 336–7
Mechanic, D., 35
Medical Research Council (MRC), 129,
    131–2, 307, 308
mental health, effect of unemployment
    on, 242
mentally handicapped people, com-
    munity care for, 148–9

middle class
    availability of health care in middle-
        class areas, 79, 267
    GP consultations, 70–71, 80, 268
    patterns of child-rearing, 113
    use of hospital services, 80
milk, school, 176–7, 336–7
Miller, F. J. W., 121
Ministry of Agriculture, Fisheries and
    Food, 293
Moran, G., 347
morbidity rates
    and choice of indicators of health, 37,
        223–4
    class and, 53–6, 232–6
    in Norway, 94–5, 245, 281
    trends in, 64–5, 262–4
Morgan, M., 77, 309
MORI poll, 333
Morris, A. C., 313
Morris, Jane, 344
Morris, J. N., 2, 5, 34, 36, 67, 86, 106,
    109, 115, 140, 144, 153, 258, 260,
    292, 294, 307
Morrison, S. L., 105
mortality rates
    causes of death, 44–8, 230–32
    and choice of indicators of health, 37,
        223
    for elderly, 63, 229–30
    housing tenure and, 52, 236–9
    infant and childhood, 62–3, 66–7, 228–
        9
    international comparisons, 82–5, 89,
        274–7
    maternal, 62, 66
    in men, 58–61, 66, 243, 274–5
    occupational class and, 43–8, 228–32
    race, ethnicity and, 50–52, 248–54
    regional differences in, 49–50, 140–42
    sex differences in, 49, 243, 302–4
    unemployment and, 239–43
    see also infant mortality; perinatal
        mortality; Standardized Mortality
        Ratio

Moser, K. A., 238, 239, 241, 242
Moylan, S., 242
Mugford, M., 236, 258, 274, 275

Naismith, D., 299
National Advisory Committee on Nutrition Education (NACNE), 300
National Association of Health Authorities (NAHA), 20
National Child Development Study, 74, 236, 288
National Children's Bureau, 221, 250, 316, 317, 318, 330
National Extension College, 330
National Food Survey, 41, 127, 128, 131, 177, 307
National Health Service
  Black Report's support for basic principles of, 27
  consensus management in, 24
  consultation of GPs, 53–5, 69–72, 269–70
  cost-benefit analysis in, 19, 24, 26
  demographic changes and, 22
  efficiency of, 22, 23, 26
  general managers in, 24
  Griffiths Report on, 24–5
  and Gross Domestic Product, 22
  hospital closures, 16
  inequalities in availability and use of, 68–81, 267–73
  league tables in, 25
  low pay in, 23
  low spending on, 20, 22–6
  need for better liaison with police, 130
  pay-beds and, 27
  performance targets and indicators for, 25
  principle of public service and, 26–7
  and private medicine, 24–7
  and privatization of ancilliary services, 26–7
  shift of resources recommended, 136–8, 160
  under-funding of, 20–26
  use of hospital services, 72–3
  waiting lists for operations, 17, 23
  see also general practitioners
National Nutrition and Food Policy, 284–5
National Survey of Health and Development, 243, 288
natural selection as explanation of health inequalities, 105–6, 287–8
Naytia, S., 90
Nelson, M., 299
neonatal mortality
  definition, 28
  in Denmark, 89, 278
  in France, 90
  in West Germany, 93
Nethercott, S., 242
Netherlands, 82, 83, 84, 85, 87, 93–4, 101
New Earnings Survey, 166
Nichols, T., 339
Nicoll, A., 320
non-manual workers, mortality rates of, 230–31
Northern Regional Health Authority, 12
north/south gradient, 49–50, 245–7
North-Western Regional Health Authority, 344
Norway, 82, 83, 84, 87, 94–5, 102, 245, 280–81, 284–5
Nottingham Health Profile, 224, 234, 313
Noyce, J., 78
NUPE, 340
nursing, role in reducing health inequalities, 316–31
Nutbeam, D., 269, 314
nutrition
  children and, 299, 336–7
  diet as health factor, 111, 112, 292–4
  food consumption and income, 299–302
  local authority initiatives on, 337, 345, 346
  National Food Survey, 41, 127, 128, 131, 177

need for a national policy on, 337
Norwegian nutrition and food policy, 284–5
restricted choice, 299–302
school meals and, 175–80, 336–7
under-nutrition, 175–6, 299–302

obesity, 235
O'Brien, M., 68, 71
occupational class
  age composition of, 122
  alternatives to use of, 311–13
  and artefact explanation of health inequalities, 105, 286–7
  class gradient in health standards, 232–6
  and desire for day care provision, 173
  and economic factors as explanation of health inequalities, 108, 289, 297–302
  as indicator of inequality, 39, 224–5, 227–8, 311–12
  inequalities, 105–6
  mortality rates, 43–8, 186, 228–32
  need for provision of school health statistics in relation to, 127–8, 307
  and nutrition, 176, 292–4
  percentage of economically active men in different classes, 209–11
  trends in death rates, 213, 258–62
  see also class gradient in health standards; manual workers; middle class; professional workers; unskilled workers; working class
Odell, A., 329, 330
Oelman, B. J., 232
Office of Population Censuses and Surveys (OPCS), 28, 58–9, 61, 106, 117, 228, 229, 230, 232, 233, 235, 236, 237, 238, 239, 241, 243, 244, 246, 247, 252, 253, 259, 262, 263, 270, 290, 291, 292, 294, 301, 308, 309
Oppé, T., 52
Osborn, A. F., 313
Oxford City Council

city health strategy, 346
initiatives taken by, 345–7

Paddington and North Kensington District Health Authority, 326
Pamuk, E. R., 264
Parker Morris standard, 339
Paterson, L., 296
Pearson, M., 330
Pendleton, D. A., 268
perinatal mortality
  British rates compared with others, 82–5, 94, 95
  class and, 62, 115, 116
  definition, 28
  nutrition and, 175
  policies designed to reduce, 97–101
Pharaoh, P. O., 86, 144, 258, 260
Phillimore, P., 12
physical access to health services, 267–8
Piachaud, D., 333, 335
Pill, R., 296
Pillay, V., 318
Platt, S., 239
Player, David, 6–8, 217
Plowden, W. J. L., 194
Pond, C., 333
Popay, J., 327
post coding, 308–9
post-natal care, 74, 99–100
post-neonatal mortality
  class and, 100, 115, 116–17, 258–60
  definition, 28
poverty
  anti-poverty strategy, 165–9, 332–8
  'culture of poverty' thesis, 113–14, 296
  evidence of multiple deprivation, 12, 166
  need for fairer distribution of resources, 167, 349–50
  public attitudes towards, 349–50
  what is poverty?, 166–7, 333–4
  see also living standards
Power, C., 288
Powles, J., 106

pre-school education, 172–5
premature deaths, 258
Preston, S., 264
preventive services
    class gradient in use of, 73–5, 269, 271,
        272
    priority for improvement of, 134, 318,
        324–6
    screening programmes, 155 6, 159,
        269, 325
    see also ante-natal care; health edu-
        cation; immunization and vac-
        cination
primary care services, 69–72, 267–72,
    284, 348
private medicine, 24–7
professional workers
    cigarette-smoking, 111, 290
    community health spending, 78
    and family planning, 104
    and GP consultations, 70–71, 268–72
    morbidity trends, 64–5, 262–3
    mortality rates, 43–8, 228–32, 282
    sex differences in mortality, 49, 303
    sickness and medical consultation, 54–
        5
promotive services, class gradient in use
    of, 73–5
Proportional Mortality Ratios, 250
Public Health Alliance, 342
Pugh, H., 238
Purola, T., 102, 103

Rabin, M., 13
race
    and mortality, 50–52, 248–51
    and provision of health care, 79, 269,
        329–30
    see also ethnic minorities; ethnicity
race relations strategy, 330
Radical Community Medicine, 4
Radical Statistics Health Group, 329
radiography, 73
Rea (Lord), 10
Reason, L., 326

Reed, F. B., 177
regional differences
    in availability of health care, 78–9,
        268–9, 321
    deprivation and, 248
    in disease and fitness, 246
    domiciliary services, 158–9
    local health profiles, 247–9
    making clinics more responsive to
        needs, 318–20
    in mortality, 69–70, 245–7, 268
    proposed programme for ten special
        areas, 156–9
    school health, 159
    screening, 159, 325
    small area analyses and, 247–9, 308–
        11
    small area strategy, 23
    smoking, 159, 291
Registrar General, 13, 28, 58–9, 61, 63,
    105, 224, 227, 257, 286, 287, 307
Reid, D. D., 118
research initiatives on Black recom-
    mendations, 308–15
Resource Allocation Working Party
    (RAWP), 21, 139, 142, 272, 273,
    322, 341
resources
    availability and distribution, 20–27,
        272–3
    need for fairer distribution, 167–8
    percentage of GDP spent on health,
        22
    recommended allocation, 138–42
    shift towards community care re-
        commended, 136–8, 320–22
respiratory disease
    in children, 117, 118–19, 120, 121, 299
    class gradients, 48, 53, 54
    housing conditions and, 298–9
Richie, J., 268
Rickard, J. H., 78
Roberts, J. L., 245
Roll, J., 337
Rona, R. J., 180

Rose, G., 232
Rose, N., 240
Rowntree, G., 74
Royal Commission on the Distribution of Income and Wealth, 41, 107, 167, 183, 211, 212
Royal Commission on the National Health Service, 22, 145, 155
Royal Society for the Prevention of Accidents (RoSPA), 181, 182, 196
Rutter, M., 104, 147

Sackett, D. L., 38
Sakula, J., 115
Salkever, D. S., 103
Scottish Health Education Group, 323
Scottish Health Education Co-ordinating Committee, 341, 342
Scott-Samuel, A., 7, 270, 310, 341
Scott-Samuel Score, 310
screening programmes, 155–6, 159, 325
Seear (Baroness), 9
sex differences
  difficulties of classifying women in social statistics, 237–8, 311–12
  explanations of, 302–4
  international comparisons, 245, 274–6
  in morbidity, 243–5
  in mortality, 48–9, 243
  trends in, 57–8, 265–6
Sheffield City Council, initiatives taken by, 345
Sheffield Health Authority, initiatives taken by, 345
Sheiham, A., 74
SHELTER, 338
sheltered housing, 148–9
Shewry, M. C., 239, 242
Sigerist, H. E., 37
Singapore, 2
Sjolin, S., 95
Skrimshire, A., 79
Slope Index of inequality, 264
small area analyses, 225, 247–8, 308–11
  OPCS statistics for, 308

see also regional differences
Smith, Alwyn, 222
Smith, C., 2
Smith, R., 239, 308, 327, 328, 342
smoking habits, 111, 290–91
  and control policies, 325
Snaith, A. H., 78
Snowdon Working Party, 183, 191
Social Fund, 336
social
  Index, 312–13
  indicators, 224, 239, 309–13
  justice, 222–3
  mobility, 287–9
  polarization, 338
Social Science Research Council (SSRC), 2, 129, 132, 306, 307
social selection, as explanation of health inequalities, 105–6, 287–9
social services, initiatives taken by, 316–31. *See also* health and social services, strategy for improving
Social Trends, 167
social workers, and unemployment, 327
Socialist Health Association, 4
socio-economic group, 224–5
Spastics Society, 319
Spicer, C. C., 63
sporting activities, 111, 112, 294
Standardized Mortality Ratio (SMR), 28, 51, 93, 160, 161, 189, 223, 228
Stewart, G. T., 240
stillbirths, 228–9
Stirland, H., 248
Stott, N., 296
Strachan, D. P., 299
Stutz, R. N., 96
suicide, 239
Sumption, J., 333
Supplementary Benefit (SB), 333, 334, 335, 336
Supplementary Benefits Commission, 166, 171
survival chances
  of men and women, 265, 303–4

survival chances – *contd*
  of rich and poor, 11, 295–6
Susser, M. W., 36
Sweden, 82, 83, 84, 85, 86–7, 95–6, 101,
  102, 245, 281
Szalai, J., 341

Taylor, R. C., 146
Terry, P. B., 252
Thomas, H. E., 52
Thompson, I., 323
Thompson, P., 106
Thunhurst, C., 247, 249, 309, 311, 345
Titmuss, R., 19, 68, 109
Todd, J. E., 236, 269
Townsend, P., 2, 4, 5, 7, 12, 75, 76, 77,
  108, 114, 166, 179, 183, 187, 231,
  246, 247, 249, 260, 270, 307, 309,
  310, 311, 313
trade unions, 187
Trades Union Congress (TUC), 4, 319,
  341
trends, measurement problems of, 13–16,
  256–8
trends in
  adult health, 57–62, 260–65
  elderly, 14, 63, 263
  GP consultation rates, 270
  inequality in health, international,
    281–2
  infant health, 62–3, 258–60
  occupational class and health, 58–65,
    258–65
  poverty, 108, 332–5
  regional distribution of NHS re-
    sources, 272
  sex differential, 265–6
  wealth, 337–8
Trickey, A. J., 78
Tuckett, D. A., 36, 153
Tudor Hart, J., 63, 78

unemployment, 109, 110, 140, 239–43,
  attempted suicide and, 239–40
  British Regional Heart Study, evi-
    dence on, 239, 241
  as cause of child poverty, 335
  coronary heart disease and, 241
  effect on children, 240
  explanations of health differences,
    240–43
  health and social service response to,
    327–9
  mental health and, 242
  mortality and, 239–41
  nutrition and, 300
  OPCS Longitudinal Study, evidence
    on, 239, 241–2
  redundancy and consultation rates,
    242
  sickness and, 240, 242
  smoking behaviour and, 291
  social and material deprivation
    indicator, 225, 239
  suicide and, 239–40
  welfare benefits and, 336
Unemployment and Health Study
  Group, 327
United Kingdom
  cf. Denmark, 89, 278–9
  cf. Finland, 90, 91, 279–80
  cf. France, 90, 91–2, 280
  infant mortality in, 275
  mortality rates compared with other
    countries, 82–7, 101–3, 274–6
  cf. Netherlands, 93–4
  cf. Norway, 94–5, 280–81
  percentage of GDP spent on health
    services, 22
  cf. Sweden, 95–6, 281
  cf. West Germany, 92–3
United States, 83, 84, 85, 86–7, 96, 102
unskilled workers
  correlation between unskilled popu-
    lation and community health
    spending, 78
  and GP consultations, 70–71, 269–72
  morbidity trends, 64–5, 262–4
  mortality rates, 43–8, 140, 228–32
  sex differences in mortality, 49, 243–5

use of hospital services, 72

vaccination, *see* immunization and vaccination
Valkonen, T., 264, 280, 281, 282, 283
Vandeskog, G., 284
Vetter, N. J., 271
Victor, C. R., 271
victim-blaming, 348

Wadsworth, M. E. J., 243, 283
Waldron, I., 303
Walker, A., 333, 335, 340
Walker, C., 333, 335, 340
Walker, G., 248
Waller, R. E., 118
Walsh, J., 326
Warr, P., 239, 242
Watkins, S., 4
Watson, W., 36
Weale, J., 179
wealth, distribution of, 18, 19
Webb, T., 340
Webber, R., 238, 309
Wedderburn, 75, 76, 77
welfare benefits, 170–80, 322, 335–6, 337, 340
welfare state, 18
wellbeing, 224, 235, 236, 313, 314
Welsh Heart Health Survey, 314
West, R. R., 78
White, E. L., 96
White, P., 325
Whitehall Study, 11, 232, 287, 288, 295
Whitehead, M., 6, 325
Whitehouse, C. R., 267
Whitelaw, W., 9
Whitney, R., 10
Wicks, M., 188

Wildavsky, A., 194
Wilkinson, R. G., 15, 235, 256, 286, 288, 299, 306
Wilson, D., 338
Wilson, H., 120
Wilson, R. W., 96, 169
Winkler, J. T., 285
Wiseman, C., 135
women and social inequalities, 228–9, 233–4, 237–8, 243–5, 302–4, 311–13. *See also* sex differences
working conditions, 185–8, 339–40
working class
    availability of health care in working-class areas, 78–9
    GP consultations, 70–71, 80
    patterns of child rearing, 113
    use of hospital services, 80–81
    use of preventive/promotive services, 73–5
    see also class gradient in health standards; manual workers; unskilled workers
World Health Organization (WHO), 10, 34, 83, 87, 222, 223, 284, 325
    Faculty of Community Medicine, commentary on targets of, 324, 348
    healthy cities project, 342, 345, 346, 350
    targets for Health for All by the Year 2000, 17, 219, 284, 324, 326, 344, 347–8, 350
    UK commitment to targets, 219, 347–8
Wynn, M A., 98, 99–100

Young, B., 298
Young, G., 5
Yuen, P., 250

FOR THE BEST IN PAPERBACKS, LOOK FOR THE

In every corner of the world, on every subject under the sun, Penguin represents quality and variety – the very best in publishing today.

For complete information about books available from Penguin – including Pelicans, Puffins, Peregrines and Penguin Classics – and how to order them, write to us at the appropriate address below. Please note that for copyright reasons the selection of books varies from country to country.

In the United Kingdom: For a complete list of books available from Penguin in the U.K., please write to *Dept E.P., Penguin Books Ltd, Harmondsworth, Middlesex, UB7 0DA*

In the United States: For a complete list of books available from Penguin in the U.S., please write to *Dept BA, Penguin, 299 Murray Hill Parkway, East Rutherford, New Jersey 07073*

In Canada: For a complete list of books available from Penguin in Canada, please write to *Penguin Books Canada Ltd, 2801 John Street, Markham, Ontario L3R 1B4*

In Australia: For a complete list of books available from Penguin in Australia, please write to the *Marketing Department, Penguin Books Australia Ltd, P.O. Box 257, Ringwood, Victoria 3134*

In New Zealand: For a complete list of books available from Penguin in New Zealand, please write to the *Marketing Department, Penguin Books (NZ) Ltd, Private Bag, Takapuna, Auckland 9*

In India: For a complete list of books available from Penguin, please write to *Penguin Overseas Ltd, 706 Eros Apartments, 56 Nehru Place, New Delhi. 110019*

In Holland: For a complete list of books available from Penguin in Holland, please write to *Penguin Books Nederland B.V., Postbus 195, NL–1380AD Weesp, Netherlands*

In Germany: For a complete list of books available from Penguin, please write to *Penguin Books Ltd, Friedrichstrasse 10 – 12, D–6000 Frankfurt Main 1, Federal Republic of Germany*

In Spain: For a complete list of books available from Penguin in Spain, please write to *Longman Penguin España, Calle San Nicolas 15, E–28013 Madrid, Spain*